About the Authors

Maya Blake's writ eventually realised Call in 2012. Maya kids and an endless www.mayabauthor.bl www.twitter.com/ma www.facebook.com/

USA Today bestselling author **Catherine Mann** has books in print in more than twenty countries with Mills & Boon. A six-time RITA® finalist, she has won both a RITA® and Romantic Times Reviewer's Choice Award. Mother of four, Catherine lives in South Carolina where she enjoys kayaking, hiking with her dog and volunteering in animal rescue. FMI, visit: catherinemann.com

Kim Lawrence was encouraged by her husband to write when the unsocial hours of nursing didn't look attractive! He told her she could do anything she set her mind to, so Kim tried her hand at writing. Always a keen Mills & Boon reader, it seemed natural for her to write a romance novel – now she can't imagine doing anything else. She is a keen gardener and cook and enjoys running on the beach with her Jack Russell. Kim lives in Wales.

Spanish Scandals

Spanish Scandals:
Heat of
the Night

MAYA BLAKE

CATHERINE MANN

KIM LAWRENCE

MILLS & BOON

First Published in Great Britain 2020
By Mills & Boon, an imprint of HarperCollins*Publishers*
1 London Bridge Street, London, SE1 9GF

www.harpercollins.co.uk

HarperCollins *Publishers*
1st Floor, Watermarque Building, Ringsend Road
Dublin 4, Ireland

SPANISH SCANDALS: HEAT OF THE NIGHT © 2020
Harlequin Books S.A.

His Ultimate Prize © 2013 Maya Blake
For the Sake of Their Son © 2014 Catherine Mann
A Spanish Awakening © 2011 Kim Lawrence

ISBN: 978-0-263-28195-8

MIX
Paper from
responsible sources
FSC C007454

This book is produced from independently certified FSC™ paper to ensure responsible forest management.

For more information visit: www.harpercollins.co.uk/green

Printed and bound in Great Britain
by CPI Group (UK) Ltd, Croydon, CR0 4YY

HIS ULTIMATE PRIZE

MAYA BLAKE

To Lucy Gilmour, for making my dream come true, and also because I know she loves bad boys!

CHAPTER ONE

'PUT YOUR ARMS around me and hold on tight.'

The rich, deep chuckle that greeted her request sent a hot shiver down Raven Blass's spine. The same deep chuckle she continually prayed she would grow immune to. So far, her prayers had gone stubbornly unanswered.

'Trust me, *bonita*, I don't need guidance on how to hold a woman in my arms. I give instructions; I don't take them.' Rafael de Cervantes's drawled response was accompanied by a lazy drift of his finger down her bare arm and a latent heat in ice-blue eyes that constantly unnerved her with their sharp, unwavering focus.

With gritted teeth, she forced herself not to react to his touch. It was a test, another in a long line of tests he'd tried to unsettle her with in the five weeks since he'd finally called her and offered her this job.

Maintaining a neutral expression, she stood her ground. 'Well, you can do what I say, or you can stay in the car and miss your nephew's christening altogether. After agreeing to be his godfather, I'm sure you not turning up in church will go down well with your brother and Sasha.'

As she'd known it would, the mention of Sasha de Cervantes's name caused the atmosphere to shift from toying-with-danger sexual banter to watch-it iciness. Rafael's hand dropped from her arm to grip the titanium-tipped walking stick tucked between his legs, his square jaw tightening as his gaze cooled.

Deep inside, in the other place where she refused to let anyone in, something clenched hard. Ignoring it, she patted herself on the back for the hollow victory. Rafael not touching her in any way but professionally was a *good* thing.

Recite. Repeat. Recite. Repeat—

'I didn't agree…exactly.'

Her snort slipped out before she could stop it. 'Yeah, right. The likelihood of you agreeing to something you're not one hundred per cent content with is virtually nil. Unless…'

His eyes narrowed. 'Unless what?'

Unless Sasha had done the asking. 'Nothing. Shall we try again? Put your arms—'

'Unless you want me to kiss that mouth shut, I suggest you can the instructions and move closer. For a start, you're too far away for this to work. If I move the wrong way and land on top of you, I'll crush you, you being *such* a tiny thing and all.'

'I'm not *tiny*.' She moved a step closer to the open doorway of the sleek black SUV, stubbornly refusing to breathe in too much of his disconcertingly heady masculine scent. 'I'm five foot nine of solid muscle and bone and I can drop kick you in two moves. Think about that before you try anything remotely iffy on me.'

The lethal grin returned. '*Dios*, I love it when you talk dirty to me. Although my moves have never been described as *iffy* before. What does that even mean?'

'It means concentrate or this will never work.'

Rafael, damn him, gave a low laugh, unsnapped his seat belt and slid one arm around her shoulders. 'Fine. Do with me what you will, Raven. I'm putty in your hands.'

With every atom in her body she wished she could halt the stupid blush creeping up her face, but that was one reaction she'd never been able to control. In the distant past she tried every day to forget, it had been another source of callous mirth to her father and his vile friends. To one friend in particular, it had provoked an even stronger, terrifying reaction. Pushing away the unwelcome memory, she concentrated on the task at hand, *her job*.

Adjusting her position, she lowered her centre of gravity, slid an arm around Rafael's back and braced herself to hold his weight. Despite the injuries he'd sustained, he was six foot three of packed, lean muscle, his body honed to perfection from years of carefully regimented exercise. She needed every single ounce of her physiotherapist training to ensure he didn't accidentally flatten her as promised.

She felt him wince as he straightened but, when she glanced at him, his face showed no hint of the pain she knew he must feel.

The head trauma and resulting weeks-long coma he'd lain in after he'd crashed his Premier X1 racing car and ended his world championship reign eight months ago had only formed part of his injuries. He'd also sustained several pelvic fractures and a broken leg that had gone mostly untreated while he'd been unconscious, which meant his recovery had been a slow, frustrating process.

A process made worse by both his stubborn refusal to heed simple instructions and his need to test physical boundaries. Especially hers.

'Are you okay?' she asked. Because it was her job to make sure he was okay. Nothing else.

He drew himself up to his full height and tugged his bespoke hand-stitched suit into place. He slid slim fingers through longer-than-conventional hair until the sleek jet-black tresses were raked back from his high forehead. With the same insufferable indolence with which he approached everything in life, he scrutinised her face, lingered for an obscenely long moment on her mouth before stabbing her gaze with his.

'Are you asking as my physiotherapist or as the woman who continues to scorn my attentions?'

Her mouth tightened. 'As your physio, of course. I have no interest in the…in being—'

'Becoming my lover would make so many of our problems go away, Raven, don't you think? Certainly, this sexual tension you're almost choking on would be so much easier to bear if you would just let me f—'

'Are you okay *to walk*, Rafael?' she interjected forcefully, hating the way her blood heated and her heart raced at his words.

'Of course, *querida*. Thanks to your stalwart efforts this past month, I'm no longer wheelchair-bound and I have the very essence of life running through my veins. But feel free to let your fingers keep caressing my backside the way they're doing now. It's been such a long time since I felt this surge of *essence* to a particular part of my anatomy, I was beginning to fear it'd died.'

With a muted curse and even redder cheeks, she dropped her hand. The professional in her made her stay put until Rafael was fully upright and able to support himself. The female part that hated herself for this insane fever of attraction wanted to run a mile. She compromised by moving a couple of feet away, her face turned from his.

For the second time in as many minutes, his laugh mocked her. 'Spoilsport.'

She fought the need to clench her hands into agitated fists and faced him when she had herself under sufficient control. 'How long are you going to keep this up? Surely you can find something else to amuse yourself with besides this need to push my buttons?'

Just like that, his dazzling smile dropped, his eyes gleaming with a hard, cynical edge that made her shiver. 'Maybe that's what keeps me going, *guapa*. Maybe I intend to push your buttons for as long as it amuses me to do so.'

She swallowed hard and considered staring him down. But she knew how good he was at that game. Heck, Rafael was a maestro at most games. He would only welcome the challenge.

Reaching behind him to slam the car door, she started to move with him towards the entrance of the church where baby Jack's ceremony was being held. 'If you're trying to get me to resign by being intolerable, I won't,' she stated in as firm a tone as possible, hoping he'd get the hint. Aside from the need to make amends, she needed this job. Her severance package from Team Espíritu when Marco de Cervantes had sold the racing team had been more than generous, but it was fast running out in light of her mother's huge treatment bills. It would take a lot more than Rafael's sexual taunts to make her walk away.

He shrugged and fell into step beside her. 'Good. As long as you're here tormenting yourself with your guilt, I feel better.'

Acute discomfort lodged in her chest. 'I thought we weren't going to speak about that?'

'You should know by now, rules mean nothing to me. Unspoken rules mean even less. How's the guilt today, by the way?'

'Receding by the second, thanks to your insufferable tongue.'

'I must be slacking.' He took a step forward, gave a visible wince, and Raven's heart stopped, along with her feet. He raised a brow at her, the hard smile back on his face. 'Ah, there it is. Good to know I haven't lost my touch after all.'

Ice danced down her spine at his chilled tone. Before she could answer, the large bell pealed nearby. Pigeons flew out of the turrets of the tiny whitewashed church that had been on the de Cervantes's Northern Spanish estate for several hundred years.

Raven glanced around them, past the church poised at the summit of the small hill that overlooked miles of prime de Cervantes vineyards, to the graveyard beyond where Rafael's ancestors lay interred.

'Are we going to stand here all day admiring the landscape or do we actually need to go *inside* the church for this gig?' A quick glance at him showed his face studiously averted from the prominent headstones, his jaw set in steel.

She drew in a deep breath and moved towards the arched entrance to the church. 'It's not a *gig;* it's your nephew's christening. In a church. With other guests. So act accordingly.'

Another dark chuckle. 'Or what, you'll put me over your knee? Or will you just pray that I be struck down by lightning if I blaspheme?'

'I'm not rising to your baits, Rafael.' Mostly because she had an inkling of how hard this morning would be for him. According to Rafael's housekeeper, it was the first time he'd interacted with his family since his return to León from his private hospital in Barcelona. 'You can try to rile me all you want. I'm not going anywhere.'

'A martyr to the last?'

'A physiotherapist who knows how grumpy patients can be when they don't get their way.'

'What makes you think I'm not getting exactly what I want?' he rasped lazily.

'I overheard your phone call to Marco this morning… twice…to try and get out of your godfather duties. Since you're here now, I'm guessing he refused to let you?'

A tic in his jaw and a raised brow was her only answer.

'Like I said, I know a grumpy patient when I see one.' She hurried forward and opened the large heavy door.

To her relief, he didn't answer back. She hoped it was because they were within the hallowed walls of his family's chapel because she was close enough to feel his tension increase the closer they got to the altar.

De Cervantes family members and the few close friends who'd managed to gain an invitation to the christening of Sasha and Marco de Cervantes's firstborn turned to watch their slow progress up the aisle.

'Shame you're not wearing a white gown,' Rafael quipped from the side of his mouth, taking her elbow even as he smiled and winked at a well-known Spanish supermodel. But, this close, Raven could see the stress lines that faintly bracketed his mouth and the pulse throbbing at his temple. Rafael *really* did not want to be here.

'White gown?'

'Think how frenzied their imagination would be running right about now. It would almost warrant a two-page spread in *X1 Magazine*.'

'Even if I were dressed in bridal white with a crown on my

head and stars in my eyes, no one would believe you would actually go through with anything as anathema to you as a wedding, Rafael. These poor people would probably drop dead at the very thought of linking you with the word *commitment*.'

His grip tightened for a minuscule moment before that lazy smile returned. 'For once, you're right. Weddings bore me rigid and the word *marriage* should have a picture of a noose next to it in the dictionary.'

They were a few steps away from the front pew, where his brother and sister-in-law sat gazing down adoringly at their infant son. The sight of their utter devotion and contentment made her insides tighten another notch.

'I don't think that's how your brother and his wife see it.'

Rafael's jaw tightened before he shrugged. 'I'm prepared to accede that for some the Halley's Comet effect does happen. But we'll wait and see if it's a mirage or the real thing, shall we?'

Her breath caught at the wealth of cynicism in his tone. She couldn't respond because an usher was signalling the priest that it was time to start.

The ceremony was conducted in Spanish with English translations printed out on embossed gold-edged paper.

As the minutes ticked by, she noted Rafael's profile growing even tenser. Glancing down at the sheet, she realised the moment was approaching for him to take his godson for the anointing. Despite her caution to remain unmoved, her heart softened at his obvious discomfort.

'Relax. Babies are more resilient than we give them credit for. Trust me, it takes a complete idiot to drop a baby.'

She was unprepared for the icy blue eyes that sliced into her. 'Your flattery is touching but the last thing I'm thinking of is dropping my nephew.'

'You don't need to hide it, Rafael. Your tension is so thick it's suffocating.'

His eyes grew colder. 'Remember when I said weddings bore me?'

She nodded warily.

'Christenings bore me even more. Besides, I've never been good in churches. All that *piety*.' He gave a mock shudder. 'My *abuela* used to smack my hand because I could never sit still.'

'Well, I'm not your grandmother so you're spared the smacking. Besides, you're a grown man now so act like one and suck it up.'

Too late, she remembered certain words were like a naked invitation to Rafael. She was completely stunned when he didn't make the obvious remark. Or maybe it was a testament to just how deeply the whole ceremony was affecting him.

'I just want this to be over and done with so I can resume more interesting subjects.' Without due warning, his gaze dropped to the cleavage of her simple, sleeveless orange knee-length chiffon dress. The bold, heated caress resonated through her body, leaving a trail of fire that singed in delicate places. 'Like how delicious you look in that dress. Or how you'll look *out* of it.'

Heat suffused her face. It was no use pointing out how inappropriate this conversation was. Rafael knew very well what he was doing. And the unrepentant gleam in his eyes told her so.

'Rafa…' Marco de Cervantes's deep voice interrupted them.

Raven glanced up and her eyes collided with steel-grey ones which softened a touch when they lit on his brother.

Like most people who'd worked the X1 Premier circuit, she knew all about the de Cervantes brothers. Gorgeous beyond words and successful in their individual rights, they'd made scores of female hearts flutter, both on and off of the racing circuit.

Marco had been the dynamic ex-racer team boss and race car designer. And Rafael, also insanely gifted behind the wheel, had at the age of twenty-eight founded and established himself as CEO of X1 Premier Management, the multi-billion euro conglomerate that nurtured, trained and looked after racing drivers. Between them they'd won more medals and championships than any other team in the history of the sport.

The last year had changed everything for them, though. Marco had sold the team and married Sasha Fleming, the racing driver who'd won him his last Constructors' Championship and stolen his heart in the process; and Rafael had spectacularly crashed his car, nearly lost his life and stalled his racing career.

The icy jet of guilt that shot through Raven every time she thought of his accident, and her part in it, threatened to overwhelm her. Her breath caught as she desperately tried to put the incident out of her head. This was neither the time nor the place.

But then, when had timing been her strong suit?

Over and over, she'd proven that when it came to being in the wrong place at the wrong time, she took first prize every single time. At sixteen, it was what had earned her the unwanted attention that had scarred what remained of her already battered childhood.

As a grown woman of twenty-three, foolishly believing she'd put the past behind her, she'd been proved brutally wrong again when she'd met Rafael de Cervantes.

Rafael's mouth very close to her ear ripped her from her painful thoughts. 'Right, I'm up, I believe. Which means, so are you.'

Her heart leapt into her throat. 'Excuse me?'

'I can barely stand up straight, *pequeña*. It's time to do your duty and *support* me just in case it all gets too much and I keel over.'

'But you're perfectly capable—'

'Rafa...' Marco's voice held a touch of impatience.

Rafael's brow cocked and he held out his arm. With no choice but to comply or risk causing a scene, Raven stood and helped him up. As before, his arm came around her in an all-encompassing hold. And again, she felt the bounds of professionalism slip as she struggled not to feel the effortless, decidedly *erotic* sensations Rafael commanded so very easily in her. Sensations she'd tried her damnedest to stem and, failing that, ignore since the first moment she'd clapped eyes on the legendary racing driver last year.

What had she said to him—*suck it up*? She took a breath and fought to take her own advice.

They made their way to the font and Raven managed to summon a smile in answer to Sasha's open and friendly one. But all through the remainder of the ceremony, Raven was drenched with the feeling that maybe, just maybe, in her haste to assuage her guilt and make amends, she'd made a mistake. Had she, by pushing Rafael to take her on as his personal physiotherapist, jumped from the frying fan into the proverbial fire?

Rafael repeated the words that bound the small person sleeping peacefully in the elegant but frilly Moses basket to him. He firmed lips that wanted to curl in self-derision.

Who was he to become *godfather* to another human being?

Everything he touched turned to dust eventually. Sooner or later he ruined everything good in his life. He'd tried to tell his brother over and over since he'd dropped the bombshell on him a month ago. Hell, as late as this morning he'd tried to get Marco to see sense and change his mind about making him godfather.

But Marco, snug in his newfound love-cocoon, had blithely ignored his request to appoint someone else his son's godfather. Apparently, reality hath no blind spots like a man in love.

Was that a saying? If not, it needed to be.

He was no one's hero. He was the last person any father should entrust with his child.

He gazed down into his nephew's sweet, innocent face. How long before Jack de Cervantes recognised him for what he was? An empty shell. A heartless bastard who'd only succeeded at two things—driving fast cars and seducing fast women.

He shifted on his feet. Pain ricocheted through his hip and pelvis. Ignoring it, he gave a mental shrug, limped forward and took the ladle the priest passed him. Scooping water out of the large bowl, he poised it over his nephew's head.

At the priest's nod, he tipped the ladle.

The scream of protest sent a tiny wave of satisfaction through him. Hopefully his innocent nephew would take a look at him and run screaming every time he saw him. Because Rafael knew that if he had anything at all to do with his brother's child, the poor boy's life too would be ruined.

As well-wishers gathered around to soothe the wailing child, he dropped the ladle back into the bowl, stepped back and forced his gaze away from his nephew's adorable curls and plump cheeks.

Beside him, he heard Raven's long indrawn breath and, grabbing the very welcome distraction, he let his gaze drift to her.

Magnet-like, her hazel eyes sought and found his. Her throat moved in a visible swallow that made his fingers itch to slide over that smooth column of flesh. Follow it down to that delectable, infinitely tempting valley between her plump breasts.

Not here, not now, he thought regrettably. What was between the two of them would not be played out here in this place where dark memories—both living and dead—lingered everywhere he looked, ready to pounce on him should he even begin to let them…

He tensed at the whirr of an electronic wheelchair, kept his gaze fixed on Raven even as his spine stiffened almost painfully. Thankfully the wheelchair stopped several feet behind him and he heard the familiar voice exchange greetings with other family members. With every pulse of icy blood through his veins, Rafael wished himself elsewhere…anywhere but here, where the thick candles and fragrant flowers above the nave reminded him of other candles and flowers placed in a shrine not very far away from where he stood—a constant reminder of what he'd done. A reminder that because of him, because of callous destruction, this was his mother's final resting place.

His beloved Mamá…

His breath caught as Sasha, his sister-in-law, came towards him, her now quietened son in her arm.

Sasha…something else he'd ruined.

Dios…

'He's got a set of lungs on him, hasn't he?' she laughed, her face radiant in the light slanting through the church windows. 'He almost raised the roof with all that wailing.'

He took in the perfect picture mother and child made and something caught in his chest. He'd denied his mother this— the chance to meet her grandchild.

'Rafael?'

He focused and summoned a half-smile. '*Sí*, my poor eardrums are still bleeding.'

She laughed again as her eyes rolled. 'Oh, come on, my little champ's not that bad. Besides, Marco tells me he takes after you, and I don't find that hard to believe at all.' She sobered, her gaze running over him before piercing blue eyes captured his in frank, no nonsense assessment. 'So…how are you? And don't give me a glib answer.'

'Thoroughly bored of everyone asking me how I am.' He raised his walking stick and gestured to his frame. 'See for yourself, *piqueña*. My clever physiotherapist tells me I'm between phases two and three on the recovery scale. *Dios* knows what that means. All I know is that I'm still a broken, broken man.' In more ways than he cared to count.

She gently rubbed her son's back. 'You're far from broken. And we ask because we care about you.'

'*Sí*, I get that. But I prefer all this caring to be from afar. The up-close-and-personal kind gives me the…what do you English call it…the *willies*?'

Her eyes dimmed but her smile remained in place. 'Too bad. We're not going to stop because you bristle every time we come near.' Her determined gaze shifted to Raven, who was chatting to another guest. 'And I hope you're not giving her a hard time. From what I hear, she's the best physio there is.'

Despite telling himself it wasn't the time or place, he couldn't stop his gaze from tracing the perfect lines of Raven Blass's body. And it *was* a perfect body, honed by hours and hours of gruelling physical exercise. She hadn't been lying when she said she was solid muscle and bone. But Rafael knew, from being up close and personal, that there was soft femininity where there needed to be. Which, all in all, presented a more-than-pleasing package that had snagged his attention with shocking intensity the first time he'd laid eyes on her in his racing paddock almost eighteen months ago.

Of course, he'd been left in no uncertain terms that, despite all indications of a *very* mutual attraction, Raven had no intention of letting herself explore that attraction. Her reaction to it had been viscerally blunt.

She'd gone out of her way to hammer her rejection home… right at the time when he'd been in no state to be rejected…

His jaw tightened. 'How I choose to treat my physiotherapist is really none of your business, Sasha.'

A hint of sadness flitted through her eyes before she looked down at her son. 'Despite what you might think, I'm still your friend, so stop trying to push me away because, in case you need reminding, I push back.' She glanced back at him with a look of steely determination.

He sighed. 'I'd forgotten how stubborn you are.'

'It's okay. I'm happy to remind you when you need reminding. Your equally demanding godson demands your presence at the villa, so we'll see you both there in half an hour. No excuses.'

'If we must,' Rafael responded in a bored drawl.

Sasha's lips firmed. 'You must. Or I'll have to leave my guests and come and fetch you personally. And Marco wouldn't like that at all.'

'I stopped being terrified of my big brother long before I lost my baby teeth, *piqueña*.'

'Yes, but I know you wouldn't want to disappoint him. Also, don't forget about Raven.'

He glanced over his shoulder at the woman in question, who now stood with her head bent as she spoke to one of the altar boys. Her namesake hair fell forward as she nodded in response to something the boy said. From the close contact necessitated by her profession, Rafael knew exactly how silky and luxuriant her hair felt against his skin. He'd long stopped resenting the kick in his groin when he looked at her. In fact he welcomed it. He'd lost a lot after his accident, not just a percentage of his physical mobility. With each groin kick, he ferociously celebrated the return of his libido.

'What about Raven?' he asked.

'I've seen her in action during her training sessions. She's been known to reduce grown men to tears. I bet I can convince her to hog-tie you to the SUV and deliver you to the villa if you carry on being difficult.'

Rafael loosened his grip on his walking stick and gave a grim smile. '*Dios*, did someone hack into my temporary Internet files and discover I have a thing for dominatrixes? Because you two seem bent on pushing that hot, sweet button.'

Sasha's smile widened. 'I see you haven't lost your dirty sense of humour. That's something to celebrate, at least. See you at the villa.'

Without waiting for an answer, she marched off towards Marco, who was shaking hands with the priest. His brother's arm enfolded her immediately. Rafael gritted his teeth against the disconcerting pang and accompanying guilt that niggled him.

He'd robbed his family of so much…

'So, which is it to be—compliance without question or physical restraints?' Raven strolled towards him, her gaze cool and collected.

The mental picture that flashed into his mind made his

heart beat just that little bit faster. Nerves which his doctors had advised him might never heal again stirred, as they'd been stirring for several days now. The very male satisfaction the sensation brought sent a shaft of fire through his veins. 'You heard?'

'It was difficult not to. You don't revere your surroundings enough to keep your voice down when you air your... peccadilloes.'

The laughter that ripped from his throat felt surprisingly great. He'd had nothing to laugh about for far longer than he cared to remember. Several heads turned to watch him but he didn't care. He was more intrigued by the blush that spread over Raven's face. He leaned in close. 'Do you think the angels are about to strike me down? Will you save me if they do?' he asked sotto voce.

'No, Rafael. I think, based on your debauched past and irreverent present, all the saints will agree by now you're beyond redemption. No one can save you.'

Despite his bitter self-condemnation moments ago, hearing the words repeated so starkly caused Rafael's chest to tighten. All traces of mirth were stripped from his soul as he recalled similar words, uttered by the same voice, this same woman eight months ago. And then, as now, he felt the black chasm of despair yawn before him, growing ever-wider, sucking at his empty soul until only darkness remained. Because knowingly or unknowingly, she'd struck a very large, very raw nerve.

'Then tell me, Raven, if I'm beyond redemption, what the hell are you doing here?'

CHAPTER TWO

I'M NOT HERE to save you, if that's what you think.

The words hovered like heat striations in Raven's brain an hour later as she stood on the large sun-baked terrace of Marco and Sasha's home. This time the rich surroundings of the architecturally stunning Casa León failed to awe her as they usually did.

I'm not here to save you...

She snorted. What a load of bull. That was *exactly* why she'd begged Marco to let her visit Rafael in hospital once he'd woken from his coma all those months ago. It was why she'd flown to León from London five weeks ago, after months of trying to contact Rafael and being stonily ignored by him; and why she'd begged him to let her treat him when she found out what an appalling job his carers were doing—not because they were incompetent, but because Rafael didn't seem inclined in any way to want to get better, and they'd been too intimidated to go against his wishes. It was most definitely why she continued to suffer his inappropriate, irreverent taunts.

She wanted to make things right...wanted to take back every single word she'd said to him eight months ago, right before he'd climbed into the cockpit of his car and crashed it into a solid concrete wall minutes later.

Because it wasn't Rafael's fault that she hadn't been able to curb her stupid, crazy delusional feelings until it was almost too late. It wasn't his fault that, despite all signs that he was nothing but a carbon copy of her heartless playboy father, she hadn't been able to stop herself from lusting after him—

No, scratch that. Not a carbon copy. Rafael was no one's copy. He was a breed in his own right. With a smile that could slice a woman's heart wide open, make a woman swoon with bliss even as she knew her heart was being slowly crushed. He possessed more charm in his little finger than most wannabe playboys, including her father, held in their entire bodies.

But she'd seen first-hand the devastation that charm could cause. Swarthy Spanish Lothario or a middle-aged English playboy, she knew the effect would be the same.

Her mother was broken, continued to suffer because of the very lethal thrall Raven's father held over her.

And although she knew after five weeks in his company that Rafael's attitude would never manifest in sexual malice, he was in no way less dangerous to her peace of mind. Truth be told, the more she suffered his blatant sexual taunts, the more certain she was that she wanted to see beneath his outwardly glossy façade.

With every atom of her being, Raven wished she'd known this on his unfortunate race day. But, tormented by her mother's suffering, her control when it came to Rafael had slipped badly. Instead of walking away with dignified indifference, she'd lashed out. Unforgivably—

'So deep in thought. Dare I think those thoughts are about me?' Warm air from warmer lips washed over her right lobe.

'Why would you think that?' she asked, sucking in a deep, sustaining breath before she faced the man who seemed to have set up residence in her thoughts.

'Because I've studied you enough to recognise your frowns. Two lines mean you're unhappy because I'm not listening to you drone on about how many squats or abdominal crunches you expect me to perform. Three lines mean your thoughts are of a personal nature, mostly likely you're in turmoil about our last conversation before my accident.' He held out a glass of champagne, his blue eyes thankfully no longer charged with the frosty fury they'd held at the chapel. 'You're wearing a three-line frown now.'

She took the proffered drink and glanced away, unable quite to meet his gaze. 'You think I'm that easy to read?'

'The fact that you're not denying what I say tells me everything I need to know. Your guilt is eating you alive. Admit it,' he said conversationally, before taking a sip of his drink. 'And it kills you even more that I can't remember the accident itself but can remember every single word you said to me only minutes before it happened, doesn't it?'

Her insides twisted with regret. 'I...Rafael...I'm sorry...'

'As I told you in Barcelona, *I'm sorry* won't quite cut it. I need a lot more from you than mere words, *mi corazon*.'

Her heart flipped and dived into her stomach. 'And I told you, I won't debase myself like a cheap paddock bunny just to prove how sorry I am for what I said.'

'Even though you meant every single word?'

'Look, I know I shouldn't have—'

'You meant them then, and you still believe them now. So we shall continue as we are. I push, you push back; we both drown in sexual tension. We'll see who breaks first.'

Her fingers tightened around the cold glass. 'Is this all really a game to you?' The man in turmoil she'd glimpsed at the chapel seemed very distant now. But she'd seen him, knew there was something else going on beneath all the sexual gloss.

'Of course it is. How else do you expect me to pass the time?'

'Your racing career may be stalled for the moment but, for a man of your wealth and power, there are a thousand ways you can find fulfilment.'

A dull look entered his eyes but disappeared a split second later. '*Fulfilment*...how New Age. Next you'll be recommending I practise Transcendental Meditation to get in touch with my chakra.'

'Meditation isn't such a bad thing. I could teach you...'

His mocking laugh stopped her in her tracks. 'Will we braid each other's hair too? Maybe share a joint or two while we're at it?'

She tried to hide her irritation and cocked her head. 'You know something? I have no idea what all those girls see in you. You're cocky, arrogant and dismissive of things you know nothing about.'

'I don't waste my time learning things that hold no interest for me. Women hold my interest so I make it a point to study them. And I know plenty about women like you.'

She stiffened. 'What do you mean, women like me?'

'You take pleasure in hiding behind affront, you take everything so personally and pretend to get all twisted up by the slightest hint of a challenge. It's obvious you've had a… traumatic experience in the past—'

'That's like a psychic predicting someone's been hurt in the past. By virtue of sheer coincidence and indisputable reality, half of relationships end badly, so it stands to reason that most people have had *traumatic experiences*. If you're thinking of taking up clairvoyance, you'll need to do better than that.'

His bared teeth held the predatory smile of one who knew he had his prey cornered. '*Claro*, let's do it this way. I'll make a *psychic* prediction. If I'm wrong, feel free to throw that glass of vintage champagne in my face.'

'I'd never make a scene like that, especially not at your nephew's christening.'

The reminder of where they were made him stiffen slightly but it didn't stop him moving closer until his broad shoulders and streamlined body blocked out the rest of the party. Breath catching, Raven could see nothing but him, smell nothing but the heady, spicy scent that clung to his skin and seemed to weave around her every time she came within touching distance.

As if he knew his effect on her, his smile widened. 'No one will see my humiliation *if* I get it wrong.'

Afraid of what he'd uncover, she started to shake her head, but Rafael was already speaking.

'You've been hurt by a man, someone you really wanted to depend on, someone you wanted to *be there* for you.' He waited, his eyes moving to the fingers clenched around her glass. When she didn't move he leaned in closer. 'Since that relationship ended, you've decided to take the tired *all men are bastards* route. You'd like nothing more than to find yourself a nice, safe man, someone who *understands* you.' His gaze moved to her face, his incisive stare probing so deep Raven wanted to take a step back. With sheer strength of will, she stood her ground. 'You hate yourself for being attracted to me but, deep inside, you enjoy our little skirmishes because the challenge of sparring with me makes your heart beat just that little bit faster.' His gaze traced her hopefully impassive face down to her throat.

For a blind moment, Raven wished she'd worn her hair down because even she could feel the wild tattoo of her pulse surging underneath the skin at her throat.

She tried to speak but the accuracy of his prediction had frozen her tongue.

'Since my face is still dry, I'll take it Psychic Rafa is accurate on all accounts?'

His arrogance finally loosened her tongue. 'Don't flatter yourself. I told you when you started playing these games that I wouldn't participate. I know you're challenged by any woman who doesn't fall for your charms, but not everyone subscribes to the OMG-Rafael de Cervantes-makes-my-knickers-wet Fan Club.'

Rafael's smile was blinding, but it held a speculation that made her hackles rise. '*Pequeña*, since there's only one way to *test* that you're not a member, I now have something to look forward to. And just like that, my days suddenly seem brighter.'

Heat punched its way through her pelvis but, before Raven could answer, a deep throat cleared behind them.

Marco de Cervantes was as tall as his brother and just as visually stunning to look at but he wore his good looks with a smouldering grace where Rafael wholeheartedly embraced his irreverent playboy status.

Marco nodded to Raven, and glanced at his brother.

'I need to talk to you. You don't mind if I borrow him for five minutes, do you, Raven?'

Relief spiked, headier than the champagne she'd barely drunk. 'Not at all. We weren't discussing anything important.'

Rafael's eyes narrowed at the thin insult, his icy blue eyes promising retribution just before they cleared into their usual deceptively indolent look.

Lifting her glass in a mocking salute, she walked away, piercingly aware that he tracked her every step. Out of his intoxicating, domineering sphere, she heaved in a breath of pure relief and pasted a smile on her face as Sasha beckoned her.

Rafael turned to his brother, mild irritation prickling his skin. 'What's on your mind?' He discarded his champagne and wished he had something stronger.

'You need another hobby besides trying to rile your physiotherapist.'

His irritation grew as Raven disappeared from sight, pulled towards a group of guests by Sasha. 'What's it to you? And why the hell does everyone feel the need to poke their nose into my business?'

Marco shrugged away the question. 'Consider the matter dropped. The old man's been asking for you.' Grey eyes bored sharply into his. 'I think it's time.'

Every bone in his body turned excruciatingly rigid. 'That's for me to decide, surely?' And if he didn't feel he was ready to ask for forgiveness, who was anybody to decide otherwise?

'There's been enough hurt all around, Rafa. It's time to move things forward.'

He spiked tense fingers through his hair. 'You wouldn't be trying to save me again by any chance, would you, brother?'

An impatient look passed through Marco's eyes. 'From the look of things, you don't need saving. Besides, I cut the apron strings when I realised you were driving me so nuts that I was in danger of strangling you with them.'

Rafael beckoned the waiter over and exchanged his untouched champagne for a crystal tumbler of Patrón. 'In that case, we're copacetic. Was there anything else?'

Marco's gaze stayed on him for several seconds before he nodded. 'You sent for the papers for the X1 All-Star event coming up?'

Rafael downed the drink, welcoming the warmth that coursed through his chest. 'Unless I'm mistaken, I'm still the CEO of X1 Premier Management. The events start in three weeks. You delegated some of the event's organisation but it's time for me to take the reins again.'

His brother's gaze probed, worry lurking within. 'Are you sure you don't want to sit this one out—?'

'I'm sure. Don't second-guess me, *mi hermano*. I understand that my racing career may be in question—' He stopped as a chill surged through his veins, obliterating the warmth of moments before. Although he didn't remember his accident, he'd seen pictures of the wreckage in vivid detail. He was very much aware that *lucky to be alive* didn't begin to describe his condition. 'The racing side of my career may be up for debate,' he repeated, beating back the wave of desolation that swelled up inside his chest, 'but my brain still functions perfectly. As for my body…' He looked over as a flash of orange caught his eye. The resulting kick gave him a surge of satisfaction. 'My body will be in top condition before very long.'

Marco nodded. 'I'm happy to hear it. According to Raven, you're on the road to complete recovery.'

'Really?' Rafael made a mental note to have a short, precise conversation with his physio about sharing confidential information.

'…*Dios*, are you listening to me? Never mind, I think it'll be safer for me not to know which part of your anatomy you're thinking with right at this moment. *Bueno*, I'll be in touch later in the week to discuss other business.'

'No need to wait till next week. I can tell you now that I'm back. I own fifty per cent of our business, after all. No reason why you should continue to shoulder my responsibilities.

Come to think of it, you should take a vacation with your family, let me handle things for a while.' He glanced over to where Sasha stood chatting to Raven. As if sensing their attention, both women turned towards them. Marco's face dissolved in a look so cheesy, Rafael barely stopped himself from making retching noises.

'Are you sure?' Marco asked without taking his eyes off his wife. 'Sasha's been on my back about taking some time off. It would be great to take the yacht to the island for a bit.' They joint owned a three-mile island paradise in the Bahamas, a place neither of them had visited in a very long time.

'Great. Do it. I'll handle things here,' Rafael responded.

His brother looked sceptical.

'This is a one-time offer, set to expire in ten seconds,' he pressed as his sister-in-law and his physiotherapist started walking towards them. For the first time he noticed Raven's open-toed high heels and saw the way they made her long legs go on for ever. Sasha said something to her. Her responding smile made his throat dry.

Hell, he had it bad if he was behaving like a hormonal teenager around a woman who clearly had *man issues*.

He barely felt it when Marco slapped his shoulder. 'I'll set things in motion first thing in the morning. I owe you one, brother.'

Rafael nodded, relieved that the disturbing subject of his father had been dropped.

'What are you looking so pleased about?' Sasha asked her husband as they drew level with them.

'I have news that's guaranteed to make you adore me even more than you already do.' He kissed her soundly on the lips before leading her away.

Rafael saw Raven looking after them. 'I do believe if they had a *like* button attached to their backs you would be pressing it right about now?'

Her outraged gasp made him curb a smile. He loved to rile her. Rafael didn't hide from the fact that while he was busy riling Raven Blass, he was busy not thinking about what this place did to him, and that gained him a reprieve from the torment of his memories.

She faced him, bristling with irritation and censure. 'Whereas if you had a *like* button I'd personally start a worldwide petition to have it obliterated and replaced with one that said *loathe*.'

He took her elbow and, despite her resistance, he led her to an exquisitely laid out buffet table. 'We'll discuss my various buttons later. Right now you need to eat something before you wither away. I noticed you didn't eat any breakfast this morning.'

She glared at him. 'I had my usual bowl of muesli and fresh fruit.'

'Was that before or after you spent two hours on my beach contorting yourself in unthinkable shapes in the name of exercise?'

'It's called Krav Maga. It works the mind as well as the body.'

He let his gaze rake her from top to toe. 'I don't dispute the effects on the body. But I don't think it's quite working on the mind.'

He stopped another outraged gasp by stuffing a piece of chicken into her mouth. Her only option, other than spitting it out, was to chew, but that didn't stop her glaring fiercely at him.

Rafael was so busy enjoying the way he got under her skin that he didn't hear the low hum of the electric wheelchair until it was too late.

'*Buenos tardes, mi hijo.* I've been looking for you.' The greeting was low and deep. It didn't hold any censure or hatred or flaying judgement. In fact it sounded just exactly as it would were a loving father greeting his beloved son.

But every nerve of Rafael's being screeched with white-hot pain. His fist clenched around his walking stick until the metal dug excruciatingly into his palm. For the life of him, he couldn't let go. He sucked in a breath as his vision blurred. Before the red haze completely dulled his vision, he saw Raven's concerned look as her eyes darted between him and the wheelchair-bound figure.

'Rafael?'

He couldn't find the words to respond to the greeting. Nor could he find the words to stem Raven's escalating concern.

Dios mío, he couldn't even find the courage to turn around. Because how the hell could he explain to Raven that he and he alone was responsible for making his father a quadriplegic?

CHAPTER THREE

'DO YOU WANT to talk about it?'

'The *therapy* in your job title pertains only to my body, not my mind. You'll do well to remember that.'

Raven should've heeded the icy warning, should've just kept her hands on the wheel of the luxury SUV and kept driving towards the stunning glass and steel structure that was Rafael's home on the other side of the de Cervantes estate from his brother's villa.

But her senses jumped at the aura of acute pain that had engulfed Rafael the moment he'd turned around to face the old man in the electric wheelchair. The same pain that surrounded him now. Grey lips were pinched into a thin line, his jaw carved from stone and fingers clamped around his walking stick in a white-knuckled grip. Even his breathing had changed. His broad chest rose and fell in an uncharacteristically shallow rhythm that screamed his agitation.

She pulled over next to a tall acacia tree, one of several hundred that lined the long winding driveway and extended into the exquisitely designed landscape beyond. Behind them, the iron gates, manned by twenty-four-hour security, swung shut.

Narrowed eyes focused with laser-like intensity on her. 'What the hell do you think you're doing?'

'I've stopped because we need to talk about what just happened. Your mental health affects your body's recovery just as much as your physiotherapy regime.'

'Healthy mind, healthy body? That's a piss-poor way of trying to extract the hot gossip, Raven *mía*. You'll need to do much better than that. Why don't you just come out and ask for the juicy details?'

She blew a breath, refusing to rise to the bait. 'Would you tell me if I asked you that?'

'No.'

'Rafael—'

Arctic-chilled eyes narrowed even further. 'In case you didn't already guess, that was my father. Our relationship comes under the subject line of *kryptonite—keep the hell out* to any and all parties.'

'So you can dissect my personal life all you want but yours is off limits?'

His smile was just as icy. 'Certain aspects of my personal life are wide open to you. All you have to do is say the word and I'll be happy to educate you in how we can fully explore it.'

'That is not what I meant.'

'You've taken pains to establish boundaries between us since the moment we met. This is one of *my* boundaries. Attempt to breach it at your peril.'

She frowned. 'Or what? You'll fall back on your default setting of sexual innuendo and taunts? Rafael, I'm only trying to help you.'

His hand slashed through the air in a movement so far removed from his normal laid-back indolence her mouth dropped open. 'I do not need your help unless it's the help I've hired you to provide. Right now I want you to shut up and *drive.*' He clipped out the final word in a hard bite that sent a chill down her spine.

After waiting a minute to steady her own shot nerves, she set the SUV back onto the road, aware of his continued shallow breathing and gritted-jaw iciness. Her fingers clenched over the titanium steering wheel and she practised some nerve-calming breaths of her own.

From the very first, Rafael had known which buttons to push. He'd instinctively known that the subject of sex was anathema to her and had therefore honed in on it with the precision of a laser-guided missile.

Seeing his intense reaction to his father—and she'd known immediately the nearly all-grey-haired man in the wheelchair was his father—had hammered home what she'd been surprised to learn this morning at the chapel, and had somewhat confirmed at Marco's villa: that Rafael, as much as he pretended to be shallow and sex pest-y, had a depth he rarely showed to the world.

Was that why she was so driven to pay penance for the way she'd treated him several months ago—because deep down she thought he was worth saving?

Raven shied away from the probing thought and brought the car to a stop at the end of the driveway.

The wide solid glass door that led into the house swung open and Diego, one of the many staff Rafael employed to run his luxurious home, came down the steps to open her door. In silence, she handed him the car keys and turned to find Rafael rounding the bonnet. The sun glinting off the silver paint cast his face into sharp relief. Her breath snagged in her chest at the masculine, tortured beauty of him. She didn't offer to assist him as he climbed the shallow steps into the house.

In the marble-floored hallway, he shrugged off his suit jacket, handed it to Diego and pulled his shirt tails impatiently from his trousers. At the glimpse of tanned golden flesh a pulse of heat shot through her belly. Sucking in a breath, she looked away, focusing on an abstract painting that took up one entire rectangular pillar in the hallway for an infinitesimal second before she glanced his away again, to find him shoving an agitated hand through his hair.

'Do you need—?' she started.

'Unless I'm growing senile, today's Sunday. Did we not agree we'd give the Florence Nightingale routine a rest on Sundays?'

Annoyance rose to mingle with her concern. 'No, *you* came up with that decree. I never agreed to it.'

Handing his walking stick to a still-hovering Diego, he

started to unbutton his shirt. 'It's a great thing I'm the boss then, isn't it?'

Her mouth dried as several inches of stunning flesh assaulted her senses. When her brain started to short-circuit, she pulled her gaze away. 'Undressing in the hallway, Rafael, really?' She tried to inject as much indifference into her tone as possible but was aware her voice had become unhealthily screechy. 'What do you think—that I'm going to run away in virginal outrage?'

His shameless grin didn't hide the strain and tension beneath. 'At twenty-four, I seriously doubt there's anything virginal about you. No, *mi dulzura,* I'm hoping you'll stay and cheer me on through my striptease.'

The sound that emerged from her throat made his grin widen. 'Don't you want to heal completely? That limp will not go away until you work hard to strengthen your core muscles and realign the bones that were damaged during the accident. If you'd just focus on that we can be rid of each other sooner rather than later.'

Although she thought she saw his shoulders stiffen as he turned to give his shirt to Diego, his grin was still in place when he faced her. 'You're under the impression that I want to be shot of you but you couldn't be further from the truth. I want you right here with me every day.'

'So I can be your whipping girl?'

'I've never been a fan of whips, myself. Handcuffs, blindfolds, the odd paddle, certainly…but whips?' He gave a mock shudder. 'No, not my thing.'

His hand went to the top of his trousers. Deft fingers freed his button, followed by the loud, distinct sound of his zip lowering. She froze. Diego didn't bat an eyelid. 'For goodness' sake, what *are* you doing, Rafael?'

He toed off his shoes and socks. 'I thought it was obvious. I'm going for a swim. Care to join me?'

'I…no, thank you.' The way her temperature had shot up, she'd need a cold shower, not the sultry warmth of Rafael's azure infinity pool. 'But we'll need to talk when you're done. I'll come and find you—' She nearly choked when he dropped his trousers and stepped out of them. The way his designer cotton boxer shorts cupped his impressive man package made all oxygen flee from her lungs. Utterly captivated by the man whose sculpted body, even after the accident that had laid him flat for months, was still the best-looking she'd even seen or worked with, Raven could no more stop herself from staring than she could fly to the moon.

His thighs and legs bore scars from his accident, his calves solid powerful muscle that made the physio in her thrilled to be working with such a manly specimen. Dear Lord, even his feet were sexy, and she'd never been one to pay attention to feet unless they were directly related to her profession.

Helplessly, her gaze travelled back up, past his golden, sculpted chest and wide, athletic shoulders to collide with icy blue eyes.

'My, my, if I didn't enjoy it so much I'd be offended to be treated like a piece of meat.'

She snapped back to her senses to see Diego disappearing up the granite banister-less staircase leading to Rafael's vast first floor suite. The click of his walking stick drew attention back to the man in question. One brow was raised in silent query.

'What do you expect if you insist on making an exhibition of yourself?'

One step brought him within touching distance. 'That's the beauty of free will, *querida*. The ability to walk away when a situation displeases you.'

'If I did that every time you attempted to rile me, I'd never get any work done and you'd still be in the pathetic shape I found you in five weeks ago.'

Another step. Raven breathed in and clenched her fists against the warm, wicked scent that assailed her senses.

'You know what drew me to you when you first joined Team Espíritu?' he breathed.

'I'm sure you're going to enlighten me.'

'Your eyes flash with the deepest hypnotic fire when you're all riled up but your body screams *stay away.* Even the most seductive woman can't pull that off as easily as you can. I'm infinitely fascinated to know what happened to make you this way.'

'Personal subjects are off the table. Besides, I thought you had me all worked out?'

His gaze dropped to her lips. She pressed them together to stop their insane tingling. 'I know the general parameters of your inner angst. But I can't help but feel there's another layer, a deeper reason why you want me with every cell in your body but would chop off your hand before you would even bring yourself to touch me in any but a professional way.'

The ice that encased her soul came from so deep, so dark a place that she'd stopped trying to fathom the depths of it. 'Enjoy your swim, Rafael. I'll come by later to discuss the next steps of your regime.'

'Of course, Mistress Raven. I look forward to the many and varied ways you intend to *whip* me into shape.' With a step sideways that still managed to encroach on her body space and bring even more of his pulsing body heat slapping against her, he adjusted the walking stick and sauntered away in a slow, languid walk.

Hell, even a limping Rafael de Cervantes managed to move with a swagger that made her heart race. Tearing her traitorous gaze away from his tight butt, she hurried up the floating staircase to her room. Gritting her teeth against the firestorm of emotions that threatened to batter her to pieces, she changed into her workout gear. The simple act of donning the familiar attire calmed her jangling nerves.

But she couldn't forget that, once again, Rafael had cut through the outer layer of her defences and almost struck bone, almost peeled back layers she didn't want uncovered.

She pushed the niggling sensation away and shoved her feet into comfortable trainers. After a minute's debate, she decided on the gym instead of her preferred outdoor regime. Even though the day was edging towards evening, the Spanish sun blazed far too hot for the gruelling exercise she needed to restore balance to her equilibrium.

She took the specially installed lift that divided her suite from Rafael's to the sub-basement level where the state-of-the-art gym was located. It was the only room in the whole house that didn't have an exhibitionist's view to the outside.

Rafael's house held no concrete walls, only thick glass interspersed with steel and chrome pillars. At first the feeling of exposure had preyed on her nerves, but now the beauty of the architecturally stunning design had won her over. Nevertheless, right this minute she was grateful for the enclosed space of the gym. Here she didn't need to compose herself, didn't need to to hold back her punches as she slammed her gloved fist into the punching bag. Pain repeatedly shot up her arms, and gradually cleared her mind.

She was here to do her job. Which started and ended with helping Rafael heal properly and regain the utmost mobility. Once she achieved her aim and made peace with her part in his accident, she could walk away from the crazy, bone-deep, completely insane attraction she felt for the man who was in every shape and form the epitome of the man who'd fathered her.

The man whose playboy lifestyle had mattered to him on so deep a level he'd turned his back on his parental responsibilities until they'd been forced on him by the authorities. The same man who'd stood by and barely blinked while his friends had tried to put their hands on her.

Punch!

Her hand slipped. The bag continued its lethal trajectory towards her. Only her ingrained training made her sidestep the heavy-moving bag before it knocked her off her feet. Chest heaving, she tugged off the gloves and went to the climbing frame and chalked her hands.

Clamping her lids shut, she regulated her breathing and forced herself to focus.

Rafael would not derail her. She'd made a colossal mistake and vocalised her roiling disgust for his lifestyle at the most inappropriate moment. Whatever the papers had said, Raven knew deep down she was partly, if not wholly, responsible for putting Rafael in the dangerous frame of mind that had caused his accident. She also knew things could've turned out a million times worse than they had. This was her penance. She would help him get back on his feet. Then she would leave and get on with the rest of her life.

Reaching high, she grabbed the first handhold.

By the time she reached the top seven minutes later, her new course of action was clearly formulated.

'I've laid out the itinerary for the next three months. If you cooperate, I'm confident I can get you back to full health and one hundred per cent mobility with little or no after-effects,' she started crisply as she opened the door and entered Rafael's study. She approached his desk, only to stop when she noticed his attention was caught on the papers strewn on his glass-topped desk.

'I'm talking to you, Rafael.'

'I heard you,' he muttered, and held out his hand for the sheet without looking up. After a cursory glance, he started to shake his head. 'This isn't going to work.' He slapped it down and picked up his own papers.

Raven waited a beat. When he didn't look up, she fought a sharp retort. 'May I ask why not?'

'I have several events to host and meetings to attend between now and when the X1 season starts. Your itinerary requires that I stand still.'

She frowned. 'No, it doesn't.'

'It might as well. You've upped the regime from two to three times a day with sports massages thrown in there that would require me to be stationary. And was that *acupuncture*

I saw in there?' His derisive tone made her hackles rise higher.
'I'll be travelling a lot in the next three months. You're sorely
mistaken if you think I intend to take time off to sit around
being pricked and prodded.'

She watched the light glint off his damp hair. 'What do
you mean, you'll be travelling a lot? You're supposed to be
recuperating.'

Steely blue eyes met hers and instantly Raven was reminded of the unwavering determination that had seen him
win several racing championships since he'd turned professional at nineteen.

'I have a multi-billion-dollar company to run, or have you
forgotten?'

'No, I haven't. But wasn't…isn't Marco in charge for the
time being? He told me he had everything in hand when we
discussed my helping you—'

His eyes narrowed. 'What else did you discuss with my
brother?'

Mouth dry, she withstood his stare. 'What do you mean?'

'I expected an element of confidentiality when I hired
you…'

'What *exactly* are you accusing me of?'

'You will not discuss details of my health with anyone else
but me, is that clear?'

'I didn't—'

'You're glowing.' His gaze raked her face down to her neck
and back up again.

'Excuse me?'

'You look…flushed. If I weren't painfully aware of the
unlikelihood of it, I'd have said you had just tumbled from
a horizontal marathon in a lover's bed. Not quite tumbled to
within an inch of your life, more like—'

'Can we get back to this, please?' She waved the sheet in
his face then slammed it back in front of him.

He shrugged and sat back in his plush leather chair, the
cool, calm businessman back in place. 'Marco has his own

company to run…and a new family to attend to. Besides, he's taking a well-earned break, so I'm managing his company as well.'

A wave of shock nearly rendered her speechless. 'And you didn't think to speak to me before you decided all this?'

'I wasn't aware I needed your permission to live my life or run my business.' His voice, a stiletto-thin blade, skimmed close to her skin.

She took a breath and searched for calm, a state which she'd concluded long ago was near on impossible when in Rafael's presence. 'It's part of the contract we agreed. If you're going to take on any substantial amount of work I'll need to know so I can formulate your therapy accordingly. For goodness' sake, you can't go from zero to full-time work in the space of an afternoon. And I really don't know what you were thinking, telling your brother you'd take on this amount of work for the next goodness knows how long!'

Rafael's gaze dropped to her annoyed almost-pout and fought not to continue downward to the agitated heaving of her breasts. Peachy…the smooth skin of her throat glowed a faint golden-pink. He'd long been fascinated by how a woman with jet-black hair such as hers could have skin so pale it was almost translucent. He knew she took care to stay out of the sun and practised her exercises before daybreak.

An image of her, streamlined, sleek and poised upside down in a martial arts pose, slammed into his brain. The groin-hardening effect made him grip his pen harder. His gaze fell once more on her lips and it was all he could do not to round his desk, clasp her face in his hands and taste her. Or maybe coax her round to him, pull down that prim little skirt she'd donned and discover the delights underneath.

Dios, focus!

'Luckily, I don't answer to you, *mi dulzura*.' He certainly had no intention of enlightening her on what he'd been working steadily on for over a month; what he hadn't stopped thinking of since he'd woken from his coma.

Because finding a way to occupy his mind was the only sure way of keeping his many and varied demons at bay.

'...I hope to hell you're not thinking of adding racing to this insane schedule.' She paled a little as she said it and the usual kick of satisfaction surged.

'And what if I am?' He moderated his voice despite the cold fist of pain that lodged in his gut. Unless a miracle happened, his racing career was over. A part of him had accepted that. Deep inside his soul, however, it was another matter.

'I'm hoping it won't come to that. Because you know as well as I do, you're in no shape to get into a racing cockpit.'

He raised an interested brow. 'And how exactly do you intend to stop me?'

Her delectable lips parted but no words emerged, and her eyes took on a haunted look that made him grit his teeth. 'I can't, I suppose. But I think you'll agree you're not in the best shape.'

'Physically or mentally?'

'Only you can judge your mental state but, as your physiotherapist, I'd say you're not ready.'

He finally got his body under enough control to stand. He caught her sharp inhalation when he rounded the desk and perched on the edge next to where she stood. Hazel eyes, wide and spirited, glared at him.

Taking the sheet from her hand, he dropped it on the table, reached across—slowly, so she wouldn't bolt—and traced his forefinger along her jaw. 'Your eyes are so huge right now. You're almost shaking with worry for me. Yet you try and make me think you detest the very ground I walk on.'

Her hand rose to intercept his finger but, instead of pushing it away, she kept a hold of it, imploring eyes boring into his. 'I don't detest you, Rafael. If I did, I wouldn't be here. I'll admit we're...different but—' her shoulders rose and fell under the thin layer of her cotton top '—I'm willing to put aside our differences to help you recuperate properly. And racing before you're ready...come on, you know that's crazy.

Besides, think of your family, of Sasha. Do you think you're being fair to them, putting them through this?'

He froze. 'I've never responded well to emotional black-mail. And leave Sasha out of this. I'll tell you what, if you don't want me to race, you'll have to find other ways to keep me entertained.'

She dropped his hand as if it burned, just like he'd known she would. 'Why does everything always circle back to sex with you?'

'I didn't actually mean that sexually, but what the hell, let's go with it.'

'Stop doing that!'

'Doing what, *mi encantador*?'

'Pretending you're a male bimbo whore.'

'Are you saying I'm not?' He pretended astonishment, the fizz of getting under her skin headier than the most potent wine.

She nodded at the papers on his desk. 'You just reminded me that you run a multi-billion-dollar corporation. I don't care how great you claim to be in bed; you couldn't have made it without using some upstairs skills.'

He leaned back on the table when a twinge of pain shot through his left hip. 'How do you know?'

'You shouldn't sit like that. You're putting too much pres-sure on your hip.'

Annoyance replaced his buzz. He didn't deny that Raven had made much progress where his previous physios had failed. After all, it was the reason Team Espíritu had hired her as his personal therapist last year. She was the best around and got impressive results with her rigorous regime. But she'd always been able to brush him off as if he were a pesky fly.

He remained in his exact position, raising a daring brow when her gaze collided with his. His blood thickened when she took the dare and stepped closer.

Without warning, her hand shot out and grabbed his hip. Her thumb dug into his hipbone where the pain radiated from.

A few rotations of pressure-based massage and he wanted to moan with relief.

'Why do you fight me when you know I'm the best person to help you get better?' she breathed.

'Because my *mamá* told me I never took the easy way out. You will never get me to ask how high when you say jump.'

She paused for a second, then continued to massage his hip. 'You never talk about your mother,' she murmured.

Tension rippled through him. 'I never talk about anyone in my family. The prying all comes from you, *bonita*. You've made it a mission to upturn every single rock in my life.'

'And yet I don't feel in any way enlightened about your life.'

'Maybe because I'm an empty vessel.' He tried damn hard not to let the acid-like guilt bleed through his voice.

'No, you're not. You just like to pretend you are. Have you considered that by pretending to be something you're not, all you're doing is attracting attention to the very thing you wish to avoid?'

'That's deep. And I presume that thought challenges you endlessly?'

Her hand had moved dangerously close to his fly. If she looked down or moved her actions a few inches west, she'd realise that, despite their verbal sparring skimming the murkier waters of his personal life, he was no less excited by her touch.

In fact, he wasn't ashamed to admit that he found the return of his libido exhilarating. For a few weeks after he'd emerged from his coma it'd been touch and go. His doctors had cautioned him that he might not resume complete sexual function. Raven Blass's appearance in his hospital room five weeks ago had blown that misdiagnosis straight out of the water.

'No,' she responded. 'I know better than to issue challenges to you.'

'You're such a buzzkill,' he said, but he felt relieved that she'd decided to leave the matter of his mother alone.

He saw the faintest trace of a smile on her face before it disappeared. Her fingers moved away, rounded his hip and settled into his back. The movement brought her closer still, her chest mere inches from his. Firm, relief-bringing fingers dug into his muscle. Again he suppressed a moan of relief.

'I know. But think how smug I'd feel if you got back into racing before you were ready and reversed your progress. You'd never hear the end of it if you proved me right.'

The sultry movement of her mouth was a siren call he didn't try very hard to resist. His forefinger was gliding over her mouth before he could stop himself. Her fingers stilled before digging painfully into his back. The rush of her breath over his finger sent his pulse thundering.

'Or I could die. And this relentless song and dance could be over between us. Once and for all.'

CHAPTER FOUR

THE CALM DELIVERY of his words, spoken with barely a flicker of those lush jet eyelashes, froze her to the core.

'Is that what you want? To die?' Her words were no more than a whisper, coated with the shock that held her immobile.

'We all have to die some time.'

'But why, Rafael? Why do you wish to hurry the process when every rational human being fights to stay alive?'

'*Mi tesoro*, rational isn't exactly what most people think when they look at me.'

'That's not an answer.' She realised she was hanging on to him with a death claw but, for the life of her, Raven couldn't let go. She feared her legs would fail her if she did. And hell, she wasn't even sure *why* Rafael's explanation was so important to her. For all she knew, it was another statement meant to titillate and shock. But, looking closer, her blood grew colder. Something in his expression wasn't quite right. Or, rather, it was too right, as if he held his statement with some conviction. 'What is it, Rafael? Please tell me why you said that.'

'Quid pro quo, sweetheart. If I bare my soul, will you bear yours?'

'Would that give you something to live for?'

Raven could've sworn she heard the snap of his jaw as he went rigid in her arms. Grasping her by the elbows, he set her away from him and straightened to his impressive six foot three inches. His lids shuttered his expression and he returned to the seat behind his desk.

'The amateur head-shrinking session is over, *chiquita*. Modify your regime to accommodate travel and liaise with Diego if you'll need special equipment for where we'll be travelling. We leave on Wednesday.' He reeled off their intended destinations before picking up a glossy photo of the latest Cervantes sports car.

Knowing she wouldn't make any more headway with him, she turned to leave.

'Oh, and Raven?'

'Yes?'

'We'll be attending several high profile events, so make sure you pack something other than kick-boxing shorts, trainers and tank tops. As delectable as they are, they won't suit.'

Raven fought the need to smash her fist into the nearest priceless vase as she left Rafael's study. Not because he would see her, although the glass walls meant he would, but because *not* losing control was paramount if she wished to maintain her equilibrium.

She'd fought long and hard to channel her tumultuous emotions into useful energy when, at sixteen, she'd realised how very little her father cared for her. For far too long, she'd been so angry with the world for taking her mother away and replacing her with a useless, despicable parent, she'd let her temper get the better of her.

Rafael could do his worst. She would not let him needle her further.

Taking the sheet into the vast living room, she spent the next hour revising Rafael's regime and speaking to Diego about organising the equipment she would need. Again she felt unease and a healthy amount of frustrated anger at Rafael's decision to return to X1 racing. She didn't shy away from the blunt truth that she herself wanted to avoid the inevitable return.

Even though she'd been paid handsomely by Team Espíritu and treated well by the team, she'd always felt ill at ease in that world. She didn't have to dig deep to recognise the reason.

Sexual promiscuity had been almost a given in the paddock. Hell, some even considered it a challenge to sleep with as many bodies as possible during one race season.

She'd received more than her fair share of unwanted male attention and, by the end of her first season, she'd known she was in danger of earning a *frigid* badge. Ironically, it was Sasha Fleming's catapult into the limelight as the team's lead racer that had lessened male interest in her. For the first time, female paddock professionals were seen as more than just the next notch on a bedpost.

'A two-line frown. I don't know whether to be pleased or disappointed.'

She looked up to find Rafael standing a few feet away, two drinks in his hand and his walking stick dangling from his arm. He held one out to her and she accepted and thanked him for the cold lime based cocktail she'd grown to love since coming to Leon.

'I was thinking about how it would be to return to the X1 circuit.'

'Shouldn't that warrant a three-line frown since I feature in there somewhere?'

'Wow, are you really that self-centred? A psychologist would have a field day with you, you know that?'

With a very confident, very careless shrug, he sank into the seat next to her. 'They'd have to fight off hordes of adoring fans first. Not to mention you.'

'Me? Why would I mind?'

'You're very possessive about me. If you had your way, I'd stay right here, doing your every bidding and following you around like a besotted puppy.'

Eternally thankful she'd swallowed her first sip, Raven stared open-mouthed. Several seconds passed before she could close her mouth. 'I'm stunned speechless.'

'Enough for me to sneak a kiss on you?'

Blood rushed to her head and much lower, between her legs, a throbbing started that should've shamed her. Instead, she exhaled and decided to give herself a break. A girl could only withstand so many shocks in one day.

'Earth to Raven. I don't know how to interpret a wish for a kiss when you go into a trance at the thought of one.'

'I…what?'

'I said kiss me.'

'No. I don't think that's a good idea.'

'It's a great idea. Look at me; I can barely walk. *You'd* be taking advantage of *me*.' His smile held a harsh edge that made the Rafael de Cervantes charm even more lethal.

'Whatever. It's not going to happen. Now, is there anything else I can help you with?'

His sigh was heavy and exaggerated. 'Bianca is almost ready to serve dinner. I figure we have twenty minutes to burn. Shall we be very English and talk about the weather before then?'

'The weather is fantastic. Now, let's talk about your return to X1. I don't wish to get personal…'

His low laugh made heat rush into her face.

'What I mean is…you'll have to be careful when it comes to being…um…'

'Just spit it out, Raven.'

'Fine. Sex. You can't have sex.'

He clutched his chest, then tapped carefully on his sculpted muscle. '*Dios*, I think my heart just stopped. You can't *say* things like that.'

'I mean it. The last thing you need to be doing is chasing after paddock bunnies. You could reverse any progress we've made in the last few weeks. Your pelvis needs time to heal properly. You do want to get better, don't you?'

'Yes, but at what cost? My libido could just shrivel away and die,' he returned without the barest hint of shame while she…she'd grown so hot she had to take a hasty sip of her drink.

'It won't.' She set her glass down on the table. 'Not unless you put too much stress on your body by taking on too much. Look, I'm not asking for much. I'm saying keep your…keep it in your pants for just a little bit longer, until you're more fully recovered.'

He opened his mouth but she raised her hand before he could speak. 'And please don't say you need sex to recover. Despite what you want everyone to think, you're not a sex addict. In fact you were one of the most disciplined men I knew when it came to dedication to racing. All I'm saying is apply that same discipline to your...needs, at least for the time being.'

Sensual masculine lips tilted at the corners. 'I think there was a compliment in there somewhere. Fine, I'll take your lecture under advisement.'

'You need to do more than that, Rafael. Your injuries are too serious to take recovery lightly.'

He shoved a hand through his hair. '*Dios*, did I call you a buzzkill earlier?'

'I believe you did.'

'Congratulations, you've just been upgraded to manhood-killer. Ah, here comes Bianca. Let's hope she's got something to revive me after that complete emasculation.'

'Yeah, my heart bleeds.'

Rafael tried to follow what the financial newsreader was saying on the large high definition screen on his plane. He failed.

Opposite him, ensconced in the club chair, Raven twirled a pen between her lips as she read and made notes on a piece of paper. On any other woman he'd have ridiculed such a blatant sexual ploy. But he knew the woman opposite him was unaware of what she was doing. And its totally groin-hardening effect on him.

Giving up on finding out how the Dow-Jones was doing, he turned off the TV and settled back in his seat.

She raised her head and looked at him with those stunning hazel eyes. 'What?'

'How did you get into physiotherapy?'

She regarded him for several seconds before she depressed the top of her pen. 'The random kindness of strangers.'

He raised an eyebrow.

She shrugged. 'A chance meeting with an ex-PE teacher in my local park when I was seventeen changed my life.'

'Was he hot?'

She rolled her eyes. '*She* realised I loved to exercise but I had no interest in being an athlete. We met and talked a few times. About a month later she took me to the local sports centre where professional athletes trained and introduced me to their head coach. By the end of the day I knew what I wanted to be.'

'And she did this all out of the goodness of her heart?'

'She realised I had...anger issues and worked to give me focus. She didn't have to, so yes, I guess she did.'

He held back the need to enlighten her that nothing in life came free; that every deed held a steep price. 'What were you angry about?' he asked instead.

'Life. My lot. What do most teenagers get angry about at that age?'

'I don't know. I was on the brink of realising my dream and getting ready to step into my very first X1 racing car when I seventeen. I was pretty happy with life at that age.' Blissfully ignorant of the consequences fate had in store for him.

'Of course you were. Well, some of us weren't that lucky.'

'Not all luck is good. Some comes from the devil himself, *bonita*. So, you achieved your light bulb moment, then what?'

Her gaze slid from his. He forced himself to remain quiet.

'Although my teacher helped direct my vision, I couldn't really do anything about it. Not at seventeen. I spent most of that year counting the days until my eighteenth birthday.'

'Why?'

He saw her reticence. Wondered why he was probing when he never intended to get as personal himself.

After a minute, she answered. 'Because turning eighteen meant I could make my own decisions, get myself away from…situations I didn't like.'

Rafael knew she wouldn't elaborate more than that. He respected that but it didn't stop him from speculating. And the directions his thoughts led him made his fist tighten on his armchair.

Raven's attitude towards sex and to him in particular had always puzzled him, not because of the women who had fallen over their feet to get to him since he'd shot up and grown broader shoulders at sixteen.

No, what had always intrigued him was the naked attraction he saw in her eyes, coupled with the fortress she put in place to ensure that attraction never got acted upon.

It didn't take a genius to know something had happened to make her that way. Her little morsel of information pointed to something in her childhood. He tensed, suddenly deciding to hell with respecting her boundaries.

'What happened to you? Were you abused?' he rasped, his fingernails digging into the armrest.

She froze. Darkened eyes shot to his before she glanced out of the porthole. When she returned her gaze to his, the haunted look had receded but not altogether disappeared. 'Have you ever heard of the term—the gift of the gab?'

He nodded.

'Well, my father could make the world's most famous orators look like amateurs. His silver tongue could charm an atom into splitting, so the term *abuse* never could stick, especially if the social worker who dealt with any allegation happened to be a woman. So technically, no, I wasn't abused.'

His teeth gritted so hard his jaw ached. Inhaling deeply, he forced himself to relax. 'What the hell did he do to you?'

She blinked, looked around as if realising where they were, or rather *who* she was with. Her features closed into neutral and she snapped the pen back out. Lowering her gaze, she snatched up her papers from her lap and tapped them into a neat sheaf. 'It doesn't matter. I'm no longer in that situation.'

Rafael almost laughed. Almost told her being out of the situation didn't mean she was out of its control. The past had tentacles that stretched to infinity. He was in the prime place to know.

His father...his mother. Not a day went by that the memories didn't burn behind his retinas—a permanent reminder only death would wipe away. They plagued him in his wakeful hours and followed him into his nightmares. He could never get away from what he'd done to them. No matter how far he went, how much he drank or how many women he let use his body.

'I've revised the regime.' Raven interrupted his thoughts, her tone crisp, businesslike. Her lightly glossed lips were set in a firm line and her whole demeanour shrieked step back in a way that made him want to reach across and *ruffle* her.

Grateful for something else to focus on rather than his dark past, he settled deeper into his seat and just watched her.

She flicked a glance at him and returned her gaze to the papers. 'I've ensured that we'll have a clear hour every morning for a thorough physio session. You already know that if you sit or stand for extended periods of time your body will seize up so I'll recommend some simple exercises for when you're in meetings, although the ideal situation would be for you not to *be* in meetings for extended periods.'

'I'll see about scheduling video conferences for some of the meetings.'

Her head snapped up, surprise reflected in her gaze. 'You will?'

'Don't sound so surprised. My boundless vanity draws the line at cutting my nose off to spite my face. You should know that by now.'

'If you can video conference, then why do you need to be there in the first place?'

'Like any other organisation, there's always a hotshot usurper waiting in the wings, ready to push you off into the great abyss at the slightest hint of weakness. I've grown attached to my pedestal.'

'You speak as if you're decrepit.'

'I haven't had sex in months. I *feel* decrepit. And with your decree of no sex, I feel as if my life has no purpose.'

'You mean you miss your fans and just want to resume basking in their admiration?'

'I'm a simple man, Raven. I love feeling wanted.'

Her lips compressed again, although he saw the shadows had faded from beneath her eyes and her colour had returned to her cheeks. He barely stopped himself from feeling inordinately pleased by the achievement.

She stared down again at the sheet in her hand. 'Why Monaco?'

'Why not? It's the glamour capital of motor racing. Most of the current and ex-drivers live there. It affords the best platform for the launch of the All-Star event.'

'Will there be any actual racing?' she asked.

He caught the wariness in her tone and suppressed another smile. Like it or not, Raven Blass was worried about him.

Just like Marco. Just like Sasha… Just like his father. He had no right to that level of concern from them. From anyone.

The tiny fizz of pleasure disappeared.

'There won't be any actual racing until we get to Monza in two weeks' time.' His brisk tone made her eyes widen. Rafael didn't bother to hide his annoyance. 'Racing is my life, Raven. I haven't decided whether or not I'll ever get behind another steering wheel but that decision will be mine to make and mine alone. So stop the mental hand-wringing and concentrate on making me fit again, *sí*?'

The large, luxurious private jet banked left and Raven felt her heart lurch with it. Below them, the dazzling vista of the Côte d'Azure glittered in the late winter sunshine. With little over a month before the racing season started, the drivers would be in various stages of pre-season tests in Barcelona.

Which was where Rafael would've been had he not had his accident.

At nearly thirty-one, he'd been in his prime as a racing driver and had commanded respect and admiration all over the world. He still did if the million plus followers he commanded on social media and adoring fans from the racing paddock were anything to go by. But Raven hadn't considered how he must be feeling to be out of the racing circuit for the coming year. And what it would do to him if he could never race again.

'I'm sorry. I didn't mean to make this any harder for you than it already is,' she murmured.

She braced herself for his usual innuendo-laden comeback.

'*Gracias*,' was all he came out with instead. 'I appreciate that.'

Before she could respond, a stewardess emerged from behind a curtain to announce they would be landing in minutes.

'Time for the crazy circus to begin. You ready?' He raised a brow at her.

'Sure. After living with you for five weeks, Rafael, I think I'm ready for anything.'

His deep laugh tugged at a place inside her she'd carefully hidden but he seemed to lay bare with very little effort.

'Let's hope you don't end up eating those words, *querida*.'

'I probably will, but…promise me one thing?'

He stilled and his eyes gleamed dangerously at her from across the marble-topped table between them. Finally he nodded.

'Promise me you'll let me know if it all gets too much. No glib or gloss. I can't do my job properly if you don't tell me what's going on.'

His eyes narrowed. 'This job, it's that important to you?'

'Yes, it is. I…I'm here to make amends. I can't ever take back what I said to you, and you don't remember if what I said played a part in your accident. Your recovery is important to me, yes.'

'Hasn't anyone told you being in a hurry to fall on your sword is an invitation to a shameless opportunist like me?'

'Rafael—'

He made a dismissive gesture. 'You won't need me to report my well-being to you, *querida*. You'll be with me twenty-four seven.'

The plane, lending perfect punctuation to his words, chose that moment to touch down. Rafael was up and heading towards the doors before the jet was fully stationary.

Jumping up, she hurried after him.

And realised—once a thousand flashlights exploded in her face on exit—that he hadn't been joking when he'd referred to the circus.

Monaco in late winter was just as glorious as it was during the summer race weekend but with an added bonus of considerably fewer people. But for the paparazzi dogging their every move, Raven could've convinced herself she was on holiday.

After a series of introductions and short but numerous meetings, they were finally driven higher and higher into the mountains above Monte Carlo. Glancing out at the spectacular view spread beneath them, her senses came alive at the beauty around her. It was different to the rugged gorgeousness of Rafael's estate in León, but breathtaking nonetheless.

'Don't you usually stay at the Hôtel de France?' She referred to the exquisite five-star hotel where all his meetings had taken place with the upper echelons of his X1 Premier Management team.

'I prefer to stay there during the race season. But not this time.'

She wondered at the cryptic remark until they arrived at their destination. Wrought iron gates swung wide to reveal a jaw-droppingly stunning art deco villa. The design wasn't unique to the French Riviera but several marked add-ons—large windows and a hint of steel and chrome here and there—made it stand out from the usual.

'Who lives here?' she asked.

'For the next few days, you and me and the usual number of complementary staff. It used to belong to an Austrian countess. I'm toying with the idea of buying it, making this my permanent base.'

She faced him in surprise. 'You're considering leaving León?'

He shrugged, seeming carefree, but his expression was shuttered. 'I haven't really lived full time in León for a very long time. It won't be a big deal.'

'Have you discussed it with Marco and Sasha? Won't they mind?'

'They'd be relieved not to have an invalid cluttering up the place, I expect.'

She suspected his brother and wife thought nothing of the sort but chose not to express that opinion. 'But…it's your home. Won't you miss it?'

'It's only bricks and mortar, *bonita*.'

Realising he meant it, she frowned. '*Is* there a place you actually call home?'

Raven was unprepared for the darkness that swept over his features. In a blink of an eye it was gone, his face restored to its rugged, breathtaking handsomeness that set so many female hearts aflutter whenever the spectacular Rafael de Cervantes made an appearance.

'Rafael?' she probed when he remained silent.

'A long time ago, I did. But, like everything else in my life, I trashed it completely and utterly. Now—' he pushed the door of the limo open, stepped out and held out a hand for her '—come in and tell me what you think. I read somewhere that a woman's opinion is priceless when choosing a house, especially a woman you're not sleeping with. Personally, I disagree with that assertion but I've been known to be wrong once or twice.'

She managed to hold her tongue until the trio of staff who greeted them at the door had taken up their luggage. The minute they were alone, she faced Rafael in the large open style living room, which had an exquisitely moulded ceiling that extended over two floors. Once again—and she was beginning to notice a pattern—the room consisted mostly of windows, although this villa had a few solid walls.

'What did you mean when you said you've trashed everything in your life?' she asked.

He flung his walking stick into the nearest chair and made his way slowly towards her. Stopping a mere foot away, he glanced down at her.

'I was hoping you'd forgotten that.'

'I haven't, and I don't really think you meant me to.'

His smile was fleeting, poignant, and barely touched his eyes. 'I guess my probing on the plane makes you feel you're entitled to a certain...reciprocity?'

'No, I don't. I shared a little of my past with you because I wanted to. You don't have to feel obliged to return the favour but I'd like to know all the same.'

'Tell me what you think of the villa first.'

Her gaze took in the various OTT abstract art and cutting edge sculptures and high-spec lighting and shrugged. Every item in the room shrieked opulence a little too loudly. 'I like it but I don't love it. I think it's trying too hard to be something it's not. I don't think it suits you.'

He glanced around at the plush leather chairs and carefully placed art and sculptures, the high-tech gadgets and priceless rugs.

'Hmm, you could be right. Although that single armchair looks perfect for...de-stressing.'

'Answer my question, Rafael. Why don't you have a home any more?'

His smile dimmed slowly until only raw, untrammelled pain reflected in his eyes. He held his breath for a long, interminable moment, then he slowly exhaled. 'Because, *querida*, everything that meant a damn to me went up in a ball of flames eight years ago.'

CHAPTER FIVE

THE GLITTERING BALLROOM of the Hôtel de France had been re-designed to look like a car showroom, albeit a very expensive car showroom, complete with elaborately elegant priceless chandeliers.

A vintage Bentley MkVI Donington Special from Rafael's own car collection gleamed beneath a spotlight in the centre of the room.

Raven stood to one side as guests continued to stream in from the Automobile Club de Monaco where the X1 All-Star event had kicked off with an opening by the resident head of the Monégasque royal family.

Glancing at the door, she caught sight of Rafael as he chatted to the head of one of the largest car manufacturers in the world. Dressed in a black tuxedo with the customary studded shirt and bow tie, it was the most formal she'd seen him. The sheer stomach-clenching magnetism he exuded made her clutch her champagne flute harder to stem the fierce reaction that threatened to rock her off her feet.

As she watched he laughed in response to a joke. Looking at him, it was hard to believe he was the same man who, for a minuscule moment in time, had bared a part of his soul to her at the villa three days ago. The moment had been fleeting—as most of those moments were with Rafael. Hell, he hadn't even bothered to elaborate after that one cryptic statement about the ball of flames. But his pain had been unmistakable, visceral in a way that had cut through her defences.

Far from recoiling from the man he'd revealed, she'd wanted to draw closer, ease his pain.

I'm going loopy.

He glanced over suddenly and held up three fingers. Her

fingers flew up her face to touch her forehead before she could stop herself. Feeling a wave of heat creep up at his knowing smile, she flung a vaguely rude sign his way and turned her back on him.

He found her minutes later. 'Are you avoiding me?'

'Nope. You seem to be in your element. How's your hip?'

'Not well enough to attempt a paso doble but I'm holding my own.'

'You never told me what all of this is in aid of.'

'Have you never been to an All-Star event?' he asked.

She shook her head. 'I don't tend to involve myself in out of season activities. I've heard of it, but only in vague terms.'

'So what *do* you do when the season ends?' He latched onto the revelation.

Raven bit the inside of her lip, then decided she had nothing to lose by revealing just a little bit more about her personal life. 'I work with injured soldiers, mostly from Afghanistan and Iraq.'

His eyes narrowed slightly, a solemn look descending over his face. 'This must seem so very pointless and horribly ostentatious to you in comparison.'

'Since I don't know exactly what *this* is, I'm prepared to reserve judgement.'

'*This* is nothing but a huge elaborate scheme to get rich people to preen and back-slap while reaching into their pockets to fund a few charities.'

'Good heavens, in that case I condemn you all to Hades,' she said around the smile she couldn't seem to stop.

'Some of us would feel at home there,' he murmured. The bleakness in his voice made her glance up at him but his features gave nothing away.

Deciding to let it go, she glanced around the glittering ballroom. 'It must be nice to click your fingers and have everything fall into place for you like this.'

'Not quite...everything.' His gaze dropped to her lips before returning to capture hers.

Her pulse kicked hard. She fought to pull her gaze away from his but it only went as far as his mouth. 'Well…consider yourself fortunate, gluttony being a sin and all that.' She attempted another smile. When Rafael's own mouth curved into a smile, her heart did a hugely silly dance then proceeded to bash itself against her ribcage.

He beckoned a waiter, took Raven's champagne and exchanged it for a fresher-looking glass. He stopped her with a restraining hand on her arm when she went to sip it.

'Take it easy. It may look like champagne but it's not.'

She eyed the drink warily. 'What is it?'

'It's called Delirium. Don't worry, it's not as sinister or as sleazy as it sounds. Sip it slowly, tell me what you think.'

She did and nearly choked on the tart, potent taste. Almost immediately, the tartness disappeared to leave her tongue tingling with a thousand sensations that made her eyes widen. 'Oh my goodness, it's incredible. What's in it?'

'Edible gold dust and the tiniest drop of adrenaline.'

'You're kidding!'

'About the adrenaline, *sí*, but not the gold dust. Although, in my opinion, it's wasted in the drink. I can think of much better uses for it.' Again his words held a note quite different from his usual innuendo-laden tone.

The ground didn't quite shift but Raven felt a distinct rumble and decided to proceed with caution. 'You were about to tell me about the All-Star event.'

'It's an event I hold every year to get all the racing drivers across various racing formulas together before the season starts. Here we can be just friends, instead of championship competitors, while raising money. It's also an opportunity for retired motor racers to still feel part of the sport for as long as they want to.'

'How many events are there in total?'

'Six races in six countries.' He waved to a grey-haired man who stood with a towering brunette with the hugest diamond ring Raven had ever seen adorning her finger. When the couple beckoned them over, Rafael sighed and took her elbow.

Raven's irritation at having to share Rafael was absurd considering he was the host. But, short of being rude, she had no choice but to let herself be led to the couple.

'Rafael!' the brunette's husky voice gushed a second before she threw herself into Rafael's arms. Dropping Raven's arm, he deftly caught the woman before she could unbalance him and laughed off her throaty murmurs of apology.

They conversed in fluent French as Raven stood to the side.

'Let me introduce you—Sergey Ivanov and his wife, Chantilly. Sergey owns the Black Rock team.'

'And I own his heart,' Chantilly gushed. But even while she planted an open-mouthed kiss on her husband, her eyes were gobbling up Rafael.

Raven tried not to retch as she murmured what she hoped were appropriate conversational responses. After ten unbearable minutes, she was about to make her excuses and escape to the ladies' room when she saw Chantilly reach into her bag. With her husband deep in conversation with Rafael, neither man noticed as she withdrew an expensive lipstick and pulled closer to Rafael.

Raven barely held back her horrified gasp as she saw what Chantilly was doing.

'Did she write her number on your walking stick?' she asked the moment the couple walked away.

He lifted the stick and peered at it. 'Hmm, I believe she did. Interesting…'

Irrational anger bubbled up through her. 'Excuse me.' She barely spat out the words before marching off to the ladies' room. She forced calming breaths into her lungs, calling on every control-restoring technique she knew to help her regain her equanimity.

But when she couldn't even summon up the will to make conversation on the ride back to the villa, she knew she'd failed.

At the door, she bit out a terse goodnight, nearly tripping over the hem of the black sequined gown she'd hastily shopped for in Monaco that morning. She was unused to such elaborate, expensive outfits, as was her credit card, but as she went up to her room, the slide of the seductive material over her heated skin was unmistakable.

Or was it Rafael's gaze on her bare back that caused sensations to skitter all over her body?

She didn't care. All she cared about was getting away from the man who, in more ways than she was willing to admit, was cut from the same cloth as her father.

'I can feel the volcanic waves rising off your body,' Rafael drawled as they finished the last of his exercises next to the large, sparkling infinity pool the next morning. 'I hope your outrage didn't keep you up all night?' His blatant amusement set her teeth on edge.

She stepped back from the bench she'd set up outside, and especially from the man whose potent sweat-mingled scent made her head swim. Taking a deep breath, she fought the feeling.

'Are you seriously so without a moral compass that you don't see anything wrong with a married woman slipping you her phone number right in front of her husband?' she asked, her insides twisting with raw acid.

'Your claws are showing again, *piqueña*.'

'I don't have claws, certainly not where you're concerned. I'm merely disgusted.'

From his position lying flat on the bench, he rose smoothly into a sitting position. 'But you could be so much more if you'd just say the word.'

Flinging a towel onto a nearby chair, she whirled to face him. She tried to tell herself her heart pumped with outrage but underlying that was another emotion she flatly refused to examine. 'For the thousandth time, I'm here to make sure you heal properly, not be your sex pet!'

He rubbed his chin thoughtfully in the morning light, a smile teasing his lips. 'Sex pet. *Dios*, the sound of that makes my pulse race, especially seeing as you're just the right size and shape for a pet.' He shut his eyes, one long arm lifting to trace the air. 'I can just see my hand gliding over that glorious raven hair, sliding down the side of your elegant neck. Of course, you'd gasp in outrage. That's when I'd slide my finger over your full, sexily kissable mouth. And if you were to nip it with just the right amount of pressure—'

She gulped. 'Dammit, Rafael—'

'Shh! Don't spoil my fantasy. The sweat trickling down your chest now just makes me want to undo those no-nonsense buttons and follow it with my tongue.'

Raven glanced down and, sure enough, a bead of sweat was making its way between her breasts. Heat slammed inside her, setting off trails of fire everywhere it touched as if seeking an outlet. This wasn't good. Fires like this eventually escaped, sought the oxygen they needed to burn. Oxygen that looked temptingly, deliciously like the half-naked man in front of her. She could never let it escape, never let it burn because she had a feeling this particular conflagration would be nearly impossible to put out.

She'd more than learned her lesson. She'd been burned badly. Never again.

'Rafael, unless you want to spend the rest of the morning sitting here burning to a crisp, I suggest you zip it and help me get you indoors.'

With a put-upon sigh, he opened his eyes. His low laugh bounced on the morning air before ricocheting through parts of her she didn't want to think about or even acknowledge. 'All right, sex pet. I'll keep my lustful thoughts to myself. But if at any time you want a demonstration, don't hesitate to ask.'

'I won't.'

His smile grew even more wicked, more dangerous than she felt able to cope with. 'You won't hesitate?'

'I won't ask,' she stated firmly, dragging her eyes from the sweat-sheened torso that gleamed mere feet from her.

For several seconds he held her gaze, challenging her with the unabashed heat in his eyes, as if daring her to refuse him.

Raven stood before him, bracing herself and silently praying he would give up or move. Or something!

Finally, he dropped his gaze and reached for his walking stick. With the other hand he pulled her closer and braced his arm over her waist.

'So, you're concerned about my moral compass?' he asked in a droll voice.

'Don't let it go to your head. Sergey seems like a decent man. Are you not concerned about how he'll feel when he finds out you're intending to call his wife for a tryst?'

His laugh was deep and long.

'A *tryst*? That sounds so…decadent.'

She leaned forward, hoping her hair would hide the renewed flush of her cheeks. 'Don't mock me, Rafael. I can still ensure you never walk again.'

'Spoilsport.' He gave a dramatic sigh. 'Before you unleash your many weapons on me, I have no intention of calling or *trysting* with Chantilly. It's a little dance we do. She slips notes and numbers in my pocket. Sergey and I pretend we don't notice.'

She stopped dead. 'You mean he knows?'

His expression was world-weary and full of cynicism. 'He's old enough to be her grandfather, *bonita*. He knows she's not with him for his virility and good looks. Sorry if that bursts your happy little moral bubble.'

The rest of the slow journey to his study was conducted in silence. Raven concentrated hard on ignoring the relief fizzing through her.

She succeeded only because with every step his body bumped against her, his warm, tensile body making her so hyper-aware of her own increased heartbeat. His scent washed over her. She swallowed, the knowledge that it was wrong to feel this way about her patient doing nothing to stop the arrows of lust shooting into her abdomen.

By the time the reached the long sofa that faced the large floor-to-ceiling window in his study, Raven wasn't sure which one of them was breathing heavier.

Rafael slumped into the seat and rested his head on the back of the sofa. Lines of strain bracketed his mouth. Her heart lurched for him.

'Are you okay?'

'Nothing a new hip won't sort out.'

'I can get you some painkillers to ease the pain?'

His jaw clenched. 'No.' From day one, Rafael had refused pain relief, opting for physical therapy to heal his body.

'You have three meetings tomorrow before we leave. I think you should cancel them. Your pelvis isn't as fluid as it could be…and please, no *double entendre*. I mean it. I…I advise you to rethink and let Marco to take over.'

Every last trace of mirth left his face and eyes. His jaw clenched tight and he speared her with suddenly cold eyes. 'I'm not cancelling anything. And my brother and Sasha will be staying exactly where they are.'

The sudden descent into iciness made her shiver. 'Is it true you tried to break them up?' she blurted before she could stop herself.

His gaze grew colder. 'You're straying into none-of-your-business territory, *chiquita*.'

'I thought we were past that? After all, you seem to feel free to stray into my life whenever you feel like it. I'm merely returning the gesture.'

He locked gazes with her for endless seconds. Then he shrugged. 'Okay. Yes, I tried to break them up.'

'Why?'

'Because it seemed like a great idea at the time. Obviously, it didn't work.'

'It wasn't because you loved her?'

Why was she doing this? Asking questions she was fairly certain she didn't want answers to.

'Love? Yes, love. I did it out of love. Twisted, isn't it? If you had a lover too, I'd probably try to separate you from him.'

She frowned. 'Why would you do that?'

He laughed, a half bitter, half amused sound that chilled her nerves. 'Haven't you noticed yet, Raven? I like chaos. I like to cause as much damage as possible wherever I go. Haven't you learned this of me by now? I'm trouble with a capital T.'

She tried for a shrug. 'Some women go for that sort of thing, I hear.'

'But not you, *si*? You remind me of one of the girls I went to Sunday school with.'

Shock held her rigid. 'You went to Sunday school?'

He nodded, the unholy gleam in his eyes lightening the blue depths. 'Religiously. My mother was very keen I got into heaven.'

She laughed at the very idea. She knew no one more devilish in temperament and looks than Rafael de Cervantes.

His grin widened. 'The idea of me in heaven is laughable?'

'In the extreme. You'd corrupt all the other angels within seconds.'

'And they'd love every minute of it.'

'I bet.'

Laughter faded, slowly replaced by an incisive look that should've been her first warning. 'You hide your pain underneath a veneer of blistering efficiency.'

'While you hide yours under the cover of irreverent, sometimes callous charm.'

He reached out a hand for her, and Raven found herself moving towards him, his aura drawing her in like a moth to a flame.

When he patted the seat next to him, she sat down. 'What a pair we are,' he muttered.

She shrugged. 'I guess we must do what we need to do to protect ourselves.'

'From the outside world, yes. But we know what the other is. So there's no need for pretence with us.'

His smile slowly faded to leave a serious, probing look that made her whole body tingle. Slowly he reached out and clasped his hand around her nape. Effortlessly, he drew her forward. She wet her lips before she could stop herself. His groan echoed the deep, dark one inside her.

'What do you want from me, Rafael?' she muttered, her tongue feeling thick in her mouth.

'Nothing you aren't prepared to give me.'

'Don't pretend you won't take more than your fair share.'

His head dropped an inch closer. 'What can I say, I'm a greedy, greedy bastard.'

'What the hell am I doing?'

'Letting go. Living a little. Just because you were hurt before doesn't mean you have to stop living. Pleasure, in the right circumstances, with the right person, can be the most exhilarating experience in life.'

'But you're the exact opposite of the right person, I can't even see how you can say that with a straight face.'

'*Sí*, I'm the devil. You would never be satisfied with a Normal Norman. You'd be bored rigid in three seconds flat.'

He kissed her before she could countermand his assertion. As first kisses with the devil went, it was soul-stealing and Raven was eternally grateful she was sitting down.

Because Rafael devoured her as if she were his favourite fruit. No millimetre of her mouth went unkissed. When he was done ravaging her lips, he delved between to boldly slide his tongue into her mouth. The toe-curling sensation made her fingers bite hard into his bicep. She needed something solid to hold on to. Unfortunately, Rafael—unyielding, warm— no, hot—heady, sexily irreverent Rafael—was the last anchor she should've been seeking. And yet she couldn't pull away, couldn't summon even the smallest protest as she let him devour her lips.

'*Dios*, you taste even better than I imagined.' He only gave her a chance to snatch a quick breath before he pounced again.

One hand caught her waist, his fingers digging into her flesh to hold her still as he angled his head to go even deeper. Her moan felt ripped from her very soul.

He started to lean her back on the sofa, then he stilled suddenly. Between their lips, the sound of his pained hiss was smothered but Raven recognised it all the same.

Reality came crashing down on her, her dulled brain clamouring to make sense of what she'd let happen. Slowly, painfully, he straightened until he was upright again.

Raven wanted to reach across and help but she was too weak with thwarted lust, too stunned from the realisation that she was still as hopelessly attracted to Rafael as she'd been the first time she was introduced to him as his physiotherapist.

'Shut up,' he ground out hoarsely.

'I didn't say anything.'

'No, but I can hear you thinking. Loudly, noisily. I've never had to compete with a woman mentally working out the Fibonacci Sequence while I was trying to get her naked. And you know what? It's not sexy. It's quite deafeningly unsexy, actually.'

She slid agitated hands into her hair. 'You're being offensive.'

'And you're ruining this electric buzz with all that overthinking. I would much prefer it if you'd shut up and strip for me.'

Her mouth dropped open. Actually dropped opened in a gob-smacked, un-pretty mess that she couldn't stop. 'I really don't know how you managed to snag girlfriend after girlfriend with that insufferable attitude.'

'It's the same way I've snagged you, *piqueña*. It's why you're leaning towards me right now, unable to look away from me as you imagine what it would be like to have me inside you, buried deep, riding us both to ecstasy.'

She jumped back, and her breath whooshed out of her lungs.

'And now you're going to blush.'

As if on cue, heat rose and engulfed her face. 'Crap.'

He laughed, actually laughed at her. Raven had never felt so humiliated. Or so…so hot as he grasped the bottom of his T-shirt.

'Here, I'll go first, shall I? One item of clothing each until we're in flagrante. Deal?'

She wanted to walk out, wanted to tell him what to do with his tight, muscle-packed body and sheer masculine perfection. She wanted to have enough willpower to turn her back on all the things his glinting blue eyes promised. This wasn't her. She wasn't the type of girl who fell casually into sex as if she were choosing the latest hair accessory from a supermarket shelf. So why couldn't she move? Why did every single instinct she had scream at her to move closer to Rafael, to touch, experience the seductive pleasure he promised, instead of running as far as her marathon-trained legs could carry her?

A long-suffering sigh filled with extreme impatience shattered her thoughts. Her gaze sharpened in time to see his hands drop.

'Fine, I get the message. You're about to fall on your puritanical sword, deny yourself pleasure just so you can crawl back into your cold bed and pat yourself on the back. Aren't you?'

'I wasn't…' But she *had* been thinking that, hadn't she? 'Maybe,' she admitted. 'Besides being totally unprofessional, I can't very well advocate no sex for you and then be the one who…who makes you suffer a setback.'

He shook his head, a genuine baffled look on his face. Reaching over carefully, he took her face in his hand. '*Sí*, I get it. More restraint. More suffering for both of us. You're twenty-four so I'm sure you're not a virgin, but are you sure you weren't an inquisitor in a past life?'

Since there was no way she wanted to confirm her virginity, she focused on the second part of his statement. 'I know you don't believe it, but I'm only looking out for you.'

'By torturing me to death? Or is there something else at play here?'

'By making sure you heal as quickly and efficiently as possible.'

He dropped his hand. 'Where's the fun in that?'

Raven kicked herself for immediately missing his touch. 'God, you're unbearable! And what do you mean, "there's something else at play"?'

'Ah. Finally, some fire. Do you have any idea how incredibly hot you look when you're riled?'

Desire dragged low through her abdomen at his heated, husky words. 'You're getting off topic. And that compliment is so clichéd, even a three-year-old wouldn't believe you.'

'Cliché doesn't make it any less true. But yes, I'll get to the point. You like to hide behind a prickly exterior, holding the world at bay because you're afraid.'

'I'm not prickly and I'm most definitely not afraid.'

'You over-think every single move you make.'

'It's called being sensible,' she retorted.

'You're living half a life. Every bone in your body wants to be on the bed with me, yet you're afraid to let yourself just be.'

'Just because I don't put myself about like you doesn't mean I'm not living.'

His lips twisted. 'I wouldn't be this frustrated if I'd been putting it about like you suggest. And don't forget, I was in a coma for several weeks. Have mercy on my poor, withered c—'

'If you finish that sentence I'm walking out of here right now!'

'The C-word offends you?'

'No, your blatant lies do. There's nothing withered or poor about you.'

'*Gracias*…I think.' He tilted his head. 'Now you're about to deflate my ego thoroughly, aren't you?'

'Your ego is Teflon-coated and self-inflating. It doesn't need any help from me.'

He let out an impatient sigh. '*Dios*, Raven, are you going to talk me into another coma or are we going to have a conversation about what's really going on here?'

She shoved her hands onto her hips. 'There's nothing going on. You want to get on with making up for lost time and I happen to be the willing body you've chosen.'

His hands dropped. 'Would it make you feel better if I said yes? It would help you get through the morning-after hand-wringing if you feel righteous anger for being used?'

She gasped. 'I didn't say that.'

He moved further away. 'You didn't have to. *Santa Maria!* We haven't been to bed yet, and already you're seeking excuses to ease your guilt. How long are you going to let your father win?'

Her gasp was a hoarse sound that scraped her throat raw. 'That's low, Rafael.'

'No lower than the way you treat yourself. Have a little pride. You're a beautiful woman, with a powerfully sexual nature you choose to suppress underneath a staid exterior. But, underneath all that togetherness, your true nature is dying to leap out. To be set free.'

'And you're the man to do it? How convenient for you.'

His face remained sober. 'For both of us. I'm willing to rise to the task. I'm very good at it, too. Trust me.'

'Trust you. The self-proclaimed damaged man who is trouble with a capital T?'

'Think of all the experience I'd bring to the task. You couldn't find a better candidate to bed you if you tried.'

She shut her eyes. Despair wove through her because, deep down, she knew he was right. Her body hadn't reacted to anyone this strongly since…heavens, since never! But that was no excuse to throw well-served caution to the wind. 'No. It's not going to happen.'

He was silent for so long her nerves were stretched to the max by the time he spoke. 'What did your father do to you?'

'What makes you think this is about my father, not about an ex?'

'The first cut is the deepest, no?'

She looked around the too posh living room, at the priceless pieces of furniture that most people would give their eye teeth to own.

She didn't belong here. Her presence in Rafael's life was temporary, transient. Baring her soul to a man who didn't possess one was out of the question. Regardless of what she'd told herself she'd seen in his eyes last night, they were nothing more than ships passing in the night.

In a few weeks she would be gone and Rafael would return, healed, to his regular life. 'Yes, the first cut is the deepest, and yes, my father hurt me. Badly. But my scars don't dictate who I am. I am free to choose who to be with, who I have sex with. And I don't want to have it with you.'

CHAPTER SIX

RAFAEL TOOK HER rejection with more grace than she'd given him credit for, especially considering his reaction to her rejection the day of his last X1 race.

Later that day, after shrugging off her terse pronouncement, they strolled into an exclusive rooftop restaurant overlooking Casino Square. Although a whisper of tension flowed between them, Rafael was as charming as ever.

'So, what are your plans after you're done fixing me?' he asked after the first course had been served.

A strange twinge attacked her insides. Pushing it away, she speared her fork through a plump shrimp. 'I'll either get the agency that allocated me the X1 contract to find me another driver to work with, or I'll find one on my own. I could also try the army facility to see if they need a full-time physiotherapist. I have a few possibilities and I figure after you, every other patient would be a breeze to work with.'

Blue eyes gleamed at her across the table. '*Gracias, bonita.*'

She eyed him suspiciously. 'What are you thanking me for, exactly?'

'I've obviously become a yardstick by which you measure your future clients. I consider it an honour.'

She rolled her eyes and found herself grinning when he laughed. Shaking her head, she took another mouthful of her delicious shrimp pasta. 'I knew you were trouble from day one.'

His laughter slowly disappeared. '*Sí,*' he murmured. 'What did you call me? A useless waste of space who was taking up valuable oxygen more worthy human beings were entitled to?'

Her fork clattered onto her plate. 'You remember? Every single word?' she whispered.

His smile was sharp and deadly, the easy camaraderie from moments before completely annihilated as the tension that had lurked solidified into a palpable wall. 'What can I say, *querida*, you cut me to the bone.'

'Was that…was that why…?' She couldn't quite frame the words.

'Why I attempted to turn myself and my car into a Rubik's Cube the next day? Ask me again when I remember anything from the accident.'

She shut her eyes for a brief second, a shudder of guilt and regret raking over her. 'Please believe me, I don't usually lay into anyone quite like that. That day…' She paused, unwilling to bare her whole life to him. But then she realised she owed him an explanation of some sort. 'It was a *very* difficult day.'

'In what way was it difficult?' he probed immediately.

'My mother called me the evening before the race, just before the team dinner where you—'

'When I *dared* to ask you out?' he asked.

Her gaze dropped as she felt a prickle behind her eyelids. 'Her relationship with my father has always been…tempestuous.' That was putting it mildly but she couldn't elaborate any further. 'When she called, she was very upset… She has…moments like that. She wanted to see him. Nothing I said would calm her down. So I called my father—the father I haven't spoken to in years.'

Rafael's brow hitched up a fraction but he didn't interrupt her.

'He wouldn't lift a finger to help. He was too busy, he said. But I could hear the sound of a party in the background. I swallowed my pride and begged him. He refused. When I called my mother to try to explain, her mood…escalated. I was trying to get her some help when you found me and asked me to dinner.'

'So you attempted to slice the skin off my bones because of bad timing?' His words were light but the chilling ice in his eyes told her he hadn't forgiven her. 'What about the dozen times before then?'

She blew out a breath. 'I've just told you the effect my father has on me and on my mother. Do you honestly think I'd ever want to associate myself personally with a man who reminds me of every despicable trait I witnessed growing up?'

'Watch it, *piqueña*,' he murmured softly. 'You didn't think I was despicable when we kissed this morning.'

A wave of heat crept up her face. 'That was a mistake.'

'Also, you may have claws, but I have teeth. Sharp ones and I'm heartless enough to use them.'

She didn't doubt it. For him to have succeeded in securing several championships over the past decade, he had to have a ruthless streak somewhere beneath the indolent playboy demeanour. Certainly, she'd seen his dedication and absolute focus during the racing season.

'I'm sorry, Rafael. But I didn't really understand why you wanted to go out with me. There were dozens more willing girls who would've jumped at the chance to be with you.' If she were being honest, she still didn't understand why he continued to try and goad her into bed. The only thing she could think of was...no, it didn't make sense. 'I'm hardly your Mount Everest.'

'You're not. Been there, done that.'

Her eyes fell to the jagged scar on his forearm. It might have been ugly at one time but now it just blended into the frustratingly captivating masterpiece that was Rafael de Cervantes. 'You've been to a lot of places, done a lot of things.'

'You've been listening to gossip.'

'Before I came to work for you last year, the agency sent me a dossier on you. Is it true that scar on your arm was from a bull goring you?' She pounced on the change of subject all the more because here was her chance to learn more about Rafael.

'*Sí*, and I thanked the bull for the unique, exhilarating experience.'

She suppressed a shudder. 'What is it exactly that you crave? The thrill of the chase? The rush of adrenaline?'

'It's conquering the fear of the unknown.'

His words were so stark, so raw, her breath caught in her lungs.

'What do you mean?'

'I don't like mysteries, *querida*. Take you, for instance. From the moment we met, you held me at arm's length. No woman's ever done that, not effectively anyway, and definitely not for as long as you have, and this isn't arrogance talking. It's just never happened. You were an enigma to me. I wanted to smash aside all your barriers. Instead you built them up higher. You intrigued me to the point I couldn't see anything beyond having you.'

She had never been able to explain the phenomenon of ice and heat that filled her whenever she was in Rafael's presence. She couldn't explain it now the sensation had increased a thousandfold. 'I don't know that I want to be described that way. You make me sound like I'd become your worst nightmare.'

'You had. I wanted to confront it. Turn it into a dream I liked.'

'God, Rafael. Do you hear how twisted that sounds?'

His laugh was nowhere near a normal sound. 'I'm sorry I don't fit your ideal of the right guy.'

'I'm not looking for a right guy. I'm not looking for a guy, period. I just want to do my job.'

'It's not just that though, is it?' He beckoned the waiter and ordered an espresso for himself and a white coffee for her. 'You're here because you want to do penance.'

'And you've been fighting me and trying to drive me away ever since I arrived.'

'If I'd wanted to be rid of you, I would've succeeded.'

'So you want me to stay?'

He shrugged. 'One of the many discoveries I made while stuck in a hospital bed was this—I like being alone. But I don't like being alone in León.'

She sensed the revelation behind the statement. 'Another of your nightmare scenarios?'

He didn't deny it. He just shrugged. 'Tell me more about your mother.'

'Tell me about yours.'

'She's dead.'

In what felt like mere seconds between one and the other, another forceful blow punched through her middle at the stark announcement. 'How—?'

The word stuck in her throat when he shook his head and picked up his newly delivered espresso. 'You're one of a handful of people outside of my family circle I've disclosed that to. It's not a state secret, but it's not a subject I wish to discuss either, so don't ask any more questions. And yes, I know it's hypocritical of me to demand everything from you and give nothing in return, but we both know I do what I like. Your mother?'

She moistened her lips and tried to arrange her thoughts. 'For what it's worth, I'm sorry about your mother.' She sucked in a deep breath and slowly exhaled. All of a sudden, it wasn't so bad to reveal just that little bit more. Because Rafael had shared *something*.

'Mine is alive but barely conscious half the time. You know why? Because she's completely and utterly hung up on a man who can go for months, sometimes years without giving her a single thought. And yet he only has to crook his finger to have her falling into his lap. At least you know your mother loved you. Do you know how devastating it is to find out your own mother would gladly give you away for free if she could have her one true obsession?'

'Is that why you lived with your father?'

'No. Aside from her obsession with my father, she was also diagnosed with severe bipolar disorder when I was seven. For a few years she took the prescribed medication, but as I got older, she would miss a few days here and there. Then days would turn into weeks, then she would stop altogether.'

His frown was thunderous. 'Did you not have any relatives that could step in?'

'None that wanted to add the burden of a pre-teen on top of the responsibilities they already had. And, frankly, I felt I was better off on my own. By ten I could take care of myself. Unfortunately, my mother couldn't. One day she had an episode in a shop. The police were called. Social services got involved. Eventually they tracked down my father and threatened to report him to the authorities when he wouldn't step up.' Bitterness made her throat raw. 'They *made* him take me. And you know what? Every day until I turned eighteen I wished they hadn't.'

'Did he hurt you?' he rasped.

'Not at first. When I initially arrived at his doorstep, he didn't even care enough to resent me for my sudden appearance in his life.' She laughed. 'And he was rich enough that I had my every material need catered for.'

'But?' he demanded.

Ice drenched her skin as the dark memory surged, its oily tentacles reaching for her.

A tinkle of laughter from a table nearby slammed her back into the present. Chilled and exposed, she rubbed her hands over her arms. 'I don't want to relive it, Rafael.'

His jaw tightened. 'It was that bad?'

'Worse.'

His fingers curled around the small, fragile cup in his white knuckled grip before he carefully set it back in its saucer. '*Dios mío*. When did it—?'

'Rafael...please...'

He sucked in a sharp breath, his gaze still fiercely probing as he sat back in his seat. After several seconds, he nodded and pushed back his chair.

Silently he held out his hand. Before the start of the evening she'd have hesitated. But after what she'd shared with him, after seeing his reaction to how she'd grown up, a tiny voice urged her to trust him a little.

She placed her hand in his and let him help her up. 'I should be helping you, not the other way round.'

'Let's forget we're patient and specialist, just for a few hours, *sí*?' The low, rough demand made her breath snag in her throat.

When she glanced up at him, he watched her with hooded eyes that held no hint of their usual teasing. Swallowing, she nodded.

They walked in the unseasonably warm evening along the dock that held some of the world's most extravagant and elegant yachts. Or they tried to walk. Rafael was stopped several times along the way by wealthy Monégasques and visiting celebrities. Again and again, Raven tried not to be enthralled by the sight of his breathtaking smile and easy charm. Even when a paparazzo's camera lens flashed nearby he didn't seem to care. But then she caught the clenched fist around his walking stick. She wasn't surprised when he signalled his driver a few moments later.

When she glanced at him, he merely shrugged. 'We have an early flight in the morning. Don't want you to accuse me of depriving you of your beauty sleep.'

She waited until they were in the car, leaving the bright lights of Monte Carlo behind. 'You strive to put a brave face on it all, don't you?'

'A brave face?'

'I saw how the paparazzi affected you just now. And even though you stopped to speak to people, you didn't really want to be there.'

He tilted his head. 'Your powers of deduction are astounding.'

'Don't dismiss me like that, Rafael,' she murmured. 'You've changed.'

Although his expression didn't alter, she saw his shoulders stiffen beneath his expensive cotton shirt.

'Of course I have, *querida*. My hip no longer works and I carry a walking stick.'

'I don't mean physically. You turned away from the cameras at the airport too. You answer their questions but you no longer bask in the limelight. Oh, the playboy is very much a part of your DNA, probably always will be, but…something's changed.'

'*Sí*, I've turned into a decrepit recluse who's been banned from having a bed partner.'

She ignored the quip. 'I bet you're not going to buy that villa, are you?'

The corner of his mouth lifted in a mirthless smile. 'You assume correctly,' he replied, his gaze steady on her face. 'You were right, it's a little too…stalker-ish for me. I think the owner studied what I liked and tried to replicate it without taking the location into consideration. It's slightly creepy, actually. Besides that, Monaco is great for a visit but not somewhere I prefer to live. But then neither is León.'

'Why?'

'Too many bad memories,' he stated.

Somewhere inside, Raven reeled at the easy access he seemed to be giving her. A strong need to know the man made her probe further. 'Your father?'

He paled a little beneath his tan, but he nodded after several seconds. '*Sí*. Amongst other things. He moved to Barcelona after…for a while, but he's back in León now. Seeing him there reminds me of what a disappointment I've been to my family.'

She gasped. 'A disappointment? How…why? You've won eight world championships and ten Constructors' Championships for Team Espíritu. How in the world can that be termed a failure?'

'Those are just trophies, *querida*.'

'Trophies coveted by the some of the world's most disciplined athletes.'

'Why, Raven, I almost think you're trying to make me feel better about myself.'

'You've achieved a lot in your life. Self-deprecation is one thing. Dismissing your achievements out of hand is an insult to the team that has always supported you. Now, if you're talking about your private life…'

'What if I said I was?'

'I've met your father, albeit very briefly. I saw no trace of disappointment when he tried to talk to you. And, as far as I can see, Marco and Sasha worship the ground you walk on, despite you saying you tried to break them up.'

He lifted a hand, his knuckles brushing her cheeks before she knew what he was doing. 'That may have been an over-exaggeration. Was I annoyed when I woke up from my coma to find my best friend had fallen for my brother? *Sí.* But I'm a big boy, I'll learn to adapt. As for worshipping the ground I walk on—appearances can be deceptive. I've done things—things I'm not proud of; things that haunt me in the middle of the night, or in the middle of the day when I smile and shake hands with people who think I'm their golden boy. They don't know what I've done.'

'What have you done, Rafael? Tell me.'

He shook his head, a bleak expression stamped on his face that sent a bolt of apprehension through her.

'Did you notice the condition my father is in?'

She frowned. 'You mean his wheelchair? Of course I did.'

'What if I told you I put him in that wheelchair?'

Rafael looked into her face, trying to read her reaction while at the same time trying to decipher exactly why he was spilling his guts when he never, ever talked about what he'd done eight years ago.

The car passed under a streetlamp and illuminated for a moment her pale, shocked face. 'H…How did you put him in the wheelchair?'

A deep tremor went through him, signalling the rise of the blistering pain that seemed to live just below his skin. 'Take a wild guess.'

'A car accident?'

He nodded, his peculiar fascination with her escalating

when she made a move as if to touch him. At the last moment, she dropped her hand.

'Where did it happen?'

'On the racing track in León. Eight years ago. I walked away unscathed. My father has never walked since.'

This time when she lifted her hand he caught it before she could lower it and twined his around her slender fingers. The surge of pain diminished a little when her fingers tightened.

'I'm so sorry,' she murmured.

His smile felt broken. 'You don't want to know whose fault it was?'

'I'm not going to force you to relive the emotional pain, Rafael. Like you said, I'm not that type of therapist. But one thing I do know is that, contrary to what you might think, your family...your father, from what I saw, is more forgiving than you realise.'

His father might be forgiving of Rafael's role in making him wheelchair-bound, but the other, darker reason would be more unthinkable to forgive. Hell, he hadn't even dreamed of seeking forgiveness. He deserved every baptism of hellfire he lived through every morning when he opened his eyes. 'That's the problem with family. Forgiveness may be readily provided but the crime is never forgotten.'

'Unfortunately, I wouldn't know. Dysfunctional doesn't even apply to me because I had two people who were connected to me by genetics but who were never family.'

The car was drawing up to the villa when he lifted their entwined fingers to his lips. A soft gasp escaped her when he kissed her knuckles. 'Then count yourself lucky.'

Two hours later, Rafael stretched and held in a grimace of pain when he tried to rise from his chair. He eyed the walking stick leaning against his desk and with an impatient hand he reached for it.

Pelvis, fractured in three places...broken leg...multiple cracked ribs...severe brain swelling...lucky to be alive.

The doctor's recital of his injuries when he'd woken from his coma should've shocked him. It hadn't. He'd known for as long as he could remember that he had the luck of the devil. He'd exploited that trait mercilessly when he was younger, and then honed it into becoming the best racing driver around when he was older. No matter how many hairy situations he put himself in, he seemed to come out, if not completely whole, then alive.

Recalling his conversation earlier with Raven, he paused in the hallway. *I'm not going to force you to relive the emotional pain.*

Little did she know that he relived it every waking moment and most nights in his vivid nightmares. He might have cheated death countless times, but his penance was to relive the devastation he'd brought to his family over and over again.

His phone pinged and before he glanced at it he knew who it was.

His father…

He deleted the message, unread. *Dios*, even if they wanted to grant it, who was he to accept their forgiveness—?

The sound in the library next to his study attracted his attention.

Raven's lusciously heady perfume drew him to the room before he could stop himself. 'It's almost midnight. What are you doing up?'

'I was looking for something to read. The only reading material I have upstairs is boring clinical stuff, and my tablet is charging, so…'

He glanced down at the papers in his hand. He had no idea what he was doing, no idea where this project would take him but… He debated for a few seconds and made up his mind. Closing the distance between them, he stopped in front of her.

'Here.' He tossed a bound sheaf of papers at her, which she managed to catch before they spilled everywhere.

'What is this?'

One corner of his mouth lifted in a dangerous little half-smile that always made her forget to breathe. 'Two articles for *X1 Magazine*…and something new I'm working on.'

'Something new? I didn't know you wrote outside of your monthly *CEO's Snippets*.'

He shrugged. 'Three months ago—while I was trussed up like a turkey in a hospital bed—I was approached by a couple of publishing houses to write my memoirs.' He laughed. 'I guess they figured a has-been like me would jump at the chance to lay it all out there before the moths set in.'

She glanced down at the thick inch of paper between her fingers. 'And you agreed?' she asked as she started to leaf through the pages.

'I said I'd think about it. I had time on my hands after all.'

She read, then read some more. On the third page, she looked up. 'This isn't your memoirs, unless you were a girl who grew up in Valencia in the late forties.'

'*Bonita*, you're getting ahead of yourself. *Por favor*, contain yourself and let me finish.'

She stared up at him. Rafael gave himself a mental slap against the need to keep staring into those mesmerising eyes. 'I started writing and realised fiction suited me much better than non-fiction. I told them no to the memoir.'

'And?' she prompted when he lapsed into silence. 'You told them about this?'

'No. I've told no one about this. Except you.'

Surprise registered in her eyes before she glanced back down at the papers. 'Are you sure you want me to read it?'

'It's pure fiction. No deep, dark secrets in there for you to hold over my head.'

Wide hazel eyes, alluring and daring at the same time, rose to lock on his. 'Are you sure?'

'If you're thinking of flipping through the pages for X-rated material, I'm afraid you'll be disappointed.'

Her blush was a slow wave of heat that he wanted to trace with his fingers. For a woman so fierce in her dedication to her craft and so determined to succeed despite her past, she blushed with an innocence that made him painfully erect. Despite his intense discomfort, he wanted to continue to bait her so she blushed for him again.

Unable to help himself, he lowered his gaze to the shallow rise and fall of her chest.

When she cleared her throat delicately, he forced his gaze upwards. 'So what are you looking for—an honest critique? I'm sure I can read whatever it is you've written and give an honest view, if that's what you want?'

He smiled at her prim tone and forced himself to step back before he gave in to the need to kiss her. Their kiss had only opened up a craving to experience the heady sensation again. But, aside from the insane physical attraction, he was feeling a peculiar pull to Raven Blass he wasn't completely comfortable with.

Keeping his distance from her was impossible considering her role in his life, but he wasn't a hormonal teenager any longer and he refused to make any move towards her that reminded her of her sleazebag father.

If anything was going to happen between them, Raven had to make the first move...or indicate in clear and precise terms that she wanted him to.

'*Gracias*, it is. I await your thoughts on my efforts with bated breath.'

CHAPTER SEVEN

THEIR EARLY MORNING departure to Italy, accompanied by Rafael's executive assistant and a trio of ex-racers, meant that Raven had no chance to discuss Rafael's manuscript with him at any point. A fact for which she was more than thankful.

The story of the young girl was both uplifting and heartbreaking. Rafael's language was lyrical and poignant, clever and funny in a way that had made her feel each and every word, every expression.

Reading his work, she'd felt just that little bit closer to him. Raven wasn't sure if she was more frightened or insane for feeling like that. It was that floundering feeling that had made her take a seat as far away from Rafael as possible.

But even though she made the right noises with the guy next to her—whose name she couldn't immediately remember—she couldn't get Rafael's story out of her head.

Nor could she deny his talent. She'd learned very early on, after reading an unauthorised biography on him before accepting the job as his physiotherapist last year, that Rafael had a magic touch in most endeavours he undertook in his life. That he'd dedicated his life to racing had only meant that the sport had benefited endlessly.

His regular contribution to X1 Premier Management's monthly magazine already garnered a subscription said to be in the millions. If he chose to dedicate his life to writing fiction his fan base would become insane.

And you would probably be his adoring number one fan.

Without warning, Rafael's gaze swung towards her. The sizzling *knowledge* in that look sent sharp arrows of need racing to her pelvis. Her pulse hammered at her throat, her skin tingling with the chemistry of what she felt for Rafael.

'...you ever been to Monza?' The German ex-racer seated next to her—Axel Jung, she remembered his name now—stared at her with blatant interest.

She shook her head but couldn't tear her gaze away from the formidable, intensely charismatic man whose gaze held her prisoner from across the aisle. 'Um, no, I was Rafael's physio last year but Monza wasn't on the race calendar so I missed it.'

'You're in for a treat. It's one of the best racetracks in the world.'

She swallowed and tried to dismiss the intensity of Rafael's stare. 'Yes, so I've been told. The old track was even more spectacular, from the pictures I've seen of it.'

Axel's chuckle helped her break eye contact with Rafael but not before she saw his gaze swing to Axel and back to her.

'If you liked danger with your spectacular view, that was the track to race on,' Axel said.

She made an effort to turn her attention to him and almost regretted it when she glimpsed his deepening interest. 'I suspect that's why it's a thrill for most drivers?' she ventured.

He nodded eagerly. 'I don't know a driver who hasn't dreamt of driving at Monza, either on the old or the new track. The tickets for Monza's All-Star event sold out within minutes of going online.'

Raven had a feeling it had something to do with Rafael's presence, this being one of his first public appearances since his accident. 'That's great for the charity, then?'

'Yes, it is. I'd be honoured if you'll permit me to show you around Monza.' He drew closer. His smile widened, lending his blond-haired, blue-eyed features a boyish charm.

'I'm there to work, I'm afraid. And you'll be driving I expect?'

Axel, a two-time world champion twenty-five years ago, nodded. 'Rafael and I have a friendly rivalry that seems to draw the crowd.' He laughed. The fondness in his voice was clear. 'He's a special one, that one. The playboy thing is just a front. Don't let it fool you. Deep down, there beats the heart

of a genius forged in steel. A fierce leader who would fight to
the death for what he believes in.'

Having her instincts confirmed that there was more to
Rafael than met the eye made her slow to respond. A quick
glance at him showed him in deep conversation with a member of his All-Star team. 'I...'

'He single-handedly brought the board members to his way
of thinking two years ago when they tried to put off new safety
measures for drivers,' Axel said.

'*Safety?*' Raven asked in surprise. 'But I thought...'

'You think because we love speed and hurtle around racetracks at two hundred and fifty miles per hour we think less
of safety? Ask any driver. The opposite is true. We manage
to take the risks we do *because* of people like Rafael and the
work they do to ensure drivers' safety.'

Feeling wave after wave of astonishment roll through her,
she glanced again at Rafael, only to find his attention fixed
on her, his blue eyes narrowed to speculative slits. He glanced
away again and resumed his conversation.

The floundering feeling escalated. 'Excuse me,' she murmured to Axel when the stewardess entered to take drinks orders. Standing, she made her way towards the large bedroom
and the en suite bathroom.

After splashing water on her wrists, she re-knotted her hair
in a secure bun and left the bathroom, only to stumble to a halt.

Rafael stood, back braced solidly against the bedroom door.
His presence in the enclosed space, larger than life and equally
as imposing, dried her mouth.

Heart hammering, she stayed where she was, away from the
danger radiating from him. 'I...is there something you need?'

He folded his arms and angled his head. '*Need?* No.' He
remained in front of the door.

Raven licked her lips and immediately regretted it. 'Can
we return to the cabin, then?'

'Not just yet,' he rasped, then just stood there, watching her
with a predatory gleam that made her nape tighten.

Silence stretched for several minutes as he stayed put, seemingly in no hurry to go anywhere, or speak, for that matter.

She searched her mind for what he could possibly want, and felt her heart lurch with disappointment. 'You're not in here because you want to make sure your playboy status is intact, are you?'

'What was Axel saying to you?'

She waved him away. 'Nothing for you to worry about.' He remained in place, that infuriatingly well-defined eyebrow arched. 'Okay, if you must know, he told me that beneath all that lady-killer persona, you're really a Boy Scout. Oh, and he also offered to show me Monza.'

He glanced away but she saw his jaw tighten. 'I hope you told him no?'

'Maybe.' She started to move towards him in the hope that he'd get the hint and move. He remained, rock-still and immovable.

'Stay away from him,' he said, his voice low but no less forcefully lethal.

Her pulse spiked higher. 'Sexually, socially or just for the hell of it?'

With a swiftness she wouldn't have attributed to him considering his injuries, he reached forward, grabbed her arms, whirled her round and reversed their position. Her lungs expended their oxygen supply as she found herself trapped between the hard, polished wood and Rafael's equally hard, warm body.

One hand gripped her nape while the other settled firmly on her waist. Heat ratcheted several notches. Inhaling only made matters worse because Rafael's scent, potent and delicious, attacked her senses with rabid fervour.

'He was looking at you as if he wanted to serve you up on his sauerkraut.'

'And what, you're jealous?'

'Not if you tell me you're not thinking of falling into the clutches of an ex-racer more than twice your age.'

'Axel's only in his mid-forties. And I'm touched you're looking out for me.'

Blue eyes deepened by his blue long-sleeved shirt and navy jeans narrowed even further. 'And he also likes to think he's slick with the ladies.'

'Scared of the competition?'

'Scared I'm going to have to toss his ass out of the plane without a parachute if you don't tell me you'll stay away from him.' Without warning, one thigh wedged between hers. The heat emanating from him made her whole body feel as if it were on fire. Second by inexorable second, he pressed closer against her. His hard chest brushed against hers, stinging sensitive nipples to life. Raven fought a moan and tried to decide whether defiance or acquiescence was her best path.

'Is this what it means to be caught between a rock and a hard place?' she asked, unable to resist baiting him just a little.

His laugh sent a skitter of pleasure through her. 'You're making jokes, *querida*?'

'You're laughing, aren't you?'

'*Sí*,' he agreed. The hand on her waist moved a fraction higher, dug deeper in an almost possessive hold on her ribcage. 'But I'm still waiting for an answer.'

A small voice cautioned her against throwing more fuel onto the flames.

'I spoke to him for fifteen minutes, but I barely remember what he looks like,' she whispered against seriously tempting lips a hair's breadth from hers. 'But why do you care? Really?'

'You were the first person I told about my father outside my family. You haven't condemned me…yet. In my own small way, I'm trying to return the favour by saving you from a potentially unfortunate situation.'

'By trapping me here and threatening to toss a man out of the plane?'

'It's my Latin blood, *piqueña*. It takes me from zero to

growly in less than five seconds.' He closed the gap between their lips and their bodies.

A fervid moan rose from her chest as sensation crashed over her head. Her knees turned liquid and she would've lost her balance had she not been trapped so powerfully against a towering pile of formidable maleness. As they were, with his thigh wedged so firmly between hers, she felt the heat from his leg caress her intimately. Friction, urgent and undeniable, made her pulse race faster. Even more when his tongue delved between her lips. Like the first time they'd kissed, Rafael seemed bent on devouring her. Although she'd been kissed, she'd never been kissed quite like this, with a dedication so intense she felt as if she were being consumed.

When he finally let her up for air, it was to allow her a single breath before he pounced again. Her hands, which had miraculously risen to glide over his shoulders, finally found the wherewithal to push him away.

'Rafael…'

'No, not yet.' His lips swooped, but she managed to turn her head just in time. He settled for nibbling the corner of her mouth, a caress so erotic she throbbed low down with the sensation.

'We need to stop. Everyone out there will think we're in here…doing…having…'

'*Sex*…saying it doesn't make you a dirty, dirty girl, Raven.' His thigh moved, inserting itself even more firmly between hers. Again friction caused sensation to explode in her belly.

She flushed. 'I know that.'

'Then say it,' he commanded, pulling back to stare into her eyes.

Defiance surged back on a wave of desperation. 'Sex. Sex, sex, *sex*—'

He kissed her silent, and damn, but did she enjoy it. When he finally raised his head she was thoroughly and dangerously breathless. 'It's okay, you've made your point. Although I can't say that'll dissuade our fellow travellers from thinking we've joined the Mile High Club.'

A growl of frustration rumbled out before she could stop it. 'Why couldn't you leave this alone until we landed?'

'The same reason you're still caressing my shoulders even though you're protesting my presence here with you.'

She dropped her hands and swore she could feel her skin tingling in protest.

'I...this is crazy,' she muttered under her breath.

'*Sí*, but we can't help ourselves where the other is concerned. Are you ready to go back?'

A shaky nod was all she could manage before he withdrew his thigh from between hers. The loss of his support and heat made her want to cry out in protest. She stopped herself in time and checked to see if her buttons had come undone.

With a sigh of relief, she stepped away from the door.

Rafael was very close behind her when they exited the bedroom. 'You didn't tell me what you thought of the story.'

She looked over her shoulder. 'I thought it was incredible.'

He stilled, an arrested look on his face. 'You enjoyed it?'

'Very much. The girl has an amazing spirit. I can't wait to find out more about her journey.' She glanced at him. 'That is if you intend to continue with it?'

A look passed over his face, gone too quickly before she could decipher it. 'With such a rousing endorsement, how could I not? As it happens, I have a few more chapters.'

Pleasure fizzed through her. 'Will you let me read it?'

He smiled. 'You mean you want to read more, despite the lack of X-rated material?'

She huffed in irritation. 'Why did I think a lovely conversation with you would last more than five seconds?'

His low laugh curled around her senses. She was so lost in it, she didn't realise he had led her away from Axel until he pushed her into the seat next to his.

The Monza circuit, perched on the outskirts of the small namesake town, was situated north of Milan. The view from above as Rafael's helicopter pilot flew over the racetrack was spectacular.

A riot of colour from the different sponsor logos and team colours defied the late winter greyness. She felt the palpable excitement from small teams readying the race cars before they landed.

Casting a glance at Rafael, she couldn't immediately see his reaction due to wraparound shades and noise-cancelling headphones, but his shoulders, the same ones she'd caressed barely ninety minutes ago, tensed the closer they got to the landing pad. If they'd been alone she would've placed her hand on his—an incredible development considering this time last week the thought of touching him set her teeth on edge—but she didn't want to attract undue attention. The paddock would supply enough gossip to fuel this event and the rest of the X1 season as it was.

Cameras flashed as soon as the helicopter touched down and demanding questions were lobbed towards them the moment the doors opened.

Are you returning to racing, Rafael?

Will you be officially announcing your retirement today or is this the start of your comeback?

Is it true you're suffering from post-traumatic stress disorder?

His jaw was set in concrete even though his lips were curved in a smile as he stepped out of the helicopter and waved a lazy hand at the cameras.

A luxurious four-by-four was parked a few feet away. He held the door open for Raven and slid in after her.

'I don't know how you can stand them without wanting to punch someone in the face,' Raven found herself murmuring as she watched a particularly ambitious paparazzo hop onto the back of a scooter and race after them.

'They help raise the profile of the sport. They're a necessary evil.'

'Even when they're intrusive to the point of personal violation?'

'When I engage them, I engage them on my terms. It's a skill I learned early.'

With a surprise, she realised that everything the press knew about Rafael was something he'd chosen to share with them, not some sleazy gossip they'd dug up. To the common spectator, Rafael lived his life in the public eye but in the past few weeks she'd discovered he had secrets...secrets he shared with no one, not even his family.

'You give them just enough to keep them interested and to keep them from prying deeper.'

Stunning blue eyes returned her stare with amusement and a hint of respect. 'That is just so, my clever Raven.'

'So, what pierces that armour, Rafael?'

His smile dimmed. 'I could tell you but I'd have to sleep with you.'

Raven's heart lurched and then sped up when, for a single second, she found herself contemplating if that was a barter worth considering. *Sleeping with Rafael*...

A tiny electric shock that zapped her system left her speechless.

'Since you're not slapping my face in outrage, dare I hope the suggestion isn't as repulsive as you found it previously?'

'I...I never thought you were repulsive,' she replied. 'You may have been a little too intense with your interest, that's all.'

'You dislike my intensity?'

She opened her mouth to say *yes,* and found herself pausing. 'I wasn't used to it. And I didn't like that you had everyone falling over themselves for you and yet you weren't satisfied.'

'But now we've spent some time together you think you *understand* me?' His tone held a hint of derision that chilled her a little.

'I don't claim to understand you but I think I know you a little better, yes.'

The warmth slowly left his eyes to be replaced by a look so neutral he seemed like a total stranger.

Their vehicle pulled up in front of the expansive, stunning motor home that had been set up to accommodate the Italian All-Star event. Several dignitaries from the sports world waited to greet Rafael. He reached for the door handle and turned to her before alighting.

'Don't let that knowledge go to your head, *querida*. I'd hate for you to be disappointed once you realise I won't hesitate to take advantage of that little chink in your armour. Underneath all this, there is only a core of nothingness that will stun you to your soul.'

He got out before she could respond. Before she drew another breath, he'd transformed into Rafael de Cervantes, world champion and charm aficionado. She watched women and *men* fall over themselves to be in his company. Basking in the adoration, he disappeared into the motor home without a backward glance.

Rafael waved away yet another offer of vintage champagne and cast his gaze around for Raven.

He'd been too harsh, he knew. Had he—finally—scared her away for good? The thought didn't please him as it should have.

But she'd strayed far too close, encroaching on a deep dark place he liked to keep to himself. He hadn't been joking when he'd warned her about the core of nothingness. How could he? What would be the point in revealing that grotesque, unthinkable secret?

She would hate you, and you don't want that.

His gut tightened but he pushed the thought away.

No one could hate him more than he hated himself. It was better that he ensured Raven harboured no illusions. Although she'd probably claim not to be, she was the type to see the good in everyone. If she didn't she wouldn't have asked for help from a deplorable father who had subjected her to *dios* knew what to save her mother. He suspected that, deep down, she'd hoped her father would reveal himself to be something other than he was.

Rafael wasn't and would never be a knight in shining armour. Not to her and not to any other woman. He took what he wanted and he didn't give a damn.

Above the heads of the two men he was talking to, he saw Chantilly enter the room on her husband's arm. She zeroed in on him with an openly predatory look, her heavily made-up eyes promising filthy decadence.

Rafael felt nothing. Or rather he felt…different. On further examining his reaction, he realised the sensation he was feeling wasn't the cheap thrill of playing games with Sergey's wife. It was self-loathing for having played it in the first place.

He looked away without acknowledging her look and cast his gaze around the room one more time. Realising he still searched for Raven—where the hell was she?—he made a sound of impatience under his breath.

'Is everything all right?' the chairman of the All-Star event asked him.

'The old racetrack has been carefully inspected as I requested?'

The white-haired man nodded. 'Of course. Every single inch of it. You still haven't told us whether you'll be participating.'

Tightness seized his chest. He forced himself to take a breath and smile. 'The event is only beginning, Adriano. I'll let you old folks have some fun first.'

'Less of the old, if you please.'

The laughter smoothed over his non-answer but the tightness didn't decrease. Nor did his temper when he looked up a third time and found Raven standing at the far end of the room with Axel.

She'd changed from jeans into yet another pair of trousers, made of a faintly shimmery material, and a black clingy top that threw her gym-fit body into relief when she moved.

The sound of a nearby engine revving provided the perfect excuse for Axel to lean in closer to whisper into her ear. Whatever the German was saying to her had her smiling and nodding. Obviously encouraged, her companion moved even closer, one hand brushing her shoulder as he spoke.

Rafael moved without recognising an intention to do so, a feat in itself considering his hip was growing stiffer from standing for too long. 'Raven, there you are.'

She turned to him. 'Did you want me?' she asked, then flushed slightly.

'Of course I want you,' he replied. 'Why else are you here, if not to come when I want you?'

A spurt of anger entered her eyes. 'What can I do for you?'

'I need your physio services. What else?'

She frowned. 'According to your itinerary, you're working until ten o'clock tonight. Which is why I scheduled a swim therapy for you afterwards and a proper physio session in the morning.'

His eyes stayed on hers. 'My schedule is fluid and right now I need you.'

'Ah, actually, I'm glad you're here, Rafael,' Axel said.

'Really? And why's that, Jung?'

The other man cleared his throat. 'I was hoping to convince you to let my team borrow Raven's services for a few hours. Our regular physiotherapist came down with a stomach bug and had to stay at the hotel.'

'Out of the question,' Rafael replied without a single glance in his direction.

'Rafael!'

'Need I remind you what your contract states?' he asked her.

'I don't need reminding, but surely—'

He shifted sideways deliberately in a move to get her attention. And succeeded immediately. 'What happened?' she demanded, her keen eyes trailing down his body, making a visual inspection.

'You were right. This whole thing has simply worn me out. I think I'll have an early night.' He turned towards the door. 'Are you coming?'

'I…yes, of course.' Concern was etched into her face. Rafael wanted to reassure her that his hip wasn't painful enough to warrant that level of worry.

But he didn't because he couldn't guarantee that she wouldn't wish to stay, return to Axel. The disconcerting feeling unsettled him further.

'I was away for just over an hour. Please tell me you didn't try and do anything foolish to your body in that time.'

'Where were you, exactly?'

'Excuse me?'

'Were you with Jung all that time?' he asked, an unfamiliar feeling in his chest.

'Are we seriously doing this again?'

'How else would he have got it into his mind to poach you?'

'He wasn't…isn't trying to poach me. He was telling the truth. His team's physio was sent back to his hotel because he fell ill. But they think it's just a twenty-four hour virus. I didn't see the harm in agreeing to give my professional opinion.'

'You should've spoken to me first.'

'In the mood you were in? You bit my head off because I got too close again. I won't be your personal punchbag for whenever you feel the need to strike out.'

He sucked in a weary breath and Raven forced herself to look at him properly for the first time. Not that it was a hardship.

It was clear he was in pain. His skin was slightly clammy and stress lines flared from his eyes. 'What the hell did you do to yourself?' she asked softly.

'You should've stuck around if you were concerned.'

She didn't get the opportunity to answer as they'd arrived at the helipad. The blades were already whirring when she took her seat beside Rafael for the short trip to their hotel in Milan.

As they exited the lift towards their exclusive penthouse suite, she turned to him. 'Lean on me.'

When he didn't argue or make a suggestive comment, she knew he was suffering. Raven was thankful she'd had the forethought to ring ahead to make sure the equipment she needed had been set up.

Back in their hotel, after Rafael stripped to his boxers, she started with a firm sports massage to relax his limbs before she went to work on the strained hip muscles.

By the time she was done, a fine sheen of sweat had broken over his face. Pouring a glass of water, she handed it to him.

He drank and handed the glass back to her.

'I don't like seeing you with other men. It drives me slightly nuts,' he said abruptly.

She stilled in the act of putting away a weighted leg brace. 'You can't have all the toys in the playground, Rafael.'

'I just want one toy. The one sitting on top of the tree that everyone says I can't have.'

'What you can't do is to keep shaking the tree in the hope that the toy will fall into your lap. That's cheating.'

'It's not cheating; it's taking the initiative. Anyway, you can't be with Axel.'

She stopped, head tilted to the side, before she tucked a strand of hair behind one ear. 'Okay, I'll play. Why can't I be with him?'

He gave a pained grimace. 'He has a ridiculous name, for a start. Think how ridiculous your future kids would find you. Raven and Axel Jung. Doesn't rhyme.'

'And I have to have a man whose name rhymes with mine, why?'

'Synergy in all things. Take you and me.'

'You and me?' she parroted.

'*Sí.* Rafa and Raven rolls right off the tongue. It was meant to be.'

She passed him a towel. 'I'd suspect you were on some sort

of high, but you didn't touch a drop of alcohol at the mixer and you've refused any pain medication.'

'I'm completely rational. And completely right.'

'It must be hunger making you delirious then.' She handed him the walking stick and walked beside him to the living room. 'Room service?'

With a sigh, he sank into the nearest wide velvet sofa, nodded and put his head back on the chair.

'What would you like?' she asked.

'You choose.'

'Would you like me to spoon-feed you when it arrives, too?'

His grin was a study in mind-melting hotness and unashamed sexual arrogance. 'You're not the first to offer, *querida*. But I may just make you the first to succeed in that task.'

Rolling her eyes, she ordered two steaks with a green salad for them. Then, on impulse, she ordered a Côte du Rhone.

The wine wouldn't exactly lay him flat but it might let him relax enough to get a good night's sleep, especially since he refused to take any medication.

After she'd placed the order, she set the phone down and approached the seating area.

Rafael patted the space beside him.

Very deliberately, and sensibly, she thought, she chose the seat furthest from him and ignored his low mocking laugh.

'So, care to tell me what happened today?'

He stilled, then his eyes grew hooded. 'First day back on the job. Everyone was clamouring for the boss.'

Raven got the feeling it was a little bit more than that but she wisely kept it to herself. 'What are the races in aid of this year?' she asked, changing the subject.

He tensed further, wrong-footing her assumption that this was a safe subject.

For the longest time, she thought he wouldn't answer. 'XPM started a foundation five years ago for the victims of road accidents and their families. But we soon realised that giving away money doesn't really help. Educating about safety was a better route to go. So we've extended the programme to testing road and vehicle safety, with special concentration on young drivers.'

'Was…was it because of what happened with your father?'

His eyes darkened. 'Surprisingly, no. It was because a boy racer wiped out a family of six because he wasn't aware of how powerful the machine underneath him really was. I knew exactly how powerful the car I drove was so my transgression didn't come from ignorance.'

'Where did it come from?'

'Arrogance. Pride. I owned the world and could do as I pleased, including ignoring signs of danger.' His face remained impassive, this slightly self-loathing playboy who wore his faults freely on his chest and dared the world to judge him. His phone rang just then. He checked the screen, tensed and pressed the off button. 'Speak of the devil and he appears,' he murmured. His voice was low and pensive with an unmistakable thread of pain.

Raven frowned. 'That was your father?'

'*Sí*,' he replied simply.

'And you didn't answer.'

The eyes he raised to her were dark and stormy. 'I didn't want to interrupt our stimulating conversation. You were saying…?'

She searched her memory banks and tried to pull together the threads of what they'd been talking about. 'You used the past tense when you said you owned the world? You no longer think that?'

'World domination is overrated. Mo' power mo' problems.' Although he smiled, the tortured pain remained.

'Is that why you won't forgive yourself? Because you think you should've known better.'

'My, my, is it Psychology 101?'

She pressed her lips together. 'It is, isn't it?'

'If I said yes, would you make it all better?'

'If you said yes you would feel better all on your own.' The doorbell rang and she looked towards the door. 'Think about that while I serve our feast.'

The emotions raging within him didn't disappear from his eyes as she went to the door to let the waiter in.

By unspoken agreement they stuck to safer subjects as they ate—once again, Rafael taking her refusal to feed him with equanimity.

When she refused a second glass of wine, he set the bottle down and twirled his glass, his gaze focused on the contents.

'So where is this island of yours that Marco and Sasha have gone to?'

'There are a string of islands near Great Exuma. We own one of them.'

'Wow, what does it feel like to own your own island?'

'Much like it feels to own a car, or a handbag, or a pen. They're all just possessions.'

'Possessions most people spend their lives dreaming about.'

'Are you one of those people? Do you dream of finding a man to take you from your everyday drudgery to a life filled with luxury?'

'First of all, I don't consider what I do drudgery. Secondly, while I think dreams are worth having, I set more store by the hard work that *propels* the achievement of that dream.'

'So I can't sway you with the promise of a private island of your very own?'

'Nah, I have a thing about private islands.'

His brow rose. 'A *thing*?'

She nodded. 'I saw a TV show once where a group of people crashed onto one and spent a hellishly long time trying to get off the damned rock.' Her mock shudder made him grin. 'A concrete jungle and the promise of a mocha latte every morning suits me just fine.'

He raised his glass. 'To concrete jungles and the euphoria of wall-to-wall coffee shops.'

'Indeed.' She clinked glasses with him. Then it dawned

on her how easy the atmosphere had become between them;
how much more she wanted to stay where she was, getting to
know this compelling man who spelled trouble for her. The
thought forced her to push her chair back. 'I think I'll head
to bed now. Goodnight, Rafael.'

If he noticed the sudden chill in her voice, he didn't react to
it. 'Before you go, I have something for you,' he said, pointing
to the elegant console table that stood outside the suite's study.

Seeing the neat stack of papers, Raven felt a leap of pleasure. Going to the table, she picked up the papers and, sure
enough, it was the continuation of Ana's story.

'Did you write all of this last night?' she asked him.

He shrugged. 'The muse struck when I was awake. No big
deal.' But she could tell it was. His gaze was hooded and his
smile a little tight. It was almost…almost as if he was nervous about her reading it.

'Thanks for trusting me with this, Rafael.'

He looked startled for a moment, then he nodded. '*De nada.*
Buenas noches, bonita,' he replied simply.

The distinct lack of *naughty* left her floundering for a moment. Then she forced herself to walk towards her suite.

'Raven?' His voice stopped her beside the wide, elegant
double doors leading into the hallway. When she turned, his
gaze had dropped to assess the contents of his wine glass.

'Yes?'

'Don't flirt with Jung.'

Her pulse raced. Later, when she was safely in her cool bed,
she tried to convince herself it was the effects of the wine that
made her say, 'Quid pro quo, my friend. If I'm not allowed to
flirt, then no more numbers on your walking stick. Agreed?'

Blue eyes lifted, regarded her steadily, their brilliance and
intensity as unnerving as they'd been the very first time she'd
looked into them. After a full minute, he nodded. 'Agreed.'

CHAPTER EIGHT

SHE FOUND HIM in the penthouse pool the next morning. She stood, awestruck, as Rafael cleaved the water in rapid, powerful strokes, his sleek muscles moving in perfect symmetry. He turned his head just before he dived under and executed a turn and, for a split second, Raven became the focus of piercing blue eyes.

One length, two lengths…three.

After completing the fourth, he stopped at the far end, flipped onto this back and swam lazily towards her. 'Are you going to stand there all day or are you going to join in? We leave for the racetrack in half an hour.'

'I'm not coming in, thank you. We were supposed to have a full physio session this morning.'

'I was up and raring to go, *bonita*. You were not.'

It was the first time ever that Raven had overslept or been late for an appointment. She couldn't stem the heat that crawled up into her face as she recalled the reason why. When she'd found herself unable to sleep, she'd opened up Rafael's manuscript and delved back between the pages. If anything, the story had been even better the second time round, renewed fascination with Ana, the heroine, keeping her awake.

'I was only ten minutes late.'

He stopped on the step just beneath where she stood and sluiced a hand through his hair. 'Ten throwaway minutes to you is a lifetime to me.' He hauled himself out of the pool. Raven couldn't stop herself from ogling extremely well-toned biceps and a tight, streamlined body. Even the scars he'd sustained on his legs and especially his hip were filled with character that made her want to trace her fingers over it, test his skin's texture for herself.

She forced herself to look away before the fierce flames rising could totally engulf her. He grabbed the towel she tossed to him and rubbed it lazily over his body.

'Well, since you had the full therapy session last night, I don't see the harm in reversing the regime.'

He glanced over and winked. 'My thoughts exactly.'

Suspicion skittered along her spine. 'You're surprisingly chipper this morning.' Looking closer, she saw that his face had lost its strained edge, and when he turned to toss the towel aside, his movement had lost last night's stiffness.

'It's amazing what a good night's sleep can do. I feel as if I have a new lease of life.' He picked up his walking stick and came towards her, a sexy, melt-your-panties-off grin firmly in place. 'Come, we'll have breakfast and I can tell you how to make your tardiness up to me.'

'Anything less than a pound of flesh and I'll probably die of shock,' she muttered.

He laughed. The sound floated along her skin then sank in with pleasure-giving intensity. 'You wound me. I was thinking more along the lines of your thoughts on the manuscript.'

She didn't answer immediately. She was too caught up in watching the ripple of muscle as he sauntered out of the pool area—and through his bedroom, where discarded clothes and twisted sheets made her temperature rise higher—towards the sun-dappled balcony where their breakfast had been laid out.

Goodness knew how she managed not to stare like some hormonal schoolgirl.

'Wow, should I take your silence to mean it was sheer dross?'

Focus! She sat down at the table, snapped out her napkin and laid it over her lap, wishing she could throw a blanket over her erotic thoughts just as easily.

He poured her coffee—mocha latte—and added a dash of cinnamon, just the way she liked it. Raven decided she was *not* going to read anything into Rafael's intimate knowledge of how she took her caffeine. But inside she felt a long held-in tightness spring free, accompanied by the faintest spark of fear.

'It wasn't dross. I'm sure you know that. I love Ana's transition from girl into woman. And that first meeting with Carlos was what every girl dreams of. I'm happy she's putting her dark past behind her...'

'But?' He scythed through her ambivalence.

'But I think Carlos is coming on too strong, too fast. He risks overwhelming Ana just a little bit.'

He picked up his own coffee and eyed her over the rim. 'But I think she has a backbone of steel. Do you not think she has what it takes to stay?'

Raven nodded. 'I think she does. She sees him as a challenge...welcomes it to some extent, but I'm still a little scared for her.'

'You're invested in her. Which is what a writer wants, isn't it? Maybe she needs to be pushed out of her comfort zone to see what she really wants.'

'I notice she likes racing, just like Carlos.'

He stilled. '*Sí*. It is a racing thriller, after all.'

Raven carefully set her cup down and picked up a slice of toast. 'She wouldn't, by chance, be modelled on your sister-in-law, would she?' she asked, keeping her voice level.

He shrugged. 'Sasha is one of the best female drivers I've known. What's your point?'

She didn't know how to articulate what it made her feel. Hell, she couldn't grasp the roiling feelings herself. All she knew was that she didn't want Rafael to be thinking of a specific woman when he wrote the story.

'I just think you would appeal to a wider audience if the character wasn't so...specific.'

'You mean, it would appeal to you?'

The toast fell from her hand. 'I don't know what you mean.'

'Are you going to play this game? Really?'

The words, so similar to those she'd thrown at him, made heat crawl up her face. 'Fine. Touché.' She hardened her spine and forced out the next words. 'But you know what I'm trying to say.'

'Are we still talking about my manuscript?' he asked, a trace of a smile on his lips.

'We've taken a slight detour.'

'A detour that touches on our…friendship and the adjustments I need to make in order for it to advance?'

Her hands shook at how quickly they'd strayed into dangerous territory. She couldn't look into his probing gaze so she studiously buttered her toast. 'Y…yes.'

He stayed silent for so long she was forced to glance up. Blue eyes pinned her to her chair. 'Don't expect me to turn into something I'm not, *querida*.'

'Take a first step. You might surprise yourself.'

'And you, *piqueña*, how are you surprising yourself?'

The question, unexpected and lightning-quick, sent a bolt of shock through her. She floundered, unsure of what to say. 'I…I'm not sure…'

'Well, make sure. If I'm to bend over backwards to accommodate you, you have to give something back, *si*?'

That pulse of fear intensified. Opening up to Rafael in Monaco, telling him things she'd never told another human soul, had left her feeling raw and exposed.

Now, by daring her in his oh-so-sexy way to open up even more, he threatened to take it a whole lot further, luring her with a promise she knew deep down he wouldn't keep. That was the essence of playboys. They exuded charisma, invited confidences until they had you in their grasp.

And yet the rare glimpses she'd caught of Rafael threatened that long-held belief. He was alluding to the fact that playboys could have hearts of gold. Raven wasn't sure she was ready to handle that nugget of information.

For years, her mother had believed it—believed it still— and look where it'd got her. If she let Rafael in and he did a number on her, she wasn't sure who she would hate more— Rafael…or herself.

'You don't have to turn into something else. All I ask is to see a little bit more, make my choice with a clear, if not total, view of the facts. Because I can't have sex with you for the sake of it. I would hate myself and I would hate you.'

'Ah, but we're already having sex, *mi amor*. All that's left is for our bodies to catch up.'

Of course, she could *really* have done without that thought in her head. Because, suddenly, it was all she could think about.

She walked beside Rafael along the long paddock an hour later, watching as he stopped at every single All-Star garage to greet and exchange info with the crew. From her stint as his physio last year, Raven knew just how meticulous a driver he was. He understood the minutiae of racing to the last detail and could probably recite the inner workings of a turbo engine in his sleep.

Which was why his accident, judged to be the result of human error—his—had stunned everyone. Some had speculated that it had been the effects of partying hard that had finally done him in. But, in the last few weeks, she'd caught occasional glimpses of the man underneath and knew Rafael de Cervantes wasn't all gloss. He rarely drank more than a glass of champagne at any event and she knew he'd banned smoking in the paddock a few years back.

What she didn't know was how deep the Rafael de Cervantes well ran, or how monstrous the demons were that chased him. It was clear he was haunted by something in his past. At first she'd thought it was his father. But even though that particular revelation had been painful to him, it had been when she'd mentioned his mother that the real pain had surfaced, just for a moment.

She glanced at him, a little overwhelmed by the many facets she had previously been too riled up to see. Rafael had traits she abhorred, traits that reminded her of the man whose DNA ran through her veins.

But he was also so much more.

'I can hear you thinking again.'

'Unfortunately, my active brain cells refuse to subside into bimbo mode just because I'm in your presence.' She cast a telling glance at a groupie who'd just obtained an autograph and was squealing in delight as she ran to her friends.

'You can wow me with your superior intelligence later,' he said as they approached the last garage in the paddock.

The first thing she noticed was the age group of this particular crew. Aside from two older supervisors, everyone else ranged from early to late teens. The other thing that struck her was their synchronicity and clear pride in what they were doing.

When Rafael greeted them, they responded as if he were their supreme deity come to life. She wasn't surprised by their reaction. What surprised her was Rafael's almost bashful response as they gathered around him. Then it all disappeared as he started to speak. Started to teach.

They hung on his every word, and took turns asking him challenging questions, which he threw right back to them. Respect shone from their eyes and the depth of understanding he'd managed to impart in the space of the hour before the race started left Raven reeling.

'Close your mouth, *piqueña*. You'll catch flies,' he quipped as he led her away from the garage towards the VIP Paddock Club.

Her mouth snapped shut. 'That was incredible, the way you got them to listen, got them to apply knowledge they'd forgotten they had.'

'They're a talented bunch. And they love racing. All there is to learn is a respect for speed.' He shrugged. 'It wasn't hard.'

'No. You're a natural teacher.'

'I learned from the best.'

'Marco?'

He shook his head and held the door open to let her into the lift that whisked them up to the top floor VIP lounge. From there they had a panoramic view over the entire race circuit.

Rafael bypassed several A-listers who'd paid thousands of euros to attend this exclusive event and led her into a private roped-off area. He held out a chair for her then sat down opposite her. 'My father. He gave me my first go-kart when I was five. There's nothing about engines that he doesn't know. By the time I was nine, I could dismantle and reassemble a carburetor without assistance.'

'I didn't know your father raced.'

'He didn't. My grandfather had a small hotel business and wanted my father to study business so he could help him run it. But he never lost his love of racing. The moment his business grew successful enough, he enrolled Marco, then me in learning the sport. And he took us to all the European races, much to my mother's distress.'

The pang of envy for what she'd never had made her feel small so she pushed it away. Especially given what she knew of the strain between father and son now.

'That sounds just like what happened to Carlos in your story.'

He glanced at her with a tense smile. 'Does it?'

'Yes.' When he just shrugged, she decided not to pursue the subject of his story. 'So your father took you to all the races? Sounds like an idyllic childhood.'

'Sure, if you're prepared to forgive the fact that back then I was so intent on winning I didn't feel any compunction in crashing into every single car in front of me just to put them out of business. I was disqualified more times than I actually won races.'

'But I'm guessing your father persevered. He saw the raw talent and did everything he could to nurture it.' Something her own father hadn't even come close to attempting with her.

'Sí, he showed me the difference between winning at all costs and winning with integrity. And I repaid that by making sure he would never be able to drive a car again.' His face was taut with pain, his eyes bleak with a haunting expression that cracked across her heart.

'I saw how things were between you two at Jack's christening, but have you spoken to him at all since the accident?'

He tensed, waited for the waiter who'd brought their drinks to leave before he answered. 'Of course I have.'

'I mean about what happened.'

'What would be the point?'

'To find out how he feels about it?'

'How he *feels*? Trust me, I have a fair idea.'

Recalling the look on his father's face, she shook her head. 'Maybe you don't. Perhaps you should talk to him again. Or maybe let *him* talk to you. He could have something to say to you instead of you thinking it only works the other way round.'

He frowned suddenly. 'You're head shrinking me again. And how the hell did we get onto this subject anyway? It's boring me.'

'Don't,' she said softly.

A glaze of ice sharpened his blue eyes. 'Don't what?'

'Don't trivialise it. You'll have to tackle it sooner or later.'

'Like you have tackled your father?'

Her breath shut off in her chest. 'This is different.'

'How?' He had to raise his voice to be heard over the sound of engines leaving the garages to line up on the racetrack. Rafael barely glanced at them, his attention riveted on her face.

'Despite everything that's happened, your father loves you enough to want to connect with you. My father doesn't care if I'm alive or dead. He never has, and he never will.'

Rafael saw the depth of pain that slashed across her features before she turned to watch the action unfolding on the racetrack. He wanted to say something, but found he had no words of wisdom or of comfort to give her.

Because he didn't agree with the redeeming quality she seemed to want to find in him. He had no doubt that if she knew the extent of his sins, she wouldn't be so quick to offer her comfort.

An icy vice threatened to crush his chest, just as it did every time he thought of his mother. He'd awoken this morning with her screams ringing in his ears, the image of her lifeless eyes imprinted on his retinas.

No, he had no words of comfort. He'd trashed everything good in his life, and had come close to dismantling his relationship with his brother last year. The last thing he wanted to do was admit to Raven that part of his refusal to speak to his father was because he didn't want to discover whether he was irredeemably trashed in his father's eyes too.

His gaze flicked to the cars lining up on the track. Unlike the normal grand prix races when the cars lined up according to their qualifying time, the six All-Star cars were lined up side by side.

Team El Camino's red and black racer, driven by the young driver he'd been working with, was the first off the mark. Rafael felt a spurt of pride, which he immediately doused.

He had no right to feel pride. All he'd done was take what his father had taught him and passed it on. His father deserved the credit here, not him.

'Don't be so hard on yourself.'

Irrational anger sprang up within him. The fact that she seemed so determined to make him feel better when she was content to wallow in her own *daddy issues* filled him with anger. The fact that he was sexually frustrated—heck, he was going on eight months without having had sex—was setting his teeth on edge. The fact that he was up here, cooling his heels when he wanted more than anything to be down there... behind the wheel of a racing car—

Ice chilled his veins as he acknowledged the full extent of what he was feeling.

'Rafael?'

He didn't respond or turn towards her. Instead he watched the screen as Axel Jung threatened to take the lead from the young driver.

'Rafael, are you okay?'

'Do me a favour, *querida*, and stop talking. You're holding a mirror up to my numerous flaws. There's only so much I can take before I have to revert to type. And since you don't want that, I suggest you let me absorb a few of them and concentrate on enjoying this race, *si*?'

Far from doing what he expected of her, which was to retreat into sullen silence or—from experience with other women—flounce off in feminine affront, she merely picked up the remote that operated the giant screen in their section and turned it on. Then she picked up the menu, asked him what he wanted for lunch, then ordered it for them, her face set in smooth, neutral lines.

He waited several minutes, despising the emotion that ate away his insides like acid on metal. Guilt. An emotion he didn't like to acknowledge.

Guilt for upsetting her. 'I'm sorry,' he said.

A shapely eyebrow lifted in his direction, then she nodded. 'It's okay. I don't like dredging up my past either. I guess I should learn to respect yours.'

'But I seem to invite you to dig, which is very unlike me.' He frowned.

A tiny, perfect smile played around lips he remembered tasting. A craving such as he'd never known punched through him. Right in that moment, all he wanted to do was taste her again. Keep on tasting her until there were no clothes between them. Then he would taste her in the most elemental way possible. Right between her legs.

He would so enjoy watching her come. Again and again. And again.

Normally, he would have been thrilled by the natural path of his thoughts, but Rafael admitted his need held a previously unknown edge to it…an almost desperate craving he'd never experienced before. He wanted Raven. And yet a part of him was terrified by the depth of his need.

Forcing himself not to analyse it too closely, he returned

his attention to the track and felt a further spurt of discontentment when he saw Axel Jung had taken the lead.

Lunch was delivered and they ate in truce-like silence.

When Axel Jung took the race by a half second, Rafael tried to force back his black mood. As the CEO of the company organising the event, he had to step up to the podium and say a few words.

'If your jaw tightens any further, you'll do yourself an injury,' Raven murmured next to him.

'I'm smiling, *querida*, like the great racer slash CEO that I am,' he muttered back, turning towards her.

This close, her perfume filled his nostrils and invaded his senses. She gave a laugh and raised a sceptical brow. 'We both know you want to throw your toys out of the pram because the team you silently support came second. You're supposed to be unbiased, remember?'

He moved closer to her, felt the brush of her arm against his side and the depth of need intensified. 'I am unbiased. I just wanted my young driver to win, that's all,' he said, unrepentant.

Her teasing laugh and the way she bumped his shoulder in playful admonition unravelled him further. He glanced down into her face and his breath strangled at her breathtaking beauty.

A shout made him turn. Axel had stepped off the podium and was making his way towards them. Or Raven in particular, if the interest in his eyes was anything to go by.

Before conscious thought formed, Rafael moved, deliberately blocking the German from accessing the woman beside him. *His woman.*

'Congratulations, Jung. I think the press want their interview now.' He deftly turned the German towards the waiting paparazzi. As moves went, Rafael thought it was supremely smooth, but Raven's gasp told him the grace had been lost on her.

'Did you just do what I think you did?'

'That depends. Did you want him to come over here and slobber all over you?'

She shuddered. 'No, but I'm not sure I wanted a blatant territory-marking from you either.'

He wanted to tell her that he wished the whole paddock knew to keep away from her. But he knew it wouldn't go down well. It would also point out just how much he detested the idea of Raven with any other man. 'Point taken.'

Her eyes widened. 'Wow, I'm not sure whether to feel suspicious or special that you've conceded a point to me.'

'You should feel special.' His gaze trapped and held hers. 'Very special.'

Raven returned his stare, trying to summon a tiny bit of ire beneath all the high octane, breath-stealing emotions coursing through her. But the excitement licking along her nerve endings put the effort to shame.

Something of her feelings must have shown on her face because his eyes darkened dramatically. His gaze dropped to her lips, the heated pulse beating a wild rhythm in her neck, then back to her face.

Calmly, he breathed out and gave her a slow, electrifying smile. Eyes still locked on hers, he pulled out his phone and spoke in clear tones. Unfortunately, Spanish wasn't her forte so she had no clue what he was saying. But she made out the word *avión,* which made her even more curious.

'What was that about?' she asked when he hung up.

'I've arranged for our things to be packed. I thought we might head to Mexico a couple of days earlier than the rest of the racers.'

'Won't you be needed?'

'Possibly, but for the next two days I'm taking your advice and delegating. Does this make you happy?'

There was a deeper question beneath the stated one, a hungry gleam in his eyes that boldly proclaimed his intention should she agree to what he was proposing.

In a single heartbeat, Raven accepted it. 'Yes.'

It was almost a relief to let go of the angst and the rigid control. At least for a while. She knew without a shadow of a doubt that it would return a hundredfold soon enough.

It was almost a relief to let go of the anger and the rigid control. Except for a while. She knew without a shadow of a doubt that it's not that no longer enough.

CHAPTER NINE

SHE WAS GOING to take a lover. She was going to lose her virginity to the very man she'd run a mile from last year. The man who would most likely break her heart into a tiny million pieces long before this thing between them was over.

Nerves threatened to eat her up as their tiny seaplane banked and headed towards the private beachfront of the stunning villa Rafael owned in Los Cabos, Mexico. By now she knew all about the eighteen-bedroom villa, the lower level sauna and steam room, the two swimming pools and the names of every member of the construction crew who'd built the villa to Rafael's exact specification three years ago.

Because she'd needed to babble, to fill her head with white noise to distract her from the urge to spill the fact that she hadn't done this before. The closer they drew to their destination, the higher panic had flared beneath the surface of her outward calm.

Rafael's experience with women was world-renowned. What if she made a spectacular fool of herself? What if he was so put off by her inexperience he recoiled from her? To silence the voices, she babbled some more, found out that he had a staff of five who managed the villa and that he practised his handicap on the legendary golf course nearby when the occasion suited him.

In direct contrast to her nervous chirping, Rafael had been circumspect, his watchful silence unlike anything she'd ever known. Although he'd answered her questions with inexhaustible patience, his eyes had remained riveted on her the whole time, occasionally dropping to her lips as if he couldn't wait to taste, to devour.

They touched down on the water and powered to a stop next

to a large wooden jetty. After alighting, they headed towards
an open-topped jeep for the short drive to the villa.

Even though she felt as if she knew the property inside and
out, Raven wasn't prepared for the sheer, jaw-dropping beauty
of the adobe white-washed walls, the highly polished exposed
beams and almost ever-present sea views from the windows of
the mission-style villa. Spanish-influenced paintings adorned
the walls, lending a rich tapestry to the luxurious interior.

In her bedroom, rich fabrics in earthy colours formed the
backdrop to a mostly white theme set against warm terracotta
floors. But one item drew her attention.

'What's this for?' She touched the black high-powered tele-
scope that stood before one large window.

He came and stood behind her, bringing that warm, evoca-
tive scent that she'd come to associate with him and only him.
It took an insane amount of willpower not to lean back into
his hard-packed body.

'The waters around here are well-known grounds for sperm
whales. They tend to come closer to shore first thing in the
morning. If you're lucky you'll spot a few while we're here.'

Again the sombre, almost guarded response caught her off-
guard. She glanced at him over her shoulder. He returned her
stare with an intensity that made her breath catch. After a full
minute, he lifted his hand and drifted warm fingers down her
cheek in a soothing, belly-melting gesture.

'You're nervous, *bonita*. Don't be. I promise it will be
good.'

Her laugh was aimed at herself as much as at him. 'That's
easy for you to say.'

His finger touched and stayed on the pulse jumping in her
throat. 'It isn't. I haven't done this for a long time, too. Hell,
I don't know if the equipment works.'

He gave a wry smile when her brows shot up. 'You don't?'

'You will be the first since a while before the accident.'

'But I felt...I know you...'

'Can get a hard-on? *Sí*, but I'm yet to test the practical integrity of the machinery.'

'Oh, so I'm to be your guinea pig?' she teased, a little appeased that she wasn't the only one climbing walls about the prospect of them together.

'Guinea pigs don't have mouths like yours, or eyes the colour of a desert oasis. Or breasts that cry out to be suckled. Or the most perfect heart-shaped ass that makes me want to put you face down and straddle—'

'Okay, I get it. I'm hotter than a Greek furnace.' Her eyes strayed to the perfectly made up bed, her imagination running wild. She swallowed. 'I…I'd like a tour of the outside now, if you don't mind.'

His finger drifted up to the corner of her mouth, pressed gently before he put his finger to his own lips and groaned.

'If that's what you want.'

She nodded.

He didn't heed her request right away. He leaned down, placed his lips at the juncture between her neck and shoulder and ran his tongue over her thundering pulse. He answered her groan with one of his own, then he reluctantly stepped back. Raven was glad when he offered his arm because her legs had grown decidedly shaky.

The heeled leather boots she'd worn with her jeans and black-edged white shirt clicked alongside his heavier tread as they went outside.

On one side, an extensive stretch of grass led to a large thatched poolside bar surrounded by potted palm trees.

Beside it, an area clearly designated for relaxing featured a hot tub under long bales of white linen that had been intertwined to form a stunning canopy that offered shade. After the chill of Europe, it was a balm to feel the sun on her face.

'Come, there's something I want to show you.' There was heated anticipation in the low rumble that fluttered over her skin, feeding her own sizzling emotions.

Rafael led her across the grass and down shallow steps to

the private, secluded beach. All through the tour, his hand had been drifting up and down her back, stealing her thoughts and playing havoc with her pulse.

Which meant that she was totally unprepared for the sight that confronted her when he led her round a rock-sheltered cove.

The thick timber four-poster canopy had been erected right on the shore, with a massive day bed suspended by thick intertwined ropes. The sight was so vividly breathtaking, and so unexpectedly raw and pagan, she stopped in her tracks.

There was only one reason for the bed.

Sex. Outdoor sex.

Heat engulfed her whole body as Rafael's gaze met and trapped hers.

'The high rocks shield even the most determined lenses. And see those?' He indicated three discreetly placed floodlights pointing out towards the water. 'They come on at night and send a glare out to sea so any cunning paparazzi out there get nothing but glare when they try and get pictures of the villa.'

She swallowed hard. 'Even so, I can't imagine doing…it so blatantly.'

He caught her hand in his and kissed her palm. 'Never say never. Now, I believe we have a therapy session to work through?'

The fact that she'd forgotten her main reason for being there made her uncomfortable.

She hastened to cover it up. 'Yes, and don't hate me, but we'll need to step things up a bit.'

'Do with me what you will, *querida*. I'm but putty in your hands.'

He led the way back into the villa and into his bedroom. The setting sun threw orange shades across the king-size wooden-framed bed that seemed to dominate the room. When he threw his walking stick on the exquisitely designed recliner facing the double doors leading to a large balcony, she was reminded again why she was here with Rafael in the first place.

She'd cautioned him against sex only a handful of days ago, and yet here she was, unable to think beyond the raging need to strip every piece of clothing from his body.

Guilt ate away inside her.

'I can hear you thinking again. And I don't feel warm and fuzzy about the direction of your thoughts.' He started to unbutton his shirt.

She tried and failed not to let her eyes linger over his muscular chest and down over his washboard stomach, following the faint line of hair that disappeared beneath his jeans.

'Is this where we hold hands and pray about whether we should have sex or not?'

He was back. The irreverent, sexy, endlessly charismatic man who had women the world over falling at his feet.

Or was he?

A careful look into his eyes showed not the gleam of irreverence but a quietly speculative look beneath his words. 'Are you afraid you'll hate sex with me? Or afraid you'll love it so much you'll beg to become a groupie?'

She shook her head. 'As much as I want it to be easy, I've never taken a decision lightly. And I don't think you should either. It's not just me I'm thinking about here, Rafael. What if all this turns around on you? What if we do this and you get even more damaged?'

'Then I'll learn to live with it. Come here,' he said, holding out his hand. Although his mouth was smiling, his eyes held a very firm command.

She had to dig her toes in to stay put. 'You'll live with it because you think you deserve all the bad things that happen to you?'

His smile slowly eroded until only a trace remained. 'Raven, it's time to stop being my therapist and just be my lover.'

'Rafael…'

'Come. Here.'

He held still, hands outstretched. Almost against her will, she found herself moving forward. He waited until she was within touching distance. Then he lunged for her, sliding his fingers between hers to entrap her.

With his other hand he pulled her close, his fingers spreading over her bottom. Moving forward, he backed her against the wall, enclosing her thighs between his. 'I've got you now. No escape. Now, are you going to undress or do you need help?'

She gnawed on her lower lip, rioting emotions tearing her apart. 'I was so sure I wanted this, Rafael, but I'll never forgive myself if I make things worse for you—'

He growled, 'Damn it, just get naked, will you?'

When she remained still, he took the task into his own hands. For a man who hadn't slept with a woman for almost a year, he didn't seem to lack the skill needed to undress her.

She was down to her bra and knickers within seconds. One deft flick of his fingers disposed of her bra. Slowly he took one step back, then another.

'*Dios*, I knew you would be worth it,' he rasped, his fiercely intent gaze making her skin heat up and pucker in all the right places. Grabbing her by the waist, he reversed their positions and walked her back towards the bed. At the back of her mind she knew she needed to tell him about her lack of experience. But words were in short supply when confronted with the perfection that was Rafael's muscled torso.

With one firm push, she lay sprawled on the bed. He placed one knee on the bed, pushed forward, then winced as he positioned himself over her.

Her concerned gasp drowned beneath his kiss. The kiss that rocked her to her very soul. His tongue pushed inside, warm, insistent and pulse-melting as he showed her the extent of his mastery. Unable to bear the torrent of sensation, she jerked, her hands flailing as she tried to find purchase. He moved over her, pinned her more firmly to the bed with his hips flush against her. When he winced again, she wrenched her mouth from his.

'Before you say it, I'm fine. Dampen the mood with another virtuous monologue and I will spank you. Hard.'

She flushed deep and fierce, but it didn't keep her silent. 'I can't…I can't stop caring about your well-being just because it's inconvenient for you. Just tell me if you're okay.'

'I'm okay. But if I had to, I'd cut off my arm just to be inside you, to feel you close around me like you'd never let me go.'

'Bloody hell, do you practice those lines or do they really just fall off your lips?'

'If I plan to relaunch myself as a multimillion euro best-selling writer, *bonita*, then a way with words is a must.' He sobered. 'But that doesn't mean I don't mean them. I mean every single word I say to you.'

Her heart stuttered, then thundered wildly. 'Rafael…' Her eyes drifted shut.

'I'm lethal. I know.' He settled himself more firmly until she felt his rigid size against the fabric of her knickers. He rocked forward and the relentless pressure on her clitoris made a few dozen stars explode behind her closed eyelids.

'You're beyond lethal,' she breathed shakily. 'You're everything I should be running away from.'

His mouth drifted down her cheek to her jaw and back again. He pressed another kiss to the corner of her mouth, then she felt him move away. 'Hey, open your eyes.'

Reluctantly, she obeyed, already missing his mouth on her.

His gaze was solemn. 'Don't run, Raven. I'm broken and cannot chase after you. Not just yet.'

Her breath caught. 'Would you really? Chase after me?'

'Most definitely. Because I get extremely grumpy when I'm cheated out of an orgasm.'

The slap she aimed at his arm was half-hearted because his mouth was descending to wreak havoc on hers once more. When he finally allowed her to breathe, she was mindless with pleasure.

'I've wanted you for so long, I can't remember when I didn't want you.'

'But…why? Because I was the only paddock bunny who wouldn't fall into your bed?'

She expected a clever quip about his irresistibility. Instead, his gaze turned serious. 'Because within that tainted, false existence, you managed to remain pure. Nothing touched you. I craved that purity. I wanted to touch it, to see what it felt like. But you wouldn't even give me the time of day.'

'Because you had enough groupies hanging around you. I…I also thought you were with Sasha.'

He groaned. 'I guess I played the playboy game a little too well.'

'You mean you weren't?'

'I grew jaded a long time ago but some cloaks are more difficult to cast off than others.'

At her half-snort, he laughed. 'Do you know this is the longest I've been in a bedroom with a woman without one of us halfway to an orgasm?'

She knew that he meant the woman, not him. 'How trying for you.'

He pushed against her once more, his erection a fierce, rigid presence. '*Sí*. It's very trying. You should do something about it before my poor body gives out.' He trailed his mouth over hers before planting a row of kisses along her jaw.

'You really are incorrigible,' she gasped.

'Yes, I am,' he murmured, slowly licking his way down her neck to her pulse. 'I am incorrigible. And I deserve to be punished. Mercilessly.' He slid a hand to caress her belly, then lower to boldly cup her. 'Show me who's boss, my stern, sensible Raven. Give me the punishment I deserve.'

Her breath snagged in her chest. The same chest where her heart hammered like a piston about to burst its casing.

His fingers pressed harder, rhythmic, unrelenting. This time the explosion of heat stemmed from her very core and radiated throughout her body. Her legs parted wider, inviting him to embed himself even deeper. Her restless fingers traced the line of his jeans and found firm skin. Her fingers slipped an inch beneath and he moaned. The sound vibrated along her nerves as heat oozed between her legs.

Her hips undulated in sync with the movement of his fingers, and in that moment, Raven felt as if she were melting from the inside out. She moaned at the intensity of it.

'That's it, *precioso*, give it up for me,' he murmured in her ear, then bit on her lobe. Her cry echoed in the room, the sound as alien to her as the feelings coursing through her body. When his hot mouth trailed down her neck, over her shoulder blades, she held her breath, at once dreading and anticipating the sensation of his stubble roughness on her breast.

With a hungry lunge, he sucked one nipple into his mouth and drew hard on it. At the same time, one firm finger pressed on her most sensitive spot.

'Oh God!' Pleasure exploded in a fiery sensation that made her hips buck straight off the bed. She felt Rafael move off her and alongside her, but the pressure of his fingers and mouth didn't abate. Her climax dragged out until she feared she would expire from it. When her tremors subsided, he left her breasts to plant a forceful kiss on her lips. She fought to breathe.

Heavens, he was too much.

She opened her eyes to find his gaze on hers, intense and purposeful. 'If you're thinking of concocting a means of escape now you've come, know now I have no intention of letting that happen.'

'Why would I want to escape? Unless I'm mistaken, the best is yet to come. Yes?'

The relieved exhalation made her guess he'd suspected she was feeling overwhelmed. 'You have no idea. Kiss me.'

Raven's fingers curled into his nape, glorying in the luxurious heat of his skin as she complied with the heated request.

No, she didn't want to escape. Touching him felt so good, so incredibly pleasurable, that fleeing was the last thing on her mind. The thought surprised her, almost tripping out of her mouth. She curbed it in time. Rafael's head was already swollen by the thought that he could turn her on. Admitting how totally enthralled she was by him would make him even more insufferable. Although, the way she was feeling right now, she wouldn't be surprised if his sharp intellect worked it out before long—

'You're thinking again.'

She stared into blue eyes filled with raw hunger and masculine affront. Slowly she let her fingers drift through his hair, experiencing a keen sense of feminine satisfaction when he groaned. 'What are you going to do about it?'

His lips parted in a feral smile. 'Don't challenge a man on the knife-edge of need, sweetheart. You might regret it. If you survive the consequences.'

Without giving her time to answer, he pulled her down on top of him, both hands imprisoning her to his body as he fell back on the bed. Unerringly, his mouth found hers.

Raven stopped thinking.

And gave herself over to sensation. Rafael's pelvic bone might have been broken and pieced back together but there was nothing wrong with his arms. He lifted her above him and held her in place while he feasted on her breasts. When he was done, he lifted even higher. 'Take off your panties for me.'

With shaky fingers she drew them off, experienced a momentary stab of self-consciousness, which was promptly washed away when he positioned her legs on either side of him and looked up at her.

'You might want to hold onto something,' he murmured huskily, taking a sharp bite of the tender skin of her inner thigh.

The statement wasn't a casual boast. At the first brush of his tongue on her sex, her whole body arched and shook. She would've catapulted off him had he not been holding her hips in an iron grip.

Pain shot through fingers which had grasped the wooden

headboard at his warning. He licked, sucked and tortured her with a skill that left her reeling and hanging on for dear life.

When she tumbled headlong into another firestorm, he caught her in his arms and caressed her body until she could breathe again. Then he left her for a moment.

The sound of foil ripping drew her hazy gaze to him. The sight of his erection in his fist made her sex swell all over again.

He caught her stare and sent her a lethal smile. 'Next time, you get to do it.'

Raven didn't know what to do with that. Nor did she know how to find the correct words to tell him she'd never done it before. In the end, they just spilled out.

'Rafael, I'm a virgin.'

He stilled, shock darkening his eyes. A look flitted through his eyes a second before he shut them. The hand he raked through his hair was decidedly shaky.

He sucked in a long harsh breath, then opened his eyes. The raw hunger hadn't abated but the fisted, white-knuckled hand on his thigh showed he was making an inhuman effort to contain it. 'Do you want to stop?' he rasped, jaw clenched as he fought for control.

The thought of stopping made her insides scream in rejection. 'No. I don't. But I wanted you to know before…before it happened.'

He exhaled slowly. His hand unclenched, then clenched again as his gaze slid hungrily over her. 'I can guess your reasons for remaining celibate. What happened to you would make anyone swear off sex. I know the chemistry between us is insane, but you need to be sure you want to do this now, with me.'

'Would you rather I do it with someone else?' she quipped lightly, although the very thought of anyone but Rafael touching her made her shudder in rejection.

He lunged for her, firm hands grasping her shoulders in a rigid hold before she could take another breath.

'Not unless that *someone else* wishes to get his throat ripped out,' he bit out. He pinned her to the bed and devoured her with an anger-tinged, lethally aroused intensity that made fire roar through her body.

By the time he parted her legs and looked deep into her eyes, she was almost lost.

'I'd planned for you to be on top our first time. But I think this will be easier on you.'

His bent arms caged her as he probed her entrance, his gaze searching hers with every inch he slid inside her. The momentary tightening that made her breath catch stilled his forward momentum.

'Raven?' he croaked, tension screaming through his body as he framed her face in gentle hands.

'I'm okay.'

'That makes one of us.'

Her fingers tried to smooth back his hair but the silky strands refused to stay in place. 'I…can I do anything?'

His laugh was tinged with pain. '*Sí*, you could stop being so damned sexy.' He pushed another fraction and her breath hitched again. '*Dios*, I'm sorry,' he murmured, bending to place a reverent kiss on her lips.

Raven didn't know what was in store for her but she knew her body was screaming with the need to find out. With a deep breath—because, hell, no pain no gain—she pushed her hip upward. His cursed groan met her hiss of pain, which quickly disappeared to be replaced by a feeling so phenomenal words failed her.

'Raven!' Rafael's response was half praise, half reproach. Tentatively, she moved again.

He growled. 'Damn it, woman. *Stay still.*'

'Why?'

'Because this will be over sooner than you'd like if you don't.'

Heart hammering, she inhaled and gasped when the tips

of her breasts brushed his sweat-filmed chest. 'But at least we know the equipment is working, right?'

He pushed the last few inches until he was firmly seated inside her. Sensation as she'd never known flooded her. At her cry of delight, he pulled out slowly and repeated the thrust. Her head slammed back against the pillow, her fingers clenching hard in his hair as she held on for mercy.

Yep, there was nothing faulty in Rafael's equipment.

With another hungry groan, he increased the tempo, murmuring hot, erotic encouragement in her ear as she started to meet his hips with tiny thrusts of her own.

This time when she came the explosion was so forceful, so completely annihilating, she wasn't sure whether she would ever recover.

Rafael plucked her hands from his hair and pinned them on the bed, then proceeded to dominate her senses once more until she was orgasming again and again.

When she heard his final guttural groan of release, she was sure she'd gone insane with pleasure overload.

'*Dios...*' His voice was rough. Mildly shocked. 'This must be what heaven feels like.'

A bolt of pleasure, pure and true, went through her.

Don't get carried away, Raven.

To bring herself down to earth, she searched her mind for something innocuous to say.

'If you break out into *At Last*, I'll personally make sure you never walk again.'

His laugh was deep, full and extremely contagious. She found herself joining in as he collapsed onto his side and pulled her body into his.

They laughed until they were both out of breath. Then he fisted a hand through her hair and tugged her face up to his. After kissing her breathless, he released her.

'I was thinking more along the lines of *Again and Again and Again*. If there's a song like that, I'll need to learn the lyrics. If there isn't I might need to write one.' He cupped her nape and pulled her down for another unending kiss that left her breathless and seriously afraid for her sanity. 'I love kissing you,' he rasped.

A bolt of something strong and unfamiliar went through her, followed swiftly by a threat of apprehension. Steadying a hand on his chest, she pulled herself up.

'Where do you think you're going?' he asked.

She averted her gaze from his and fought to find reason in all this madness. 'I need to get up.'

'No. You need to look after me, and my needs demand that, after what you've just done to me, I stay in this bed. Which means you have to stay too.'

Unable to resist, she glanced down his body and swallowed the hungry need that coursed through her. It was unthinkable that she would want him again, so voraciously, so soon. But she did.

'If you carry on licking your lips and eyeing me like that, I'll have to teach you this lesson all over again.'

She blinked. 'I can't…we can't…it's too soon.'

'As you rightly noted, the equipment works so I most certainly can, *pequeña*.' He moved and she saw his fleeting grimace. 'But maybe you need to go on top this time.' He held out his hand and she swayed towards him.

'This is crazy, Rafael,' she protested feebly, even as she let him arrange her over him.

'But crazy good, no?'

She melted into his arms. 'Crazy good, yes.'

'Tell me what really happened with your father. What did he do to make you yearn for your eighteenth birthday?'

Rafael couldn't believe the words tumbling out of his mouth. But then again, he couldn't believe a lot that had happened in the last twenty-four hours. From the moment he'd placed the phone call to set things in motion to fly them to Mexico, he'd felt control and reason slipping out of his grasp.

Not that he'd had much in the way of control when it came

to the woman drifting in and out of sleep only a heartbeat away. Sure, he used the Los Cabos villa for entertaining. But it was mostly on business, never for pleasure. And he'd never let a woman stay over. Until now.

Her raven-black hair spread over his arm and he couldn't resist putting his nose to the silky strands, inhaling the peach-scented shampoo as he waited for the answer to the question that invited shared confidences he wasn't sure he wanted to reciprocate. But what the hell? She'd pried more information out of him in the last few weeks than he'd ever released in years.

A little reciprocity didn't hurt.

She turned towards him and spoke in a low, quiet voice. 'Remember I told you he barely acknowledged my existence at first?'

He nodded.

'Over time, as I got older, that began to change. I noticed from the way he looked at me. I thought I was imagining it. Then I overheard the housekeeper saying something to my father's driver.'

'What did she say?'

'That my father didn't really believe I was his daughter. I couldn't be because I looked nothing like him—he has ash-blond hair and blue eyes. I inherited my mother's colouring. Between fourteen and fifteen, I shot up in height and grew breasts. I tried not to link that and the fact that he'd started entertaining more and more at his house instead of at his private club.'

Rafael's hand tightened into a fist out of her sight and he fought to maintain a regular breathing pattern as she continued.

'He encouraged me to stay up at the weekend, help him *host* his parties. When I refused, he got angry, but he didn't take his anger out on me. The housekeeper's son, who was the general handyman, got fired when my father saw me talking to him, then the gardener went, then his driver of fifteen years. I got the hint and decided to do as I was told. By the time I turned sixteen, he was entertaining a few nights during the week and most weekends, and the outfits he wanted me to wear to those parties got…skimpier.'

Rafael's sucked-in breath made her glance up, her eyes wary. Swiftly he kissed her and nudged her nose with his to continue. But the white-hot rage inside him blazed higher.

'I knew I had to do something. I asked for the housekeeper's help, even though I knew I was putting her livelihood in jeopardy. Luckily, she was willing to help. We forged my father's signature and got a DNA test done. When the results came I showed them to him. He was angry, of course, but he couldn't refute the evidence any longer.'

'And did things get better?'

She shrugged but Rafael knew the gesture was anything but uncaring. 'For a time, he reverted to his old, cold indifference. I was hoping he'd take his partying out of the house but they continued…'

Her lids descended and he saw her lips tremble. Spearing his fingers in her hair, he tilted her face until she was forced to look at him. Haunting memory lurked in the green depths. 'Raven, what happened?'

'His…his male friends began to take notice of me.'

'*Que diablos!*' He could no longer stem the tide of anger. Right that moment, he wanted nothing more than to track down her bastard of a father and drive his fist into the man's face. 'They didn't take it further than just noticing, did they?'

The longer she stayed silent, the harder his breathing got.

Ignoring the pain throbbing in his groin and hip, he hauled himself against the headboard and dragged her up. Tilting her jaw, he forced her to look into his eyes. 'Did they?'

Her lower lip trembled. 'One of them did. One day after a party, I thought everyone had left. He…he came into my room and tried to force himself on me. I'd started training at the gym so I knew a few moves. I managed to struggle free and kicked him where it hurt most.'

He passed his thumb over her lips until they stopped trembling. '*Bueno*. Good girl.'

'I ran out of my room. My father was waiting in the hallway. I thought he was coming to help me because he'd heard me scream. But he wasn't...'

Rafael's blood ran cold. 'What was he doing?'

'He knew exactly why his friend had come to my room. In fact, I don't think his friend could've found my room without help.' She shuddered and goose bumps raced over her arms. He pulled her close and wrapped his arms around her.

'Did you report it to the authorities?' he asked.

She shook her head. 'I'd reported him a few times in the past and been ignored. I knew once again it would be his word against mine. I bought a baseball bat and slept with it under my pillow instead and I moved out on my eighteenth birthday.'

'Where is he now?' He entertained thoughts of tracking down the bastard, wielding his own baseball bat.

'I hadn't spoken to him until I called him last year to help my mother but, the last I heard, he'd lost all his money in some Ponzi scheme and is living with his mistress somewhere in Scotland.'

Rafael filed that piece of information away. When she gave another shudder, he kissed her again, a little deeper this time. He made sure when she shuddered again minutes later it was with a different reaction, one that set his blood singing again.

On impulse, he got out of bed and tugged her upright.

'What are you doing?' she asked.

He went into his dressing room and came out with a dark blue T-shirt. 'Put that on.'

'Why? Where are we going?'

'You'll find out in a minute.' He pulled on his shorts and grabbed her hand.

Five minutes later, she pulled at his grip. 'No, I'm not going on there.' She dug her feet into the sand when he would've tumbled her onto the wide beach bed.

'Of course you are. You've been dying to try it since we

got here.' He set down the vintage champagne and flutes he'd grabbed from the kitchen.

'Rafael, it's the middle of the night,' she protested, although her glance slid to the white-canopied bed that gleamed under the moon and starlit night.

'Where's your sense of adventure?'

'Back upstairs, where it doesn't run the risk of being eaten by sharks.'

He let go of her hand and started uncorking the champagne. 'Unless sharks have developed a way of walking on sand, you'll have to come up with a better excuse.'

'I'm not wearing any knickers. I don't want to catch cold.'

His grin was utterly shameless. 'That's a very good reason.' He popped the cork, poured out a glass of golden liquid and handed it to her. Setting the bottle down, he shucked off his shorts and got onto the bed. Casting her a hot glance, he patted the space beside him. 'I'll be your body blanket. If I fail completely in my task you'll be free to return to the safety of my bed.'

He saw her battle for a response. But his insistent patting finally won through. The mixture of hunger, innocence and vulnerability on her face touched a part of him he'd long thought dead. When she set her glass down and slid into his arms, Rafael swore to make her forget everything about her bastard of a father. If only for a few hours.

Why taking on that task meant so much to him, he refused to consider.

He made love to her with a slow, leisurely tempo even though everything inside him clamoured for quick, fiery satisfaction.

When she came apart in his arms, he let himself be swept away into his own release. Sleep wasn't far behind and, gathering her close, he kissed her temple and pulled the cashmere blanket over them.

CHAPTER TEN

THE INTRUSION OF light behind her eyelids came with firm, warm lips brushing her jaw.

'Wake up, *querida*…'

'Hmm, no…don't want to…'

A soft deep laugh. 'Come on, wake up or you'll miss the sunrise.'

'Sun…no…' She wanted to stay just as she was, suspended between dream and reality, entranced by the sultry air on her face and hard, firm…aroused male curved around her.

'Open your eyes. I promise you, it's spectacular.'

She opened her eyes, simply because she couldn't resist him, and found herself gazing into deep blue eyes. Eyes she'd looked into many times. But still her heart caught as if it'd been tugged by a powerful string.

'*Buenos días*,' Rafael murmured. 'Look.' He nodded beyond the canopy to the east. She followed his gaze and froze at the sheer beauty of the gathering sunrise. Orange, yellow and blue where the light faded, it was nature at its most spectacular and she lay there, enfolded in Rafael's arms, silent and in complete awe as the sun spread its stunning rays across the sky.

'Wow,' she whispered.

'Indeed. Does that win me Brownie points?' he whispered hotly into her ear.

Turning from the sight, she looked again into mesmerising eyes. And once again she felt her heart stutter in awe.

'It depends what you intend to use the points for.'

'To get you to come yachting with me today. My yacht is moored at the Marina. We can take her out for the day.'

More alone time with Rafael. *Too much…too much…*

She should've heeded the screeching voice of caution. But

Raven had a feeling she was already too far gone. 'I'd love to. On one condition.'

He mock frowned. '*Condition*...my second least favourite word.'

'What's your least favourite?'

'*No.*'

She laughed. 'That figures. Well, I need to exercise. Then *you* need to have your session. Then we'll go yachting.'

With a quick, hard kiss, he released her and sat back. 'You can do your exercise right here on the beach.'

She felt heat rise. 'While you watch?'

'I'm a harmless audience. Besides, I want to see if this Krav Maga is worth all the hype.'

She bit her lip and hesitated.

'What?' he demanded.

'I...I'm not wearing any knickers, remember?'

His laugh was shameless and filled with predatory anticipation. 'Kinky Krav Maga...sounds even better.' He lounged back against the plump pillows, folded golden muscled arms and waited.

It was the hottest, most erotic exercise routine Raven had ever performed.

The rest of the day went like a dream. Rafael's yacht was the last word in luxury. With a crew of four, they sailed around the Los Cabos islands, stopped at a seafront restaurant for a lunch of cerviche and sweet potato fries, then sunbathed on the twenty-foot deck until it got too hot. Then he encouraged her to join him in the shower below deck.

She clung to him in the aftermath of another pulse-destroying orgasm.

'Hmm...I have a feeling you won't be needing my services for much longer.'

He raised his head from where he'd been kissing her damp shoulder and stared deep into her eyes. 'What makes you say that?'

'You haven't used your cane all day, and your...um...stamina seems to be endless.'

His frown was immediate, edged with tension that seeped into the atmosphere. 'You're signed on for another three months. Don't make any plans to break the contract just yet.' He moved away and grabbed two towels. He handed her one and wrapped the other around her waist, his movements jerky.

'I wasn't making plans. I was just commenting that your movements are a little more fluid. And you haven't used the cane all day today. I think it's a great sign. You should be pleased.'

'Should I?'

His icy tone made alarm skitter over her. 'What's the matter?'

He smoothed a hand over the steamed up mirror and met her gaze over his shoulder. 'Why should anything be wrong?'

'I've just given you the equivalent of an almost clean bill of health. You're reacting as if I've just told you your puppy has died.'

He whirled to face her. 'This clean bill of health, will it pass the X1 training board and see me reinstated as a race driver?'

Her breath caught. 'You're thinking of going back to racing?'

'You sound surprised.'

She licked her lips. 'Well, I am. I thought since Marco had sold the team, and Sasha had quit—'

'What are you saying, that I should follow the family tradition and quit while I'm ahead?'

'No...but—'

'You don't think I can hack it?'

'Stop putting words in my mouth, Rafael. You're almost done with phase three of the physio regime. I'm just trying to find out what your plans are so I can work with you to achieve them.'

He stalked to where she stood and gripped her nape in a

firm hold. His kiss was hot, ravaging and rage-tinged. 'Right now, my only plan is to be inside you again.'

She barely stopped herself from dissolving into a puddle of need. 'And afterwards? We can't stay here indefinitely, indulging in wall-to-wall shagging.'

His eyes narrowed, his grip tightening. 'Are you trying to set a time limit on what's happening between us? Is that what all this is about?'

The shard of steel that lodged in her chest made her breath catch. 'I don't know what you mean.'

'Don't you? From the start you've tried to manage what was happening between us, tried to define it into something you can deal with. Now you want to set a time limit on it so you can walk away once the time comes, *si*?'

'Are you saying you're not? Am I not just one more challenge to you? Can we please not delude ourselves into thinking this is anything more than sex?'

He sucked in a breath as if he'd been punched. Stepping back, he dropped his hand and left the bathroom.

Raven trailed after him into the large, exquisite gold and cream cabin. He was pulling on a pair of boxers, which he followed with cargo shorts and a white T-shirt.

Feeling exposed, she slipped on her underwear and the lilac flowered slip dress she'd worn to go sailing. 'I'm not sure what's going on here, Rafael. Or why you're annoyed with me. I may not know the rules of this sleeping together thing but even I know there is a time limit when it comes to your affairs—'

'*Affairs*? Is that what we're doing, having an affair?' he asked with a cocked eyebrow. 'How quaint.'

'Will you please stop mocking me and tell me what's really bothering you?'

He slammed the drawer he'd just opened none too gently. 'I don't like time limits. I don't being head-shrunk. And I don't like the woman I'm sleeping with hinting that she'll be leaving me the day after we start sleeping together. There, does that sum things up for you?'

'So you want to be the one to call the shots? To dictate when this aff...*liaison* starts and ends?'

He dragged a hand through his damp hair and glared at her. '*Santo cielo*, why are we even having this argument?' he shouted.

'I have no idea but you started it!' she yelled back.

His eyes widened at her tone, then he sighed. 'Forgive me, I'm used to having things my way, *pequeña*. You have every right to shout at me when I step out of line.'

'Thanks, I will.'

He laughed, and just like that the tension broke. Striding to her, he tugged her into his arms and proceeded to kiss the fight out of both of them. They sailed back to the villa shortly after and, once again, she let him coax her into spending part of the night on the beach bed.

They were halfway through their breakfast when the delivery arrived.

'What is it?'

'I've got something for you.' The gleam in his eyes was pure wickedness. Her heartbeat escalated as she eyed the large gold-ribboned package sitting on the floor beside their breakfast table.

'Don't worry, you'll enjoy it,' he promised with a smile so sexy, and so deliciously decadent, her toes curled.

Even though the subject quickly changed to their plans for the rest of the day, Raven's gaze strayed time and again to the package. But Rafael, as she'd discovered in the past two nights, was skilled in delayed gratification. He was also skilled in being the perfect host. She was stunned when she discovered how many details he'd picked up through their conversation. When he shepherded her towards the SUV mid-morning, she gaped in surprise when she found out he'd organised the hang-gliding trip she'd casually mentioned was on her list of things to do.

She'd barely descended from that high when he whisked her by helicopter to the Mayan encampment she'd been dying to explore.

'You're seriously scaring me now by how utterly close I am to adoring you for this,' she said in hushed tones as they were ushered into the hallowed grounds of the ancient burial site.

His breath hissed out. When she glanced at him, he'd paled a little.

'Rafael? Are you in pain?' He'd left his walking stick back at the villa and nothing from his gait told her he'd suffered a mishap. All the same...

He shook his head. A second later the look had disappeared. 'It's nothing.'

She stopped as the full import of her words struck her. Wide-eyed, she turned to him. 'No, I didn't mean...I was only joking...'

'Were you?' The intensity of his gaze pinned her where she stood.

'Yes! Ignore me, I'm babbling because you've made two dreams come true today.'

'So you don't adore me?'

She opened her mouth to refute the comment and found she couldn't speak. Because she realised she did adore him, and more than a little. The Rafael she'd come to know in the past few weeks had a depth she'd never got the chance to explore last year. She felt a connection to this Rafael, and not just because he'd been her first lover.

The depth of the feeling rampaging through her made her shake her head.

One corner of his mouth lifted in a mirthless smile. Then he nodded to the tour guide looking their way.

'Now that we've established that you *don't* adore me, I think you need to go see your artefacts.'

She felt a stab of disappointment. 'Aren't you coming?'

'Been there, done that.' He pulled the phone from his pocket. 'The drivers and cars arrive this afternoon. I need to return a few calls.' He walked away before she could reply.

Disappointment morphed into something else. Something she couldn't put her finger on but which confused the hell out of her. The more she tried to grasp it, the further away it slithered from her.

He was waiting when she finally emerged. Back in the helicopter, he pulled her close and sealed his lips over hers, his mouth hungry and demanding.

She was breathless when he finally pulled away. 'What was that for?' she asked huskily.

His lids swept down over his eyes. 'Maybe I want you to adore me, just a little.'

Rafael watched her breath catch all over again and wondered just what the hell he was doing. Why he was letting the angst riding underneath his skin get to him.

So she didn't adore him. Big deal. There were thousands of women out there who were more than willing to fall into his bed should he wish them to.

But none like the woman in his arms. None like the woman who refused to mould into a being he understood, could predict. Most women would be halfway to falling in love with him by now; would be secretly or not so secretly making plans on how to prolong their presence in his life.

When he wasn't kissing her breathless—a diversionary tactic he'd grown to enjoy immensely—Raven seemed to be counting the days, hell, the minutes until she could walk away from him.

The notion unsettled him enough to make him want to probe, to find an answer.

Had she glimpsed the darkness in his soul? Had opening up to her in Monaco and again in Monza made him into a man she could sleep with but not a man she wanted in her life for the long-term?

The long-term? Santa María. Had he finally lost all common sense? Certainly, reality had slid back these past two days. Being with her had been like living some sort of dream. A dream where he could look at himself in the mirror without being revolted by what stared back at him.

A dream where he could continue the secret writing project he'd started before his accident without feeling as if he was tainting the very memory he wanted to preserve.

He stared down into her face, a face flushed with pleasure from the activities of the day or, he thought semi-cockily, from kissing him. All at once he wanted to blurt his very innermost secret to her.

He stopped himself just in time.

Permanent wasn't part of his vocabulary. He wasn't about to seek it out now. And, really, he should thank his lucky stars because Raven knew his flaws and had adequately cautioned herself against getting too close.

So why did the thought not please him?

His phone rang and he happily abandoned the questions that threatened to flood him. But he didn't abandon his hold on the soft body of the woman next to him. Delight curled in his chest when she slid closer.

'De Cervantes,' he answered.

The conversation was short and succinct. And it raised every single hair on his nape to full, electrifying attention. Feeling slightly numb, he ended the call.

'What's happened?' she asked.

'One of the drivers has pulled out of the remaining races.'

'Can they do that, pull out without warning?'

He shook his head. 'I've never had a driver pull out before. Normally I have them begging to race.' She didn't miss the frown in his voice. 'But he's just been offered a race seat for the coming season and it's an opportunity of a lifetime. I recognise how important that is to a young driver.'

'So what does that mean for your event?' she asked, pulling back to stare up into his face.

He looked down but didn't really see her. The thoughts tumbling through his head both terrified and excited him at the same time.

'They can find a replacement if they search hard enough...'

Raven pulled away further. He wanted to tug her back but he couldn't seem to summon the strength it took because of the feelings rushing through him.

'Or?'

'Or...the general consensus is that I should step in.'

'No,' she said. Naked fear pulsed through the single word.

He finally focused on her, felt a burn in his stomach from the impact of her searing look. 'No?'

'You're not ready.'

'Shouldn't *I* be the judge of that? And didn't you say yourself I was almost healed?' he asked.

'Yes, *almost!* As your physiotherapist, I strongly do not recommend it. You could reverse everything you've achieved in the last several weeks...'

'If I crash?'

She paled a little, and he felt a tug of guilt for pushing her. 'I won't answer that. What I will say is that you're the head of X1 Premier Management. All you need to do is make a single phone call and any one of dozens of drivers will fly out and take your driver's place. You don't have to do this. *Please don't do it.*'

The naked plea in her eyes struck deep. The unsettling angst of a moment before subsided as he traced his finger down her face.

'Dare I believe that you care about me, just a little bit?' He couldn't stop the question from spilling out. But, once it was out there, he *needed* to know.

'I care, Rafael. More than a little bit, I think.' The naked truth struck them both. Their eyes met, locked.

Breaths held until the banking helicopter jolted them. The sight of the villa sprawled beneath them made Rafael want to swear. Instead he activated his phone again.

'Angelo—' he addressed his second-in-command '—call around the teams, find out if there's any driver who isn't testing and offer them a place on the newly available seat on the All-Star event. You know which guys I rate the most. Tell them they're guaranteed a spread in the next issue of *X1 Magazine* and my personal endorsement of whatever charity they choose. Oh, and I want a driver on his way to the racetrack in Los Cabos by the end of the day.' He ended the call and looked down at her.

'Now what?' he asked softly as the helicopter blades slowed to a halt.

Her smile held such radiance he found it hard to breathe. 'Now, I may let myself adore you a little bit more…see where it takes me.'

He regretted that he wasn't healed enough to swing her into his arms and carry her off to his lair. But he was well enough to drag her from the helicopter to his bedroom. And he made sure he kept her fully occupied until neither of them could move.

'You never told me what was in the package,' Raven murmured, drifting somewhere between *I-can't-move* satiation and a drugging need to experience that mind-bending pleasure all over again.

The wicked grin he sent her way made her heart pound all over again. He left the bed and she could no more help herself from visually devouring him than she could stop breathing.

He picked up the package from the foot of the bed and returned it to her. 'This may just buy me a few more Brownie points.'

That got her attention. She dragged herself up to lean on one elbow. The sight of his naked chest threatened to fry her brain cells. 'What is it?' Her mind whirled with the possibilities, then latched onto what she wanted it to be. Could it be the rest of his manuscript?

Her senses now on a high, she stared down at the box,

feeling like a kid on Christmas morning. 'What's in the box, Rafael?'

He lifted the lid. All she could see were sheaves of wrapping paper. 'See for yourself.'

Carefully, she lifted the sheer paper. The first items made her heart knock in her chest. And not in a good way. Praying she was dreaming, she nudged the material aside with her finger and looked underneath. Each layer held more of the same.

'Naughty underwear? *That's* what you got me?' Raven let the garments drop back into the box, unable to stem the cold wave of hurt that washed over her. She wasn't even sure why it hurt so much. But it felt as if she'd climbed a mountain only to look back and find out that she'd only taken a few steps.

He looked genuinely stunned. 'You don't like it?'

'What's wrong with my own underwear?'

His perplexed look deepened. For the first time, Rafael looked seriously nonplussed. It would have been funny had it not been so far from funny.

'I didn't…I just wanted to…' He stopped, a flush lighting his high cheekbones.

If someone had told her as little as a week ago that she'd be sitting in bed discussing naughty lingerie with Rafael, she'd have laughed herself blind.

Now, she forced herself to glance at the lacy silks and delicate satin bows that didn't seem as if they would stand up to any overt pressure.

'That's not even my size, Rafael. I'm a size twelve, remember?'

His flush deepened. 'I have a feeling you'll punch me when I tell you I don't have a clue what size underwear you wear or what yours look like. By the time I get to your panties, I'm nearly insane with lust. Damn it. I've got it spectacularly wrong, haven't I?'

'Not all wrong. You got my favourite colours right.'

He picked up the package and flung it across the room.

Then he tugged her close. 'Is there any way I can make you forget the last ten minutes?'

Against her will and certainly against her better judgement, she glanced at the lilac silk material caught over a chair back. It seemed so delicate and forlorn.

'I don't need expensive lingerie to feel sexy. If you don't want me as I am—'

He caught her chin between his fingers. 'I do,' he breathed. 'Let me prove it...' His head started to descend.

Raven's gaze swung once more to the basque. Pulling herself from his arms, she walked, naked, to the garment and plucked it off the chair. Carefully, she rubbed the material between her fingers and turned. Rafael's breath caught as she slowly traced the warm silk over her body.

A glance from beneath her lashes showed a definite effect on him.

Pure feminine power washed away her misgivings. With a wanton smile she'd never have believed herself capable of, she sauntered back towards him.

'You need to understand one thing, Rafael.'

He nodded but his eyes were riveted on her breasts. '*Si*?'

'You promise never to buy me lingerie again as long as we're together. I choose my own underwear.'

He swallowed and nodded.

Raven glanced down at the panties and shook her head. 'I can't believe you thought I was a size eight,' she muttered.

'*Por favor!* Forgive me.' He wet his lips in such a blatantly sexual way, a blush suffused her whole body.

'You're just saying that so I hurry back to bed.'

'*Si*. And you can forget the lingerie if you wish.'

'And give up the chance to see you sweat. No can do.' She slowly, deliberately swept her hair to one side before sliding the lace-trimmed garment over her head.

She nearly bottled it then, but the scorching intensity in his eyes had the direct effect of firing up her courage. The soft lilac tulle basque hugged her breasts in such a blatant caress, she bit her lower lip to stop a moan of excitement. She turned, then glanced back over her shoulder.

'Are you going to help me with the laces?' she rasped.

'*Dios mío*, what are you trying to do?'

'Teach you a lesson.'

He got off the bed, almost a little too eager for his punishment. 'Turn around,' he instructed.

She did, and heard him hiss out a breath as he pulled the delicate laces and tied it.

'Once again, I have no knickers.'

His moan was a heartfelt balm to her soul.

Turning, she placed her hands on her hips, feminine power fuelling her desire as she saw her effect on him.

When he stumbled back and sank onto the side of the bed, she laughed. 'Hoisted by your own petard, Rafael?'

She took a step towards him and gloried in the slide of the silk on her skin. She would never don anything like this again. Naughty lingerie wasn't really her style but, just for tonight, she would allow herself this experience.

His face was strained like the steely erection that jutted from between his legs. Heat oozed between her thighs, made her movements slow as the magnetic force between them pulled her inexorably into his orbit.

When she reached him, she raked her fingers down his chest. 'You won't see me like this again, Rafael, so look your fill.'

His features altered, a look of regret passing through his eyes that made her stomach hollow out. 'You're breathtaking without it, Raven. How can I make this up to you?'

Her heart thundered at the sincerity in his voice. 'You don't need to. Just see me as I am.'

He inhaled, long and deep, and dropped his head between her breasts. For a long moment, Raven held him close. Then his breathing altered. Hers followed as lust sizzled, rose to the fore once more.

She pushed him back on the bed and climbed on top of him. By the time he donned the condom, they were both nearly insane with need. She'd barely positioned her thighs on either side of him when he thrust hard and deep inside her. Raven lost all coherent thought.

In the sizzling, excruciatingly heady aftermath, she curled into him but found she couldn't breathe, even after his deft fingers pulled the basque from her body and flung it away. She'd always known that Rafael's dominance was larger than life. But she'd trusted herself not to get pulled into his devastating, fast-spinning orbit. Her emotions were fast skittering out of control. How long had she watched her mother experience the same devastation over and over? Now she was running the same risk—

'What is it?' he demanded, his intuitiveness almost scary.

'Nothing…' she started to say, then stopped. 'How many times have you done this?' she blurted.

'I think I definitely need a definition of *this,* otherwise I'll have to plead the fifth.'

'Bought risqué underwear for a woman?'

His lids dropped for a second before rising to spear her with that intense blue. 'Never.'

Her snort was borne of disbelief and a sharp pang she didn't want to touch with a dozen bargepoles. She shook her head and started to move away.

He caught her back easily. A shiver ran through her when his finger slid under her chin and tilted her head up. Almost afraid, she looked into his eyes.

'I've never lied to you, Raven. I'm skilled in evading subjects I don't wish to discuss, but I have never and will never lie to you. Understood?'

She was stunned by how much she wanted to believe him, how much she wanted to be the first at something in his life. 'Why haven't you done this before?'

Surprise flared in his eyes. 'You're asking me why I haven't bought lingerie for a woman before?'

She pursed her lips. 'It seems the kind of thing ruthless playboys specialise in.'

His own lips flattened at the label, then he shrugged and relaxed onto the pillows. 'Not specialise. I have knowledge of it because I'm always the recipient. The assumption has always been that I would prefer the bedroom unveiling to be a knock-my-brains-out surprise, not a joint enterprise. I haven't felt the inclination to alter that assumption.'

A small fizz of pleasure started in her belly. Which was really foolish because she knew this particular experiment had been a means to an end for him.

Unwilling to face up to what all this meant, she buried her face in his neck. 'I'm glad.'

'Enough to forgive my grievous error?'

'That depends.'

'On?'

'On whether you'll give me what I expected to find in the box when I opened it.' She told him.

Another peculiar look crossed his face. 'The story has reached a crossroads.'

'Are you saying I did all of that for nothing?'

He pushed her firmly onto her back and leaned his powerful, endlessly intoxicating body over hers. Unable to resist, she let her hands wander at will over smooth muscle.

'For nothing? No, *bonita*, it was most definitely not for nothing. I think you could be the key to unlocking everything.'

Although she went into his arms at his urging, Raven sensed he wasn't as in control as he made out. She'd heard a different note in his voice—part vulnerability, part bravado. She slid her hand up and down his back in a strong need to comfort him. The persistent voice that had cautioned against getting too deep was receding—almost as if it knew the path she'd chosen. She would live in this fantasy now.

This magic, this overwhelming sense that she was exactly

where she wanted to be, was too great to deny. Reality would encroach soon enough.

So where was the harm in experiencing it for a little while longer?

CHAPTER ELEVEN

IT TURNED OUT a little while was all she would get.

Things started to go wrong the moment the helicopter touched down at the Autódromo Hermanos Rodríguez in Mexico City the next morning. The replacement driver Angelo had lined up didn't turn up. As the day went on with no immediate solution, Raven felt the pressure mount as everyone turned to Rafael for a solution.

Even though this was primarily a charity event, high profile sponsors had channelled millions of euros into it in the hope of gaining maximum exposure, courtesy of the sold-out events. Racing five cars instead of the usual six would make the headlines and throw negative publicity on the event—something X1 Premier Management and Rafael in particular couldn't afford to let happen.

Already the paparazzi, sensing blood in the water, were sniffing around, cameras and microphones poised to capture any salacious gossip.

She recalled how they'd decimated Sasha de Cervantes and her gut churned at the thought of what that type of publicity could do to Rafael.

As if she'd conjured him up, Rafael walked past the window, his pace carrying him from one end of the air-conditioned VIP lounge to the other, his gait remarkably improved despite the physical stress she'd put on his body in the last three days.

Feeling a blush creep up her face, she glanced away before he or any of the other management team hastily assembled for the meeting could guess at her thoughts.

Angelo, Rafael's assistant, approached him, a phone in his

hand. Rafael listened for several seconds, his tension increasing with each breath he took.

'Tell him if he threatens me with a lawsuit one more time, I'll personally see to it that his brand of vodka never leaves the icy wilderness of Siberia...*bueno*, I'm pleased you're finally seeing things my way. We will find a driver, and your logo will be emblazoned on the side pod just as we agreed.'

He hung up, glanced around the room and caught a few nervous gazes. 'They want to play dirty; I'm more than happy to oblige.'

A three-time world champion, now in his early sixties, cleared his throat. 'The race starts in three hours. I don't see that we have much of a choice here. You all but agreed to step in two days ago when we were a driver short. I'm not sure what changed your mind but perhaps you'd revisit the idea of racing?'

Raven half rose out of her seat, the scrape of her chair on the tiled floor drawing attention from the rest of the room.

She collapsed back into her seat when Rafael's fierce gaze settled on her. When the quick shake of her head didn't seem to register, she cleared her throat.

His eyes narrowed. Then he turned, slowly, deliberately away from her.

A block of ice wedged in her chest and her stomach hollowed out. From very far away, she heard him address the race coordinator and chief engineer of the driverless team.

'I have a couple of spare seats around here somewhere. Angelo will arrange to supply you with one to fit into the car. I'll be along in ten minutes to go over race strategy with you.' He looked around the room, the devil's own grin spreading over his face. 'Gentlemen, let's go racing.'

The explosion of excitement that burst through the room drowned out her horrified gasp. Manly slaps of his shoulder and offers of congratulations echoed through her numb senses.

When someone suggested a quick press conference, Raven

finally found the strength to stand and approach him as the room emptied.

'R...Rafael, can I talk to you?'

'Now is not a good time, *bonita*.' His voice was brusque to the point of rudeness.

The endearment she was beginning to adore suddenly grated. But she refused to be dismissed. 'I think this is a bad idea.'

'*Sí*, I knew you would think so. But I can't help what you think. Needs must and I stand to become embroiled in all sorts of legal wrangling if this isn't sorted out.'

She frowned. 'But it was the driver who broke the contract. Isn't he liable?'

'No, he isn't. XPM is staging this event, so I'm responsible. I should've taken more time to ensure contingencies were in place before we arrived. Everyone here knows someone's dropped the ball. Unfortunately, they're looking at me to pick it up and run with it.' He was the hard businessman, the ruthless racer who'd held a finite edge over his competitors for years.

He was certainly nothing like the lover who'd taken her to the heights of ecstasy.

She fought to regain her own professionalism, to put aside the hurt splintering her insides. 'As your physiotherapist, I'll have to recommend that you don't race.'

'Your recommendation is duly noted. Is that all?'

Her fists clenched in futile anger. Anger she wanted to let loose but couldn't. Her days of lashing out were far, far behind her. 'No, that's not all! This is crazy. You're risking your health, not to mention your life, Rafael.'

His smile was tight and tension-filled. 'And *you* are running the risk of overstepping, *querida*. I won't be tacky enough to point out just what your role is in my life considering the lines have been blurred somewhat, but I expect you to recognise the proper time and place for voicing disagreement.'

The blunt words hit her like a slap in the face. Regret momentarily tightened his face, then it smoothed once again into the outward mask of almost bored indifference.

It took every ounce of self-control to contain her composure. 'No, you're right. Pardon me for thinking of your health first.' She indicated the frenzy outside, the racetrack and the baking heat under which the cars gleamed. 'Off you go, then. And good luck.'

He reached forward and grabbed her arm when she'd have turned away.

'Aren't you forgetting something?'

'What?' She made herself look into his eyes, determined not to be cowed by the storm of fear rolling through her gut. He returned her look with one that momentarily confused her. Had her thoughts been clearer, Raven would've sworn Rafael was scared out of his wits.

'As my physio, you need to come with me, attend to my needs until I'm in the cockpit. Have you forgotten your role already?'

She had. Whether intentionally or through mental blockage, she'd tried to put her role eight months ago as Rafael's race physio out of her mind. Because every time she thought of it, she remembered their last row. Her rash, heated words; the stunned look on his face as he'd absorbed her bone-stripping insults before he'd walked out to his car. They'd been in a situation like this, momentarily alone in a place that buzzed with suppressed energy. His race suit had been open and around his neck she'd spied his customary chain with the cross on it. The cross he kissed before each race.

In the months since, she'd remembered vividly that Rafael hadn't kissed his cross that day…

Now, Raven was in favour of forgetting all about it. All she wanted to do right now was find a dark corner, stay there and not come out until the blasted race was over. Watching his crash that day had been one of the most heart-wrenching experiences of her life. She would give anything not to be put in that position again.

But she had a job to do. Sucking a sustaining breath, she nodded. 'Of course, whatever you need.' Pulling herself from his grasp, she walked towards the bar and picked up two bottles of mineral water. She handed him one. 'We're a little late off the mark in trying to hydrate you sufficiently so I'd suggest you get as much liquid in as possible.'

He took the bottle from her but made no move to drink the water.

'You think I'm making the wrong decision.' It wasn't a question.

'What I think is no longer relevant, remember?' Her gaze dropped meaningfully to the bottle.

He uncapped it and drank without taking his gaze off her face. She felt the heavy force of his stare but studiously avoided eye contact. When he finished and tossed the empty bottle aside, she handed him the second bottle.

'Drink this one in about ten minutes.' She started to walk towards the door, eager to get away from the clamouring need to throw herself in his path, to stop him putting himself in any danger.

Too late, she realised the media had camped outside the door, eager to jump on the latest news of Rafael's return.

Is this the start of your comeback?

Are you sure you can take the pressure?

Which team will you be driving for when the X1 season starts next month?

Rafael fielded their questions without breaking a sweat, all the while keeping a firm hold on her elbow. Every time she tried to free herself, he held on tighter.

Raven spotted the keen reporter from the corner of her eye.

Is there a new woman in your life?

Without the barest hint of affront, he smiled. 'If I told you that you'd stop hounding me, then my life would no longer be worth living, would it?'

The paparazzi, normally a vicious thrill-seeking lot, actually laughed. Raven marvelled at the spectacle. Then berated herself for failing to realise the obvious. Sooner or later, everyone, man, woman or child, fell under Rafael's uniquely enthralling spell.

She'd fooled herself into believing she could fall only a little, that she could go only so far before, wisely and safely, she pulled back from the dizzying precipice.

How wrong she'd been. Wasn't she right now experiencing the very depths of hell because she couldn't stand the thought of him being hurt again?

Hadn't she spent half the night awake, her stomach tied in knots as she'd wondered why so beautiful a man suffered tortured dreams because of his choices and his determination to shut everyone out?

She hadn't missed the phone calls from his father that he'd avoided, or the one from Marco yesterday that he'd swiftly ended when she entered the room.

Pain stabbed deep as she acknowledged that she'd come to adore him just a little bit more than she'd planned to. She'd probably started adoring him the moment he'd answered her call and agreed to see her in Barcelona seven weeks ago.

Because by allowing her in just that little bit meant he didn't hate her as much as he should. Or maybe he didn't hate her at all.

Or maybe she was deluding herself.

'A three-line frown. Stop it or I'll have to do something drastic, like confirm to them just who the new woman in my life is. Personally, I don't mind drastic but I have a feeling you wouldn't enjoy being eaten alive by the paparazzi.'

She'd been walking alongside him without conscious thought as to where they were going. The sound of the engine revving made her jump. 'No, I wouldn't.'

'*Bueno*, then behave.'

They'd arrived at the garage of the defected racer. Rafael grabbed the nearest sound-cancelling headphones and passed them to her.

She was about to put them on when she spotted Chantilly,

lounging with a bored look on her face on the other side of the garage. The second she spotted Rafael, she came to vivacious life.

'Damn it, your frown just deepened. What did I say about behaving?'

'What's she doing here? In this garage, I mean?'

Rafael followed her gaze to Chantilly, then glanced back at her. 'Her husband owns this team.'

The single swear word escaped before she could stop it. A slow grin spread over Rafael's face but it didn't pack the same charismatic punch as it usually did. Examining him closer, she noted the lines of strain around his mouth.

'Sheath your claws, *chiquita*. I told you, I have no interest in her. Not after discovering the delights of fresh English roses.' A pulse of heat from his eyes calmed her somewhat but it was gone far too quickly for her to feel its warmth.

The chief engineer called out for Rafael and, with another haunted look down at her, he went over to discuss telemetry reports with the team.

The ninety minutes before the race passed with excruciating slowness. With every second that counted down, Raven's insides knotted harder. The walk across the sun-baked pit lane into the race lane felt like walking the most terrifying gauntlet.

She hitched the emergency bag higher on her shoulder and took her place beside Rafael's car, making sure to keep the umbrella above his head to protect his suit-clad body from overheating. She ignored the sweat trickling down her own back to check for signs of distress on him.

'If you feel your hip tightening, try those pelvic rotations we practised by flexing your spine. I know you don't have much room in the cockpit but give it a try anyway,' she said, trying desperately to hang on to a modicum of professionalism.

He nodded but didn't look up. His attention was fixed on the dials on his steering wheel. When the first red light flashed on, signalling it was time to clear the track, Raven opened her mouth to say something…anything, but her throat had closed up.

She took one step back, and another.

'Rafael…' she whispered.

His head swung towards her, ice-blue eyes capturing hers for a single naked second.

The stark emptiness in his eyes made her heart freeze over.

Rafael fought to regulate his breathing. Shards of memories pierced his mind, drenching his spine and palms in cold sweat.

His fight with Marco the night before the Hungary race… *You're dishonouring Mamá's memory by continuing with this reckless behaviour…*

Sasha's voice joined the clamouring…*it's not okay for you to let everyone think you're a bastard.*

And Raven's condemning truth…*you're a useless waste of space…who cares about nothing but himself and his own vacuous pleasures…*

He tried to clear his mind but he knew it wouldn't be that easy. Those words had carried him into that near fatal corner that day in Hungary because he'd known they all spoke the truth. What they hadn't known was that the day had held another meaning for him. It was emblazoned into his memory like a hot iron brand.

That day in Hungary had been exactly eight years to the day he'd charmed his mother into the ride that had ended her life…the day he'd let partying too hard snuff out a life he'd now happily give his own to have returned.

Looking into Raven's eyes just now, he'd known she was recalling her words, too; he'd seen the naked fear and remorse in her eyes. But he hadn't been able to offer reassurance.

How could he, when he knew deep down she was right? Since his mother's death, he'd lived in the special place in hell he'd reserved for himself. That *no trespassing* place where no one and nothing was allowed to touch him.

It was a place he planned on staying…

No matter how horrifyingly lonely…

His gaze darted to the lights as they lit up. Jaw tight, he tried to empty his mind of all thought, but her face kept intruding…her pleading eyes boring into his ravaged soul despite every effort to block her out.

Que diablos!

He stepped on the accelerator a touch later than he'd planned and cursed again as Axel Jung and Matteo, the teenage driver, shot past him on either side. Even in a showcase event like this one, a fraction of a second was all it took to fall behind.

Adrenaline and age-old reflexes kicked in but Rafael knew he was already at a disadvantage. He eyed the gap to the right on the second corner, and calculated that he could slot himself in there if he was quick enough. He pressed his foot down and felt his pulse jump when Axel, in a bid to cut him off, positioned himself in front of him.

In a move he'd perfected long before he'd been tall enough to fit into an X1 cockpit, he flicked his wrist and dashed down the left side of the track. Too late, Axel tried to cover his mistake but Rafael was already a nose ahead of the German. From the corner of his eye, he saw the other driver flick him a dirty gesture.

Where normally he'd have grinned with delight behind his helmet, Rafael merely gestured back and pressed down even harder on the accelerator, desperately trying to outrun his demons the way he had that day in Hungary.

You're not all bad…

Yes, he was. Even his father looked at him with pity and sadness.

His father…the man he'd put in a wheelchair. The man who kept calling and leaving him messages because Rafael was too afraid…too ashamed to talk to him.

The car shot forward faster. Inside his helmet, his race engineer's voice cautioned him on the upcoming bend. The words barely registered before disappearing under the heavy weight of his thoughts. He took the bend without lifting off the throttle or easing back on his speed.

He heard the muted roar of the appreciative crowd but the spark of excitement he'd expected from the recognition that he was still in fine racing form, that his accident hadn't made him lose what was most important to him, didn't manifest.

That was when the panic started.

For as long as he could recall, that excitement had been present. No matter what else was going on in his life, racing was the one thing that had always…*always* given him a thrill, given him a reason to push forward.

Fear clutched his chest as he searched for and found only emptiness. In front of him, Matteo had made a mistake that had cost him a few milliseconds, bringing Rafael into passing distance of him.

He could pass him, using the same move he'd used in Hungary. He had nothing to lose. The grin that spread over his face felt alien yet oddly calming, as did the black haze that started to wash over his eyes.

He had nothing to lose…

'Rafael, your liquid level readings show you haven't taken a drink in the last thirty minutes.'

Her voice…husky, low, and filled with fearful apprehension, shot into his head with the power of a thunderclap. He gasped as he felt himself yanked back from the edge, from the dark abyss he'd been staring into.

For a single second, he hated her for intruding.

'Rafael?'

Sucking in a breath, he glanced up and realised Matteo had regained his speed and was streaking ahead. And still, Rafael felt…nothing.

'Rafael, please respond.' A shaky plea.

He didn't, because he couldn't speak, but he took a drink and kept his foot on the pedal until the race was over.

The shoulder slaps of congratulations for coming in second washed right over him. On the podium, he smiled, congratulated Axel and even felt a little spurt of pride when Matteo took the top step, but all through it he was numb.

The moment he stepped off the podium, he ripped off his race suit. He brushed away the engineer's request for a post race analysis, his every sense shrieking warning of imminent disaster.

He rushed out of the garage, for the first time in his life ignoring the media pen, the paparazzi and news anchors who raced after him for a sound bite.

Relief rushed through him as he entered his motor home and slammed the door shut behind him.

'Rafael?'

Dios mío. Had he lost it so completely he was now hearing her voice in his head? Bile surged through his stomach and leapt into his throat. He barely made it to the bathroom before he retched with a violence that made his eyes water.

For several minutes he hunched over the bowl, feelings coursing through him that he couldn't name. No...he knew what those feelings were, it was just that he'd never allowed them room in his life.

He was a racing driver. Racing was his lifeblood. Therefore he had no room for despair or fear. He was used to success, to adrenaline-fuelled excitement. To pride and satisfaction in what he did. So why the hell was he puking his guts out while fear churned through his veins?

Because, *diablo*, he *had* finally parted ways with reality.

With a stark laugh and a shake of his head, he cleaned up after himself, rinsed his mouth thoroughly...

And turned to find Raven in the doorway, her face deathly pale and her gorgeous eyes wide with panic.

'*Madre de dios.* What the hell are you doing here?'

CHAPTER TWELVE

'ARE YOU ALL right?' Raven asked, making a small movement forward.

Rafael instinctively stepped back from her. If she touched him, she would know. And whatever else he was...*or wasn't*, the last thing he wanted Raven Blass, this infuriatingly bright, mind-bendingly sexy woman, to see was his fear.

He took another step back, feeling more exposed than he'd ever felt in his life.

The water he'd splashed over his face chilled his skin. 'Am I all right? Sure. I puke my guts out after every race. Didn't you know that?'

'No you don't.' She took another step closer and, instantly, another more urgent need surged to the fore. The need to grab her, plaster her warm, giving body against his, use her to stem the tide of icy numbness spreading over him.

Use her...

Bile threatened to rise again and he swallowed hard. He stepped past her, entered the bedroom and started to undress.

'Tell me what's wrong.'

Rafael glanced down at his hands and realised they were shaking. The realisation stunned him so completely, his whole body shuddered before he could control himself. The idea that he was losing control so completely, so unstoppably, made irrational anger whip up inside him.

'Stop it, Raven. Stop trying to save me. You've done your penance.'

'Excuse me?' Her voice was hushed but strong.

'That's what you've wanted since you phoned me up two months ago, isn't it? To hear that I forgive you for what you think you did to cause my accident?'

'What I think…' She sucked in a sharp breath. 'Are you saying you remember why you crashed?'

He firmed his lips. *Brava*, Rafael. 'Perhaps I do. Or perhaps I'm just tired of watching you fall on your sword over and over again. I wouldn't be surprised if that was why you gave me your virginity, considering you didn't like me much before then.'

He felt like the lowest form of life when her colour receded completely. But, *dios*, admiringly she rallied.

'You're trying to push me away by being hateful. But I won't leave until you tell me what happened out there today.'

'What do you mean, what happened? I raced. I came second. Considering I've been out of the game for nearly a year, I think that's a commendable start, don't you?'

He shucked his suit and peeled off the fire-retardant long-sleeved gear. Her eyes darkened but she didn't lose her determination.

'Aside from the fact that you didn't hydrate nearly enough, why did you not pass Matteo the half a dozen times you had the chance?'

'What are you talking about? After he recovered his mistake in Sector 4 there was never a chance to pass Matteo…'

'Of course there was. He damaged his front wing when he went too close to the pit wall on his exit but you stayed behind him when you could've passed. And many times you came close to passing him but you pulled back every time. Your race engineer tried to talk to you but you didn't respond.'

He froze, scrambled around to supply the adequate information to refute her words and came up blank. Panic cloaked his skin, sank its claws deeper into him.

'Are you saying you don't remember?' she almost whispered, her voice thick with emotion.

Rafael couldn't breathe. 'I…no, I don't remember.'

The black haze crowded his mind, encroaching rapidly with each excruciating second. He knew he was in deep trouble when he didn't stop her from touching him, from pulling him down to sit on the king-sized bed.

'Rafael, you're freezing. And you're shaking!'

His laugh was hollow. '*Sí*. In case you haven't guessed yet, *querida*, I'm a hot mess right now.'

'Oh God!' She threw her arms around him, her warm hands pressing into his skin.

Another series of shudders raked through him, setting his teeth chattering. Her fingers speared through his hair, pulling him down into the crook of her neck. He wanted to move, *needed* to move. But he stayed right where he was, selfishly absorbing her warmth, her heady scent, inhaling her very essence as if that would save him. But nothing could save him. He was beyond redemption in more ways than he could count.

Blanking out behind the wheel had cemented the realisation.

And still he found himself leaning into her, his lips finding that soft, sweet spot below her ear lobe where he knew she loved to be kissed. He kissed it, felt her try to shift away, and trapped her in his arms.

'Rafael…'

He trailed his mouth down her neck, to the pulse that jumped when he flicked his tongue against it.

The shaking receded a little, the numbness fading under the pulse of seductive heat that was all Raven. Greedily, he tried to grab onto it, to delay the encroaching darkness beneath the bliss of her touch. With a deep groan, he moved to cup her breasts.

Only to fall into a deeper hell when she pulled away and rushed to her feet.

'Sex isn't going to make this problem go away.'

Darkness prowled closer. 'I know, but a guy can still dream, can't he?'

'No, it's time for reality. We need to discuss what happened. When I saw you throwing up, I thought it was a panic attack. But I think it's more than that,' she said.

Ice snapped through him, freezing him once more to the soul. 'Leave it, Raven.'

'No, you need help, Rafael.'

He couldn't hold her gaze—she saw far too much—so he concentrated on his clenched fists. 'And you think you're the one to offer that help?'

He knew his tone was unduly harsh but he had gone beyond remorse. He was in his special frozen place.

'What happened?' Her voice pleaded for understanding.

Since he was at a loss himself, he contemplated silence. Then he contemplated seduction. When bile threatened, he contemplated pleading for mercy.

Through frozen lips, he found himself speaking. 'I remembered everything about the race in Hungary.'

He looked up to see her hands fly to her lips. He gave a grim smile and stared back down at his hands. Hands that shook uncontrollably.

'You know what I remember most about it?'

She shook her head.

'As I went to the wall, I knew, no matter what happened, no matter how hard I tried, I wasn't going to die.'

'You mean you...*wanted* to die?' Horror coated her words.

He shrugged. 'It doesn't matter what I wanted. I knew it wasn't going to happen. My expertise lies in many other areas. Killing myself isn't one of them.'

'I don't... Explain, please.'

He raised his head, took in her tall, proud figure and felt a moment of regret that he'd messed this up too. She was one thing he'd have fought to hang on to, if it hadn't been too late for him.

'I've been dicing with death since I was old enough to walk. If a situation has an element of danger, I'm there. Being born with racing imprinted into my DNA was just a bonus.'

'Even if it ends up consuming you so thoroughly it kills you?'

The look that came over his face was so gut-wrenchingly

stark she felt pain resonate inside her. 'Sorry, I didn't mean it like that—'

He shook his head. 'I won't die from racing.'

'Are you retiring?'

He dashed the hope in her question. 'No. Regardless of everything that's happened, I still crave it. I've been spared death so far. It seems I'm destined for other things.'

A frown formed. 'What do you mean?'

'Haven't you guessed it yet? My skill lies in killing everything I come into contact with. If you haven't woken to the fact that all I'll bring to your doorstep is utter chaos then you're not as bright as I thought.'

'That sounds like…are you trying to warn me off you?'

He laughed. '*Sí*, I am. Which in itself is strange. Normally, I just take what I want and leave the husk behind.'

Pain darkened her eyes. 'Why are you doing this?'

'Doing what, *querida*?'

'Trying to belittle what we have, and don't use that endearment any more. It's a beautiful word you've made tacky because you don't really mean it. You're trying to paint yourself in a vile light, trying to put me off you so I'll walk away.'

'I'm not *trying*. I'm telling you I'm not a great bet for you. I always escape unscathed but everyone I come into contact with sooner or later suffers for it.'

'You make yourself sound as if you've got a contagious disease. Stop it. And no one suffered today. You still need to address exactly what happened during the race but no one had an accident.'

'That's where you're wrong. At the start, when I realised I was getting squeezed out, I contemplated a move that would've taken Matteo out. For a moment, I forgot that I was supposed to be his teacher. I forgot the reason I'm staging the All-Star event in the first place. In that cockpit, I was just a racer, programmed to win.'

'But isn't that what racers do?'

'He's only nineteen, Raven! And I came within a whisker

of taking him out. Do you know his mother is here today? Can you imagine how devastated she'd have been if I'd crossed that line?'

'But you didn't cross it. You pulled back before you did any damage.'

'Yeah, and you know how I felt? Nothing. No remorse, no victory, no sympathy. I felt nothing.'

'Because there was something else going on. You say you remembered your crash in Hungary but then you blanked out the rest of the race. That could be a form of PTSD.'

He raked a hand through his hair. '*Santo cielo!* Stop trying to make excuses for me. Stop trying to make me the sort of man you'll fall for. There is nothing beneath this shell.'

Raven's heart lurched, then thundered so hard she was surprised it didn't burst out of her chest. Surprised she managed to keep breathing, to keep standing upright despite the knee-weakening realisation that it was too late.

She had fallen hard. So very, very hard for Rafael.

'And if I don't fall in with your plan to drive me away? You know me well enough by now to know I'm no pushover.'

He speared her with a vicious look meant to flay the skin from her flesh, and maybe a few weeks ago she'd have heeded the warning, but she'd found, when it came to Rafael, she was made of sterner stuff than that.

'No, but I'm a complete bastard when I'm pushed to the edge, *chiquita*. Are you prepared for that?' he parried.

'You'll have to do more than throw words at me. I *know* you, Rafael. I see beyond your so-called shell. And I know, despite what you say, you love your family and would do anything for them. I also know that you're pissed off right now because you're terrified of what's happening with you. But I'm not walking away, no matter how much you try to push me. I won't let you.'

Anger hissed through his teeth. Rising from the bed, he stalked, albeit with a barely visible limp, to the drawer that held his clothes and pulled it open. 'A few days ago, you were counting the days until this thing between us ended. Now I'm trying to end it and you've suddenly gone ostrich on me?' He returned with a handful of clothes.

'I'm not burying my head in the sand—far from it. I'm trying to understand. What have you done that's so viciously cruel that you think I'll walk away from you?'

He froze before her, his whole body stiffening into marble stillness. Only his lips moved, but even then no words emerged.

A chord of fear struck her. 'Rafael?'

'What does your mother mean to you?' he rasped.

Although she wondered at the change of subject, her answer was immediate. 'Everything. She's the only family I have. She may think I'm her enemy half the time because she doesn't want to be where she is, and she may blame me some of the time, imagining I'm the reason my father doesn't want her, but the times she's lucid, she's a wonderful human being and I love her unconditionally, regardless of what persona she is on any given day. The thought of her, safe and a phone call away, makes me happy. I'll do anything for her…' Her words drifted to nothing when she saw the look on his face. He'd grown paler with each word she'd uttered, the jeans he'd pulled from the drawer crushed in his vice-like grip. His face, hewn from a mask of pain so visceral, made her step towards him.

He stepped back swiftly, evoking a vivid image of carrying the contagion she'd accused him of seconds ago.

'Well, stay away from me, then, and enjoy that luxury. Because once you have me in your life, you may not have her for long.' His voice came from far away, as if from the shell he'd referred to moments ago.

'What on earth are you talking about?'

'You know I put my father in a wheelchair eight years ago. But, even before that, my life was on a slippery downward slope.'

'You've let yourself suffer enough. You have to learn to forgive yourself, Rafael.'

His head went back as if she'd struck him. 'Forgive myself? For not only crippling my own father but for taking away the one person he treasured the most?'

'What did you do?'

'*I killed my mother,* Raven. I put her in my car, drove too fast into a sharp corner and executed a perfect somersault that snuffed her out within minutes.'

The horror that engulfed her had nothing to do with his emotionless recounting of events. No, the dismay that rocked through her stemmed from knowing just how much more he'd suffered, how he'd buried it all under the perfect front.

His laugh was a harsh, cruel sound. 'Now that's more like it. That look of horror is what I expect. Maybe now you'll listen to me when I suggest you stay away from me.'

He pulled on his jeans, fished out a black polo shirt and shrugged into it.

Reeling as she was from the news he'd delivered, it took her a moment to realise what he was saying into his phone.

'You're leaving Mexico?' she asked when he hung up.

'The race is over. The next one isn't for another four days.'

She started in surprise. 'Where are you going?'

He gave her a grim smile. 'No. The twenty questions is over, *quer*—' He stopped, looked around, then shoved more things into the large bag he'd placed on the bed.

Scrambling wildly, she said, 'What about your physio sessions?'

'I've just endured a two-hour race. I hardly think I'm going to crumble into a million little pieces if I go without a session for a few days.'

Her lips firmed but the questions hammered in her mind. 'No, you won't. As long as you're not attempting to skydive over any volcanoes?'

'Been there, done that.'

His phone rang. He stared at it for several seconds, pain rippling in tides over his face. Finally, sucking in a deep breath, he answered it.

'*Sí*, Papá?' he rasped.

Raven's heart caught. The faint hope that help for Rafael would come from another angle was stymied when the conversation grew heated with bursts of staccato responses.

Rafael grew tenser with each passing moment until his body was as taut as a bow.

The moment he hung up, he reached for his bag. The action held an air of permanence about it that terrified her.

'So, I'll see you at the track in Rio?' she asked, hating herself for the desperation in her voice.

He gave her a smile that didn't reach his eyes. He started to answer but his phone rang again. He stared into her eyes, his expression inscrutable save for the tinge of relief she glimpsed before he masked it.

'No, you won't. *Adios, bonita.*'

He pressed the *answer* button, raised the phone to his ear and walked out of the door.

Rafael told himself to keep moving. To walk away before he brought chaos to her life. Time was running out for him.

He knew he wasn't ready to give up racing. Just as he knew it was his guilt that was causing the feelings rushing through him. For him to hang onto the only thing that kept him sane, he had to try to make amends.

No, racing wasn't the only thing that kept him sane. If he admitted nothing else, he would admit that.

Raven Blass kept him sane, made him laugh, made him feel things he hadn't felt in a long time. But for her sake he had to walk away. Keep walking away. He was toxic in this state.

He couldn't allow himself to be swayed into thinking he was anything else but what she'd first thought him to be.

As for what he planned to do... His father had summoned him.

Since he had nothing to lose, he saw no reason to refuse the summons. Just as he saw no reason to examine why his heart felt as if it would burst out of his chest with every step he took away from her.

Gritting his teeth, he walked out, threw a *'no comment'* to a stunned media before he stepped up in his helicopter and buckled himself in. He had no heart. So he had nothing to worry about.

Raven got the email an hour later. She'd been fired. Rafael de Cervantes no longer needed her services. She would be paid her full contract fee and an insanely hefty bonus for her inconvenience. Et cetera…et cetera…

Thing was, she wasn't surprised. Or even hurt. The man she'd fallen in love with was in full retreat mode because she'd got under his skin, had glimpsed the ravaged soul of the outwardly irreverent but desperately lonely playboy who had been grappling with monstrous demons.

She could've fought to stay, cited contract clauses and notice periods, but she knew first-hand how intransigent Rafael could be. And she knew offering her help when it was unwelcome would only set back the progress she'd made.

So she sent an email response. She would leave on one condition. That he let her recommend a physio who could help.

His curt text message agreeing to the condition made her heart contract painfully. Her next request was flatly refused.

No, Rafael stated, he had no wish to see her. But he wished her good luck with her future endeavours.

Raven watched the remaining All-Star events like most people did around the world—from the comfort of her couch. Except she had an extra reason to watch. She told herself she was making sure Rafael's new physio was doing a good enough job. It only took a glimpse of Rafael walking down the paddock en route to his car at the Montreal race to know that he hadn't suffered any setbacks.

At least not physically.

His haggard features told a different story. That and his studious avoidance of the media.

Her heart clenched as she devoured images of him; called herself ten kinds of fool when she froze his latest image and let her gaze settle on his hauntingly beautiful face.

The icy blue eyes staring into the camera still held the hint of devilish irreverence that was never far away but a raw desperation lurked there too, one that made tears prick her eyes. With a shaky hand, she pressed the release button and sat, numb, as the rest of the race unfolded.

Whatever Rafael had been running from still chased him with vicious relentlessness. The thought made her heart ache so painfully, she was halfway to picking up the phone when she stopped herself.

What would she say to him that she hadn't said before? He'd made it painfully clear he didn't want her interfering in his life. Like all his relationships, she'd been a means to an end, a sexual panacea to make him forget. She had no choice but to accept it was over.

She needed to put the past in the past and move on.

Which was why she nearly binned the invitation that arrived a week later.

The All-Star event's last race was taking place in Monaco. To be followed by an All-Star gala in honour of the drivers who'd given up their time to raise money for the road safety programme.

The only thing that stopped her from throwing the invitation away was the hand-written note from Sasha de Cervantes on behalf of her and her husband.

Sasha had been a good friend to her when she'd first joined the X1 Premier. Raven knew she'd put her friendship with Rafael on the line because of her and it had almost caused an irreparable rift between them. Certainly, she knew that not admitting Raven's role in Rafael's accident was what had caused the initial friction between Sasha and Marco.

So although attending the gala would mean she ran the risk of coming face to face with Rafael, Raven slid the invitation and the accompanying first class aeroplane ticket into her bag, then spent the next three days desperately trying to stop her heart from beating itself into exhaustion every time she thought of returning to Monaco.

Rafael stood before the door leading to the study at Casa León, where his father waited. Contrary to his intentions when he'd left Mexico two weeks ago, he hadn't made the trip to León. The indescribable need that had assailed him as he'd lifted off the racetrack in Mexico had led him down another path. A path which had brought him an infinitesimal amount of comfort. Comfort and the courage to grasp the door before him…and open it.

His father was seated behind his ancient desk in the room that seemed to have fallen into a time warp décor-wise.

'*Buenos tardes,* Papá.'

'*Mi hijo,*' his father replied. My son. 'It's good to see you.'

Guilt and sadness welled in Rafael's chest as he let his gaze rest properly on his father for the first time in eight years. His hair had turned almost completely grey and his limbs, paralysed thanks to Rafael, appeared shrunken. But his eyes, grey and sharp like Marco's, sparked with keen intellect and an expression Rafael thought he'd never see again. Or maybe it was just wishful thinking. 'Is it?' he asked, his throat tight with all the emotions he held within.

'It's always good to see you. I've missed you. I miss you every day.'

Rafael advanced into the room on shaky legs, inhaling an even shakier breath. 'How can you say that after all I've done?'

'What exactly do you think you've done, Rafa?'

He let out a harsh laugh and speared a hand through his hair. '*Por favor*, Papá. Condemn me to hell. It's where I belong, after all.'

'I think you've done a good job all by yourself. Now it's time to end this.'

'End this?'

His father nodded to a file on his desk. 'Sit down and read that.'

The hand he reached across the desk felt as feeble as a new-born's. The file contained a three-page report, one he read with growing disbelief.

'What is this?' he rasped through numb lips.

'It's the truth of what happened to your car that day, Rafael. You're not responsible for your mother's death.'

Shock hollowed his stomach. 'No…it can't be. Please tell me you're not making this up in some attempt to make me feel less guilty.'

'As your father, it's my duty to comfort you when you feel bad. It's also my duty to make you see the truth in front of your own eyes. You've been so bent on punishing yourself you've failed to listen to reason or contemplate the evidence. You told me when you first drove the car that you felt something wasn't right. That's what made your brother decide to investigate further. It turned out your hunch was right.'

'It says here all fifteen models of that car have been re-called for the same error. But it doesn't excuse the fact that I was running on fumes that day, high from partying even though my body was exhausted from being up almost twenty-four hours straight.'

'All things you'd been doing since you hit late puberty. All those things combined, while it gave me nightmares as a father, didn't make me think for a second that you would be dangerous behind a steering wheel or I wouldn't have bought you such a powerful machine, and I certainly wouldn't have allowed my beloved Ana in the car with you.'

The pure truth behind his father's words hit him square in the solar plexus. He stumbled backward and sagged onto the ancient leather armchair.

'I can't…I don't know what to say.' His head dropped into his hands and he felt tears prick his eyes.

'Let it go, Rafa. You've punished yourself enough over this. Your mamá wouldn't want this for you.'

The sob choked him, hot and tight and cathartic. Once it started, he couldn't seem to make it stop. He didn't even have the strength to lift his head when he heard the haunting whine of his father's wheelchair.

'Enough, son…enough.'

He looked up through a mist of tears. 'Forgive me, Papá.'

His father's smile touched him in a way that went beyond the physical. 'There's nothing to forgive. There never was.'

Footsteps sounded and Marco walked in, cradling his son, with Sasha right behind him.

She stopped dead when she saw him, her eyes widening in disbelief. 'Good grief, I never thought I'd live to see the day you'd be reduced to tears, Rafa. Quick, Marco, activate your phone's camera. We'll make a killing on YouTube.'

Marco laughed, their father snorted, even baby Jack chimed in with a hearty gurgle.

'So, we're all good here?' Marco asked several minutes later, his grey eyes probing as they darted between his father and his brother.

Rafael's gaze met his father's and the unconditional love he saw made the tightness in his chest give way just a tiny bit further. 'We're getting there.'

He had a feeling he'd never get there completely. Not while he felt a part of himself still missing.

'Pacing a crater through that carpet won't make the next few hours of your life any easier. You're screwed ten ways to Sunday. Accept that now and you'll be fine.'

Rafael glared at the amusement on his brother's face and clenched his fist. 'Don't you have an adoring wife somewhere who's waiting for you to swoon over her?' He walked over to the balcony overlooking the immense ballroom and scoured the crowd again, his stomach clenching when he didn't spot the figure he sought.

'Sí,' Marco replied smugly. 'But watching you twist yourself into knots is fun, too.'

'Keep it up and I'll be twisting my fist into your face.'

Marco grinned, an expression that had been rare in the years after his own personal tragedy of losing his unborn child. Sasha had brought the smile back to his brother's face. A smile that was now rubbing him a dozen different wrong ways.

As if he knew he was skating close to the edge, Marco sobered. 'If it helps, I messed up with Sasha, too.'

'It doesn't. Sasha is a soft touch. I'm not surprised she was fooled by those puppy-dog eyes of yours.'

Marco laughed. 'You're in more trouble than I thought if you're that deluded.' When his brother tapped him on the shoulder, Rafael was ready with a pithy response. Instead he saw Marco nod over his shoulder.

'Your Armageddon is here. I'd wish you luck but I've always thought you were dealt more than your fair share at birth. So I'll just suggest you don't balls it up…'

Rafael had stopped listening. His attention, his whole being was focused on the figure framed in the double doors of the ballroom.

Her black silky hair was caught up in a high, elaborate bun that made her sleek neck seem longer. And her dress, a simple but classy white gown threaded with gold sequined lines, followed her curves in a loving caress that made his mouth dry.

The vision of her, so stunning, so held together while he was falling apart inside, made his fingers tighten over the banister railing.

He watched Sasha approach and hug her. Her smile made his breath catch and, once again, Rafael felt a bolt of dismay at the thought of what he'd thrown away.

A waiter offered her a glass of champagne. She was about to take a sip when her gaze rose and collided with his.

The force of emotion that shot through him galvanised his frozen feet. He was moving along the balcony and the stairs before he'd taken a full breath.

Sasha saw him approach, gave him a stern *don't-mess-this-up-or-I'll-castrate-you* look and melted away into the crowd. Raven made no move to walk away, and he wasn't sure whether he was relieved or disturbed because her face gave nothing away.

No pleasure. No censure. Just a careful social mask that made his heart twist.

'You're late.' Ah, *brava*, Rafa. *Brava*.

'My flight out of London was delayed due to fog. I explained to Sasha. She's forgiven me.'

The not-so-subtle barb found its mark. *I'm not here for you.*

He wanted to touch, wanted to feel the warmth of her skin so badly, he had to swallow several times before he could speak.

'I need to talk to you.'

Her eyes widened. 'Why? I thought you said all you had to say in Mexico.'

He tried for a careless shrug. 'Perhaps I have a few more things to say.'

She glanced away and gave her still-full glass to a passing waiter. 'I don't want to hear it. We were never friends, not really. And you fired me from being your physio. That leaves us nothing in common.'

'I'm seeing a therapist,' he blurted out.

Shocked eyes returned to his. 'You are?'

His smile felt false and painful. 'Yes, I figured I must be the only high-profile figure without the requisite head-shrinker as an accessory. Now I'm a fully fledged, card-carrying whack-job. But I still want to talk to you.'

She pressed lightly glossed lips together and shook her head. 'I don't think it's a good idea.'

Feeling the ground rock under him, he reached out and captured her wrist. 'You were right.'

Her breath caught. 'About what?' she whispered.

He started to answer but a burst of laughter from nearby guests stopped him. 'Not here.' He pulled her towards the doors and breathed in relief when she didn't resist. The lift ride up to his VIP suite was made in silence. After shutting the door, he threw his key card on a nearby table and shrugged off his tuxedo jacket.

'You were right about everything.'

She turned from the window overlooking the stunning marina. Her gaze slid over him, a hasty assessment which nevertheless made the blood thrum in his veins.

'Even I can't take responsibility for *everything*.'

'According to my shrink, I'm suffering from a combination of survivor's guilt and PTSD. Together, they make for one sexy but volatile cocktail of emotions.'

She licked her lips then curved them into a quick smile. An impersonal smile. She started to move towards the door. 'Well, I'm happy that you're getting some help. If that's all, I'll return downstairs. I don't wish to be rude to Sasha—'

'I also spoke to my father.'

She froze. He took advantage of her hesitation and stalked after her. Catching her around the waist, he pulled her body into his. She gave the tiniest gasp but didn't fight to get away.

Rafael took that as a good sign. 'I finally flew to León and spoke to my father.' He gave her the gist of their family meeting.

'Why are you telling me all this, Rafael?' she whispered.

He pulled her closer until he felt the sweet curve of her bottom against his groin. For a quick second, he lost himself in her scent, breathed her in and let her warm his frozen soul. The past three weeks had shown him there was an even worse hell than the one he'd previously inhabited. Because in that one he'd lost Raven.

Hell without Raven was a whole new reality. One he was desperate to escape.

'You made me face up to my flaws, to seek help before I hurt anyone else.' He couldn't stop himself from brushing his lips against her nape.

Her delicate shudder gave him hope but her next words dashed them completely. 'So you wanted to thank me? I accept your gratitude. Let me go, please.'

He held on tight. 'I'm seeking help, Raven, learning to change. But I need you. Without you, all this will be for nothing.'

She finally turned in his arms. The look on her face threatened to stop his breath. 'You can't do this because of me. You should want to seek help for yourself.'

'*Sí*, even I get that. But nothing I do will have any meaning unless you're part of that change.'

'What exactly are you saying?' she whispered.

Go for broke, Rafa. Hell, there was nothing left to lose. No, scratch that. There was everything to lose. Without her, his life had no meaning. So he took the biggest gamble he'd ever taken.

'*Lo siento.* I got it horribly wrong. I'm sorry.'

'What did you get wrong?'

'Not seeing the treasure I had in you until it was too late.'

She shook her head and grimaced. 'I'm no treasure, Rafael. I am just as damaged as you. I fooled myself into thinking a half-life was better than letting myself feel. You made me see that I'd let my father's treatment of me cloud my judgement so I pushed everyone away.'

His hand tightened on her waist. 'You know what I want to do?'

She shook her head.

'I want to track him down and ram my fist so far down his throat, he'll never speak again.'

'Don't let your shrink hear you say that.'

His smile felt grim and tight. 'I said I was trying to change. I never said I was aiming for saint of the year.' He sobered. 'I'm disgusted that my behaviour brought up what happened to you when you lived with him.'

'That's just it. Deep down I knew you were nothing like him but I'd programmed myself so thoroughly I let myself grasp the excuse when everyone told me you were nothing but a ruthless playboy.'

'And of course I went out of my way to prove them right.'

'If you were, you'd never have agreed to stop flirting with other women. Never have refused Chantilly's blatant invitation.'

Raven saw the flash of self-disgust and pain in his eyes.

'There was a time when I wouldn't have.'

'Past tense. You're a better man now. A better person.'

'Because of you.' His knuckle brushed down her cheek in a gesture so soft and gentle, tears threatened.

Despite the foolish hope that threatened, Raven's heart remained frozen. She couldn't remain here. If she did, she'd end up making a total fool of herself.

'I have to go—'

'I love you,' he rasped in a whisper so fierce it sizzled around the room.

'I…*what*?'

His heartbreakingly beautiful face contorted in a grimace. 'I'm still broken, *querida*, not so much on the outside any more, but I'm a long way from being perfect. And I know it's selfish of me but I want you so very desperately that I have to ask you to consider taking a chance on me, flawed and hideous as I am.' Acute vulnerability shone from his eyes and, when he grasped her arms, Raven felt the tremor in his fingers.

'You love me?'

'I have no right to, and I can't promise that I won't be a complete bastard on occasion, but *sí*, I love you. And I'll do anything to make you agree to hitch a ride with this broken wagon.'

'Rafael…'

He kissed her silent, as if he was afraid of what she'd say. She kissed him back, infusing every single drop of what she felt into the act. Somehow, he got the message.

He pulled back sharply, the question blazing its intensity in his eyes.

'Yes, my gorgeous man. I love you too.'

A frenzied tearing of clothes followed that sweet, soul-shaking confession. They made love right there in the living room, on the plush, expensive rug helpfully supplied by the five-star hotel.

She held her breath as Rafael slid on the sheath and prowled his naked body over hers. Hardly believing that this beautiful man was hers, she caressed her fingers down his firm cheek. He turned his head and kissed her palm, then, being the shameless opportunist he was, he kissed his way down her arm to her shoulder, then over her chest to capture one rigid nipple in his mouth.

At the same time, he parted her thighs with his and entered her in one bold thrust. Their coupling was fast, furious, their need for each other a raging fire that swiftly burned out of control.

When they'd caught their breaths, Rafael moved, picked her up and walked her into the bedroom.

'Should you be doing that?' she asked.

'I'm a renewed man. I can move mountains.' He let go of her and she tumbled onto the bed. Before she got totally lost in the effortlessly skilled seduction she knew he was aiming her way, she placed a hand on his lips.

'We haven't talked about your racing.'

His settled his long frame next to hers, his eyes serious. 'I think I need to concentrate on getting myself mentally in shape before I get behind the wheel. I've turned down a seat for this season.'

Knowing what it must have taken for him to turn down what he loved doing, her heart swelled. 'You take care of the mental aspect. I'll make sure your body is whipped into shape in time for next year's season.'

He grinned and tugged her close. 'I'd expect no less from my take-no-prisoners future wife.'

Her breath stalled. 'Is that a proposal, Rafael?'

'It's whatever you want it to be. If you don't think I'll make a good enough husband, you can take me as your sex slave. Or your boy toy. Or your f—'

She stopped him with a kiss before he finished. His incorrigible laugh promised retribution. And, for the life of her, Raven couldn't think of a better way to be punished.

'Sasha is going to hate me for disappearing from her gala,' she said an hour later.

'No, she's not. I begged her to send you the invitation. We both agreed I owe her big.'

She mock glared at him. 'You're right, you haven't changed one little bit.'

He laughed, a rich sound that made her soul sing. When he stared deep into her eyes her heart turned over. 'I have something to show you.'

Curious, she watched him reach into his drawer and pull out a sheaf of papers.

'You finished it?'

'Yes,' he answered. There was no laughter in his voice, no shameless lust monster lurking behind the stunning blue eyes.

There was only a careful, almost painfully hopeful expectancy.

She took the papers from him. Seeing the one word title, her heart caught—*Mamá*.

'I knew it. I knew Ana and Carlos were your parents.'

Two hours later, she looked up, tears streaming down her face. He'd sat with her back tucked against his front, in watchful silence while she read, all the while knowing he'd been reading his words alongside her.

The sheen of tears in his eyes rocked her soul.

'It's beautiful, Rafael.'

'*Gracias*. I hope, wherever she is, she forgives me for what I did.'

'She's your mother. That's what mothers do. And I promise to remind you of that whenever the nightmares threaten.'

The look in his eyes made hers fill all over again. '*Mi corazon*. I don't deserve you.'

Her smile was watery. 'No, you don't. But I'll let you have me anyway.'

EPILOGUE

'SO WHAT DO I get for winning the bet?' Raven asked as they stood in another luxurious room, surrounded by well-heeled guests, the very best vintage champagne and excellent food.

'What more could you possibly want, *mi amor*? You have my slavish adoration by day and my hot body by night.'

'Yes, but do you know how draining it's been to reassure you every day for the last three months that your book will be a smashing success? That more than one person will turn up at this launch?'

Rafael mock frowned. 'Have I been that needy?'

'Yes, you have, but don't think I wasn't fooled by what that neediness got you. You owe me big.'

'I seem to owe everyone big. Okay, how about…' He whispered a very hot, very dirty suggestion of payment. She was still blushing several minutes later when they both heard the whine of an electric wheelchair.

Rafael's father stopped beside them. An electronic copy of Rafael's book had been programmed into a tablet on his wheelchair, and the front page showed a picture of Rafael's mother, her face creased in a stunning smile as she laughed into the camera.

Rafael told her he'd taken that picture the year before she died.

'Carlos, please tell your son to stop worrying about his book. He thinks one of us has been bribing the critics to give it rave reviews.'

Carlos smiled and glanced at his son. Then he started to speak to him in Spanish. Slowly, Rafael's smile disappeared until his face was transformed into a look of intense love and gratitude. With a shaky hand, he touched his father's shoulder, then bent forward and kissed both his cheeks.

'*Gracias,* Papá.' His voice was rough as he straightened.

Carlos nodded, his own eyes holding a sheen of tears as he rolled his chair away.

'What did he say?'

'He's proud of me. And my mother would be too if she were here.'

As hard as she blinked, the tears welled. 'Damn it, you de Cervantes men sure know how to ruin a girl's make up.'

He caught her around the waist and pulled her close into his hard body.

'You're now a de Cervantes too. You can't take back your vows.'

She gave a mock grimace. She was still getting used to her new name, just as she was getting used to wearing the exquisite engagement and wedding ring set that had belonged to Rafael's mother. 'Raven de Cervantes is such a mouthful.'

'Hmm…' He nuzzled her neck, instantly melting her insides. 'We could shorten it.'

'You mean like just initials or a symbol like that rock star?'

'Not quite.'

'What have you in mind?' she asked, her fingers toying with buttons she couldn't wait to undo later. The promise of exploring the flesh underneath made her hot.

He worked along her jaw until he reached the side of her mouth. With a whisper-soft kiss, he raised his head and looked directly into her eyes. 'How about just…*amor querida*?'

Her heart, her soul and the rest of her body melted into him.

When his thumb brushed her cheek, she blinked back tears.

'That works. That works very well for me.'

* * * * *

FOR THE SAKE
OF THEIR SON

CATHERINE MANN

For my children.

One

Elliot Starc had faced danger his whole life. First at the hands of his heavy-fisted father. Later as a Formula One race car driver who used his world travels to feed information to Interpol.

But he'd never expected to be kidnapped. Especially not in the middle of his best friend's bachelor party.

Mad as hell, Elliot struggled back to consciousness, only to realize his wrists were cuffed. Numb. He struggled against the restraints while trying to get his bearings, but his brain was still disoriented. Last he remembered, he'd been in Atlanta, Georgia, at a bachelor party and now he was cuffed and blindfolded, for God's sake. What the hell? He only knew that he was in the back of a vehicle that smelled of leather and luxury. Noise offered him little to go on. Just the purr of a finely tuned engine. The pop of an opening soda can. A low hum of music so faint it must be on a headset.

"He's awake," a deep voice whispered softly, too softly to be identified.

"Damn it," another voice hissed.

"Hey," Elliot shouted, except it wasn't a shout. More of a hoarse croak. He cleared his throat and tried again. "Whatever the hell is going on here, we can talk ransom—"

A long buzz sounded. Unmistakable. The closing of a privacy window. Then silence. Solitude, no chance of shouting jack to anyone in this…

A limo, perhaps? Who kidnapped someone using a limousine?

Once they stopped, he would be ready, though. The second he could see, he wouldn't even need his hands. He was trained in seven different forms of self-defense. He could use his feet, his shoulders and his body weight.

He would be damned before he let himself ever be helpless in a fight.

They'd pulled off an interstate at least twenty minutes ago, driving into the country as best he could tell. He had no way of judging north, south or west. He could be anywhere from Florida to Mississippi to South Carolina, and God knows he had enemies in every part of the world from his work with Interpol and his triumphs over competitors in the racing world.

And he had plenty of pissed-off ex-girlfriends…. He winced at the thought of females and Carolina so close together. Home. Too many memories. Bad ones—with just a single bright spot in the form of Lucy Ann Joyner, but he'd wrecked even that.

Crap.

Back to the present. Sunlight was just beginning to filter through the blindfold, sparking behind his eyes like shards of glinting glass.

One thing was certain. This car had good shock absorbers. Otherwise the rutted road they were traveling would have rattled his teeth.

Although his teeth were clenched mighty damn tight right now.

Even now, he still couldn't figure out how he'd been blindsided near the end of Rowan Boothe's bachelor party in an Atlanta casino. Elliot had ducked into the back to find a vintage Scotch. Before he could wrap his hand around the neck of the bottle, someone had knocked him out.

If only he knew the motive for his kidnapping. Was someone after his money? Or had someone uncovered his secret dealings with Interpol? If so, did they plan to exploit that connection?

He'd lived his life to the fullest, determined to do better than his wrong-side-of-the-tracks upbringing. He only had one regret: how his lifelong friendship with Lucy Ann had crashed and burned more fiercely than when he'd been sideswiped at the Australian Grand Prix last year—

The car jerked to a halt. He braced his feet to keep from rolling off onto the floor. He forced himself to stay relaxed so his abductors would think he was still asleep.

His muscles tensed for action, eager for the opportunity to confront his adversaries. Ready to pay back. He was trained from his work with Interpol, with lightning-fast instincts honed in his racing career. He wouldn't go down without a fight.

Since he'd left his dirt-poor roots behind, he'd been beating the odds. He'd dodged juvie by landing in a military reform school where he'd connected with a lifelong group of friends. Misfits like himself who disdained rules while living by a strict code of justice. They'd grown up to take different life paths, but stayed connected through their friendship and freelance work for Interpol. Not that they'd been much help to him while someone was nabbing him a few feet away from the bachelor party they were all attending.

The car door opened and someone leaned over him. Something tugged at the back of his brain, a sense that he should know this person. He scrambled to untangle the mystery before it was too late.

His blindfold was tugged up and off, and he took in the inside of a black limo, just as he'd suspected. His abductors, however, were a total surprise.

"Hello, Elliot, my man," said his old high school pal Malcolm Douglas, who'd asked him to fetch that bottle of Scotch back at the bachelor party. "Waking up okay?"

Conrad Hughes—another traitorous bastard friend—patted his face. "You look plenty awake to me."

Elliot bit back a curse. He'd been kidnapped by his own comrades from the bachelor party. "Somebody want to tell me what's going on here?"

He eyed Conrad and Malcolm, both of whom had been living it up with him at the casino well past midnight. Morning sunshine streamed over them, oak trees sprawling behind them. The scent of Carolina jasmine carried on the breeze. Why were they taking him on this strange road trip?

"Well?" he pressed again when neither of them answered. "What the hell are you two up to?" he asked, his anger barely contained. He wanted to kick their asses. "I hope you have a good reason for taking me out to the middle of nowhere."

Conrad clapped him on the back. "You'll see soon enough."

Elliot angled out of the car, hard as hell with his hands

cuffed in front of him. His loafers hit the dirt road, rocks and dust shifting under his feet as he stood in the middle of nowhere in a dense forest of pines and oaks. "You'll tell me now or I'll beat the crap out of both of you."

Malcolm lounged against the side of the black stretch limo. "Good luck trying with your hands cuffed. Keep talking like that and we'll hang on to the key for a good long while."

"Ha—funny—not." Elliot ground his teeth in frustration. "Isn't it supposed to be the groom who gets pranked?"

Conrad grinned. "Oh, don't worry. Rowan should be waking up and finding his new tattoo right about now."

Extending his cuffed wrists, Elliot asked, "And the reason for this? I'm not the one getting married."

Ever.

Malcolm pushed away, jerking his head to the side, gesturing toward the path leading into the dense cluster of more pine trees with an occasional magnolia reaching for the sun. "Instead of telling you why, we'll just let you look. Walk with us."

As if he had any choice. His friends clearly had some kind of game planned and they intended to see it through regardless. Sure, he'd been in a bear of a mood since his breakup with Gianna. Hell, even before that. Since Lucy Ann had quit her job as his assistant and walked out of his life for good.

God, he really needed to pour out some frustration behind the wheel, full out, racing to…anywhere.

A few steps deeper into the woods, his blood hummed with recognition. The land was more mature than the last time he'd been here, but he knew the area well enough. Home. Or rather it used to be home, back when he was a poor kid with a drunken father. This small South Carolina farm town outside of Columbia had been called God's land.

Elliot considered it a corner of hell.

Although hell was brimming with sunshine today.

He stepped toward a clearing and onto a familiar dirt driveway, with a ranch-style cabin and a fat oak at least a hundred years old in the middle. A tree he'd played under as a kid, wishing he could stay here forever because this little haven in hell was a lot safer than his home.

He'd hidden with Lucy Ann Joyner here at her aunt's farmhouse. Both of them enjoying the sanctuary of this place, even if only for a few hours. Why were his buds taking him down this memory lane detour?

Branches rustled, a creaking sound carrying on the breeze, drawing his gaze. A swing dangled from a thick branch, moving back and forth as a woman swayed, her back to them. He stopped cold. Suddenly the meaning of this journey was crystal clear. His friends were forcing a confrontation eleven months in the making since he and Lucy Ann were both too stubborn to take the first step.

Did she know he was coming? He swallowed hard at the notion that maybe she wanted him here after all. That her decision to slice him out of her life had changed. But if she had, then why not just drive up to the house?

He wasn't sure the past year could be that easily forgotten, but his gut twisted tight over just the thought of talking to her again.

His eyes soaked in the sight of her, taking her in like parched earth with water. He stared at the slim feminine back, the light brown hair swishing just past her shoulders. Damn, but it had been a long eleven months without her. His lifelong pal had bolted after one reckless—incredible—night that had ruined their friendship forever.

He'd given her space and still hadn't heard from her.

In the span of a day, the one person he'd trusted above everyone else had cut him off. He'd never let anyone get that close to him—not even his friends from the military reform school. He and Lucy Ann had a history, a shared link that went beyond a regular friendship.

Or so he'd thought.

As if drawn by a magnet, he walked closer to the swing, to the woman. His hands still linked in front of him, he moved silently, watching her. The bared lines of her throat evoked memories of her jasmine scent. The way her dress slipped ever so slightly off one shoulder reminded him of years past when she'd worn hand-me-downs from neighbors.

The rope tugged at the branch as she toe-tapped, back and forth. A gust of wind turned the swing spinning to face him.

His feet stumbled to a halt.

Yes, it was Lucy Ann, but not just her. Lucy Ann stared back at him with wide eyes, shocked eyes. She'd clearly been kept every bit as much in the dark as he had. Before he could finish processing his disappointment that she hadn't helped arrange this, his eyes took in the biggest shocker of all.

Lucy Ann's arms were curved around an infant swaddled in a blue plaid blanket as she breast-fed him.

Lucy Ann clutched her baby boy to her chest and stared in shock at Elliot Starc, her childhood friend, her former boss. Her onetime lover.

The father of her child.

She'd scripted the moment she would tell him about their son a million times in her mind, but never had it played out like this, with him showing up out of the blue. Handcuffed? Clearly, he hadn't planned on coming to see her. She'd tempted fate in waiting so long to tell him, then he'd pulled one of his disappearing acts and she couldn't find him.

Now there was no avoiding him.

Part of her ached to run to Elliot and trust in the friendship they'd once shared, a friendship built here, in the wooded farmland outside Columbia, South Carolina. But another part of her—the part that saw his two friends lurking and the handcuffs on her old pal—told her all she needed to know. Elliot hadn't suddenly seen the light and come running to apologize for being a first-class jerk. He'd been dragged kicking and screaming.

Well, screw him. She had her pride, too.

Only the baby in her arms kept her from bolting altogether into her aunt's cabin up the hill. Lucy Ann eased Eli from her breast and adjusted her clothes in place. Shifting her son to her shoulder, she patted his back, her eyes staying locked on Elliot, trying to gauge his mood.

The way his eyes narrowed told her loud and clear that she couldn't delay her explanation any longer. She should have told him about Eli sooner. In the early days of her pregnancy, she'd tried and chickened out. Then she'd gotten angry over his speedy rebound engagement to the goddess Gianna, and that made it easier to keep her distance a while longer. She wouldn't be the cause of breaking up his engagement—rat bastard. She would tell him once he was married and wouldn't feel obligated to offer her anything. Even though the thought of him marrying that too-perfect bombshell heiress made her vaguely nauseous.

Now, Elliot was here, so damn tall and muscular, his sandy brown hair closely shorn. His shoulders filled out the black button-down shirt, his jeans slung low on his hips. His five o'clock shadow and narrowed green eyes gave him a bad-boy air he'd worked his whole life to live up to.

She knew every inch of him, down to a scar on his elbow he'd told everyone he got from falling off his bike but he'd really gotten from the buckle on his father's belt during a beating. They shared so much history, and now they shared a child.

Standing, she pulled her gaze from him and focused on his old boarding school friends behind him, brooding Conrad Hughes and charmer Malcolm Douglas. Of course they'd dragged him here. These days both of them had sunk so deep into a pool of marital bliss, they seemed to think everyone else wanted to plunge in headfirst. No doubt they'd brought Elliot here with just that in mind.

Not a freakin' chance.

She wasn't even interested in dipping her toes into those waters and certainly not with Elliot, the biggest playboy in the free world.

"Gentlemen, do you think you could uncuff him, then leave so he and I can talk civilly?"

Conrad—a casino owner—fished out a key from his pocket and held it up. "Can do." He looked at Elliot. "I trust you're not going to do anything stupid like try to start a fight over our little prank here."

Prank? This was her life and they were playing with it. Anger sparked in her veins.

Elliot pulled a tight smile. "Of course not. I'm out-numbered. Now just undo the handcuffs. My arms are too numb to hit either of you anyway."

Malcolm plucked the keys from Conrad and opened the cuffs. Elliot massaged his wrists for a moment, still silent, then stretched his arms over his head.

Did he have to keep getting hotter every year? Especially not fair when she hadn't even had time to shower since yesterday thanks to her son's erratic sleeping schedule.

Moistening her dry mouth, Lucy Ann searched for a way to dispel the awkward air. "Malcolm, Conrad, I realize you meant well with this, but perhaps it's time for you both to leave. Elliot and I clearly have some things to discuss."

Eli burped. Lucy Ann rolled her eyes and cradled her son in the crook of her arm, too aware of the weight of Elliot's stare.

Malcolm thumped Elliot on the back. "You can thank us later."

Conrad leveled a somber steady look her way. "Call if you need anything. I mean that."

Without another word, both men disappeared back into the wooded perimeter as quickly as they'd arrived. For the first time in eleven months, she was alone with Elliot.

Well, not totally alone. She clutched Eli closer until he squirmed.

Elliot stuffed his hands in his pockets, still keeping his distance. "How long have you been staying with your aunt?"

"Since I left Monte Carlo." She'd been here the whole time, if he'd only bothered to look. Where else would she go? She had money saved up, but staying here made the most sense economically.

"How are you supporting yourself?"

"That's not your business." She lifted her chin. He had the ability to find out anything he wanted to know about her if he'd just looked, thanks to his Interpol connections.

Apparently, he hadn't even bothered to try. And that's what hurt the most. All these months, she'd thought he would check up on her. He would have seen she was pregnant. He would have wondered.

He would have come.

"Not my business?" He stalked a step closer, only a hint of anger showing in his carefully guarded eyes. "Really? I think we both know why it is so very much my business."

"I have plenty saved up from my years working for you." He'd insisted on paying her an outlandish salary to be his personal assistant. "And I'm doing virtual work to subsidize my income. I build and maintain websites. I make enough to get by." Her patience ran out with this small talk, the avoidance of discussing the baby sleeping in her arms. "You've had months to ask these questions and chose to remain silent. If anyone has a right to be angry, it's me."

"You didn't call either, and you have a much more compelling reason to communicate." He nodded toward Eli. "He is mine."

"You sound sure."

"I know you. I see the truth in your eyes," he said simply.

She couldn't argue with that. She swallowed once, twice, to clear her throat and gather her nerve. "His name is Eli. And yes, he's your son, two months old."

Elliot pulled his hands from his pockets. "I want to hold him."

Her stomach leaped into her throat. She'd envisioned this moment so many times, but living in it? She never could have imagined how deeply the emotions would rattle her. She passed over Eli to his father, watching Elliot's face. For once, she couldn't read him at all. So strange, considering how they'd once been so in sync they could finish each other's sentences, read a thought from a glance across a room.

Now, he was like a stranger.

Face a blank slate, Elliot held their son in broad, capable hands, palmed the baby's bottom and head as he studied the tiny cherub features. Eli still wore his blue footed sleeper from bedtime, his blond hair glistening as the sun sent dappled rays through the branches. The moment looked like a fairy tale, but felt so far from that her heart broke over how this should have, could have been.

Finally, Elliot looked up at her, his blasé mask sliding away to reveal eyes filled with ragged pain. His throat moved in a slow gulp of emotion. "Why did you keep this—Eli—from me?"

Guilt and frustration gnawed at her. She'd tried to contact him but knew she hadn't tried hard enough. Her pride… Damn it all. Her excuses all sounded weak now, even to her own ears.

"You were engaged to someone else. I didn't want to interfere in that."

"You never intended to tell me at all?" His voice went hoarse with disbelief, his eyes shooting back down to his son sleeping against his chest so contentedly as if he'd been there all along.

"Of course I planned to explain—after you were married." She dried her damp palms on her sundress. "I refused to be responsible for breaking up your great love match."

Okay, she couldn't keep the cynicism out of that last part, but he deserved it for his rebound relationship.

"My engagement to Gianna ended months ago. Why didn't you contact me?"

He had a point there. She ached to run, but he had her son. And as much as she hated to admit it to herself, she'd missed Elliot. They'd been so much a part of each other's lives for so long. The past months apart had been like a kind of withdrawal.

"Half the time I couldn't find you and the other half, your new personal secretary couldn't figure out where you were." And hadn't that pissed her off something fierce? Then worried her, because she knew about his sporadic missions for Interpol, and she also knew his reckless spirit.

"You can't have tried very hard, Lucy Ann. All you had to do was speak with any of my friends." His eyes narrowed. "Or did you? Is that why they brought me here today, because you reached out to them?"

She'd considered doing just that many times, only to balk at the last second. She wouldn't be manipulative. She'd planned to tell him face-to-face. And soon.

"I wish I could say yes, but I'm afraid not. One of them must have been checking up on me even if you never saw the need."

Oops. Where had that bitter jab come from?

He cocked an eyebrow. "This is about Eli. Not about the two of us."

"There is no 'two of us' anymore." She touched her son's head lightly, aching to take him back in her arms. "You ended that when you ran away scared after we had a reckless night of sex."

"I do *not* run away."

"Excuse me if your almighty ego is bruised." She crossed her arms over her chest, feeling as though they were in fifth grade again, arguing over whether the basketball was in or out of bounds.

Elliot sighed, looking around at the empty clearing. The limo's engine roared to life, then faded as it drove away without him. He turned back to Lucy Ann. "This isn't accomplishing anything. We need to talk reasonably about our child's future."

"I agree." Of course they had to talk, but right now her

heart was in her throat. She could barely think straight. She scooped her baby from his arms. "We'll talk tomorrow when we're both less rattled."

"How do I know you won't just disappear with my son?" He let go of Eli with obvious reluctance.

His son.

Already his voice echoed with possessiveness.

She clasped her son closer, breathing in the powder-fresh familiarity of him, the soft skin of his cheek pressed against her neck reassuringly. She could and she would manage her feelings for Elliot. Nothing and no one could be allowed to interfere with her child's future.

"I've been here all this time, Elliot. You just never chose to look." A bitter pill to swallow. She gestured up the empty dirt road. "Even now, you didn't choose. Your friends dumped you here on my doorstep."

Elliot walked a slow circle around her, his hand snagging the rope holding the swing until he stopped beside her. He had a way of moving with such fluidity, every step controlled, a strange contradiction in a man who always lived on the edge. Always flirting with chaos.

Her skin tingled to life with the memory of his touch, the wind teasing her with a hint of aftershave and musk.

She cleared her throat. "Elliot, I really think you should—"

"Lucy Ann," he interrupted, "in case it's escaped your notice, my friends left me here. Alone. No car." He leaned in closer, his hand still holding the rope for balance, so close she could almost feel the rasp of his five o'clock shadow. "So regardless of whether or not we talk, for now, you're stuck with me."

Two

Elliot held himself completely still, a feat of supreme control given the frustration racing through his veins. That Lucy Ann had hidden her pregnancy—his son—from him all this time threatened to send him to his knees. Somehow during this past year he'd never let go of the notion that everything would simply return to the way things had been before with them. Their friendship had carried him through the worst times of his life.

Now he knew there was no going back. Things between them had changed irrevocably.

They had a child together, a boy just inches away. Elliot clenched his hand around the rope. He needed to bide his time and proceed with caution. His lifelong friend had a million great qualities—but she was also stubborn as hell. A wrong step during this surprise meeting could have her digging in her heels.

He had to control his frustration, tamp down the anger

over all that she'd hidden from him. Staying levelheaded saved his life on more than one occasion on the racetrack. But never had the stakes been more important than now. No matter how robbed he felt, he couldn't let that show.

Life had taught him well how to hide his darker emotions.

So he waited, watching her face for some sign. The breeze lifted a strand of her hair, whipping it over his cheek. His pulse thumped harder.

"Well, Lucy Ann? What now?"

Her pupils widened in her golden-brown eyes, betraying her answering awareness a second before she bolted up from the swing. Elliot lurched forward as the swing freed. He released the rope and found his footing.

Lucy Ann glanced over her shoulder as she made her way to the graveled path. "Let's go inside."

"Where's your aunt?" He followed her, rocks crunching under his feet.

"At work." Lucy Ann walked up the steps leading to the prefab log cabin's long front porch. Time had worn the redwood look down to a rusty hue. "She still waits tables at the Pizza Shack."

"You used to send her money." He'd stumbled across the bank transaction by accident. Or maybe his accountant had made a point of letting him discover the transfers since Lucy Ann left so little for herself.

"Well, come to find out, Aunt Carla never used it," Lucy Ann said wryly, pushing the door open into the living room. The decor hadn't changed, the same brown plaid sofa with the same saggy middle, the same dusty Hummel figurines packed in a corner cabinet. He'd forgotten how Carla scoured yard sales religiously for the things, unable to afford them new.

They'd hidden here more than once as kids, then as

teenagers, plotting a way to escape their home lives. He eyed the son he'd barely met but who already filled his every plan going forward. "Your aunt's prideful, just like you."

"I accepted a job from you." She settled Eli into a portable crib by the couch.

"You worked your butt off and got your degree in computer technology." He admired the way she never took the easy way out. How she'd found a career for herself.

So why had she avoided talking to him? Surely not from any fear of confrontation. Her hair swung forward as she leaned into the baby crib, her dress clinging to her hips. His gaze hitched on the new curves.

Lucy Ann spun away from the crib and faced him again. "Are we going to keep making small talk or are you going to call a cab? I could drive you back into town."

"I'm not going anywhere."

Her eyebrows pinched together. "I thought we agreed to talk tomorrow."

"You decided. I never agreed." He dropped to sit on the sofa arm. If he sat in the middle, no telling how deep that sag would sink.

"You led me to believe..." She looked around as if searching for answers, but the Hummels stayed silent. "Damn it. You just wanted to get in the house."

Guilty as charged. "This really is the best place to discuss the future. Anywhere else and I'll have to be on the lookout for fans. We're in NASCAR country, you know. Not Formula One, but kissing cousins." He held up his hands. "Besides, my jackass buddies stranded me without my wallet."

She gasped. "You're joking."

"I wish." They must have taken it from his pocket while he was knocked out. He tamped down another surge of anger over being manipulated. If he'd just had some warning…

"Why did they do this to you—to both of us?" She sat on the other arm of the sofa, the worn width between them.

"Probably because they know how stubborn we are." He watched her face, trying to read the truth in the delicate lines, but he saw only exhaustion and dark circles. "Would you have ever told me about the baby?"

"You've asked me that already and I've answered. Of course I would have told you—" she shrugged "—eventually."

Finally he asked the question that had been plaguing him most. "How can I be sure?"

Shaking her head, she shrugged again. "You can't. You'll just have to trust me."

A wry smile tugged the corner of his mouth. "Trust has never been easy for either of us." But now that he was here and saw the truth, his decision was simple. "I want you and Eli to come with me, just for a few weeks while we make plans for the future."

"No." She crossed her arms over her chest.

"Ah, come on, Lucy Ann. Think about my request before you react."

"Okay. Thinking…" She tapped her temple, tapping, tapping. Her hand fell to her lap. "Still no."

God, her humor and spunk had lifted him out of hell so many times. He'd missed her since she'd stormed out of his life.…

But he'd also missed out on a lot more in not knowing about his son.

"I can never regain those first two months of Eli's life." A bitter pill he wasn't sure how to swallow down. "I need a chance to make up for that."

She shook her head slowly. "You can't be serious about taking a baby on the road."

"I'm dead serious." He wasn't leaving here without them. He couldn't just toss money down and go.

"Let me spell it out for you then. Elliot, this is the middle of your racing season." She spoke slowly, as she'd done when they were kids and she'd tutored him in multiplication tables. "You'll be traveling, working, running with a party crowd. I've seen it year after year, enough to know that's no environment for a baby."

And damn it, she was every bit as astute now as she'd been then. He lined up an argument, a way to bypass her concerns. "You saw my life when there wasn't a baby around—no kids around, actually. It *can* be different. *I* can be different, like other guys who bring their families on the circuit with them." He shifted to sit beside her. "I have a damn compelling reason to make changes in my life. This is the chance to show you that."

Twisting the skirt of her dress in nervous fingers, she studied him with her golden-brown gaze for so long he thought he'd won.

Then resolve hardened her eyes again. "Expecting someone to change only sets us both up for disappointment."

"Then you'll get to say 'I told you so.' You told me often enough in the past." He rested a hand on top of hers to still the nervous fidgeting, squeezing lightly. "The best that happens is I'm right and this works. We find a plan to be good parents to Eli even when we're jet-setting around the world. Remember how much fun we used to have together? I miss you, Lucy Ann."

He thumbed the inside of her wrist, measuring the speed of her pulse, the softness of her skin. He'd done

everything he could to put her out of his mind, but with
no luck. He'd been unfair to Gianna, leading her to think
he was free. So many regrets. He was tired of them.
"Lucy Ann…"

She yanked her hand free. "Stop it, Elliot. I've watched
you seduce a lot of women over the years. Your games
don't work with me. So don't even try the slick moves."

"You wound me." He clamped a hand over his heart
in an attempt at melodrama to cover his disappointment.

She snorted. "Hardly. You don't fool me with the
pained look. It's eleven months too late to be genuine."

"You would be wrong about that."

"No games." She shot to her feet. "We both need time
to regroup and think. We need to continue this conversation later."

"Fair enough then." He sat on the sofa, stretching both
arms out along the back.

She stomped her foot. "What are you doing?"

He picked up the remote from the coffee table and
leaned back again into the deepest, saggiest part. "Making myself comfortable."

"For what?"

He thumbed on the television. "If I'm going to stick
around until you're ready to talk, I might as well scout
the good stations. Any beer in the fridge? Although wait,
it's too early for that. How about coffee?"

"No." She snatched the remote control from his hand.
"And stop it. I don't know what game you're playing but
you can quit and *go*. In case that wasn't clear enough,
leave and come back later. You can take my car."

He took the remote right back and channel surfed
without looking away from the flat screen. "Thanks for
the generous offer of transportation, but you said we can't

take Eli on the road and I only just met my son. I'm not leaving him now. How about the coffee?"

"Like hell."

"I don't need cream. Black will do just fine."

"Argh!" She slumped against the archway between the living room and kitchen. "Quit being ridiculous about the coffee. You know you're not staying here."

He set aside the remote, smiling as some morning talk show droned in the background. "So you'll come with me after all. Good."

"You're crazy. You know that, right?"

"No newsflash there, sweetheart. A few too many concussions." He stood. "Forget the suitcase."

"Run that by me again?"

"Don't bother with packing. I'll buy everything you need, everything new. Let's just grab a couple of diapers for the rug rat and go."

Her acceptance was becoming more and more important by the second. He needed her with him. He had to figure out a way to tie their lives together again so his son would know a father, a mother and a normal life.

"Stop! Stop trying to control my life." She stared at him sadly. "Elliot, I appreciate all you did for me in the past, but I don't need rescuing anymore."

"Last time I checked, I wasn't offering a rescue. Just a partnership."

If humor and pigheadedness didn't work, time to go back to other tactics. No great hardship really, since the attraction crackled between them every bit as tangibly now as it had the night they'd impulsively landed in bed together after a successful win. He sauntered closer. "As I recall, last time we were together, we shared control quite…nicely. And now that I think of it, we really don't need those clothes after all."

* * *

The rough upholstery of the sofa rasped against the backs of Lucy Ann's legs, her skin oversensitive, tingling to life after just a few words from Elliot. Damn it, she refused to be seduced by him again. The way her body betrayed her infuriated her down to her toes, which curled in her sandals.

Sure, he was beach-boy handsome, mesmerizingly sexy and blindingly charming. Women around the world could attest to his allure. However, in spite of her one unforgettable moment of weakness, she refused to be one of those fawning females throwing themselves at his feet.

No matter how deeply her body betrayed her every time he walked in the room.

She shot from the sofa, pacing restlessly since she couldn't bring herself to leave her son alone, even though he slept. Damn Elliot and the draw of attraction that had plagued her since the day they'd gone skinny-dipping at fourteen and she realized they weren't kids anymore.

Shutting off those thoughts, she pivoted on the coarse shag carpet to face him. "This is not the time or the place for sexual innuendo."

"Honey—" his arms stretched along the back of the sofa "—it's never a bad time for sensuality. For nuances. For seduction."

The humor in his eyes took the edge of arrogance off his words. "If you're aiming to persuade me to leave with you, you're going about it completely the wrong way."

"There's no denying we slept together."

"Clearly." She nodded toward the Pack 'n Play where their son slept contentedly, unaware that his little world had just been turned upside down.

"There's no denying that it was good between us. Very good."

Elliot's husky words snapped her attention back to his face. There wasn't a hint of humor in sight. Awareness tingled to the roots of her hair.

Swallowing hard, she sank into an old cane rocker. "It was impulsive. We were both tipsy and sentimental and reckless." The rush of that evening sang through her memory, the celebration of his win, reminiscing about his first dirt track race, a little wine, too much whimsy, then far too few clothes.… "I refuse to regret that night or call our…encounter…a mistake since I have Eli. But I do not intend to repeat the experience."

"Now that's just a damn shame. What a waste of good sexual chemistry."

"Will you please stop?" Her hands fisted on the arms of the wooden rocker. "We got along just fine as friends for thirty years."

"Are you saying we can be friends again?" He leaned forward, elbows on his knees. "No more hiding out and keeping big fat secrets from each other?"

His words carried too much truth for comfort. "You're twisting my words around."

"God's honest truth, Lucy Ann." He sighed. "I'm trying to call a truce so we can figure out how to plan our son's future."

"By telling me to ditch my clothes? You obviously missed class the day they taught the definition of truce."

"Okay, you're right. That wasn't fair of me." He thrust his hands through his hair. "I'm not thinking as clearly as I would like. Learning about Eli has been a shock to say the least."

"I can understand that." Her hands unfurled to grip the rocker. "And I am so very sorry for any pain this has caused you."

"Given that I've lost the first two months of my son's

life, the least you can do is give me four weeks together. Since you're working from home here, you'll be able to work on the road, as well. But if going on the race circuit is a deal breaker, I'll bow out this season."

She jolted in surprise that he would risk all he'd worked so hard to achieve, a career he so deeply loved. "What about your sponsors? Your reputation?"

"This is your call."

"That's not fair to make an ultimatum like that, to put it on me."

"I'm asking, and I'm offering you choices."

Choices? Hardly. She knew how important his racing career was to him. And she couldn't help but admit to feeling a bit of pride in having helped him along the way. There was no way she could let him back out now.

She tossed up her hands. "Fine. Eli and I will travel with you on the race circuit for the next four weeks so you can figure out whatever it is you want to know and make your plans. You win. You always do."

Winning didn't feel much like a victory tonight.

Elliot poured himself a drink from the wet bar at his hotel. He and Lucy Ann had struck a bargain that he would stay at a nearby historic home that had been converted into a hotel while she made arrangements to leave in the morning. He'd called for a car service to pick him up, making use of his credit card numbers, memorized, a fact he hadn't bothered mentioning to Lucy Ann earlier. Although she should have known. Had she selectively forgotten or had she been that rattled?

The half hour waiting for the car had been spent silently staring at his son while Eli slept and Lucy Ann hid in the other room under the guise of packing.

Elliot's head was still reeling. He had been knocked

unconscious and kidnapped, and found out he had an unknown son all in one day. He tipped back the glass of bourbon, emptying it and pouring another to savor, more slowly, while he sat out on the garden balcony where he would get better cell phone reception.

He dropped into a wrought-iron chair and let the Carolina moon pour over him. His home state brought such a mix of happy and sad memories. He was always better served just staying the hell away. He tugged his cell from his waistband, tucked his Bluetooth in his ear and thumbed autodial three for Malcolm Douglas.

The ringing stopped two buzzes in. "Brother, how's it going?"

"How do you think it's going, Douglas? My head hurts and I'm pissed off." Anger was stoked back to life just thinking about his friends' arrogant stunt, the way they'd played with his life. "You could have just told me about the baby."

Malcolm chuckled softly. "Wouldn't have been half as fun that way."

"Fun? You think this is some kind of game? You're a sick bastard." The thought of them plotting this out while he partied blissfully unaware had him working hard to keep his breath steady. He and his friends had played some harsh jokes on one another in the past, but nothing like this. "How long have you known?"

"For about a week," the chart-topping musician answered unrepentantly.

"A week." Seven days he could have had with his son. Seven days his best friends kept the largest of secrets from him. Anger flamed through him. Was there nobody left in this world he could trust? He clenched his hand around the glass tumbler until it threatened to shatter. "And you said nothing at all."

"I know it seems twisted, but we talked it through," he said, all humor gone, his smooth tones completely serious for once. "We thought this was the best way. You're too good at playing it cool with advance notice. You would have just made her mad."

"Like I didn't already do that?" He set aside the half-drunk glass of bourbon, the top-shelf brand wasted on him in his current mood.

"You confronted her with honesty," Malcolm answered reasonably. "If we'd given you time to think, you'd have gotten your pride up. You would have been angry and bullish. You can be rather pigheaded, you know."

"If I'm such a jackass, then why are we still friends?"

"Because I'm a jackass, too." Malcolm paused before continuing somberly. "You would have done the same for me. I know what it's like not to see your child, to have missed out on time you can never get back…"

Malcolm's voice choked off with emotion. He and his wife had been high school sweethearts who'd had to give up a baby girl for adoption since they were too young to provide a life for their daughter. Now they had twins—a boy and a girl—they loved dearly, but they still grieved for that first child, even knowing they'd made the right decision for her.

Although Malcolm and Celia had both known about *their* child from the start.

Elliot forked his hands through his buzzed hair, kept closely shorn since he'd let his thoughts of Lucy Ann distract him and he'd caught his car on fire just before Christmas—nearly caught himself on fire, as well.

He'd scorched his hair; the call had been that damn close.

"I just can't wrap my brain around the fact she's kept his existence from me for so long."

Malcolm snorted. "I can't believe the two of you slept together."

A growl rumbled low in his throat. "You're close to overstepping the bounds of our friendship with talk like that."

"Ahhh." He chuckled. "So you do care about her more than you've let on."

"We were...friends. Lifelong friends. That's no secret." He and Lucy Ann shared so much history it was impossible to unravel events from the past without thinking about each other. "The fact that there was briefly more...I can't deny that, either."

"You must not have been up to snuff for her to run so fast."

Anger hissed between Elliot's teeth, and he resisted the urge to pitch his Bluetooth over the balcony. "Now you have crossed the line. If we were sitting in the same place right now, my fist would be in your face."

"Fair enough." Douglas laughed softly again. "Like I said. You do care more than a little, more than any 'buddy.' And you can't refute it. Admit it, Elliot. I've just played you, my friend."

No use denying he'd been outmaneuvered by someone who knew him too well.

And as for what Malcolm had said? That he cared for Lucy Ann? Cared? Yes. He had. And like every other time in his life he'd cared, things had gone south.

If he wanted to sort through this mess and create any kind of future with Eli and Lucy Ann, he had to think more and care less.

Three

Lucy Ann shaded her eyes against the rising sun. For the third time in twenty-four hours a limousine pulled up her dusty road, oak trees creating a canopy for the long driveway. The first time had occurred yesterday when Elliot had arrived, then when he'd left, and now, he was returning.

Her simple semihermit life working from home with her son was drawing to a close in another few minutes.

Aunt Carla cradled Eli in her arms. Carla never seemed to age, her hair a perpetual shade halfway between gray and brown. She refused to waste money to have it colored. Her arms were ropy and strong from years of carting around trays of pizzas and sodas. Her skin was prematurely wrinkled from too much hard work, time in the Carolina sun—and a perpetual smile.

She was a tough, good woman who'd been there for Lucy Ann all her life. Too bad Carla couldn't have been her mother. Heaven knows she'd prayed for that often enough.

Carla smiled down at little Eli, his fist curled around her finger. "I'm sure I'm going to miss you both. It's been a treat having a baby around again."

She'd never had a child of her own, but was renowned for opening her home to family members in need. She wasn't a problem-solver so much as a temporary oasis. Very temporary, as the limo drew closer down the half-mile driveway.

"You're sweet to make it sound like we haven't taken over your house." Lucy Ann tugged her roller bag through the door, *kerthunking* it over a bump, casting one last glance back at the tiny haven of Hummels and the saggy sofa.

"Sugar, you know I only wish I could've done more for you this time and when you were young." Carla swayed from side to side, wearing her standard high-waisted jeans and a seasonal shirt—a pink Easter bunny on today's tee.

"You've always been there for me." Lucy Ann sat on top of her luggage, her eyes on the nearing limo. "I don't take that for granted."

"I haven't always been there for you and we both know it," Carla answered, her eyes shadowed with memories they both didn't like to revisit.

"You did the best you could. I know that." Since Lucy Ann's mother had legal guardianship and child services wouldn't believe any of the claims of neglect, much less allegations of abuse by stepfathers, there wasn't anything Lucy Ann could do other than escape to Carla—or to Elliot.

Her mother and her last stepfather had died in a boating accident, so there was nothing to be gained from dwelling on the past. Her mom had no more power over her than Lucy Ann allowed her. "Truly, Carla, the past is best left there."

"Glad to know you feel that way. I hope you learned that from me." Carla tugged on Lucy Ann's low ponytail. "If you can forgive me, why can't you forgive Elliot?"

Good question. She slouched back with a sigh. "If I could answer that, then I guess my heart wouldn't be breaking in two right now."

Her aunt hauled her in for a one-armed hug while she cradled the baby in the other. "I would fix this for you if I could."

"Come with us," Lucy Ann blurted. "I've asked you before and I know all your reasons for saying no. You love your home and your life and weekly bingo. But will you change your mind this time?" She angled back, hoping. "Will you come with us? We're family."

"Ah, sweet niece." Carla shook her head. "This is your life, your second chance, your adventure. Be careful. Be smart. And remember you're a damn amazing woman. He would be a lucky man to win you back."

Just the thought… No. "That's not why I'm going with him." She took Eli from her aunt. "My trip is only about planning a future for my son, for figuring out a way to blend Elliot's life with my new life."

"You used to be a major part of his world."

"I was his glorified secretary." A way for him to give her money while salving her conscience. At least she'd lived frugally and used the time to earn a degree so she could be self-sufficient. The stretch limo slowed along the last patch of gravel in front of the house.

"You were his best friend and confidant… And apparently something more at least once."

"I'm not sure what point you are trying to make, but

if you're going to make it, do so fast." She nodded to the opening limo door. "We're out of time."

"You two got along fabulously for decades and there's an obvious attraction. Why can't you have more?" Her aunt tipped her head, eyeing Elliot stepping from the vehicle. The car door slammed.

Sunshine sent dappled rays along his sandy-brown hair, over his honed body in casual jeans and a white polo that fit his muscled arms. She'd leaned on those broad shoulders for years without hesitation, but now all she could think about was the delicious feel of those arms around her. The flex of those muscles as he stretched over her.

Lucy Ann tore her eyes away and back to her aunt. "Have more?" That hadn't ended well for either of them. "Are you serious?"

"Why wouldn't I be?"

"He hasn't come looking for me for nearly a year. He let me go." Something that had hurt every day of the eleven months that passed. She waved toward him talking to his chauffeur. "He's only here now because his friends threw him on my doorstep."

"You're holding back because of your pride?" Her aunt tut-tutted. "You're throwing him and a possible future away because of pride?"

"Listen to me. *He* threw *me* away." She'd been an afterthought or nuisance to people her whole life. She wouldn't let her son live the same second-class existence. Panic began to set in. "Now that I think of it, I'm not sure why I even agreed to go with him—"

"Stop. Hold on." Carla grabbed her niece by the shoulders and steadied her. "Forget I said anything at all. Of course you have every reason to be upset. Go with him and figure out how to manage your son's future. And I'll always be here if you decide to return."

"If?" Lucy Ann rolled her eyes. "You mean when."

Carla pointed to the limo and the broad-shouldered man walking toward them. "Do you really think Elliot's going to want his son to grow up here?"

"Um, I mean, I hadn't thought…"

True panic set in as Lucy Ann realized she no longer had exclusive say over her baby's life. Of course Elliot would have different plans for his child. He'd spent his entire life planning how to get out of here, devising ways to build a fortune, and he'd succeeded.

Eli was a part of that now. And no matter how much she wanted to deny it, her life could never be simple again.

Elliot sprawled in the backseat of the limo while Lucy Ann adjusted the straps on Eli's infant seat, checking each buckle to ensure it fit with obvious seasoned practice. Her loose ponytail swung forward, the dome light bringing out the hints of honey in her light brown hair.

He dug his fingers into the butter-soft leather to keep from stroking the length of her hair, to see if it was as silky as he remembered. He needed to bide his time. He had her and the baby with him. That was a huge victory, especially after their stubborn year apart.

And now?

He had to figure out a way to make her stay. To go back to the way things were…except he knew things couldn't be exactly the same. Not after they'd slept together. Although he would have to tread warily there. He couldn't see her cheering over a "friends with benefits" arrangement. He'd have to take it a step at a time to gauge her mood. She needed to be reminded of all the history they shared, all the ways they got along so well.

She tucked a homemade quilt over Eli's tiny legs before shifting to sit beside him. Elliot knocked on the driver's window and the vehicle started forward on their journey to the airport.

"Lucy Ann, you didn't have to stay up late packing that suitcase." He looked at the discarded cashmere baby blanket she left folded to the side. "I told you I would take care of buying everything he needs."

His son would never ride a secondhand bike he'd unearthed at the junkyard. A sense of possessiveness stirred inside him. He'd ordered the best of the best for his child—from the car seat to a travel bed. Clothes. Toys. A stroller. He'd consulted his friends' wives for advice— easy enough since his buddies and their wives were all propagating like rabbits these days.

Apparently, so was he.

Lucy Ann rested a hand on the faded quilt with tiny blue sailboats. "Eli doesn't know if something is expensive or a bargain. He only knows if something feels or smells familiar. He's got enough change in his life right now."

"Is that a dig at me?" He studied her, trying to get a read on her mood. She seemed more reserved than yesterday, worried even.

"Not a dig at all. It's a fact." She eyed him with confusion.

"He has you as a constant."

"Damn straight he does," she said with a mama-bear ferocity that lit a fire inside him. Her strength, the light in her eyes, stirred him.

Then it hit him. She was in protective mode because she saw him as a threat. She actually thought he might try to take her child away from her. Nothing could be further from the truth. He wanted to parent the child *with* her.

He angled his head to capture her gaze fully. "I'm not trying to take him away from you. I just want to be a part of his life."

"Of course. That was always my intention," she said, her eyes still guarded, wary. "I know trust is difficult right now, but I hope you will believe me that I want you to have regular visitation."

Ah, already she was trying to set boundaries rather than thinking about possibilities. But he knew better than to fight with her. Finesse always worked better than head-on confrontation. He pointed to the elementary school they'd attended together, the same redbrick building but with a new playground. "We share a lot of history and now we share a son. Even a year apart isn't going to erase everything else."

"I understand that."

"Do you?" He moved closer to her.

Her body went rigid as she held herself still, keeping a couple of inches of space between them. "Remember when we were children, in kindergarten?"

Following her train of thought was tougher than maneuvering through race traffic, but at least she was talking to him. "Which particular day in kindergarten?"

She looked down at her hands twisted in her lap, her nails short and painted with a pretty orange. "You were lying belly flat on a skateboard racing down a hill."

That day eased to the front of his mind. "I fell off, flat on my ass." He winced. "Broke my arm."

"All the girls wanted to sign your cast." She looked sideways at him, smiling. "Even then you were a chick magnet."

"They just wanted to use their markers," he said dismissively.

She looked up to meet his eyes fully for the first time since they'd climbed into the limousine. "I knew that your arm was already broken."

"You never said a word to me." He rubbed his forearm absently.

"You would have been embarrassed if I confronted you, and you would have lied to me. We didn't talk as openly then about our home lives." She tucked the blanket more securely around the baby's feet as Eli sucked a pacifier in his sleep. "We were new friends who shared a jelly sandwich at lunch."

"We were new friends and yet you were right about the arm." He looked at his son's tiny hands and wondered how any father could ever strike out at such innocence. Sweat beaded his forehead at even the thought.

"I told my mom though, after school," Lucy Ann's eyes fell to his wrist. "She wasn't as…distant in those days."

The weight of her gaze was like a stroke along his skin, her words salve to a past wound. "I didn't know you said anything to anyone."

"Her word didn't carry much sway, or maybe she didn't fight that hard." She shrugged, the strap of her sundress sliding. "Either way, nothing happened. So I went to the principal."

"My spunky advocate." God, he'd missed her. And yet he'd always thought he knew everything about her and here she had something new to share. "Guess that explains why they pulled me out of class to interview me about my arm."

"You didn't tell the principal the truth though, did you?

I kept waiting for something big to happen. My five-year-old imagination was running wild."

For one instant in that meeting he had considered talking, but the thoughts of afterward had frozen any words in his throat like a lodged wad of that shared jelly sandwich. "I was still too scared of what would happen to my mother if I talked. Of what he would do to her."

Sympathy flickered in her brown eyes. "We discussed so many things as kids, always avoiding anything to do with our home lives. Our friendship was a haven for me then."

He'd felt the same. But that meeting with the principal had made him bolder later, except he'd chosen the wrong person to tell. Someone loyal to his father, which only brought on another beating.

"You had your secrets, too. I could always sense when you were holding back."

"Then apparently we didn't have any secrets from each other after all." She winced, her hand going to her son's car seat. "Not until this year."

The limo jostled along a pothole on the country road. Their legs brushed and his arm shot out to rest along the back of her seat. She jolted for an instant, her breath hitching. He stared back, keeping his arm in place until her shoulders relaxed.

"Oh, Elliot." She sagged back. "We're a mess, you and I, with screwed-up pasts and not much to go on as an example for building a future."

The worry coating her words stabbed at him. He cupped her arm lightly, the feel of her so damn right tucked to him. "We need to figure out how to straighten ourselves out to be good parents. For Eli."

"It won't be all that difficult to outdo our parents."

"Eli deserves a lot better than just a step above our

folks." The feel of her hair along his wrist soothed old wounds, the way she'd always done for him. But more than that, the feel of her now, with the new memories, with that night between them...

His pulse pounded in his ears, his body stirring.... He wanted her. And right now, he didn't see a reason why they couldn't have everything. They shared a similar past and they shared a child.

He just had to convince Lucy Ann. "I agree with you there. That's why it's important for us to use this time together wisely. Figure out how to be the parents he deserves. Figure out how to be a team, the partners he needs."

"I'm here, in the car with you, committed to spending the next four weeks with you." She tipped her face up to his, the jasmine scent of her swirling all around him. "What more do you want from me?"

"I want us to be friends again, Lucy Ann," he answered honestly, his voice raw. "Friends. Not just parents passing a kid back and forth to each other. I want things the way they were before between us."

Her pupils widened with emotion. "Exactly the way we were before? Is that even possible?"

"Not exactly as before," he conceded, easy enough to do when he knew his plans for something better between them.

He angled closer, stroking her ponytail over her shoulder in a sweep he wanted to take farther down her back to her waist. He burned all the way to his gut, needing to pull her closer.

"We'll be friends and more. We can go back to that night together, pick up from there. Because heaven help me, if we're being totally honest, then yes. I want you back in my bed again."

Four

The caress of Elliot's hand along her hair sent tingles all the way to her toes. She wanted to believe the deep desire was simply a result of nearly a year without sex, but she knew her body longed for this particular man. For the pleasure of his caress over her bare skin.

Except then she wouldn't be able to think straight. Now more than ever, she needed to keep a level head for her child. She loved her son more than life, and she had some serious fences to mend with Elliot to secure a peaceful future for Eli.

Lucy Ann clasped Elliot's wrist and moved it aside. "You can't be serious."

"I'm completely serious." His fingers twisted in her ponytail.

"Let. Go. Now," she said succinctly, barely able to keep herself from grabbing his shirt and hauling him in for a kiss. "Sex will only complicate matters."

"Or it could simplify things." He released her hair slowly, his stroke tantalizing all the way down her arm.

Biting her lip, she squeezed her eyes shut, too enticed by the green glow of desire in his eyes.

"Lucy Ann?" His bourbon-smooth tones intoxicated the parched senses that had missed him every day of the past eleven months. "What are you thinking?"

Her head angled ever so slightly toward his touch. "My aunt said the same thing about the bonus of friends becoming…more."

He laughed softly, the heat of his breath warming her throat and broadcasting just how close he'd moved to her, so close he could kiss the exposed flesh. "Your aunt has always been a smart woman. Although I sure as hell didn't talk to her about you and I becoming lovers."

She opened her eyes slowly, steeling herself. "You need to quit saying things like that or I'm going to have the car stopped right now. I will walk home with my baby if I have to. You and I need boundaries for this to work."

His gaze fell to her mouth for an instant that felt stretched to eternity before he angled back, leather seat creaking. "We'll have to agree to disagree."

Her exhale was shakier than she would have liked, betraying her. "You can cut the innocent act. I've seen your playboy moves over the years. Your practiced charm isn't going to work with me." Not again, anyway. "And it wouldn't have worked before if I hadn't been so taken away by sentimentality and a particularly strong vintage liqueur."

Furrows dug deep trenches in his forehead. "Lucy Ann, I am deeply sorry if I took advantage of our friendship—"

"I told you that night. No apologies." His apologies had been mortifying then, especially when she'd been hoping for a repeat only to learn he was full of regrets. He'd stung her pride and her heart. Not that she ever intended to let him know as much. "There were two of us in bed that night, and I refuse to call it a mistake. But it won't happen again, remember? We decided that then."

Or rather *he* had decided and *she* had pretended to go along to save face over her weakness when it came to this man.

His eyes went smoky. "I remember a lot of other things about that night."

Already she could feel herself weakening, wanting to read more into his every word and slightest action. She had to stop this intimacy, this romanticism, now.

"Enough talking about the past. This is about our future. Eli's future." She put on her best logical, personal-assistant voice she'd used a million times to place distance between them. "Where are we going first? I have to confess I haven't kept track of the race dates this year."

"Races later," he said simply as the car reached the airport. "First, we have a wedding to attend."

Her gut tightened at his surprise announcement. "A wedding?"

Lucy Ann hated weddings. Even when the wedding was for a longtime friend. Elliot's high school alumni pal—Dr. Rowan Boothe—was marrying none other than an African princess, who also happened to be a Ph.D. research scientist.

She hated to feel ungrateful, though, since this was the international event of the year, with a lavish ceremony in East Africa, steeped in colorful garb and local delicacies. Invitations were coveted, and media cameras hovered at a respectable distance, monitored by an elite security team that made the packed day run smoothly well into the evening. Tuxedos, formal gowns and traditional tribal wraps provided a magnificent blend of beauty that reflected the couple's modern tastes while acknowledging time-honored customs.

Sitting at the moonlit reception on the palace lawns by the beach, her baby asleep in a stroller, Lucy Ann sipped her glass of spiced fruit juice. She kept a smile plastered on her face as if her showing up here with Elliot and their son was nothing out of the ordinary. Regional music with drums and flutes carried on the air along with laughter and celebration. She refused to let her bad mood ruin the day for the happy bride and groom. Apparently, Elliot had been "kidnapped" from Rowan's bachelor party.

Now he'd returned for the wedding—with her and the baby. No one had asked, but their eyes all made it clear they knew. The fact that he'd thrust their messed-up relationship right into the spotlight frustrated her. But he'd insisted it was better to do it sooner rather than later. Why delay the inevitable?

He'd even arranged for formal dresses for her to pick from. She'd had no choice but to oblige him since her only formals were basic black, far too somber for a wedding. She'd gravitated toward simple wear in the past, never wanting to stand out. Although in this colorful event, her pale lavender gown wasn't too glaring. Still, she felt a little conspicuous because it was strapless and floor-length with a beaded bodice. Breast-feeding had given her new cleavage.

A fact that hadn't gone unnoticed, given the heated looks Elliot kept sliding her way.

But her mood was too sour to dwell on those steamy glances. Especially when he looked so mouth-wateringly handsome in a tuxedo, freshly shaven and smiling. It was as if the past eleven months apart didn't exist, as if they'd just shared the same bed, the same glass of wine. They'd been close friends for so long, peeling him from her thoughts was easier said than done.

She just wanted the marriage festivities to be over, then hopefully she would feel less vulnerable, more in control.

Weddings were happy occasions for some, evoking dreams or bringing back happy memories. Not for her. When she saw the white lace, flowers and a towering cake, she could only remember each time her mama said "I do." All four times. Each man was worse than the one before, until child services stepped in and said drug addict stepdaddy number four had to go if Lucy Ann's mother wanted to keep her child.

Mama chose hubby.

Lucy Ann finally went to live with her aunt for good— no more dodging groping hands or awkward requests to sit on "daddy's" lap. Her aunt loved her, cared for her, but Carla had others to care for, as well—Grandma and an older bachelor uncle.

No one put Lucy Ann first or loved her most. Not until this baby. She would do anything for Eli. Anything. Even swallow her pride and let Elliot back in her life.

Still, keeping on a happy face throughout the wedding was hard. All wedding phobia aside, she worked to appreciate the wedding as an event. She had to learn the art of detaching her emotions from her brain if she expected to make it through the next four weeks with her heart intact.

"Lucy Ann?" A familiar female voice startled her, and she set her juice aside to find Hillary Donavan standing beside her.

Hillary was married to another of Elliot's school friends, Troy Donavan, more commonly known as the

Robin Hood Hacker. As a computer-savvy teen he'd wreaked all sorts of havoc. Now he was a billionaire software developer. He'd recently married Hillary, an events planner, who looked as elegant as ever in a green Grecian-style silk dress.

The red-haired beauty dropped into a chair beside the stroller. "Do you mind if I hide out here with you and the baby for a while? My part in orchestrating this nationally televised wedding is done, thank heavens."

"You did a lovely job blending local traditions with a modern flair. No doubt magazine covers will be packed with photos."

"They didn't give me much time to plan since they made their engagement announcement just after Christmas, but I'm pleased with the results. I hope they are, too."

"I'm sure they are, although they can only see each other." Lucy Ann's stomach tightened, remembering her mother's adoring looks for each new man.

"To think they were professional adversaries for so long…now the sparks between them are so tangible I'm thinking I didn't need to order the firework display for a finale."

Lucy Ann pulled a tight smile, doing her best to be polite. "Romance is in the air."

"I hope this isn't going too late for you and the little guy." She flicked her red hair over her shoulder. "You must be exhausted from your flight."

"He's asleep. We'll be fine." If she left, Elliot would feel obligated to leave, as well. And right now she was too emotionally raw to be alone with him. Surely Hillary had to have some idea of how difficult this was for her, since the alum buddies had been party to the kidnapping.

Her eyes slid to the clutch of pals, the five men who'd been sent to a military reform school together.

Their bond was tight. Unbreakable.

They stood together at the beachside under a cabana wearing matching tuxedos, all five of them too damn rich and handsome for their own good. Luckily for the susceptible female population, the other four were now firmly taken, married and completely in love with their brides. The personification of bad boys redeemed, but still edgy.

Exciting.

The Alpha Brotherhood rarely gathered in one place, but when they did, they were a sight to behold. They'd all landed in trouble with the law as teens, but they'd been sent to a military reform school rather than juvie. Computer whiz Troy Donavan had broken into the Department of Defense's computer system to expose corruption. Casino magnate Conrad Hughes had used insider trading tips to manipulate the stock market. He'd only barely redeemed himself by tanking corporations that used child-labor sweatshops in other countries. World famous soft rock/jazz musician Malcolm Douglas had been sent away on drug charges as a teenager, although she'd learned later that he'd been playing the piano in a bar underage and got nabbed in the bust.

The groom—Dr. Rowan Boothe—had a history a bit more troubled. He'd been convicted of driving while drunk. He'd been part of an accident he'd taken the blame for so his overage brother wouldn't go to jail—then his brother had died a year later driving drunk into a tree. Now Rowan used all his money to start clinics in third-world countries.

They all had their burdens to bear, and that guilt motivated them to make amends now. Through their freelance work with Interpol. Through charitable donations beyond anything anyone would believe unless they saw the accounting books.

Now, they'd all settled down and gotten married, starting families of their own. Was that a part of what compelled Elliot to push for more with her? A need to fit in with his Alpha Brothers as they moved on to the next phase of their lives?

Lucy Ann looked back at Hillary. "Did you know what Malcolm and Conrad were up to yesterday?"

"I didn't know exactly, not until Troy told me, and they were already on their way. I can't say I approve of their tactics, but it was too late for me to do anything. You appear to be okay." Hillary leaned on her elbows, angling closer, her eyes concerned. "Is that an act?"

"What do you think?"

She clasped Lucy Ann's hand. "I'm sorry. I should have realized this calm of yours is just a cover. We're kindred spirits, you and I, ever organized, even in how we show ourselves to the world." She squeezed once before letting go. "Do you want to talk? Need a shoulder? I'm here."

"There's nothing anyone can do now. It's up to Elliot and me to figure out how to move forward. If I'd let him know earlier…"

"Friend, you and I both know how difficult it can be to contact them when the colonel calls for one of their missions. They disappear. They're unreachable." She smiled sadly. "It takes something as earth-shattering as, well, a surprise baby to get them to break the code of silence."

"How do you live with that, as a part of a committed relationship?"

She couldn't bring herself to ask what it felt like to be married to a man who kept such a chunk of his life separate. She'd known as a friend and as a personal assistant that Elliot's old headmaster later recruited previous students as freelancers for Interpol. She'd kept thoughts about that segmented away, since it did not pertain to her job or their life on the race circuit.

But now, there was no denying that her life was tied to Elliot's in a much deeper way.

"I love Troy, the man he is. The man he's always been," Hillary said. "We grow, we mature, but our basic natures stay the same. And I love who that man is."

Lucy Ann could almost—almost—grasp the promise in that, except she knew Hillary helped her husband on some of those missions, doing a bit of freelance work of her own.

Lucy Ann stared down into the amber swirl of her juice glass. "Is it so wrong to want an ordinary life? I don't mean to sound ungrateful, but *normal,* boring, well, I've never had that. I crave it for myself and my child, but it feels so unattainable."

"That's a tough one, isn't it? These men are many things, but normal—delightfully boring—doesn't show up anywhere on that list."

Where did that leave her? In search of what she couldn't have? Or a hypocrite for not accepting Elliot the way he had accepted her all her life? She ran from him. As much as she swore that he pushed her away, she knew. She'd run just as fast and hard as he'd pushed.

"Thank you for the advice, Hillary."

Her friend sighed. "I'm not sure how much help I've been. But if you need to talk more, I'm here for you. I won't betray your confidences."

"I appreciate that," Lucy Ann said, and meant it, only just realizing how few female friends she'd ever had. Elliot had been her best friend and she'd allowed that to close her off to other avenues of support.

"Good, very good. We women need to stick together, make a sisterhood pact of our own." She winked before ducking toward the stroller. "Little Eli is adorable, and I'm glad you're here."

Lucy Ann appreciated the gesture, and she wanted to trust. She wanted to believe there could be a sisterhood of support in dealing with these men—even though she wouldn't be married to Elliot. Still, their lives were entwined because of their child.

A part of her still wondered, doubted. The wives of Elliot's friends had reached out initially after she left, but eventually they'd stopped. Could she really be a part of their sisterhood?

"Thank you, Hillary," she said simply, her eyes sliding back to Elliot standing with his friends.

Her hand moved protectively over to the handle of her son's stroller, her throat constricting as she took in the gleaming good looks of her baby's father. Even his laugh seemed to make the stars shimmer brighter.

And how frivolous a thought was that?

She definitely needed to keep her head on straight and her heart locked away. She refused to be anyone's obligation or burden ever again.

Elliot hoped Rowan and Mariama's marriage ceremony would soften Lucy Ann's mood. After all, weren't weddings supposed to make women sentimental? He'd watched her chatting with his friends' wives and tried to gauge her reaction. She knew them all from her time working as his assistant, and seeing this big extended family connected by friendship rather than blood should appeal to her. They'd talked about leaving their pasts behind countless times as kids.

They could fit right in here with their son. A practical decision. A fun life.

So why wasn't she smiling as the bride and groom drove away in a BMW convertible, the bride's veil trailing in the wind?

Shouldering free of the crowd, Elliot made his way toward Lucy Ann, who stood on the periphery, their son in a stroller beside her. Even though he'd arranged for a nanny who'd once worked for a British duke, Lucy Ann said she couldn't let her son stay with a total stranger. She would need to conduct her own interview tomorrow. If the woman met her standards, she could help during Eli's naps so Lucy Ann could keep up with the work obligations she hadn't been able to put on hold. The encounter still made Elliot grin when he thought of her refusing to be intimidated by the very determined Mary Poppins.

He stopped beside Lucy Ann, enjoying the way the moonlight caressed her bare shoulders. Her hair was loose and lifting in the night wind. Every breath he took drew in hints of her, of Carolina jasmine. His body throbbed to life with a reminder of what they could have together, something so damn amazing he'd spent eleven months running from the power of it.

Now, fate had landed him here with her. Running wasn't an option, and he found that for once he didn't mind fate kicking him in the ass.

Elliot rested his hand on the stroller beside hers, watching every nuance of her reaction. "Are you ready to call it a day and return to our suite, or would you like to take a walk?"

She licked her lips nervously. "Um, I think a walk, perhaps."

So she wasn't ready to be alone with him just yet? A promising sign, actually; she wanted him still, even if she wasn't ready to act on that desire. Fine, then. He could use the moon and stars to romance her, the music from a steel drum band serenading them.

"A walk it is, then, Lucy dear," he asserted.

"Where can we go with a baby?"

He glanced around at the party with guests still dancing along the cabana-filled beach. Tables of food were still laden with half shares of delicacies, fruits and meats. A fountain spewing wine echoed the rush of waves along the shore. Mansions dotted the rocky seashore, with a planked path leading to docks.

"This way." He gestured toward the shoreline boardwalk, all but deserted this late at night. "I'll push the stroller."

He stepped behind the baby carriage. Lucy Ann had no choice but to step aside or they would be stuck hip to hip, step for step.

Five minutes later, they'd left the remnants of the reception behind, the stroller wheels rumbling softly along the wooden walkway. To anyone looking from the looming mansions above, lights shining from the windows like eyes, he and Lucy Ann would appear a happy family walking with their son.

Tonight more than ever he was aware of his single status. Yet again, he'd stood to the side as another friend got married. Leaving only him as a bachelor. But he was a father now. There was no more running from fears of becoming his father. He had to be a man worthy of this child. His child with Lucy Ann.

She walked beside him, the sea breeze brushing her gauzy dress along his leg in phantom caresses. "You're quite good at managing that stroller. I'm surprised. It took me longer than I expected to get the knack of not knocking over everything in my path."

He smiled at her, stuffing down a spark of anger along with the urge to remind her that he would have helped in those early days if she'd only let him know. "It's just like maneuvering a race car."

"Of course. That makes sense."

"More sense than me being at ease with a child? I'm determined to get this right, Lucy Ann, don't doubt that for a second." Steely determination fueled his words.

"You used to say you never wanted kids of your own."

Could those words have made her wary of telling him? There had been a time when they shared everything with each other.

He reminded her, "You always insisted that you didn't want children, either."

"I didn't want to risk putting any child in my mother's path." She rubbed her hand along her collarbone, the one she'd cracked as a child. "I'm an adult now and my mother's passed away. But we're talking about *you* and your insistence that you didn't want kids."

"I didn't. Then." If things hadn't changed, he still might have said the same, but one look in Eli's wide brown eyes and his world had altered in an instant. "I don't run away from responsibilities."

"You ran away before—" She stopped short, cursing softly. "Forget I said that."

Halting, he pulled his hands from the stroller, the baby sleeping and the carriage tucked protectively between them and the railing.

Elliot took her by the shoulders. Her soft bare shoulders. So vulnerable. So…*her.* "Say it outright, Lucy Ann. I left *you* behind when I left Columbia behind, when I let myself get sloppy and caught, when I risked jail because anything seemed better than staying with my father. For a selfish instant, I forgot about what that would mean for you. And I've regretted that every day of my life."

The admission was ripped from his throat; deeper still, torn all the way from his gut. Except there was no one but Lucy Ann to hear him on the deserted walkway. Stone houses dotted the bluff, quarters for guests and staff, all structures up on the bluff with a few lights winking in the night. Most people still partied on at the reception.

"I understand that you feel guilty. Like you have to make up for things. But you need to stop thinking that way. I'm responsible for my own life." She cupped his face, her eyes softening. "Besides, if you'd stayed, you wouldn't have this amazing career that also gave me a chance to break free. So I guess it all worked out in the end."

"Yet you ended up returning home when you left me." Hell, he should be honest now while he had the chance. He didn't want to waste an instant or risk the baby waking up and interrupting them. "When I stupidly pushed you away."

Her arm dropped away again. "I returned with a degree and the ability to support myself and my child. That's significant and I appreciate it." Her hands fisted at her sides. "I don't want to be your obligation."

"You want a life of your own, other than being my assistant. I understand that." He kept his voice low, which brought her closer to listen over the crash of waves below the boardwalk. He liked having her close again. "Let's talk it through, like we would have in the old days."

"You're being so—" she scowled "—so reasonable."

"You say that like it's a dirty word. Why is that a bad thing?" Because God help him, he was feeling anything but reasonable. If she wanted passion and emotion, he was more than willing to pour all of that into seducing her. He just had to be sure before he made a move.

A wrong step could set back his cause.

"Don't try to manipulate me with all the logical reasons why I should stay. I want you to be honest about what you're thinking. What you *want* for your future."

"When it comes to the future, I don't know what I want, Lucy Ann, beyond making sure you and Eli are safe, provided for, never afraid. I'm flying by the seat of my pants here, trying my best to figure out how to get through this being-a-father thing." Honesty was ripping a hole in him. He wanted to go back to logic.

Or passion.

Her chest rose and fell faster with emotion, a flush spreading across her skin in the moon's glow. "How would things have been different if I had come to you, back when I found out I was pregnant?"

"I would have proposed right away," he said without hesitation.

"I would have said no," she answered just as quickly.

He stepped closer. "I would have been persistent in trying to wear you down."

"How would you have managed that?"

The wind tore at her dress, whipping the skirt forward to tangle in his legs, all but binding them together with silken bands.

He angled his face closer to hers, his mouth so close he could claim her if he moved even a whisker closer. "I would have tried to romance you with flowers, candy and jewels." He watched the way her pupils widened with awareness as his words heated her cheek. "Then I would have realized you're unconventional and I would have changed tactics."

"Such as?" she whispered, the scent of fruit juice on her breath, dampening her lips. "Be honest."

"Hell, Lucy Ann, if you want honesty, here it is." His hand slid up her bare arm, along her shoulder, under her hair, to cup the back of her neck, and God, it felt good to touch her after so long apart. It felt right. "I just want to kiss you again."

Five

Five

Lucy Ann gripped Elliot's shoulders, her fingers digging in deep by instinct even as her brain shouted "bad idea."

Her body melted into his, the hard planes of his muscular chest absorbing the curves of her, her breasts hypersensitive to the feel of him. And his hands… A sigh floated from her into him. His hands were gentle and warm and sure along her neck and into her hair, massaging her scalp. Her knees went weak, and he slid an arm down to band around her waist, securing her to him.

How could he crumble her defenses with just one touch of his mouth to hers? But she couldn't deny it. A moonlight stroll, a starlight kiss along the shore had her dreaming romantic notions. Made her want more.

Want him.

His tongue stroked along the seam of her mouth, and she opened without hesitation, taking him every bit as much as he took her. Stroking and tasting. There was a certain safety in the moment, out here in the open, since there was no way things could go further. Distant guest houses, the echoes of the reception carrying on the wind and of course the baby with them kept her from being totally swept away.

Her hands glided down his sides to tuck into his back pockets, to cup the taut muscles that she'd admired on more than one occasion. Hell, the whole female population had admired that butt thanks to a modeling gig he'd taken early in his career to help fund his racing. She'd ribbed him about those underwear ads, even knowing he was blindingly hot. She'd deluded herself into believing she was objective, immune to his sensuality, which went beyond mere good looks.

The man had a rugged charisma that oozed machismo.

Heaven help her, she wanted to dive right in and swim around, luxuriating in the sensations. The tingling in her breasts sparked through her, gathering lower with a familiar intensity she recognized too well after their night together.

This had to stop. Now. Because mistakes she'd made this time wouldn't just hurt her—or Elliot. They had a child to consider. A precious innocent life only a hand's reach away.

With more than a little regret, she ended the kiss, nipping his sensuous bottom lip one last time. His growl of frustration rumbled his chest against hers, but he didn't stop her. Her head fell to rest on his shoulder as she inhaled the scent of sea air tinged with the musk of his sweat. As Elliot cupped the back of her head in a broad palm, his ragged breaths reassured her he was every bit as affected by the kiss. An exciting and yet dangerous reality that confused her after the way they'd parted a year ago.

She needed space to think through this. Maybe watching the wedding and seeing all those happy couples had affected her more than she realized. Even just standing here in his arms with the feel of his arousal pressing against her stomach, she was in serious danger of making a bad choice if she stayed with him a moment longer.

Flattening her palms to his chest, Lucy Ann pushed, praying her legs would hold when he backed away.

She swayed for an instant before steeling her spine. "Elliot, this—" she gestured between them, then touched her kissed tender lips softly "—this wasn't part of our bargain when we left South Carolina. Or was it?"

The night breeze felt cooler now, the sea air chilly.

His eyes stayed inscrutable as he stuffed his hands in his tuxedo pockets, the harsh planes of his face shadowed by moonlight. "Are you accusing me of plotting a seduction?"

"*Plotting* is a harsh word," she conceded, her eyes flitting to the baby in his stroller as she scrambled to regain control of her thoughts, "but I think you're not above planning to do whatever it takes to get your way. That's who you are. Can you deny it?"

His eyes glinted with determination—and anger? "I won't deny wanting to sleep with you. The way you kissed me back gives me the impression you're on board with that notion."

Her heartbeat quickened with visions of how easy it would be to fall into bed with him. To pick up where they'd left off a year ago. If only she had any sense he wanted her for more than a connection to his son.

"That's the point, Elliot. It doesn't matter what *we* want. This month together is supposed to be about building a future for *Eli*. More of—" she gestured between them, her heart tripping over itself at just the mention of their kiss, their attraction "—playing with fire only risks an unstable future for our son. We need to recapture our friendship. Nothing more."

Her limbs felt weak at even the mention of *more*.

He arched an arrogant eyebrow. "I disagree that they're mutually exclusive."

"If you push me on this, I'll have to leave the tour and return to South Carolina." She'd seen too often how easily he seduced women. He was a charmer, without question, and she refused to be like her mother, swept away into reckless relationships again and again. She had a level head and she needed to keep it. "Elliot, do you hear me? I need to know we're on the same page about these next four weeks."

He studied her through narrowed eyes for the crash of four rolling waves before he shrugged. "I will respect your wishes, and I will keep my hands to myself." He smiled, pulling his hands from his pockets and holding them up. "Unless you change your mind, of course."

"I won't," she said quickly, almost too forcefully for her own peace of mind. That old Shakespeare quote came back to her, taunting her, *Methinks the lady doth protest too much.*

"Whoa, whoa, hold on now." Elliot patted the air. "I'm not trying to make you dig in your stubborn heels, so let's end this conversation and call it a day. We can talk more tomorrow, in the light of day."

"Less ambiance would be wise." Except she knew he looked hunky in any light, any situation.

Regardless of how much she wanted to go back, she realized that wasn't possible. They'd crossed a line the night they went too far celebrating his win and her completing her final exams.

It had never happened before she had a plan for her

own future. The catalyst had been completing her degree, feeling that for the first time since they were kids, she met him on an even footing. She'd allowed her walls to come down. She'd allowed herself to acknowledge what she'd been hiding all her adult life. She was every bit as attracted to Elliot Starc as his fawning groupies.

What if she was no different from her mother?

The thought alone had her staggering for steady ground. She grabbed the stroller just to be on the safe side. "I'm going back to the room now. It's time to settle Eli for the night. I need to catch up on some work before I go to sleep. And I do mean sleep."

"Understood," he said simply from beside her. "I'll walk back with you."

The heat of him reached her even though their bodies didn't touch. Just occupying the same space as him offered a hefty temptation right now.

She shook her head, the glide of her hair along her bared shoulders teasing her oversensitized skin. "I'd rather go alone. The palace is in sight and the area's safe."

"As you wish." He stepped back with a nod and a half bow. "We'll talk tomorrow on the way to Spain." He said it as a promise, not a request.

"Okay then," she conceded softly over her shoulder as she pushed the stroller, wheeling it toward the palace where they were staying in one of the many guest suites. Her body still hummed from the kiss, but her mind filled with questions and reservations.

She and Elliot had been platonic friends for years, comfortable with each other. As kids, they'd gone skinny-dipping, built forts in the woods, comforted each other during countless crises and disappointments. He'd been her best friend...right up to the moment he wasn't. Where had this crazy attraction between them come from?

The wheels of the stroller whirred along the walkway as fast as the memories spinning through her. That night eleven months ago when they'd been together had been spontaneous but amazing. She'd wondered if maybe there could be more between them. The whole friends-with-benefits had sounded appealing, taking it a day at a time until they sorted out the bombshell that had been dropped into their relationship: a sexual chemistry that still boggled her mind.

And yet Elliot's reaction the next day had made her realize there could be no future for them. Her euphoria had evaporated with the morning light.

She'd woken before him and gone to the kitchen to make coffee and pile some pastries on a plate. The front door to his suite had opened and she'd assumed it must be the maid. Anyone who entered the room had to have a key and a security code.

However, the woman who'd walked in hadn't been wearing a uniform. She—Gianna—had worn a trench coat and nothing else. If only it had been a crazed fan. But Lucy Ann had quickly deduced Gianna was the new female in Elliot's life. He hadn't even denied it. There was no misunderstanding.

God, it had been so damn cliché her stomach had roiled. Elliot came out of the bedroom and Gianna had turned paler than the towel around Elliot's waist.

He'd kept his calm. Apologized to Gianna for the awkward situation, but she'd burst into tears and run. He'd told Lucy Ann there was nothing between him and his girlfriend anymore, not after what happened the night before with Lucy Ann.

But she'd told him he should have let Gianna know that first, and she was a hundred percent right. He'd agreed and apologized.

That hadn't been enough for her. The fact that he could be seeing one woman, even superficially, and go to bed with another? No, no and hell, no. That was something she couldn't forgive. Not after how all those men had cheated on her mom with little regard for vows or promises. And her mother kept forgiving the first unfaithful jerk, and then the next.

If Elliot could behave this way now, how could she trust him later? What if he got "swept away" by someone else and figured he would clue her in later? She'd called him dishonorable.

And in an instant, with that one word, a lifetime friendship crumbled.

She'd thrown on her clothes and left. Elliot's engagement to Gianna a month later had only sealed Lucy Ann's resolve to stay away. They hadn't spoken again until the day he'd shown up in Carla's yard.

Now, after more impulsive kisses, she found herself wanting to crawl right back into bed with him. Lucy Ann powered the stroller closer to the party and their quarters, drawing in one deep breath of salty air after another, willing her pulse to steady. Wishing the urge to be with Elliot was as easily controlled.

With each step, she continued the chant in her brain, the vow not to repeat her mother's mistakes.

Wind tearing at his tuxedo jacket, Elliot watched Lucy Ann push the stroller down the planked walkway, then past the party. He didn't take his eyes off her or his son until he saw they'd safely reached the palace, even though he now had bodyguards watching his family 24/7. His family?

Hell, yes, his family.

Eli was his son. And Lucy Ann had been his only real

family for most of his life. No matter how angry he got at her for holding back on telling him about Eli, Elliot also couldn't forgive himself for staying away from her. He'd let her down in a major way more than once, from his teenage years up to now. She had reason not to trust him.

He needed to earn back her trust. He owed her that and so much more.

His shoulders heaving with a sigh, he started toward the wedding reception. The bride and groom had left, but the partying would go long into the night. It wasn't every day a princess got married. People would expect a celebration to end all celebrations.

A sole person peeled away from the festivities and ambled toward him. From the signature streamlined fedora, he recognized his old school pal Troy Donavan. Troy was one of the originals from their high school band, the Alpha Brotherhood, a group of misfits who found kindred spirits in one another and their need to push boundaries, to expose hypocrisy—the greatest of crimes in their eyes.

Troy pulled up alongside him, passing him a drink. "Reconciliation not going too well?"

"What makes you say that?" He took the thick cut glass filled with a locally brewed beer.

"She's returning to her room alone after a wedding." Troy tipped his glass as if in a toast toward the guests. "More people get lucky after weddings than any other event known to mankind. That's why you brought Lucy Ann here, isn't it? To get her in the romantic mood."

Had he? He'd told himself he wanted her to see his friends settling down. For her to understand he could do the same. But he wasn't sure how much he felt like sharing, especially when his thoughts were still jumbled.

"I brought Lucy Ann to the wedding because I couldn't

miss the event. The timing has more to do with how you all colluded to pull off that kidnapping stunt."

"You're still pissed off? Sorry, dude, truly," he said, wincing. "I thought you and Malcolm talked that all out."

"Blah, blah, blah, my good pals wanted to get an unguarded reaction. I heard." And it still didn't sit well. He'd trusted these guys since high school, over fifteen years, and hell, yeah, he felt like they'd let him down. "But I also heard that Lucy Ann contacted the Brotherhood over a week ago. That's a week I lost with my son. A week she was alone caring for him. Would you be okay with that?"

"Fair enough. You have reason to be angry with us." Troy nudged his fedora back on his head. "But don't forget to take some of the blame yourself. She was your friend all your life, and you just let her go. You're going to have a tough as hell time convincing her you've magically changed your mind now and you would have wanted her back even without the kid."

The truth pinched. "Tell me something I don't know."

"Okay then. Here's a bit of advice."

"Everyone seems full of it," Elliot responded, tongue in cheek.

Troy laughed softly, leaning back against a wrought-iron railing. "Fine. I'm full of it. Always have been. Now, on to my two cents."

"By all means." Elliot knocked back another swallow of the local beer.

"You're a father now." Troy rolled his glass between his palms. "Be that boy's father and let everything else fall into place."

A sigh rattled through Elliot. "You make it sound so simple."

Troy's smile faded, no joking in sight. "Think how different our lives would have been with different parents.

Things came together when Salvatore gave us direction. Be there for your son."

"Relationships aren't saved by having a child together." His parents had gotten married because he was on the way. His mother had eventually walked out and left him behind.

"True enough. But they sure as hell are broken up by fighting over the child. Be smart in how you work together when it comes to Eli and it might go a long way toward smoothing things out with Lucy Ann." Troy ran a finger along the collar of his tuxedo shirt, edging a little more air for himself around his tie. "If not, you've got a solid relationship with your kid, and that's the most important thing."

Was his focus all wrong by trying to make things right with Lucy Ann? Elliot had to admit Troy's plan made some sense. The stakes were too important to risk screwing up with his son. "When did you get to be such a relationship sage?"

"Hillary's a smart woman, and I'm smart enough to listen to her." His sober expression held only for a second longer before he returned to the more lighthearted Troy they were all accustomed to. "Now more than ever I need to listen to Hillary's needs since she's pregnant."

"Congratulations to you both." Elliot clapped Troy on the back, glad for his friend even as he wondered what it might have been like to be by Lucy Ann's side while she was expecting Eli. "Who'd have predicted all this home and hearth for us a few years ago?"

"Colonel Salvatore's going to have to find some new recruits."

"You're not pulling Interpol missions?" That surprised him. Elliot understood Hillary's stepping out of fieldwork while pregnant. But he wouldn't have thought Troy would ever back off the edge.

"There are other ways I can help with my tech work. Who knows, maybe I'll even take on the mentorship role like Salvatore someday. But I'm off the clock now and missing my wife." Troy walked backward, waving once before he sprinted toward the party.

Elliot knew his friend was right. The advice made sense. Focus on the baby. But that didn't stop him from wanting Lucy Ann in his bed again. The notion of just letting everything fall into place was completely alien to his nature. He'd never been the laid-back sort like Troy. Elliot needed to move, act, win.

He needed Lucy Ann back in his life.

For months he'd told himself the power of Lucy Ann's kiss, of the sex they'd shared nearly a year ago, had been a hazy memory distorted by alcohol. But now, with his body still throbbing from the kiss they'd just shared, his hair still mussed, the memory of their hands running frenetically—hungrily—over each other, he knew. Booze had nothing to do with the explosive chemistry between them. Although Gianna's arrival had sure as hell provided a splash of ice water on the morning-after moment.

He'd screwed up by not breaking things off with Gianna before he let anything happen between him and Lucy Ann. He still wasn't sure why he and Gianna had reconciled afterward. He hadn't been fair to either woman. The dishonor in that weighed on him every damn day.

At least he'd finally done right by Gianna when they'd broken up. Now, he had to make things right with Lucy Ann.

Their kiss ten minutes ago couldn't lead to anything more, not tonight. He accepted that. It was still too early in his campaign to win her over. But a kiss? He could have that much for now at least. A taste of her, a hint of what more they could have together.

A hint of Lucy Ann was so much more than everything with any other woman.

She was so much a part of his life. Why the hell had he let her go?

This didn't have to be complicated. Friendship. Sex. Travel the world and live an exciting life together. He had a fortune at his disposal. They could stay anywhere, hire teachers to travel with them. Eli would have the best of everything and an education gleaned from seeing the world rather than just reading about it. Surely Lucy Ann would see that positively.

How could she say no to a future so much more secure than what they'd grown up with? He'd been an idiot not to press his case with her last time. But when she'd left before, he'd thought to give her space. This time, he would be more persistent.

Besides, last time he'd been a jerk and tried to goad her into returning by making the news with moving on—a total jackass decision he never would have made if he'd thought for a second that Lucy Ann might be pregnant.

Now, he would be wiser. Smoother.

He would win her over. They'd been partners before. They could be partners again.

Lucy Ann peered out the window of the private jet as they left Africa behind.

Time for their real journey to begin. It had been challenging enough being together with his friends, celebrating the kind of happily ever after that wasn't in the cards for her. But now came the bigger challenge—finding a way to parent while Elliot competed in the Formula One circuit. A different country every week—Spain, Monaco, Canada, England. Parties and revelry and yes, decadence, too. She felt guilty for enjoying it all, but she couldn't deny that she'd missed the travel, experiencing different cultures without a concern for cost. Plus, his close-knit group of friends gave them a band of companionship no matter what corner of the earth he traveled to during racing season.

She sank deeper into the luxury of the leather sofa, the sleek chrome-and-white interior familiar from their countless trips in the past, with one tremendous exception. Their son was secured into his car seat beside her, sleeping in his new race car pj's with a lamb's wool blanket draped over his legs. She touched his impossibly soft cheek, stroking his chubby features with a soothing hand, cupping his head, the dusting of blond hair so like his father's.

Her eyes skated to Elliot standing in the open bulkhead, talking to the pilot. Her former best friend and boss grew hotter with each year that passed—not fair. That didn't stop her from taking in the sight of him in low-slung jeans and a black button-down shirt with the sleeves rolled up. Italian leather loafers. He looked every bit the world-famous race car driver and heartthrob.

How long would Elliot's resolution to build a family life for Eli last? Maybe that's what this trip was about. Proving to *him* it couldn't be done. She wouldn't keep his son from him, but she refused to expose her child to a chaotic life. Eli needed and deserved stability.

And what did she want?

She pressed a hand to her stomach, her belly full of butterflies that had nothing to do with a jolt of turbulence. Just the thought of kissing Elliot last night... She dug her fingers into the supple leather sofa to keep from reaching for him as he walked toward her.

"Would you like something to eat or drink?" he asked, pausing by the kitchenette. "Or something to read?"

She knew from prior trips that he kept a well-stocked library of the classics as well as the latest bestsellers loaded on ereaders for himself and fellow travelers. In school, he'd always won the class contest for most books read in a year. He told her once those stories offered him an escape from his day-to-day life.

"No, thank you. The brunch before we left was amazing."

True enough, although she hadn't actually eaten much. She'd been so caught up in replaying the night before. In watching his friends' happy marriages with their children and babies on the way until her heart ached from all she wanted for her son.

For herself, as well.

Elliot slid onto the sofa beside her, leaning over her to adjust the blanket covering Eli's legs. "Tell me about his routine."

She sat upright, not expecting that question at all. "You want to know about Eli's schedule? Why?"

"He's my son." His throat moved with a long swallow of emotion at the simple sentence. "I should know what he needs."

"He has a mom, and he even has a nanny now." The British nanny was currently in the sleeping quarters reading or napping or whatever nannies did when they realized mothers needed a breather from having them around all the time.

Elliot tapped Lucy Ann's chin until she looked at him again. "And he has a dad."

"Of course," she agreed, knowing it was best for Eli,

but unused to sharing him. "If you're asking for diaper duty, you're more than welcome to it."

Would he realize her halfhearted attempt at a joke was meant to ease this tenacious tension between them? They used to be so in tune with each other.

"Diaper duty? Um, I was thinking about feeding and naps, that kind of thing."

"He breastfeeds," she said bluntly.

His eyes fell to her chest. The stroke of his gaze made her body hum as tangibly as the airplane engines.

Elliot finally cleared his throat and said, "Well, that could be problematic for me. But I can bring him to you. I can burp him afterward. He still needs to be burped, right?"

"Unless you want to be covered in baby spit-up." She crossed her arms over her chest.

He pulled his eyes up to her face. "Does he bottle-feed, too? If so, I can help out that way."

Fine, he wanted to play this game, then she would meet him point for point. "You genuinely think you can wake up during the night and then race the next day?"

"If you can function on minimal sleep, then so can I. You need to accept that we're in this together now."

He sounded serious. But then other than his playboy ways, he was a good man. A good friend. A philanthropist who chose to stay anonymous with his donations. She knew about them only through her work as his assistant.

"That's why I agreed to come with you, for Eli and in honor of our friendship in the past."

"Good, good. I'm glad you haven't forgotten those years. That friendship is something we can build on. But I'm not going to deny the attraction, Lucy Ann." He slid his arm along the back of the sofa seat, stretching his legs out in front of him. "I can't. You've always been pretty, but you looked incredible last night. Motherhood suits you."

"Flattery?" She picked up his arm and moved it to his lap. "Like flowers and candy? An obvious arm along the back? Surely you've got better moves than that."

"Are you saying compliments are wasted on you?" He picked up a lock of her hair, teasing it between two fingers. "What if I'm telling the truth about how beautiful you are and how much I want to touch you?"

She rolled her eyes, even though she could swear electricity crackled up the strand of hair he held. "I've watched your moves on women for years, remember?"

"It's not a move." He released the lock and smoothed it into the rest before crossing his arms. "If I were planning a calculated seduction for you, I would have catered a dinner, with a violin."

She crinkled her nose. "A violin? Really?"

"No privacy. Right." His emerald eyes studied her, the wheels in his brain clearly churning. "Maybe I would kiss you on the cheek, distract you by nuzzling your ear while tucking concert tickets into your pocket."

"Concert tickets?" She lifted an eyebrow with interest. They'd gone to free concerts in the park when they were teenagers.

"We would fly out to a show in another country, France or Japan perhaps."

She shook her head. "You're going way overboard. Too obvious. Rein it in, be personal."

"Flowers…" He snapped his fingers. "No wait. A single flower, something different, like a sprig of jasmine because the scent reminds me of you."

That silenced her for a moment. "You know my perfume?"

He dipped his head toward her ever so slightly as if

catching a whiff of her fragrance even now. "I know you smell like home in all the good ways. And I have some very good memories of home. They all include you."

Damn him, he was getting to her. His words affected her but she refused to let him see that. She schooled her features, smiling slightly. "Your moves have improved."

"I'm only speaking the truth." His words rang with honesty, his eyes heated with attraction.

"I do appreciate that about you, how we used to be able to tell each other anything." Their friendship had given her more than support. He'd given her hope that they could leave their pasts behind in a cloud of dust. "If we can agree to be honest now, that will work best."

"And no more secrets."

She could swear a whisper of hurt smoked through his eyes.

Guilt stabbed through her all over again. She owed him and there was no escaping that. "I truly am sorry I held back about Eli. That was wrong of me. Can you forgive me?"

"I have to, don't I?"

"No." She swallowed hard. "You don't."

"If I want us to be at peace—" he reached out and took her hand, the calluses on his fingertips a sweet abrasion along her skin "—then yes, I do."

She wasn't sure how that honest answer settled within her because it implied he wasn't really okay with what she'd done. He was only moving past it out of necessity. The way he'd shrugged off all the wrongs his father had done because he had no choice.

Guilt hammered her harder with every heartbeat, and she didn't have a clue how to make this right with him. She had as little practice with forgiveness and restitution as he did.

So she simply said, "Peace is a very good thing."

"Peace doesn't have to be bland." His thumb stroked the inside of her wrist.

Her pulse kicked up under his gentle stroking. "I didn't say that."

"Your tone totally implied it. You all but said 'boring.'" His shoulder brushed hers as he settled in closer, seducing her with his words, his husky tones every bit as much as his touch. "A truce can give freedom for all sorts of things we never considered before."

"News flash, Elliot. The kissing part. We've considered that before."

"Nice." He clasped her wrist. "You're injecting some of your spunky nature into the peace. That's good. Exciting. As brilliantly shiny as your hair with those new streaks of honey added by the Carolina sun."

Ah, now she knew why he'd been playing with her hair. "Added by my hairdresser."

"Liar."

"How do you know?"

"Because I'm willing to bet you've been squirrelling away every penny you make. I can read you—most of the time." He skimmed his hand up her arm to stroke her hair back over her shoulder. "While I know that you want me, I can't gauge what you intend to do about that, because make no mistake, I want us to pursue that. I said before that motherhood agrees with you and I meant it. You drove me crazy last night in that evening gown."

He continued to stroke her arm, but she couldn't help but think if she moved even a little, his hand would brush her breast. Even the phantom notion of that touch had her tingling with need.

She worked to keep her voice dry—and to keep from grabbing him by the shirtfront and hauling him toward her. "You're taking charming to a new level. I'm impressed."

"Good. But are you seduced?"

"You're good, and I'm enticed," she said, figuring she might as well be honest. No use denying the obvious. "But Elliot, this isn't a fairy tale. Our future is not going to be some fairy tale."

He smiled slowly, his green eyes lighting with a promise as his hand slid away. "It can be."

Without another word, he leaned back and closed his eyes. Going to sleep? Her whole body was on fire from his touch, his words—his seduction. And he'd simply gone to sleep. She wanted to shout in frustration.

Worse yet, she wanted him to recline her back on the sofa and make love to her as thoroughly as he'd done eleven months ago.

Six

By nightfall in Spain, Elliot wondered how Lucy Ann would react to their lodgings for the night. The limousine wound deeper into the historic district, farther from the racetrack than they normally stayed. But he had new ideas for these next few weeks, based on what Lucy Ann had said on the plane.

After the fairy-tale discussion, inspiration had struck. He'd forced himself to make a tactical retreat so he could regroup. Best not to risk pushing her further and having her shut him down altogether before he could put his plan into action to persuade her to stay longer than the month.

Once she was tucked into the back room on the airplane to nurse Eli, Elliot had made a few calls and set the wheels in motion to change their accommodations along the way. A large bank account and a hefty dose of fame worked wonders for making things happen fast. He just hoped his new agenda would impress Lucy Ann. Winning her over was becoming more pressing by the second. Not just for Eli but because Elliot's life had been damn empty without her. He hadn't realized just how much until he had her back. The way her presence made everything around him more vibrant. Hell, even her organized nature, which he used to tease her about. She brought a focus, a grounding and a beauty to his world that he didn't want to lose again.

Failure was not an option.

He'd made himself a checklist, just like he kept for his work. People thought he was impulsive, reckless even, but there was a science to his job. Mathematics. Calculations. He studied all the details and contingencies until they became so deeply ingrained they were instinct.

Still, he refused to become complacent. He reviewed that checklist before every race as if he were a rookie driver. Now he needed to apply the same principles to winning back Lucy Ann's friendship...and more.

Their new "hotel" took shape on the top of the hill, the Spanish sunset adding the perfect dusky aura to their new accommodations.

In the seat across from him, Lucy Ann sat up straighter, looking from the window to him with confusion stamped on her lovely face.

"This isn't where you usually stay. This is...a castle."

"Exactly."

The restored medieval castle provided safety and space, privacy and romance. He could give her the fairy tale while making sure Lucy Ann and their son were protected. He could—and would—provide all the things a real partner and father provided. He would be everything his father wasn't.

"Change of plans for our stay."

"Because...?"

"We need more space and less chance of interruptions." He couldn't wait to have her all to himself. Damn, he'd missed her.

"But pandering to the paparazzi plays an important role in your PR." She hugged the diaper bag closer to her chest; the baby's bag, her camera and her computer had been the only things she'd insisted on bringing with her from home.

"Pandering?" He forced himself to focus on her words rather than the sound of her voice. Her lyrical Southern drawl was like honey along his starved senses. "That's not a word I'm particularly comfortable with. Playing along with them, perhaps. Regardless, they don't own me, and I absolutely will not allow them to have access to you and our son on anything other than our own terms."

"Wow, okay." Her eyes went wide before she grinned wryly. "But did you have to rent a castle?"

He wondered if he'd screwed up by going overboard, but her smile reassured him he'd struck gold by surprising her.

"It's a castle converted to a hotel, although yes, it's more secure and roomier." Safer, but also with romantic overtones he hoped would score points. "I thought in each place we stay, we could explore a different option for traveling with a child."

"This is…an interesting option," she conceded as the limousine cruised along the sweeping driveway leading up to the towering stone castle. Ivy scrolled up toward the turrets, the walls beneath baked brown with time. Only a few more minutes and the chauffeur would open the door.

Elliot chose his words wisely to set the stage before they went inside. "Remember how when we were kids, we hid in the woods and tossed blankets over branches? I called them forts, but you called them castles. I was cool with that as long as I got to be a knight rather than some pansy prince."

They'd climbed into those castle forts where he'd read for hours while she colored or drew pictures.

"Pansy prince?" She chuckled, tapping his chest. "You *are* anti-fairy-tale. What happened to the kid who used to lose himself in storybooks?"

He captured her finger and held on for a second before linking hands. "There are knights in fairy tales. And there are definitely castles."

"Is that what this is about?" She left her hand in his. "Showing me a fairy tale?"

"Think about coming here in the future with Eli." He stared at his son's sleeping face and images filled his head of their child walking, playing, a toddler with his hair and Lucy Ann's freckles. "Our son can pretend to be a knight or a prince, whatever he chooses, in a real castle. How freaking cool is that?"

"Very cool." A smile teased her kissable pink lips. "But this place is a long way from our tattered quilt forts in the woods."

His own smile faded. "Different from our childhood is a very good thing."

Her whole body swayed toward him, and she cupped his face. "Elliot, it's good that our child won't suffer the way we did, but what your father did to you...that had nothing to do with money."

Lucy Ann's sympathy, the pain for him that shone in her eyes, rocked the ground under him. He needed to regain control. He'd left that part of his life behind and he had no desire to revisit it even in his thoughts. So he deflected as he always did, keeping things light.

"I like it when you get prissy." He winked. "That's really sexy."

"Elliot, this isn't the time to joke around. We have some very serious decisions to make this month."

"I'm completely serious. Cross my heart." He pressed their clasped hands against his chest. "It makes me want to ruffle your feathers."

"Stop. It." She tugged free. "We're talking about Eli. Not us."

"That's why we're at a castle, for Eli," he insisted as the limousine stopped in front of the sprawling fortress. "Einstein said, 'The true sign of intelligence is not knowledge but imagination.' That's what we can offer our son with this unique lifestyle. The opportunity to explore his imagination around the world, to see those things that we only read about. You don't have to answer. Just think on it while we're here."

With the baby nursing, Lucy Ann curled up in her massive bed. She took comfort in the routine of feeding her child, the sweet softness of his precious cheek against her breast. With her life turning upside down so fast, she needed something familiar to hold on to.

The medieval decor wrapped her in a timeless fantasy she wasn't quite sure how to deal with. The castle had tapestries on the wall and sconces with bulbs that flickered like flames. Her four-poster bed had heavy drapes around it, the wooden pillars as thick as any warrior's chest. An arm's reach away waited a bassinet, a shiny reproduction of an antique wooden cradle for Eli.

Her eyes gravitated toward the tapestry across the room telling a love story about a knight romancing a maiden by a river. Elliot had chosen well. She couldn't help but be charmed by this place. Even her supper was served authentically in a trencher, with water in a goblet.

A plush, woven rug on the stone floor, along with

the low snap of the fire in the hearth, kept out the chilly spring night. The sound system piped madrigal music as if the group played in a courtyard below.

Through the slightly opened door, she saw the sitting room where Elliot was parked at a desk, his computer in front of him. Reviewing stats on his competitors? Or a million other details related to the racing season? She missed being a part of all that, but he had a new assistant, a guy who did his job so seamlessly he blended into the background.

And speaking of work, she had some of her own to complete. Once Eli finished nursing and went to bed there would be nothing for her to do but complete the two projects she hadn't been able to put on hold.

She'd expected Elliot to try to make a move on her once they got inside, but the suite had three bedrooms off the living area. One for her and one for him. The British nanny he'd hired had settled into the third, turning in after Lucy Ann made it clear Eli would stay with his mother tonight. While Mrs. Clayworth kept a professional face in place, the furrows along her forehead made it clear that she wondered at the lack of work on this job.

This whole setup delivered everything Elliot had promised, a unique luxury she could see her son enjoying someday. Any family would relish these fairy-tale accommodations. It was beyond tempting.

Elliot was beyond tempting.

Lucy Ann tore her eyes from her lifetime friend and onetime lover. This month was going to be a lot more difficult than she'd anticipated.

Desperate for some grounding in reality before she weakened, she reached for her phone, for the present, and called her aunt Carla.

* * *

She'd made it through the night, even if the covers on the bed behind her were a rumpled mess from her restless tossing and turning.

Lucy Ann sat at the desk at the tower window with her laptop, grateful to Carla for the bolstering. Too bad she couldn't come join them on this trip, but Carla was emphatic. She loved her home and her life. She was staying where she belonged.

Who could blame her? A sense of belonging was a rare gift Lucy Ann hadn't quite figured out how to capture yet. In South Carolina, she'd dreamed of getting out, and here she craved the familiarity of home.

Which made her feel like a total ingrate.

She was living the easy life, one any new mother would embrace. How ironic that at home she'd spent every day exhausted, feeling like Eli's naps were always a few minutes too short to accomplish what she needed to do. And now, she spent most of her time waiting for him to wake up.

She closed her laptop, caught up on work, dressed for the day, waiting to leave for Elliot's race. She still couldn't wrap her brain around how different this trip was from ones she'd shared with Elliot in the past. Staring out the window in their tower suite, she watched the sun cresting higher over the manicured grounds.

Last night, she'd actually slept in a castle. The restored structure was the epitome of luxury and history all rolled into one. She'd even pulled out her camera and snapped some photos to use for a client's web design. Her fingers already itched to get to the computer and play with the images, but Elliot was due back soon.

He'd gone to the track for prelim work, his race scheduled for tomorrow. Normally he arrived even earlier before an event, but the wedding had muddled his schedule. God, she hoped his concentration was rock solid. The thought of him in a wreck because she'd damaged his focus sent her stomach roiling. Why hadn't she considered this before? She should have told him about Eli earlier for so many reasons.

She was familiar with everything about his work world. She'd been his personal assistant for over a decade, in charge of every detail of his career, his life. And even in their time apart she'd kept up with him and the racing world online. Formula One racing in Spain alternated locations every year, Barcelona to Valencia and back again. She knew his preferences for routes like Valencia, with the street track bordering the harbor. She was used to being busy, in charge—not sitting around a castle twiddling her thumbs, eating fruit and cheese from medieval pottery.

Being waited on by staff, nannies and chauffeurs, being at loose ends, felt alien, to say the least. But she'd agreed to give him a chance this month. She would stick to her word.

As if conjured from her thoughts, Elliot appeared in the arched doorway between the living area and her bedroom. Jeans hugged his lean hips, his turtleneck shirt hugging a well-defined chest. Her mouth watered as she considered what he would do if she walked across the room, leaned against his chest to kiss him, tucked her hands in his back pockets and savored the chemistry simmering between them.

She swallowed hard. "Are you here for lunch?"

"I'm here for you and Eli." He held out a cashmere sweater of his. "In case you get chilly on our outing."

"Outing?" she asked to avoid taking the sweater until she could figure out what to do next.

She'd worn pieces of Elliot's clothes countless times over the years without a second thought, but the notion of wrapping his sweater around her now felt so intimate that desire pooled between her legs. However, to reject the sweater would make an issue of it, revealing feelings that made her too vulnerable, a passion she still didn't know how to control yet.

Gingerly, she took the sweater from him, the cashmere still warm from his touch. "Where are we going?"

He smiled mysteriously. "It's another surprise for you and Eli."

"Can't I even have a hint?" She hugged the sweater close, finding she was enjoying his game more than she should.

"We're going to play." He scooped his son up from the cradle in sure hands. "Right, Eli, buddy? We're going to take good care of your mama today. If she agrees to come with me, of course."

The sight of their son cradled in Elliot's broad hands brought her heart into her throat. She'd imagined moments like this, dreamed of how she would introduce him to their child. Day after day, her plan had altered as she delayed yet again.

And why? Truly, why? She still wasn't sure she understood why she'd made all the decisions she'd made these past months. She needed to use her time wisely to figure out the best way to navigate their future.

She tugged on the sweater. "Who am I to argue with such a tempting offer? Let's go play."

They left the suite and traveled down the sweeping stone stairway without a word, passing other guests as well as the staff dressed in period garb. The massive front doors even creaked as they swept open to reveal the waiting limousine.

Stepping out into the sunshine, she took in the incredible lawns. The modern-day buzz of cars and airplanes mixed with the historical landscaping that followed details down to the drawbridge over a moat.

The chauffeur opened the limo door for her. Lucy Ann slid inside, then extended her arms for her child. Elliot passed over Eli as easily as if they were a regular family.

Lucy Ann hugged her son close for a second, breathing in the baby-powder-fresh scent of him before securing Eli into his car seat. "Shouldn't you be preparing for race day?"

Getting his head together. Resting. Focusing.

"I know what I need to do," he answered as if reading her mind. He sat across from her, his long legs extended, his eyes holding hers. "That doesn't mean we can't have time together today."

"I don't want to be the cause of your exhaustion or lack of focus because you felt the need to entertain me." She'd been so hurt and angry for a year, she'd lost sight of other feelings. Race day was exciting and terrifying at the same time. "I've been a part of your world for too long to let you be reckless."

"Trust me. I have more reason than ever to be careful. You and Eli are my complete and total focus now."

There was no mistaking the certainty and resolve in his voice. Her fears eased somewhat, which made room for her questions about the day to come back to the fore. "At least tell me something about your plans for today. Starting with, where are we going?"

He leaned to open the minifridge and pulled out two water bottles. "Unless you object, we are going to the San Miguel de los Reyes Monastery."

She sat up straighter, surprised, intrigued. She took

the water bottle from him. "I'm not sure I understand your plan...."

"The monastery has been converted into a library. We've never had a chance to visit before on other trips." He twisted open his spring water. "In fact, as I look back, we both worked nonstop, all the time. As I reevaluate, I'm realizing now a little sightseeing won't set us behind."

"That's certainly a one-eighty from the past. You've always been a very driven man—no pun intended." She smiled at her halfhearted joke, feeling more than a little off balance by this change in Elliot. "I'll just say thank-you. This is a very thoughtful idea. Although I'm curious. What made you decide on this particular outing when there are so many more obvious tourist sites we haven't visited?"

"You sparked the idea when we were on the airplane, actually." He rolled the bottle between his palms. "You mentioned not believing in fairy tales anymore. That is why I chose the castle. Fairy tales are important for any kid...and I think we've both lost sight of that."

"We're adults." With adult wants and needs. Like the need to peel off his forest-green turtleneck and faded jeans.

"Even as kids, we were winging it with those fairy tales. Then we both grew jaded so young." He shrugged muscular shoulders. "So it's time for us to learn more about fairy tales so we can be good parents. Speaking of which, is Eli buckled in?"

"Of course."

"Good." He tapped on the window for the chauffeur to go. "Just in case you were wondering, I'm calling this the *Beauty and the Beast* plan."

They were honest-to-goodness going to a library. She sagged back, stunned and charmed all at once.

God, she thought she'd seen all his moves over the years—moves he'd used on other women. He'd always been more…boisterous. More obvious.

This was different. Subtle. Damn good.

"So I'm to be Belle to your beast."

"A Southern belle, yes, and you've called me a beast in the past. Besides, you know how much I enjoy books and history. I thought you might find some interesting photo opportunities along the way."

"You really are okay with a pedestrian stroll through a library." The Elliot she'd known all her life had always been on the go, scaling the tallest tree, racing down the steepest hill, looking for the edgiest challenge. But he did enjoy unwinding with a good book, too. She forgot about that side of him sometimes.

"I'm not a Cro-Magnon…even though I'm playing the beast. I do read. I even use a napkin at dinnertime." He waggled his eyebrows at her, his old playful nature more evident.

She wished she could have just slugged him on the shoulder as if they were thirteen again. Things had been simpler then on some levels—and yet not easy at all on others.

"You're right. I shouldn't have been surprised."

"Let's stop making assumptions about each other from now on about a lot of things. We've been friends for years, but even friends change, grow, even a man like me can mature when he's ready. Thanks to you and Eli, I'm ready now."

She wanted to believe him, to believe in him. She wanted to shake off a past where the people she cared about always let her down. Hundreds of times over the past eleven months she'd guessed at what his reaction would be if she told him about the baby.

She'd known he would come through for her. The part that kept haunting her, that kept her from trying... She could never figure out how she would know if he'd come through out of duty or something more.

The thought that she could yearn for more between the two of them scared her even now. She was much better off taking this one day at a time.

"Okay, Elliot—" she spread her arms wide "—I'm all-in...for our day at the monastery."

As she settled in for her date, she couldn't help wondering which was tougher: resisting the fairy-tale man who seemed content to ignore the past year or facing the reality of her lifelong friend who had every reason to be truly angry with her.

Regardless, at some point the past would catch up with both of them. They could only play games for so long before they had to deal with their shared parenthood.

Wearing a baseball cap with the brim tugged low, Elliot soaked in the sight of Lucy Ann's appreciation of the frescoes and ancient tomes as she filled a memory card with photos of the monastery turned library. He should have thought to do this for her sooner. The place was relatively deserted, a large facility with plenty of places for tourists to spread out. A school tour had passed earlier, but the echoes of giggles had faded thirty minutes ago. No one recognized him, and the bodyguards hung back unobtrusively. For all intents and purposes, he and Lucy Ann were just a regular family on vacation.

Why had he never thought to bring her to places like this before? He'd convinced himself he was taking care of her by offering her a job and a life following him around the world. But somehow he'd missed out on giving her so much more. He'd let her down when they were teenagers and he'd gotten arrested, leaving her alone to deal with her family. Now to find out he'd been selfish as an adult too. That didn't sit well with him.

So he had more to fix. He and Lucy Ann were bound by their child for life, but he didn't intend to take that part for granted. He would work his tail off to be more for her this time.

He set the brake on the stroller by a looming marble angel. "You're quiet. Anything I can get for you?"

She glanced away from her camera, looking back over her shoulder at him. "Everything's perfect. Thank you. I'm enjoying the peace. And the frescoes as well as the ornately bound books. This was a wonderful idea for how to spend the afternoon."

Yet all day long she'd kept that camera between them, snapping photos. For work? For pleasure?

Or to keep from looking at him?

Tired of the awkward silence, he pushed on, "If you're having fun, then why aren't you smiling?"

She lowered the camera slowly, pivoting to face him. Her eyes were wary. "I'm not sure what you mean."

"Lucy Ann, it's me here. Elliot. Can we pretend it's fifteen years ago and just be honest with each other?"

She nibbled her bottom lip for a moment before blurting out, "I appreciate what you're doing, that you're trying, but I keep waiting for the explosion."

He scratched over his closely shorn hair, which brought memories of sprinting away from a burning car. "I thought we cleared that up in the limo. I'm not going to wreck tomorrow."

"And I'm not talking about that now." She tucked the camera away slowly, pausing as an older couple meandered past looking at a brochure map of the museum. Once they cleared the small chapel area, she turned back to him and said softly, "I'm talking about an explosion of anger. You have to be mad at me for not telling you about Eli sooner. I accept that it was wrong of me not to try harder. I just keep wondering when the argument will happen."

God, was she really expecting him to go ballistic on her? He would never, never be like his father. He used his racing as an outlet for those aggressive feelings. He did what he needed to do to stay in control. Always.

Maybe he wasn't as focused as he claimed to be, because if he'd been thinking straight he would have realized that Lucy Ann would misunderstand. She'd spent her life on shaky ground growing up, her mother hooking up with a different boyfriend or husband every week. Beyond that, she'd always stepped in for others, a quiet warrior in her own right.

"You always did take the blame for things."

"What does that have to do with today?"

He gestured for her to sit on a pew, then joined her. "When we were kids, you took the blame for things I did—like breaking the aquarium and letting the snake loose in the school."

She smiled nostalgically. "And cutting off Sharilynn's braid. Not a nice thing to do at all, by the way."

"She was mean to you. She deserved it." He and Lucy Ann had been each other's champions in those days. "But you shouldn't have told the teacher you did it. You ended up cleaning the erasers for a week."

"I enjoyed staying after school. And my mom didn't do anything except laugh, then make me write an apology and do some extra chores." She looked down at her hands twisted in her lap. "Your father wouldn't have laughed if the school called him."

"You're right there." He scooped up her hand and held

on. It was getting easier and easier for them to be together again. As much as he hated revisiting the past, if it worked to bring her back into his life, he would walk over hot coals in hell for her. "You protected me every bit as much as I tried to protect you."

"But your risk was so much higher...with your dad." She squeezed his hand. "You did the knightly thing. That meant a lot to a scrawny girl no one noticed except to make fun of her clothes or her mom."

He looked up at Lucy Ann quickly. Somehow he'd forgotten that part of her past. He always saw her as quietly feisty. "What elementary school boy cares about someone's clothes?"

"True enough, I guess." She studied him through the sweep of long eyelashes. "I never quite understood why you decided we would be friends—before we started taking the blame for each other's transgressions."

Why? He thought back to that time, to the day he saw her sitting at the computer station, her legs swinging, too short to reach the ground. The rest of the class was running around their desks while the teacher stepped out to speak with a parent. "You were peaceful. I wasn't. We balanced each other out. We can have that again."

"You're pushing." She tugged her hand.

He held firm. "Less than a minute ago, you told me I have the right to be mad at you."

"And I have the right to apologize and walk away."

Her quick retort surprised him. The Lucy Ann of the past would have been passive rather than confrontational. Like leaving for a year and having his baby. "Yeah, you're good at that, avoiding."

"There." She looked up quickly. "Tell me off. Be angry. Do anything other than smile and pretend everything's okay between us while we tour around the world like some dream couple."

Her fire bemused him and mesmerized him. "You are the most confusing woman I have ever met."

"Good." She stood up quickly, tugging her camera bag back onto her shoulder. "Women have always fallen into your arms far too easily. Time to finish the tour."

Seven

Lucy Ann swaddled her son in a fluffy towel after his bath while the nanny, Mrs. Clayworth, placed a fresh diaper and sleeper on the changing table. After the full day touring, then dinner with the nanny so Lucy Ann could get to know her better, she felt more comfortable with the woman.

Elliot's thoughtfulness and care for their son's future touched her. He'd charmed Mrs. Clayworth, yet asked perceptive questions. The woman appeared soft and like someone out of a Disney movie, but over the hours it became clear she was more than a stereotype. More than a résumé as a pediatric nurse. She was an avid musician and a hiker who enjoyed the world travel that came with her job. She spent her days off trekking through different local sites or attending concerts.

Lucy Ann liked the woman more and more with every

minute that passed. "Mrs. Clayworth, so you really were a nanny for royalty? That had to have been exciting."

Her eyes twinkled as she held out her arms for Eli. "You have seen my list of references. But that's just about the parents." She tucked Eli against her shoulder with expert hands, patting his back. "A baby doesn't care anything about lineage or credentials. Only that he or she is dry, fed, cuddled and loved."

"I can see clearly enough that you have a gift with babies."

The nanny's patience had been admirable when, just after supper, Eli cried himself purple over a bout of gas.

"I had two of my own. The child care career started once they left for the university. I used to be a pediatric nurse and while the money was good, it wasn't enough. I had bills to pay because of my loser ex-husband, and thanks to my daughter's connections with a blue-blooded roommate, I lucked into a career I thoroughly enjoy."

Having lived the past months as a single mom, Lucy Ann sympathized. Except she had always had the safety net of calling Elliot. She'd had her aunt's help, as well. What if she'd had nowhere to go and no one's help? The thought made her stomach knot with apprehension. That didn't mean she would stay with Elliot just because of her bills—but she certainly needed to make more concrete plans.

"I want the best for my son, too."

"Well, as much as I like my job, you have to know the best can't always be bought with money."

So very true. Lucy Ann took Eli back to dress him in his teddy bear sleeper. "You remind me of my aunt."

"I hope that's a compliment." She tucked the towel into the laundry chute.

"It is. Aunt Carla is my favorite relative." Not that

there was a lot of stiff competition. She traced the ap-pliquéd teddy bear on the pj's and thought of her aunt's closet full of themed clothes. "She always wears these chipper seasonal T-shirts and sweatshirts. She has a thick Southern accent and deep-fries everything, including pickles. I know on the outside it sounds like the two of you are nothing alike, but on the inside, there's a calm-ing spirit about you both."

"Then I will most certainly take that as a compliment, love." She walked to the pitcher on the desk by the win-dow and poured a glass of water. "I respect that you're taking your time to get to know me and to see how I handle your son. Not all parents are as careful with their wee ones."

Mrs. Clayworth placed the glass beside the ornately carved rocker thoughtfully, even though Lucy Ann hadn't mentioned how thirsty she got when she nursed Eli. Money couldn't buy happiness, but having extra hands sure made life easier. She snapped Eli's sleeper up to his neck.

"I do trust Elliot's judgment. I've known him all my life. We've relied on each other for so much." There had been a time when she thought there was nothing he could do that would drive a wedge between them. "Except now there's this new dynamic to adjust to with Eli. But then you probably see that all the time."

Lucy Ann scooped up her son and settled into the wooden rocker, hoping she wasn't the only new mother to have conflicted feelings about her role. As much as she loved nursing her baby, she couldn't deny the occa-sional twinge of sadness that the same body Elliot once touched with passion had been relegated to a far more utilitarian purpose.

"You're a new mum." Mrs. Clayworth passed a burp cloth. "That's a huge and blessed change."

"My own mother wasn't much of a role model." She adjusted her shirt, and Eli hungrily latched on.

"And this favorite aunt of yours?" The nanny adjusted the bedding in the cradle, draping a fresh blanket over the end, before taking on the many other countless details in wrapping up the day.

"She helped as much as she could, but my mother resented the connection sometimes." Especially when her mom was between boyfriends and lonely. Then suddenly it wasn't so convenient to have Lucy Ann hang out with Aunt Carla. "I've been reading everything I can find on parenting. I even took some classes at the hospital, but there are too many things to cover in books or courses."

"Amen, dear."

Having this woman to lean on was…incredible, to say the least. Elliot was clearly working the fairy tale–like life from all angles.

She would be pridefully foolish to ignore the resources this woman brought to the table. Isolating herself for the past eleven months had been a mistake. Lucy Ann needed to correct that tendency and find balance. She needed to learn to accept help and let others into her life. Starting now seemed like a good idea.

She couldn't deny that all this "playing house" with Elliot was beginning to chip away at her reservations and her resolve to keep her distance. Elliot had said they needed to use this time to figure out how to parent Eli. She knew now they also needed to use this time to learn how to be in the same room with each other without melting into a pool of hormones. Time to quit running from the attraction and face it. Deal with it.

"And that's where your experience comes in. I would

be foolish not to learn from you." Lucy Ann paused, patting Eli's pedaling feet. "Why do you look so surprised?"

"Mothers seek help from me, not advice. You are a unique one."

"Would you mind staying for a while so we can talk?"

"Of course. I don't mind at all."

Lucy Ann gestured to the wingback chair on the other side of the fireplace. "I'd like to ask you a few questions."

"About babies?" she asked, sitting.

"Nope, I'd like to ask your advice on men."

The winner's trophy always felt so good in his hands, but today...the victory felt hollow in comparison with what he really wanted. More time with Lucy Ann.

Elliot held the trophy high with one hand, his helmet tucked under his other arm.

His *Beauty and the Beast* plan had gone well. They'd spent a low-key day together. Her pensive expression gave him hope he was on the right path. If she was ready to check out and return to Columbia, there would have been decisiveness on her face. But he was making headway with her. He could see that. He just needed to keep pushing forward with his plans, steady on. And try like hell to ignore the urge to kiss her every second they were together.

A wiry reporter pushed a microphone forward through the throng of fans and press all shouting congratulations. "Mr. Starc, tell us about the new lady in your life."

"Is it true she was your former assistant?"

"Where has she been this year?"

"Did she quit or was she fired?"

"Lovers' spat?"

"Which designer deserves credit for her makeover?"

Makeover? What the hell were they talking about?

To him, she was Lucy Ann—always pretty and special. And even though she had come out of her shell some in the past year, that didn't change the core essence of her, the woman he'd always known and admired.

Sure, her new curves added a bombshell quality. And the clothes his new assistant had ordered were flashier. None of that mattered to him. He'd wanted her before. He wanted her still.

The wiry reporter shoved the mic closer. "Are you sure the baby is yours?"

That question pulled him up short in anger. "I understand that the press thinks the personal life of anyone with a little fame is fair game. But when it comes to my family, I will not tolerate slanderous statements. If you want access to me, you will respect my son and his mother. And now it's time for me to celebrate with my family. Interviews are over."

He heard his assistant hiss in protest over the way he'd handled the question. The paparazzi expected to be fed, not spanked.

Shouldering through the crowd, Elliot kept his eyes locked on Lucy Ann in his private box, watching. Had she heard the questions through the speaker box? He hoped not. He didn't want anything to mar the evening he had planned. She'd actually consented to let the nanny watch Eli. Elliot would have her all to himself.

He kept walking, pushing through the throng.

"Congratulations, Starc," another reporter persisted. "How are you planning to celebrate?"

"How long do you expect your winning streak to run?"

"Is the woman and your kid the reason your engagement broke off?"

He continued to "no comment" his way all the way up the steps, into a secure hallway and to the private viewing box in the grandstand where Lucy Ann waited with a couple of honored guests, local royalty and politicians he only just managed to acknowledge with a quick greeting and thanks for attending. His entire focus locked on Lucy Ann.

"You won," she squealed, her smile enveloping him every bit as much as if she'd hugged him. Her red wraparound dress clung to her body, outlining every curve.

He would give up his trophy in a heartbeat to tug that tie with his teeth until her dress fell open.

"I think we should go." Before he embarrassed them both in front of reporters and esteemed guests.

He couldn't wait to get her alone. All he'd been able to think about during the race was getting back to Lucy Ann so he could continue his campaign. Move things closer to the point where he could kiss her as he wanted.

"Right." She leaned to pluck her purse from her seat. "The after-parties."

"Not tonight," he said softly for her ears only. "I have other plans."

"You have responsibilities to your career. I understand that."

He pulled her closer, whispering, "The press is particularly ravenous today. We need to go through the private elevator."

Her eyebrows pinched together. "I'm not so sure that's the best idea."

Damn it, was she going to bail on him before he even had a chance to get started? He would just have to figure out a way around it. "What do you propose we do instead?"

She tugged his arm, the warmth of her touch reaching through his race jacket as she pulled him closer to the observation window. "You taught me long ago that the best way to get rid of the hungry press is to feed them tidbits."

The tip of her tongue touched her top lip briefly before she arched up on her toes to kiss him. He stood stock-still in shock for a second before—hell, yeah—he was all-in. His arms banded around her waist. She leaned into him, looping her arms his neck. He could almost imagine the cameras clicking as fast as his heartbeat, picking up speed with every moment he had Lucy Ann in his arms.

He didn't know what had changed her mind, but he was damn glad.

Her fingers played along his hair and he remembered the feel of her combing her hands through it the night they'd made love. He'd kept his hair longer then, before the accident.

Lucy Ann sighed into his mouth as she began to pull back with a smile. "That should keep the media vultures happy for a good long while." She nipped his bottom lip playfully before asking, "Are you ready to celebrate your win?"

Lucy Ann stepped out onto the castle balcony, the night air cool, the stone flooring under her feet even cooler but not cold enough to send her back inside. She walked to the half wall along the balcony and let the breeze lift her hair and ruffle through her dress before turning back to the table.

Elliot was showering off the scent of gasoline. He'd already ordered supper. The meal waited for them, savory Spanish spices drifting along the air.

There was no question that Elliot had ordered the dinner spread personally. The table was laden with her favorites, right down to a flan for dessert. Elliot remembered. She'd spent so much time as his assistant making sure to remember every detail of his life, she hadn't considered he'd been paying just as close attention to her.

She trailed her fingers along the edge of her water goblet. The sounds below—other guests coming and going, laughing and talking—mingled with the sound system wafting more madrigal tunes into the night. She didn't even have the nursery monitor with her for the first time since... She couldn't remember when. Mrs. Clayworth had already planned to watch Eli tonight since Lucy Ann had expected to go to an after-race party with Elliot.

Then she'd kissed him.

Halfway through that impulsive gesture, Lucy Ann realized that holding back was no longer an option. Sleeping with Elliot again was all but inevitable. The longer she waited, the more intense the fallout would be. They needed to figure out this crazy attraction now, while their son was still young enough not to know if things didn't work out.

Her stomach knotted with nerves. But the attraction was only getting stronger the longer she denied herself. It was only a matter of time—

As if conjured from that wish, Elliot stood in the balcony doorway, so fresh from the shower his short hair still held a hint of water. He'd changed into simple black pants and a white shirt with the sleeves rolled up. With the night shadows and flickering sconce lights he had a timeless air—the Elliot from the past mixing with the man he'd become.

She wanted them both.

Lucy Ann swallowed nervously and searched for something to say to break the crackling silence between them. "I can't believe the press actually left us alone after the race."

"We did slip away out a back entrance."

"That never stopped them before."

"I ordered extra security." He stalked toward her slowly. "I don't want anyone hassling you or Eli. Our lives are private now. I'm done playing the paparazzi game. At least we know this place is secure."

"As private as the woods we hid in as kids."

How many times had he made her feel safe? As if those quilted walls could hold out the world while they huddled inside reading books and coloring pictures like regular kids.

He stopped in front of her, his hand brushing back a stray lock of her hair. "Why did you kiss me after the race?"

"To keep the press content." To let other women know he was taken? "Because I wanted to."

He tugged the lock of hair lightly. "I meant why did you bite me?"

A laugh rolled free and rode the breeze. "Oh, that. Can't have everything going your way."

"You're more confident these days." His emerald eyes glinted with curiosity—and promise.

"Motherhood has given me purpose." Even now, the need to settle her life for her child pushed her to move faster with Elliot, to figure out one way or another.

To take what she could from this time together in case everything imploded later.

"I like seeing you more comfortable in your skin." He sat on the balcony half wall with unerring balance and confidence. "Letting the rest of the world see the woman you are."

As much as she feared trusting a man—trusting Elliot—she couldn't help but wonder if he would continue trying to spin a fairy-tale future for them long beyond tonight and ignore the fact that she had been the unnoticed Cinderella all her life. She wanted a man who noticed the real her—not the fairy tale. Not the fantasy. If she was honest, she was still afraid his sexual interest had come too late to feel authentic.

"You make me sound like I was a mouse before—someone in need of a makeover, like that reporter said."

He cursed softly. "You heard their questions?"

"The TV system in the private box was piping in feed from the winner's circle." She rolled her eyes. "It was a backhanded compliment of sorts."

"Don't ever forget I saw the glow long before."

She couldn't help but ask, "If you saw my glow, then why did it take you all those years to make a move on me?"

"If I remember correctly, you made the first move."

She winced, some of her confidence fading at the thought that they could have still been just friends if she hadn't impulsively kissed him that night they'd been drunk, celebrating and nostalgic. "Thanks for reminding me how I made a fool of myself."

"You're misunderstanding." He linked fingers with her, tugging her closer. "I've always found you attractive, but you were off-limits. Something much more valuable than a lover—those are a dime a dozen. You were, you are, my friend."

She wanted to believe him. "A dime a dozen. Nice."

"Lucy Ann, stop." He squeezed her hand. "I don't want to fight with you. It doesn't have to be that way for us this time. Trust me. I have a plan."

She'd planned to seduce him, keep things light, and he was going serious on her. She tried to lighten the mood again. "What fairy tale does this night come from?"

"It could be reality."

"You disappoint me." She leaned closer until their

chests just brushed. Her breasts beaded in response. "Tonight, I want the fairy tale."

He blinked in surprise. "Okay, fair enough." He stood, tugging her to the middle of the balcony. "We're in the middle of Cinderella's ball."

Appropriate, given her thoughts earlier. "Well, the clock is definitely ticking since Eli still wakes up in the middle of the night."

"Then we should make the most of this evening." The moonlight cast a glow around them, adding to the magical air of the night. "Are you ready for supper?"

"Honestly?" She swayed in time with the classical music.

"I wouldn't have asked if I hadn't wanted to know. I don't think you know how much I want to make you happy."

She stepped closer, lifting their hands. "Then let's dance."

"I can accommodate." He brought her hand to rest on his shoulder, his palm sliding warmly along her waist. "I owe you for homecoming our sophomore year in high school. You had that pretty dress your aunt made. She showed me so I could make sure the flowers on your wrist corsage matched just the right shade of blue."

"I can't believe you still remember about a high school dance." Or that he remembered the color of her dress.

"I got arrested for car theft and stood you up." He rested his chin on top of her head. "That tends to make a night particularly memorable."

"I knew it was really your friends that night, not you."

He angled back to look in her warm chocolate-brown eyes. "Why didn't you tell me you thought that?"

"You would have argued with me about some technical detail." She teased, all the while too aware of the freshly showered scent of him. "You were even more stubborn in those days."

"I *did* steal that car." He tugged her closer and stole her breath so she couldn't speak. "And it wasn't a technicality. I wanted to take you to the dance in decent wheels. I figured the used car dealership would never know as long as I returned it in the morning."

"I wouldn't have cared what kind of car we had that night."

"I know. But I cared. And ended up spending the night in jail before the car dealer dismissed the charges—God only knows why." He laughed darkly. "That night in jail was the best night's sleep I'd gotten in a long time, being out of my father's house."

God, he was breaking her heart. Their childhoods were so damaged, had they even stood a chance at a healthy adult relationship with each other? She rested her head on his shoulder and let him talk, taking in the steady beat of his pulse to help steady her own.

"I felt like such a bastard for sleeping, for being grateful for a night's break from my dad when I'd let you down."

Let her down? He'd been her port in the storm, her safe harbor. "Elliot," she said softly, "it was a silly dance. I was more worried about how your father would react to your arrest."

"I wanted to give you everything," he said, ignoring her comment about his dad. "But I let you down time after time."

This conversation was straying so far from her plans for seduction, her plans to work out the sensual ache inside her. "This isn't the sort of thing Prince Charming says to Cinderella at the ball."

"My point is that I'm trying to give you everything

now, if you'll just let me." He nuzzled her hair. "Just tell me what you want."

Every cell in her body shouted for her to say she wanted him to peel off her dress and make love to her against the castle wall. Instead, she found herself whispering, "All I want is for Eli to be happy and to lead a normal life."

"You think this isn't normal." His feet matched steps with hers as the music flowed into their every move.

A castle? A monastery library? "Well, this isn't your average trip to a bookstore or corner library, that's for sure."

"There are playgrounds here as well as libraries. We just have to find them for Eli."

Lucy Ann felt a stab of guilt. Elliot was thinking of their son and she'd been thinking about sex. "You make it sound so simple."

"It can be."

If only she could buy into his notion of keeping things simple long-term. "Except I never contacted you about being pregnant."

"And I didn't come after you like I should have. I let my pride get stung, and hurt another woman in the process."

She hadn't considered the fact that Gianna had been wronged in this situation. "What happens in the future if you find someone else...or if I do?"

"You want monogamy?" he asked. "I can do that."

"You say that so quickly, but you're also the one spinning fairy tales and games." She looked up at him. "I'm asking honest questions now."

She wondered why she was pushing so hard for answers to questions that could send him running. Was she on a self-destructive path in spite of her plans to be with him? Then again, this level of honesty between them had been a long time coming.

His feet stopped. He cupped her face until their eyes met. "Believe this. You're the only woman I want. You're sure as hell more woman than I can handle, so if you will stay with me, then monogamy is a piece of cake."

"Are you proposing?"

"I'm proposing we stay together, sleep together, be friends, lovers, parents."

He wasn't proposing. This wasn't Cinderella's ball after all. They were making an arrangement of convenience—to enjoy sex and friendship.

She didn't believe in fairy tales, damn it. So she should take exactly what he offered. But she intended to make sure he understood that convenience did not mean she would simply follow his lead.

Eight

Lucy Ann stepped out of his arms, and a protest roared inside Elliot. Damn it, was she leaving? Rejecting him in spite of everything they'd just said to each other? He set his jaw and stuffed his hands into his pockets to keep from turning into an idiot, a fool begging her to stay.

Except she didn't move any farther away. She locked eyes with him, her pupils wide—from the dark or from desire? He sure as hell hoped for the latter. Her hand went to the tie of her silky wraparound dress and she tugged.

His jaw dropped. "Um, Lucy Ann? Are you about to, uh—?"

"Yes, Elliot, I am." She pulled open the dress, revealing red satin underwear and an enticing expanse of creamy freckled skin.

His brain went on stun. All he could do was stare—and appreciate. Her bra cupped full breasts so perfectly his hands ached to hold and test their weight, to caress her until she sighed in arousal.

She shrugged and the dress started to slide down, down—

Out here.

In the open.

He bolted forward, a last scrap of sense telling him to shield her gorgeous body. He clasped her shoulders and pulled her to him, stopping the dress from falling away. "Lucy Ann, we're on a balcony. Outside."

A purr rippled up her throat as she wriggled against his throbbing erection. "I know."

Her fragrance beckoned, along with access to silky skin. His mouth watered. That last bit of his sense was going to give up the fight any second.

"We need to go back into our suite."

"I know that, too. So take me inside. Your room or mine. You choose as long as we're together and naked very soon." She leaned into him, her breasts pressing against his chest. "Unless you've changed your mind."

The need to possess tensed all his muscles, the adrenaline rush stronger than coming into a final turn neck and neck.

"Hell, no, I haven't changed my mind. We'll go to my room because there are condoms in my nightstand. And before you ask, yes, I've been wanting and planning to take you to bed again every minute of our journey." He scooped her up into his arms and shouldered the doors open into their suite. The sitting area loomed quiet and empty. "Thank God Mrs. Claymore isn't up looking for a midnight snack."

Her hair trailing loose over his shoulder, Lucy Ann kissed his neck in a series of nibbles up to his ear. "You're supposed to be the race car driver who lives on the edge, and yet you're the one being careful. That's actually quite romantic."

"For you. Always careful for you." Except he hadn't been. He'd left her alone as a teen, gotten her pregnant and stayed away for nearly a year. He refused to let her down again in any way. She deserved better from him.

Lucy Ann deserved the best. Period.

She slid her hand behind his head and brought him closer for a kiss. He took her mouth as fully as he ached to take her body. With every step closer to his bedroom, his body throbbed harder and faster for her. The last few steps to the king-size bed felt like a mile. The massive headboard took up nearly the whole wall, the four posters carved like trees reaching up to the canopy. He was glad now he'd brought her here, a place they'd never been, a fantasy locale for a woman who deserved to be pampered, adored.

Treasured.

He set her on her feet carefully, handling her like spun glass. She tossed the dress aside in a silky flutter of red.

Nibbling her bottom lip and releasing it slowly, seductively, Lucy Ann kicked her high heels off with a flick of each foot. "One of us is *very* overdressed."

"You don't say."

"I do." She hooked her finger in the collar of his shirt and tugged down. Hard. Popping the buttons free in a burst that scattered them along the floor.

Ooooo-kay. So much for spun glass. His libido ramped into high gear. "You seem to be taking charge so nicely I thought you might help me take care of that."

He looked forward to losing more buttons in her deft hands.

"Hmm," she hummed, backing toward the bed until her knees bumped the wooden steps. "If I'm taking charge, then I want you to take off the rest of your clothes while I watch."

"I believe I can comply with that request." Shrugging off his destroyed shirt, he couldn't take his eyes from her as she settled onto the middle of the gold comforter, surrounded by tapestry pillows and a faux-fur throw. He toed off his loafers, his bare feet sinking into the thick Persian rug.

She reclined on the bed, pushing her heels into the mattress to scoot farther up until she could lean against the headboard. "You could have continued your underwear model days and made a mint, you know."

His hands stopped on his belt buckle. "You're killing the mood for me, Lucy Ann. I prefer to forget that brief chapter of my life."

"Briefs?" She giggled at her own pun. "You're right. You're definitely more of a boxers kind of guy now."

Fine, then. She seemed to want to keep this lighthearted, avoiding the heavier subjects they'd touched on while dancing. Now that he thought of it, they'd never gotten around to dinner, either. Which gave him an idea, one he'd be better off starting while he still had his clothes on.

"Stay there, just like that," he said. "I'll be right back."

Belt buckle clanking and loose, he sprinted out to the balcony. He picked up the platter of fruit and cheese and tucked the two plates of flan on top. Balancing the make-shift feast, he padded toward their room, careful not to wake the nanny or Eli.

Backing inside, he elbowed the door closed carefully. Turning, he breathed a sigh of relief to find Lucy Ann waiting. He hadn't really expected her to leave…except for a hint of an instant he'd thought about how quickly she'd run from what they shared last time.

She tipped her head to the side, her honey-streaked brown hair gliding along her shoulder like melted caramel. "You want to eat dinner now?"

He gave her his best bad boy grin. "If you're my plate, then yes, ma'am, I think this is a fine time for us to have supper."

"Okay then. Wouldn't want to mess up our clothes." She tugged off her bra and shimmied out of her panties, her lush curves bared and... Wow.

He almost dropped the damn tray.

Regaining his footing, he set the food on the edge of the bed without once taking his eyes off the long lines of her legs leading up to her caramel curls. He was definitely overdressed for what he had in mind.

He tugged off his slacks along with his boxers. His erection sprang free.

She smiled, her eyes roving over him in an appreciative sweep that made him throb harder. "Elliot?"

"Yes?" He clasped her foot in his hand, lifting it and kissing the inside of her ankle where a delicate chain with a fairy charm surprised him on such a practical woman. What else had he missed about Lucy Ann in the year they'd been apart?

"Do you know what would make this perfect?"

He kissed the inside of her calf. "Name it. I'll make it happen."

"More lights."

He looked up from her leg to her confident eyes reflecting the bedside lamp. "Lights?"

"It's been quite a while since I saw you naked, and last time was rather hurried and with bad lighting."

She was a total and complete turn-on. Everything about her.

"Can do," he said.

He placed her leg back on the bed and turned on the massive cast-iron chandelier full of replica candles that supplemented the glow of the bedside lamp. The rich colors of the bed and the heavy curtains swept back on either side somehow made Lucy Ann seem all the more pale and naked, her creamy flesh as tempting as anything he'd ever seen. The feel of her gaze on him heated his blood to molten lava, his whole body on fire for her.

But no way in hell would he let himself lose control. He took the time to reach for the bedside table, past his vintage copy of *Don Quixote*. Dipping into the drawer, he pulled out a condom. He dropped it on the bed before hitching a knee on the edge and joining her on the mattress. Taking his time, even as urgency thrummed through him, he explored every curve, enjoying the way goose bumps rose along her bared flesh.

She met him stroke for stroke, caress for caress, until he couldn't tell for certain who was mirroring whom. Their hands moved in tandem, their sighs syncing up, until they both breathed faster. He lost track of how long they just enjoyed each other, touching and seeking their fill. At some point, she rolled the condom over him, but he only half registered it since pleasure pulsed through him at her touch—and at the feel of her slick desire on his fingertips as he traced and teased between her legs.

Holding himself in check grew tougher by the second so he angled away, reaching for the platter of food on the corner of the bed.

He pushed the tray along the bed to put it in better reach. Then he plucked a strawberry and placed the plump fruit between his teeth. He slid over her, blanketing her. He throbbed between her legs, nudging, wanting. He leaned closer and pressed the strawberry to her mouth. Her lips parted to close over the plump fruit until they met in a kiss.

She bit into the strawberry and he thrust inside her. The fruity flavor burst over his taste buds at the same time sensation sparked through him. Pleasure. The feel of her clamping around him, holding him deep inside her as a "yes" hissed between her teeth. Her head pressed back into the bolster, her eyes sliding closed.

He moved as her jaw worked, chewing the strawberry. Her head arched back, her throat gliding with a slow swallow. Her breasts pushed upward, beading tight and hard.

Inviting.

Leaning on one elbow, he reached for another berry. He squeezed the fruit in his fist, dribbling the juice over her nipple. She gasped in response. He flicked his tongue over her, tasting her, rolling the beaded tip in his mouth until she moaned for more. The taste of ripe fruit and a hint of something more had him ready to come apart inside her already.

Thrusting over and over, he pushed aside the need to finish, hard and fast. Aching to make this last, for her and for him.

How could he possibly have stayed away from her for so long? For any time at all? How could he have thought for even a second he could be with anyone other than her? They were linked together. They always had been, for as far back as he could remember.

She was his, damn it.

The thought rocketed through him, followed closely by her sighs and moans of completion. Her hands flung out, twisting in the comforter, her teeth sinking deep into her bottom lip as she bit back the cry that might wake others.

Seeing the flush of pleasure wash over her skin

snapped the reins on his restraint and he came, the hot pulse jetting from him into her. Deeper, and yet somehow not deep enough as he already wanted her again.

As his arms gave way and he sank to rest fully on top of her, he could only think, damn straight, she was his.

But he hadn't been able to keep Lucy Ann before. How in the hell was he going to manage to keep the new, more confident woman in his arms?

A woman who didn't need anything from him.

Tingling with anticipation, Lucy Ann angled toward Elliot. "I need another bite now or I am absolutely going to pass out."

She gripped his wrist and guided his spoonful of flan toward her mouth as he chuckled softly. She closed her lips over it and savored the creamy caramel pudding. All of her senses were on hyperalert since she and Elliot had made love—twice. The scent of strawberries still clung to the sheets even though they'd showered together, making love in the large stone spa before coming back to bed.

Eventually, she would have to sleep or she would be a completely ineffective mother. But for now, she wasn't ready to let go of this fantasy night, making love with Elliot in a castle.

The luxurious sheets teased her already-sensitive skin, and she gave herself a moment to soak in the gorgeous surroundings. Beyond Elliot. The man was temptation enough, but he'd brought her to this decadent haven where she could stare up at carvings of a Dionysian revel on the bedposts or lose herself in the images of a colorful, wall-sized tapestry depicting a medieval feast. The figures were almost life-size, gathered around a table, an elegant lord and lady in the middle and an array of characters all around from lecherous knight to teasing serving maid. Even the scent of dried herbs and flowers that emanated from the linens immersed her in a fantasy world.

One she never wanted to end.

She scooped her spoon through the flan and offered a bite to her own sexy knight. "I have to say our dance tonight ended much better than our sophomore homecoming ever could have."

"You're right about that." He dipped his spoon into the dessert for her, picking up the rhythm of feeding each other. "Lady, you are rocking the hell out of that sheet."

He filled her whole fairy-tale fantasy well with his broad shoulders and muscular chest, the sheet wrapped around his waist. There was a timeless quality about this place that she embraced. It kept her from looking into the future. She intended to make the absolute most of this chance to be together.

They'd had sex before. They knew each other's bodies intimately. Yet there was a newness about this moment. She looked different now that she'd had a baby. Her body had changed. *She* had changed in other ways, as well. She had a growing confidence now, personally and professionally.

Lucy Ann searched Elliot's eyes…and found nothing but desire. His gaze stroked over her with appreciation and yes, even possession—stoking the heat still simmering inside her.

"I have to confess something." She angled forward to accept the next bite he fed her.

His face went somber in a flash even as he took the spoonful of flan she brought to his mouth. He swallowed, then said, "Tell me whatever you need to. I'm not going anywhere."

She carefully set her utensil onto the platter by the last strawberry, her body humming with the memory of the moment they'd shared the fruit, the moment he'd thrust inside her. The intensity of it all threatened to overwhelm her. She desperately needed to lighten the moment before they waded into deeper waters.

"I may like simplicity in many parts of my life—" she paused for effect, then stretched out like a lazy cat until the sheet slithered away from her breasts "—but I am totally addicted to expensive linens."

"God, Lucy Ann." He hauled her against his side, her nipples beading tighter at the feel of his bare skin. "You scared the hell out of me with talk of confessions."

"I'm serious as a heart attack here." She rested her cheek on his chest, the warmth of him seeping into her. "Every night when I crawled into bed—and trust me, cheap mattresses also suck a lot more than I remembered—those itchy sheets made me long for Egyptian cotton."

"Ahhh, now I understand." He tugged the comforter over them. "The fairy tale here is *The Princess and the Pea*. I will be very sure you always have the best mattresses and sheets that money can buy." He patted her butt.

"My prince," she said, joking to keep talk of the future light for now, all the while knowing that inevitably they would have to steer the conversation in another direction. "I don't think I ever said congratulations on your win today. I'm sorry you missed out on the parties tonight."

"I'm not sorry at all." He stroked back her hair, extending the length with his fingers and letting damp strands glide free. "This is exactly where I wanted to be. Celebrating with you, without clothes—best party ever."

"You do deserve to celebrate your success though. You've come a long way through sheer determination." She hooked a leg over his, enjoying the way they fit.

"Although I have to say, I've always been surprised you chose Formula One over the NASCAR route, given your early days racing the dirt-track circuit."

Why had she never thought to question him about this before? She'd simply followed, accepting. He'd always taken the lead in life and on the track.

He'd begun racing with adults at fourteen years old, then picked it up again when he graduated from the military high school in North Carolina. He was a poster boy for the reformative success of the school even without people knowing he periodically helped out Interpol.

Elliot rested his chin on her head, his breath warm on her scalp. "I guess I have a confession of my own to make. I wanted to go to college and major in English. But I had to make a living. I went back to racing after school because my credit was shot."

English? It made sense given the way he'd always kept a book close at hand, and yet she couldn't believe he'd never mentioned that dream. A whole new side of Elliot emerged, making her wonder what else he'd kept secret.

"Because of your arrest history?"

His chest rose and fell with a heavy sigh. "Because my father took out credit cards in my name."

Her eyes closing, she hugged an arm tighter around him. "I'm so sorry. Nothing should surprise me when it comes to that man, but it still sucks to hear. I'm just so glad you got away from him."

"You should be mad at me for leaving you," he repeated, his voice hoarse. "I let you down."

"I don't agree." She kissed his chest before continuing. "You did what you needed to. I missed you when they sent you to North Carolina, but I understood."

"All the same, you were still hurt by what I did. I could see that then. I can even feel it now. Tell me the truth."

So much for keeping things light. They would always have to cycle around to the weightier stuff eventually. "I understand why you needed a way out, believe me, I do. I just wish you'd spoken to me, given me an opportunity to weigh in and figure out how we could both leave. That place was bearable with you around. Without you…"

She squeezed her eyes closed, burying her face in his chest, absorbing the vibrant strength of him to ward off the chill seeping into her bones.

"I like to think if I could go back and change the past that I would. Except I did the same thing all over again. I let you go. You deserve to be put first in someone's life, someone who won't let you down."

Where was he going with this? Where did she *want* him to go?

After that, he stayed silent so long she thought for a moment he had drifted off midthought, then his hand started to rove along her spine slowly. Not in a seductive way; more of a touch of connection.

He kissed the top of her head, whispering into her hair still damp from their shared shower, "I didn't want to leave you back in high school. You have to know that." His voice went ragged with emotion. "But I didn't have anything to offer you if we left together. And I couldn't stay any longer. I just couldn't see another way out except to get arrested."

She struggled to sift through his words, to understand what he was trying to tell her. "You stole cars on purpose, hoping the cops would catch you?"

"That pretty much sums it up." His hand slid to rest on her hip, his voice strangely calm in contrast to his racing heart. "After that first night in jail, I started stealing cars on a regular basis. I didn't expect to be so good at it. I thought I would get caught much earlier."

"Why did you want to get caught?" she repeated, needing to understand, wondering how she didn't know this about him. She'd thought they told each other everything.

"I figured jail was safer than home," he said simply. "I didn't worry so much about myself with my dad, but I worried what he would do to the people around me."

"You mean me and your mother?"

He nodded against her head. "Remember when we went on that trip to the beach and my old rebuilt truck broke down?"

"You mean when the tires fell off." Only his incredible reflexes had kept them from crashing into a ditch. It had been a near miss.

"Right. When the first one fell off, I thought what crappy luck. Then the second one came off, too...."

Her stomach lurched at the memory. "We were lucky we didn't get T-boned in traffic. You had fast instincts, even then."

His arms twitched around her, holding her too tightly. "I found out that my father had taken out a life insurance policy on me."

She gasped, rising up on her elbows to look him in the eyes. His expression was completely devoid of emotion, but she could see the horror that must be on her face reflected in his eyes.

"Elliot, do you really believe your father tried to kill you?"

"I'm sure of it," he said with certainty, pushing up to sit, the covers rustling and twisting around their legs.

"You had to have been so scared."

Why hadn't he told her? Although the second she finished that thought, she already knew the answer. He didn't want to put her at risk. Debating the fact now, insisting he should have told the police, seemed moot after so long. Better to just listen and figure out why he was telling her this now.

"I didn't have the money to strike out on my own. I knew the odds of teens on the street." His head fell back against the carved headboard. "I figured the kids in juvie couldn't be as bad as my old man."

"Except you were sent to military reform school instead."

Thank heavens, too, since his life had been turned around because of his time in that school, thanks to his friends and the headmaster. The system did work for the best sometimes. Someone somewhere had seen the good deep inside of Elliot.

"I finally caught a lucky break." He cupped the back of her head, his fingers massaging her scalp. "I'm just so damn sorry I had to leave you behind. I see now I should have figured out another way."

"It all worked out—"

"Did it?" he asked, his eyes haunted. "Your mom's boyfriends... We've talked about so much over the years but we've never discussed that time when I was away."

Slowly, she realized what he was asking, and the thought that he'd worried about her, about that, for all these years... Her heart broke for him and the worries he'd had. She wondered if that's why he'd been so protective, giving her a job, keeping her with him—out of guilt?

"Elliot, the guys my mom saw were jerks, yes, and a few of them even tried to cop a feel, but none of them were violent. Some may have been perverts but they weren't rapists. So I was able to take care of myself by avoiding them. I escaped to Aunt Carla's until things settled down or until Mom and her latest guy broke up."

"You shouldn't have had to handle it yourself, to hide from your own home." Anger and guilt weighted his words and tightened his jaw until the tendons flexed along his neck. "Your mother should have been there for you. *I* should have been there."

She didn't want him to feel guilty or to feel sorry for her. Angling up, she cupped his face in her hands. "I don't want you to feel obligated to be my protector."

"I don't know what else I can be for you." His voice was ragged with emotion, his eyes haunted.

They could have been teenagers again, the two of them clinging to each other because there was so little else for them. So much pain. So much betrayal by parents who should have valued them and kept them safe. Her shared past with Elliot wrapped around her so tightly she felt bound to him in a way she couldn't find words to explain but felt compelled to express, even if only physically.

Soaking in the feel of bare flesh meeting flesh, Lucy Ann kissed Elliot, fully, deeply. She savored the taste of flan and strawberries and *him*. A far more intoxicating combination than any alcohol.

And he was all hers, for tonight.

Nine

Their tongues met and tangled as Lucy Ann angled her mouth over Elliot's. They fit so seamlessly together as she tried to give him some sort of comfort, even if only in the form of distraction. Sex didn't solve problems, but it sure made the delaying a hell of a lot more pleasurable. Her mind filled with the sensation of him, the scents of them together.

His hands banded around her waist, and he urged her over him. She swung her leg over his lap, straddling him. His arousal pressed between her legs, nudging against the tight bundle of nerves at her core.

She writhed against him, her body on fire for him. "I need… I want…"

"Tell me, Lucy Ann," he said between kisses and nips, tasting along her neck, "tell me what you want."

She didn't even know what would settle out their lives or how to untangle the mess they'd made of their world.

Not to mention their emotions. "Right now, I just need you inside me."

"That's not what I meant." He held her with those mesmerizing green eyes, familiar eyes that had been a part of her life for as long as she could remember.

"Shh, don't ruin this." She pressed two fingers to his lips. She didn't want to risk their conversation leading down a dangerous path as it had eleven months ago.

Even thinking about their fight chilled her. That argument had led to the most painful time in her life, the time without the best friend she'd ever had. They couldn't go that route again. They had Eli to consider.

And as for their own feelings?

She shied away from those thoughts, determined to live in the moment. She shifted to reach in the bedside table drawer for another condom. He plucked it from between her fingers and sheathed himself quickly, efficiently, before positioning her over him again. Slowly, carefully—blissfully—she lowered herself onto him, taking the length of him inside her until he touched just… the right…spot.

Yessss.

Her eyelids grew heavy but the way he searched her face compelled her to keep her eyes open, to stare back at him as she rolled her hips to meet his thrusts. Every stroke sent ripples of pleasure tingling through her as they synced up into a perfect rhythm. Her palms flattened against his chest, her fingers digging into the bunched muscles twitching under her touch. A purr of feminine satisfaction whispered free as she reveled in the fact that she made him feel every bit as out of control as he made her feel.

His hands dug into her hips then eased, caressing up her sides then forward to cup her breasts. She sighed at the gentle rasp of his callused fingers touching her so instinctively, his thumbs gliding over nipples until she feared she would come apart now. Too soon. She ached for this to last, to hang on to the blissful forgetfulness they could find in each other's arms. She flowed forward to cover him, moving slower, holding back.

Elliot's arms slid around her, and he drew her earlobe between his teeth. Just an earlobe. Yet her whole body tensed up with that final bit of sensation that sent her hurtling into fulfillment. Her nails dug into his shoulders, and she cried out as her release crested.

He rolled her over, and she pushed back, tumbling them again until the silver tray went crashing to the floor, the twang of pewter plates clanking. He kissed her hard, taking her cries of completion into his mouth. As orgasm gripped her again and again, his arms twitched around her, his body pulsing, his groans mingling with hers until she melted in the aftermath.

Panting, she lay beside him, her leg hitched over his hip, an arm draped over him. Her whole body was limp from exhaustion. She barely registered him pulling the comforter over her again.

Maybe they could make this friendship work, friendship combined with amazing sex. Being apart hadn't made either of them happy.

Could this be enough? Friendship and sex? Could they learn to trust each other again as they once had?

They had the rest of the month together to figure out the details. If only they could have sex until they couldn't think about the future.

His breath settled into an even pattern with a soft snore. What a time to realize she'd never slept with him before. She'd seen him nap plenty of times, falling asleep with a book on his chest, but never once had she stayed through the night with him.

For now, it was best she keep it that way. No matter how tempted she was to indulge herself, she wouldn't make the mistakes of her past again. Not with Eli to think about.

Careful not to wake her generous, sexy lover, she eased from the bed, tiptoeing around the scattered cutlery and dishes that looked a lot like the disjointed parts of her life. Beautiful pieces, but such a jumbled mess there was no way to put everything back together.

"Lucy Ann?" Elliot called in a groggy voice. He reached out for her. "Come back to bed."

She pulled on her red wraparound dress and tied it quickly before gathering her underwear. "I need to go to Eli. I'll see you in the morning."

Her bra and panties in her hand, she raced from his room and tried to convince herself she wasn't making an even bigger mess of her life by running like a coward.

"Welcome to Monte Carlo, Eli," Elliot said to his son, carrying the baby in the crook of his arm, walking the floor with his cranky child while everyone else slept. He'd heard Eli squawk and managed to scoop him up before Lucy Ann woke.

But then she was sprawled out on her bed, looking dead to the world after their trip to Monte Carlo—with a colicky kid.

The day had been so busy with travel, he hadn't had a chance to speak to Lucy Ann alone. But then she hadn't gone out of her way to make that possible, either. If he hadn't known better, he would have thought she was hiding from him.

Only there was no reason for her to do so. The sex

last night had been awesome. They hadn't argued. Hell, he didn't know what was wrong, but her silence today couldn't be missed.

Compounding matters, Eli had become progressively irritable as the day passed. By the time his private plane had landed in Monte Carlo, Elliot was ready to call a doctor. Lucy Ann and the nanny had both reassured him that Eli was simply suffering from gas and exhaustion over having his routine disrupted.

Of course that only proved Lucy Ann's point that a child shouldn't be living on the road, but damn it all, Elliot wasn't ready to admit defeat. Especially not after last night. He and Lucy Ann were so close to connecting again.

He'd hoped Monte Carlo would go a long way toward scoring points in his campaign. He owned a place here. A home with friends who lived in the area. Sure it was a condominium and his friend owned a casino. But his friend was a dad already. And the flat was spacious, with a large garden terrace. He would have to add some kind of safety feature to the railing before Eli became mobile. He scanned the bachelor pad with new eyes and he saw a million details in a different light. Rather than fat leather sofas and heavy wooden antiques, he saw sharp edges and climbing hazards.

"What do you think, Eli?" he asked his son, staring down into the tiny features all scrunched up and angry. "Are you feeling any better? I'm thinking it may be time for you to eat, but I hate to wake your mama. What do you say I get you one of those bottles with expressed milk?"

Eli blinked back up at him with wide eyes, his fists and feet pumping.

He'd always thought babies all looked the same, like

tiny old men. Except now he knew he could pick out Eli from dozens of other babies in a heartbeat.

How strange to see parts of himself and Lucy Ann mixed together in that tiny face. Yet the longer he looked, the more that mixture became just Eli. The kid had only been in his life for a week. Yet now there didn't seem to be a pre-Eli time. Any thoughts prior to seeing him were now colored by the presence of him. As if he had somehow already existed on some plane just waiting to make an appearance.

Eli's face scrunched up tighter in that sign he was about to scream bloody murder. Elliot tucked his son against his shoulder and patted his back while walking to the fridge to get one of the bottles he'd seen Lucy Ann store there.

He pulled it out, started to give it to his son...then remembered something about cold bottles not being good. He hadn't paid a lot of attention when his friends took care of baby stuff, but something must have permeated his brain. Enough so that he tugged his cell phone from his pocket and thumbed speed dial for his buddy Conrad Hughes. He always stayed up late. Conrad had said once that life as a casino magnate had permanently adjusted his internal clock.

The phone rang only once. "This is Hughes. Speak to me, Elliot."

"I need advice."

"Sure, financial? Work? Name it."

"Um, babies." He stared at the baby and the bottle on the marble slab counter. Life had definitely changed. "Maybe you should put Jayne on the line."

"I'm insulted," Conrad joked, casino bells and music drifting over the airwaves. "Ask your question. Besides, Jayne's asleep. Worn out from the kiddo."

"The nanny's sick and Lucy Ann really needs to sleep in." He swayed from side to side. "She's been trying to keep up with her work, the baby, the traveling."

"And your question?"

"Oh, right. I forgot. Sleep deprivation's kicking in, I think," he admitted, not that he would say a word to Lucy Ann after the way she was freaking out over him having a wreck.

"Happens to the best of us, brother. You were just the last man to fall."

"Back to my question. When I give the baby a bottle of this breast milk from the refrigerator, do I heat it in the microwave? And I swear if you laugh, I'm going to kick your ass later."

"I'm only laughing on the inside. Never out loud." Conrad didn't have to laugh. Amusement drenched his words.

"I can live with that." As long as he got the advice.

"Run warm water over the bottle. No microwave. Do not heat it in water on the stove," Conrad rattled off like a pro. "If he doesn't eat it all, pour it out. You can't save and reuse it. Oh, and shake it up."

"You're too good at this," Elliot couldn't resist saying as he turned on the faucet.

"Practice."

"This has to be the strangest conversation of my life." He played his fingers through the water to test the temperature and found it was warming quickly. He tucked the bottled milk underneath the spewing faucet with one hand, still holding his son to his shoulder with the other.

"It'll be commonplace before you know it."

Would it? "I hope so."

The sound of casino bells softened, as if Conrad had

gone into another room. "What about you and Lucy Ann?"

Elliot weighed his answer carefully before saying simply, "We're together."

"Together-together?" Conrad asked.

Elliot glanced through the living area at the closed bedroom door and the baby in his arms. "I'm working on it."

"You've fallen for her." His friend made it more of a statement than a question.

So why couldn't he bring himself to simply agree? "Lucy Ann and I have been best friends all our lives. We have chemistry."

Best friends. His brothers all called themselves best friends, but now he realized he'd never quite paired up with a best bud the way they all had. He was a part of the group. But Lucy Ann was his best friend, always had been.

"You'd better come up with a smoother answer than that if you ever get around to proposing to her. Women expect more than 'you're a great friend and we're super together in the sack.'"

Proposing? The word *marriage* hadn't crossed his mind, and he realized now that it should have. He should have led with that from the start. He should have been an honorable, stand-up kind of guy and offered her a ring rather than a month-long sex fest.

"I'm not that much of an idiot."

He hoped.

"So you are thinking about proposing."

He was now. The notion fit neatly in his brain, like the missing piece to a puzzle he'd been trying to complete since Lucy Ann left a year ago.

"I want my son to have a family, and I want Lucy Ann to be happy." He turned off the water and felt the bottle. Seemed warm. He shook it as instructed. "I'm just not sure I know how to make that happen. Not many long-term role models for happily ever after on my family tree."

"Marriage is work, no question." Conrad whistled softly on a long exhale. "I screwed up my own pretty bad once, so maybe I'm not the right guy to ask for advice."

Conrad and Jayne had been separated for three years before reuniting.

"But you fixed your marriage. So you're probably the best person to ask." Elliot was getting into this whole mentor notion. Why hadn't he thought to seek out some help before? He took his son and the bottle back into the living room of his bachelor pad, now strewn with baby gear. "How do you make it right when you've messed up this bad? When you've let so much time pass?"

"Grovel," Conrad said simply.

"That's it?" Elliot asked incredulously, dropping into his favorite recliner. He settled his son in the crook of his arm and tucked the bottle in his mouth. "That's your advice? Grovel?"

"It's not just a word. You owe her for being a jackass this past year. Like I said before. Relationships are work, man. Hard work. Tougher than any Interpol assignment old headmaster Colonel Salvatore could ever give us. But the payoff is huge if you can get it right."

"I hope so."

"Hey, I gotta go. Text just came in. Kid's awake and Jayne doesn't believe in nighttime nannies. So we're in the walking dead stage of parenthood right now." He didn't sound at all unhappy about it. "Don't forget. Shake the milk and burp the kid if you want to keep your suit clean."

Shake. Burp. Grovel. "I won't forget."

Lucy Ann blinked at the morning sun piercing the slight part in her curtains. She'd slept in this room in Elliot's posh Monte Carlo digs more times than she could remember. He'd even had her choose her own decor since they spent a lot of off-season time here, too.

She'd chosen an über-feminine French toile in pinks and raspberries, complete with an ornate white bed—Renaissance antiques. And the best of the best mattresses. She stretched, luxuriating in the well-rested feeling, undoubtedly a by-product of the awesome bed and even more incredible sex. She couldn't remember how long it had been since she'd woken up refreshed rather than dragging, exhausted. Certainly not since Eli had been born—

Blinking, she took in the morning sun, then gasped. "Eli!"

She jumped from the bed and raced over to the portable crib Elliot had ordered set up in advance. Had her baby slept through the night? She looked in the crib and found it empty. Her heart lurched up to her throat.

Her bare feet slipping on the hardwood floor, she raced out to the living room and stopped short. Elliot sat in his favorite recliner, holding their son. He looked so at ease with the baby cradled in the crook of his arm. An empty bottle sat on the table beside them.

Elliot toyed with his son's foot. "I have plans for you, little man. There are so many books to read. *Gulliver's Travels* and *Lord of the Rings* were favorites of mine as a kid. And we'll play with Matchbox cars when you're older. Or maybe you'll like trains or airplanes? Your choice."

Relaxing, Lucy Ann sagged against the door frame in relief. "You're gender stereotyping our child."

Glancing up, Elliot smiled at her, so handsome with a five o'clock shadow peppering his jaw and baby spit-up dotting his shoulder it was all she could do not to kiss him.

"Good morning, beautiful," he said, his eyes sliding over her silky nightshirt with an appreciation that all but mentally pulled the gown right off her. "Eli can be a chef or whatever he wants, as long as he's happy."

"Glad to hear you say that." She padded barefoot across the room and sat on the massive tapestry otto-man between the sofa and chairs. "I can't believe I slept in so late this morning."

"Eli and I managed just fine. And if I ran into prob-lems, I had plenty of backup."

"I concede you chose well with the nanny." She wasn't used to taking help with Eli, but she could get addicted to this kind of assistance quickly. "Mrs. Clayworth's amaz-ing and a great help without being intrusive."

"You're not upset that I didn't wake you?"

She swept her tangled hair back over her shoulders. "I can't think any mother of an infant would be upset over an extra two hours of sleep."

"Glad you're happy, Sleeping Beauty." His heated gaze slid over the satin clinging to her breasts.

"Ah, your fairy-tale romancing theme."

He arched an eyebrow. "You catch on fast. If you were to stay with me for the whole racing season, we could play Aladdin and his lamp."

His talk of the future made her…uncomfortable. She was just getting used to the shift in their relationship, adding a sexual level on a day-to-day basis. So she ig-nored the part about staying longer and focused on the fairy tale. "You've been fantasizing about me as a belly dancer?"

"Now that you mention it…"

"Lucky for us both, I'm rested and ready." She curled her toes into the hand-knotted silk Persian rug that would one day be littered with toys. "You're going to be a wonderful father."

As the words fell from her mouth she knew them to be true, not a doubt in her mind. And somehow she'd slid into talking about the future anyway.

"Well, I sure as hell learned a lot from my father about how not to be a dad." His gaze fell away from her and back to their child. "And the things I didn't learn, I intend to find out, even if that means taking a class or reading every parenting book on the shelves since I never had much of a role model."

Clearly, he was worried about this. She leaned forward to touch his knee. "Does that mean I'm doomed to be a crummy mother?"

"Of course not." He covered her hand with his. "Okay, I see your point. And thanks for the vote of confidence."

"For what it's worth, I do think you've had a very good role model." She linked fingers with him. "The colonel. Your old headmaster has been there for you, the way my aunt has for me. Doing the best they could within a flawed system that sent them broken children to fix."

"I don't like to think of myself as broken." His jaw clenched.

"It's okay, you know—" she rubbed his knee "—to be sad or angry about the past."

"It's a lot easier to just speed around the track, even smash into walls, rather than rage at the world." His throat moved with a long swallow.

"I'm not so sure I like that coping mechanism. I would

be so sad if anything happened to you." And wasn't that the understatement of the year? She had to admit, though, she'd been worrying more about him lately, fearing the distractions she brought to his life, also fearing he might have beat the odds one time too many.

He squeezed her hand, his eyes as serious as she'd ever seen them. "I would quit racing. For you."

"And I would never ask you to do that. Not for me."

"So you would ask for Eli?"

She churned his question around in her mind, unable to come up with an answer that didn't involve a lengthy discussion of the future.

"I think this is entirely too serious a conversation before I've had breakfast."

Scooping up her son from Elliot's arms, she made tracks for the kitchen, unable to deny the truth. Even though she stayed in the condo, she was running from him now every bit as much as she'd run eleven months ago.

Ten

Steering through the narrow streets of Monte Carlo, Elliot drove his new Mercedes S65 AMG along the cliff road leading to the Hughes mansion. His Maserati wouldn't hold a baby seat, so he'd needed a sedan that combined space and safety with his love of finely tuned automobiles. He felt downright domesticated driving Lucy Ann and their son to a lunch with friends. She was meeting with Jayne Hughes and Jayne's baby girl while he went over to the track.

Last time he'd traveled this winding road, he'd been driving Jayne and Conrad to the hospital—Conrad had been too much of a mess to climb behind the wheel of his SUV. Jayne had been in labor. She'd delivered their baby girl seventeen minutes after they'd arrived at the hospital.

How strange to think he knew more about his friend's first kid coming into the world than he knew about the birth of his own son.

His fingers clenched around the steering wheel as they wound up a cliff-side road overlooking the sea. "Tell me about the day Eli was born."

"Are you asking me because you're angry or because you want to know?"

A good question. It wouldn't help to say both probably came into play, so he opted for, "I will always regret that I wasn't there when he came into this world, that I missed out on those first days of his life. But I understand that if we're going to move forward here, I can't let that eat at me. We both are going to have to give a little here. So the answer to your question is, I want to know because I'm curious about all things relating to Eli."

She touched his knee lightly. "Thank you for being honest."

"That's the only way we're going to get through this, don't you think?"

He glanced over at her quickly, taking in the beautiful lines of her face with the sunlight streaming through the window.

Why had it taken him so long to notice?

"Okay…" She inhaled a shaky breath. "I had an appointment the week of my due date. I really expected to go longer since so many first-time moms go overdue. But the doctor was concerned about Eli's heart rate. He did an ultrasound and saw the placenta was separating from the uterine wall— Am I getting too gross for you here?"

"Keep talking," he commanded, hating that he hadn't been there to make things easier, less frightening for her. If he hadn't been so pigheaded, he would have been there to protect her. Assure her.

"The doctor scheduled me for an immediate cesarean section. I didn't even get to go home for my toothbrush," she joked in an attempt to lighten the mood.

He wasn't laughing. "That had to be scary for you. I wish I could have been with you. We helped each other through a lot of tough times over the years."

"I did try to call you," she confessed softly, "right before I went in. But your phone went straight to voice mail. I tried after, too...I assumed you were off on an Interpol secret 'walkabout' for Colonel Salvatore."

"I was." He'd done the math in his head. Knew the case he'd been working at the time.

"I know I could have pushed harder and found you." She shook her head regretfully. "I didn't even leave a message. I'm so sorry for that. You may be able to move past it, but I'm not sure I'll ever forgive myself."

He stayed silent, not sure what to say to make this right for both of them.

"What would we have done if Malcolm and Conrad hadn't kidnapped you from the bachelor party?"

Damn good question. "I like to think I would have come to my senses and checked on you. I don't know how the hell I let eleven months pass."

"Or how you found a fiancée so fast," she blurted out. "You proposed to another woman barely three months after we slept together. Yes, that's a problem for me."

He weighed his words carefully. "This may sound strange, but Gianna was the one who got shortchanged. I obviously didn't care about her the way I should have. I wasn't fair to her."

Her smile was tight. "Excuse me if I'm not overly concerned about being fair to Gianna. And from what I read in the news, she broke things off with you. Not the other way around. If she hadn't left, would you have married her?"

Stunned, he downshifted around a corner. She'd read about his breakup? She'd left, but kept tabs on him. If only he'd done the same with her, he would have known about Eli. As much as Elliot wanted to blame a remote Interpol stint for keeping him out of touch, he knew he should have followed up with Lucy Ann.

Then why hadn't he? She'd been so good to him, always there for him, always forgiving him. Damn it, he didn't deserve her— Could that have been part of why he'd stayed away? Out of guilt for taking so much from her all their lives?

That she could think he still wanted Gianna, especially after what he and Lucy Ann had just shared... Incomprehensible.

"No. I didn't want to marry her. We broke off the engagement. I knew it was inevitable. She just spoke first."

She nodded tightly. "Fine, I appreciate your honesty. I'm still not totally okay with the fact that you raced right back to her after we... Well, I'm just not okay with it. But I'm working on it."

Conrad had told him to grovel. Elliot scrounged inside himself for a way to give her what she needed.

"Fair enough. At least I know where I stand with you." He stared at the road ahead, struggling. Groveling was tougher than he'd expected after the way his father had beaten him to his knees so many times. "That was the hardest part about growing up with my old man. The uncertainty. I'm not saying it would have been okay if he'd punched me on a regular basis. But the sick feeling in my gut as I tried to gauge his moods? That was a crappy way to live."

"I'm so sorry." Her hand fell to rest on his knee again. This time she didn't pull away.

"I know. You saved my sanity back then." He placed his hand over hers. "I always knew it was you who let the air out of my dad's tires that time in sixth grade."

She sat upright. "How did you know?"

"Because you did it while I was away on that science fair trip. So I couldn't be blamed or catch the brunt of his anger." He rubbed her hand along the spot on her finger where he should have put a ring already. "Do I have the details correct?"

"That was the idea. Couldn't have your father get away with everything."

"He didn't. Not in the end." There'd never been a chance to make peace with his bastard of an old man—never a chance to confront him, either.

"I guess there's a sad sort of poetic justice that he died in a bar fight while you were off at reform school."

Her words surprised him. "You're a bloodthirsty one."

"When it comes to protecting the people in my life? Absolutely."

She was freaking amazing. He couldn't deny the rush of admiration for the woman she'd become—that she'd always been, just hidden under the weight of her own problems.

And on the heels of that thought, more guilt piled on top of him for all the ways he'd let her down. Damn it all, he had to figure out how to make this right with her. He had to pull out all the stops as Conrad advised.

Full throttle.

He had to win her over to be his wife.

Lucy Ann sat on the terrace with Jayne Hughes, wondering how a woman who'd been separated for three years could now be such a happily contented wife and new mother. What was her secret? How had they overcome the odds?

There was no denying the peaceful air that radiated off the bombshell blonde with her baby girl cradled in a sling. The Hughes family split their time between their home in Monte Carlo and a home in Africa, where Jayne worked as a nurse at a free clinic her husband funded along with another Alpha Brother. She made it all look effortless whether she was serving up luncheon on fine china or cracking open a boxed lunch under a sprawling shea butter tree.

Lucy Ann patted her colicky son on his precious little back. He seemed to have settled to sleep draped over her knees, which wasn't particularly comfortable, but she wasn't budging an inch as long as he was happy.

Jayne paused in her lengthy ramble about the latest addition to the pediatrics wing at the clinic to tug something from under the plate of petits fours. "Oh, I almost forgot to give you this pamphlet for Elliot."

"For Elliot?" She took it from Jayne, the woman's short nails hinting at her more practical side. "On breast-feeding?"

"He called Conrad with questions the other night." She adjusted her daughter to the other breast in such a smooth transition the cloth baby sling covered all. "I don't know why he didn't just look it up on Google. Anyhow, this should tell him everything he needs to know."

"Thank you." She tucked the pamphlet in her purse, careful not to disturb her son. "He didn't tell me he called your husband for help."

"He was probably too embarrassed. Men can be proud that way." She sipped her ice water, sun glinting off the Waterford crystal that Lucy Ann recalled choosing for a wedding gift to the couple.

There'd been a time when tasks like that—picking out expensive trinkets for Elliot's wealthy friends—had made her nervous. As if the wrong crystal pattern could call her out as an interloper in Elliot Starc's elegant world.

But it had taken walking away from the glitz and glamour to help her see it for what it really was…superficial trappings that didn't mean a lot in the long run. Lucy Ann was far more impressed with Jayne's nursing capabilities and her motherhood savvy than with what kind of place setting graced her table.

"There's a lot to learn about parenting," Lucy Ann acknowledged. "Especially for someone who didn't grow up around other kids." She would have been overwhelmed without Aunt Carla's help.

And wasn't it funny to think that, even though she'd traveled the globe with Elliot for a decade, she'd still learned the most important things back home in South Carolina?

"I think it's wonderful that he's trying. A lot of men would just dump all the tough stuff onto a nanny." Jayne shot a glance over her shoulder through the open balcony doors, somehow knowing Conrad had arrived without even looking.

"I just suggested that it wouldn't hurt to let someone else change the diapers," said Mr. Tall, Dark and Brooding. "Who the hell wants to change a diaper? That doesn't make me a bad human being."

Lucy Ann had to admit, "He has a point."

Jayne set her glass down. "Don't encourage him."

Conrad chuckled as he reached for his daughter. "Lucy Ann, let me know when you're done. I promised Elliot I would drive you and the kidlet back to the condo. He said he's running late at the track. Have fun, ladies. The princess and I are going to read the *Wall Street Journal*."

Conrad disappeared back into the house with his daughter, words about stocks and short sales carrying on the wind spoken in a singsong tone as if telling her a nursery rhyme.

Lucy Ann leaned back in the chair and turned her water glass on the table, watching the sunlight refracting prisms off the cut crystal. "I envy your tight-knit support group. Elliot and I didn't have a lot of friends when we were growing up. He was the kid always in trouble so parents didn't invite him over. And I was too shy to make friends."

"You're not shy anymore," Jayne pointed out.

"Not that I let people see."

"We've known you for years. I would hope you could consider us your friends, too."

They'd known each other, but she'd been Elliot's employee. It wasn't that his friends had deliberately excluded her, but Conrad had been separated for years, and only recently had the rest of them started marrying. She knew it would be easier for all of them if she made the effort here.

"We'll certainly cross paths because of Eli," Lucy Ann said simply.

"And Elliot?"

The conversation was starting to get too personal for her comfort. "We're still working on that."

"But you're making progress."

"Have you been reading the tabloids?"

"I don't bother with those." Jayne waved dismissively. "I saw the way you two looked at each other when Elliot dropped you off."

In spite of herself, Lucy Ann found herself aching to talk to someone after all, and Jayne seemed the best candidate. "He's into the thrill of the chase right now. Things will go back to normal eventually."

"I'm not so sure I agree. He seems different to me." Jayne's pensive look faded into a grin. "They all have to grow up and settle down sometime."

"What about—" She didn't feel comfortable discussing the guys' Interpol work out in the open, so she simply said, "Working with the colonel after graduation and following a call to right bigger wrongs? How do they give that up to be regular family guys?"

"Good question." Jayne pinched the silver tongs to shuffle a petit four and fruit onto a dessert plate. "Some still take an active part once they're married, but once the children start coming, things do change. They shift to pulling the strings. They become more like Salvatore."

"Mine is a bit wilder than yours." When had she started thinking of Elliot as *hers*? Although on some level he'd been hers since they were children. "I mean, seriously, he crashes cars into walls for a living."

"You've known that about him from the start. So why are things different now?"

"I don't know how to reconcile our friendship with everything else that's happened." The whole "friends with benefits" thing was easier said than done.

"By 'everything else' you mean the smoking hot sex, of course." Jayne grinned impishly before popping a grape in her mouth.

"I had forgotten how outspoken you can be."

"Comes with the territory of loving men like these. They don't always perceive subtleties."

True enough. Lucy Ann speared a chocolate strawberry and willed herself not to blush at the heated memories the fruit evoked. "Outspoken or not, I'm still no closer to an answer."

Jayne nudged the gold-rimmed china plate aside and leaned her arms on the table. "You don't have to reconcile the two ways of being. It's already done—or it will be once you stop fighting."

Could Jayne be right? Maybe the time had come to

truly give him a chance. To see if he was right. To see if they could really have a fairy-tale life together.

Fear knotted her gut, but Lucy Ann wasn't the shy little girl anymore. She was a confident woman and she was all-in.

Elliot shrugged out of his black leather jacket with a wince as he stepped into the dark apartment. He'd done his prelim runs as always, checklists complete, car scrutinized to the last detail, and yet somehow he'd damn near wiped out on a practice run.

Every muscle in his body ached from reactionary tensing. Thank goodness Lucy Ann hadn't been there as she would have been in the past as his assistant. He didn't want her worrying. He didn't want to risk a confrontation.

He tossed the jacket over his arm, walking carefully so he wouldn't wake anyone up. His foot hooked on something in the dark. He bit back a curse and looked down to find…a book? He reached to pick up an ornately bound copy of *Hansel and Gretel*. He started to stand up again and looked ahead to find a trail of books, all leading toward his bedroom. He picked up one book after the other, each a different fairy tale, until he pushed open his door.

His room was empty.

Frowning, he scanned the space and… "Aha…"

More books led to the bathroom, and now that he listened, he could hear the shower running. He set the stack on the chest of drawers and gathered up the last few "crumbs" on his trail, a copy of *Rapunzel* and a Victorian version of *Rumpelstiltskin*. Pushing his way slowly into the bathroom, he smiled at the shadowy outline behind the foggy glass wall. The multiple showerheads shot spray over Lucy Ann as she hummed. She didn't seem to notice he'd arrived.

He peeled off his clothes without making a sound and padded barefoot into the slate-tiled space. He opened the door and stepped into the steam. Lucy Ann stopped singing, but she didn't turn around. The only acknowledgment she gave to his arrival was a hand reaching for him. He linked fingers with her and stepped under the warm jets. The heat melted away the stress from his muscles, allowing a new tension to take hold. He saw the condom packet in the soap dish and realized just how thoroughly she'd thought this through.

He pressed against her back, wrapping his arms around her. Already, his erection throbbed hard and ready, pressed between them.

He sipped water from just behind her ear. "I'm trying to think of what fairy tale you're fantasizing about, and for water, I can only come up with the *Frog Prince*."

Angling her head to give him better access to her neck, she combed her fingers over his damp hair. "We're writing our own fantasy tonight."

Growling his approval, he slicked his hands over her, taking in the feel of her breasts peaking against his palms. His blood fired hotter through his veins than the water sluicing over them. He slipped a hand between her thighs, stroking satin, finding that sweet bundle of nerves. Banding his arm tighter around her waist, he continued to circle and tease, feeling her arousal lubricate his touch. She sagged back against him, her legs parting to give him easier access.

With her bottom nestled against him, he held on to control by a thread. Each roll of her hips as she milked the most from her pleasure threatened to send him over the edge. But he held back his own release, giving her hers. He tucked two fingers inside her, his thumb still working along that pebbled tightness.

Her sighs and purrs filled the cubicle, the jasmine scent of her riding the steam. Every sound of her impending arousal shot a bolt of pleasure through him, his blood pounding thicker through his veins. Until, yes, she cried out, coming apart in his arms. Her fingernails dug deep into his thighs, cutting half-moons into his flesh as she arched into her orgasm.

He savored every shiver of bliss rippling her body until he couldn't wait any longer. He took the condom from the soap tray and sheathed himself. He pressed her against the shower stall wall, her palms flattened to the stone. Standing behind her, he nudged her legs apart and angled until... He slid home, deep inside her, clamped by damp silken walls as hot and moist as the shower.

Sensation engulfed him, threatened to shake the ground under him as he pushed inside her again and again. Things moved so damn fast... He was so close... Then he heard the sound of her unraveling in his arms. The echoes of her release sent him over the edge. Ecstasy rocked his balance. He flattened a hand against the warm wall to keep from falling over as his completion pulsed until his heartbeat pounded in his ears. Shifting, he pulled out of her, keeping one arm around her.

Slowly, his world expanded beyond just the two of them, and he became aware of the water sheeting over them. The patter of droplets hitting the door and floor.

Tucking her close again, he thought about his near miss at the track today and all the relationship advice from his friends. He'd waited too long these past eleven months to make sure she stayed with him. Permanently. He wouldn't let another minute pass without moving forward with their lives.

He nuzzled her ear. "What kind of house do you want?"

"House?" she asked, her knees buckling.

He steadied her. "I want to build a real house for us, Lucy Ann. Not just condos or rented places here and there."

"Umm…" She licked her lips. The beads on her temple mingled perspiration with water. "What city would you choose?"

He had penthouse suites around the world, but nowhere he stayed long enough to call home. And none of them had the room for a boy to run and play.

"I need a home. We need a home for our son."

"You keep assuming we'll stay together."

Already his proposal was going astray. Could be because most of the blood in his brain was surging south. "Where do you want to live? I'll build two houses next door if that's the way you want it." Living near each other would give him more time to win her over, because he was fast realizing he couldn't give her up. "I have connections with a friend who restores historic homes."

She turned in his arms, pressing her fingers to his lips. "Can we just keep making love instead?"

Banding her wrist in his hand, he kissed it, determined not to let this chance slip away, not to let *her* slip away again. "Let's get married."

She leaned into him, whispering against his mouth as she stroked down between them, molding her palm to the shape of him. "You may have missed the memo…" She caressed up and down, again and again. "But you don't have to propose to get me to sleep with you."

He angled away, staring straight in her eyes, her eyelashes spiky wet. "I'm not joking, so I would appreciate it if you took my proposal seriously."

"Really? Now?" She stepped back, the water showering between them. "You mean this. For Eli, of course."

"Of course Eli factors into the equation." He studied her carefully blank expression. "But it's also because you and I fit as a couple on so many levels. We've been friends forever, and our chemistry... Well, that speaks for itself. We just have to figure out how not to fight afterward and we'll have forever locked and loaded."

The more he talked, the more it felt right.

"Forever?" Her knees folded, and she sat on the stone seat in the corner, her hair dripping water. "Do you think that's even possible for people like you and me?"

"Why shouldn't it be?" He knelt in front of her.

"Because of our pasts." She stroked over his wet hair, cupping his neck, her eyes so bittersweet they tore him to bits. "Our parents. Our own histories. I refuse to spend the rest of my life wondering when the next Gianna is going to walk through the door."

Gianna? He hadn't even thought of her other than when Lucy Ann mentioned her. But looking back, he realized how bad his engagement would have looked to her, how that must have played a role in her keeping quiet about the pregnancy.

This was likely where the groveling came in. "I'm sorry."

"For which part? The engagement? Or the fact you didn't contact me— Hell, forget I said that." She leaned forward to kiss him.

If they kissed, the discussion would be over, opportunity missed. He scooped her up in his arms and pivoted, settling her into his lap as he sat on the stone seat in the corner.

She squawked in protest but he pressed on. "You expected me to follow you? Even after you said—and I quote—'I don't ever want to lay eyes on your irresponsible ass ever again'?"

"And you've never said anything in the heat of the moment that you regretted later?"

Groveling was all well and good, but he wasn't taking the full blame for what shook down these past months. "If you regretted those words, it sure would have been helpful if you'd let me know."

"This is my whole point. We're both so proud, neither one of us could take the steps needed to repair the damage we did. Yes, I am admitting that we both were hurt. Even though you seemed to recover fast with Gianna—" she gave him that tight smile again "—I acknowledge that losing our friendship hurt you, as well. But friendship isn't enough to build a marriage on. So can we please go back to the friends-with-benefits arrangement?"

"Damn it, Lucy Ann—"

She traced his face with her fingers. "Do you know what I think?" She didn't wait for him to answer. "I think you don't believe in fairy tales after all. The dates, the romance... It has actually been a game for you after all. A challenge, a competition. Something to win. Not Cinderella or Sleeping Beauty."

"I suspect I've been led into a trap." He'd thought he'd been following all the right signs and taking the steps to fix this, but he'd only seemed to dig a bigger hole for himself.

"Well, you followed my bread crumbs." Her joke fell flat between them, her eyes so much sadder than he'd ever dreamed he could make them.

"So you're sure you don't want to marry me?"

She hesitated, her pulse leaping in her neck. "I'm sure I don't want you to propose to me."

Her rejection stunned him. Somehow he'd expected her to say yes. He'd thought... Hell, he'd taken her for granted all over again and he didn't know how to fix this. Not now. He needed time to regroup. "If I agree to stop pressing for marriage, can we keep having incredible sex with each other?"

"'Til the end of the month."

"Sex for a few weeks? You're okay with sleeping together with an exit strategy already in place?"

"That's my offer." She slid from his lap, stepping back. Away. Putting distance between them on more than just one level. "Take it or leave it."

"Lucy Ann, I'm happy as hell to take you again and again until we're both too exhausted to argue." Although right now, he couldn't deny it. He wanted more from her. "But eventually we're going to have to talk."

Eleven

Lucy sprawled on top of Elliot in bed, satiated, groggy and almost dry from their shower, but not ready for their evening together to end. Elliot seemed content to let the proposal discussion go—for tonight. So this could well be the last uncomplicated chance she had to be with him.

The ceiling fan *click, click, clicked* away their precious remaining seconds together, the lights of Monaco glittering through the open French doors, the Cote d'Azur providing a breathtaking vista. Who wouldn't want to share this life with him? Why couldn't she just accept his proposal? She hated how his offer of marriage made her clench her gut in fear. She should be happy. Celebrating. This would be the easy answer to bringing up Eli together. They were best friends. Incredible lovers. Why not go with the flow? They could take a day to see Cannes with the baby, and she could snap pictures…savor the things she'd been too busy to notice in the early years of traveling with Elliot.

Yet something held her back. She couldn't push the word *yes* free. Every time she tried, her throat closed up. She trusted him...yet the thought of reliving the past eleven months again, of living without him...

Her fingers glided along his closely shorn hair. "You could have been killed that day your hair got singed."

"You're not going to get rid of me that easily," he said with a low chuckle and a stroke down her spine.

Ice chilled the blood in her veins at his words. "That wasn't funny."

"I'm just trying to lighten the mood." He angled back to kiss the tip of her nose, then look into her eyes. "I'm okay, Lucy Ann. Not a scratch on me that day."

She'd been in South Carolina when it had happened, her belly swelling with his child and her heart heavy with the decision of when to tell him about the baby. "That doesn't make it any less terrifying."

He grinned smugly. "You do care."

"Of course I care what happens to you. I always have. There's no denying our history, our friendship, how well we know each other." How could he doubt that, no matter what else they'd been through? "But I know something else. You're only interested in me now because I'm telling you no. You don't like being the one left behind."

Breathlessly, she finished her rant, stunned at herself. Her mouth had been ahead of her brain. She hadn't even realized she felt that way until the words came rolling out.

"That's not a very nice thing to say," he said tightly.

"But is it true?" She cupped his face.

He pulled her hands down gently and kissed both palms. "I already offered to stop racing. I meant it. I'm a father now and I understand that comes with responsibilities."

Responsibilities? Is that what they were to him? But then, in a way, that's what she'd always been since he got out of reform school, since he'd offered her a job as his assistant even though at the time she hadn't been qualified for the job. He'd given it to her out of friendship—and, yes, the sense of obligation they felt to look out for each other.

That had been enough for a long time, more than either of them had gotten from anyone else in their lives. But right now with her heart in her throat, obligation didn't feel like nearly enough to build a life on.

She slid off him, the cooling breeze from the fan chilling her bared flesh. "Do whatever you want."

"What did I say wrong? You want me to quit and I offer and now you're angry?"

"I didn't say I want you to quit." She opted for the simpler answer. "I understand how important your career is to you. You have a competitive nature and that's not a bad thing. It's made you an incredibly successful man."

"You mentioned my competitiveness earlier. Lucy Ann, that's not why I—"

She rolled to her side and pressed her fingers to his mouth before he could get back to the proposal subject again. "You've channeled your edginess and your drive to win. That's not a bad thing." She tapped his bottom lip. "Enough talk. You should rest up now so you're focused for the race."

And so she could escape to her room, away from the building temptation to take what he offered and worry about the consequences later. Except with Elliot's muscled arm draped over her waist, she couldn't quite bring herself to move out of his embrace. His hand moved along her back soothingly. Slowly, her body began to relax, melting into the fantastic mattress.

"Lucy Ann? You're right, you know." Elliot's words were so low she almost didn't hear him.

"Right about what?" she asked, groggy, almost asleep.

"I like to win— Wait. Scratch that. I *need* to win."

Opening her eyes, she didn't move, just stared at his chest and listened. There was no escaping this conversation. Wherever it led them.

"There are two kinds of people in the world. Ones who have known physical pain and those who never will. Being beaten…" He swallowed hard, his heart hammering so loudly she could feel her pulse sync up with his, racing, knowing just what that word *beating* meant to him growing up. "That does something to your soul. Changes you. You can heal. You can move on. But you're forever changed by that moment you finally break, crying for it to stop."

His voice stayed emotionless, but what he said sliced through her all the more because of the steely control he forced on himself.

Her hand fluttered to rest on his heart as she pressed a kiss to his shoulder. "Oh, God, Elliot—"

"Don't speak. Not yet." He linked his fingers with hers. "The thing is, we all like to think we're strong enough to hold out when that person brings on the belt, the shoe, the branch, or hell, even a hand used as a weapon. And there's a rush in holding out at first, deluding yourself into believing you can actually win."

She willed herself to stay completely still, barely breathing, while he poured out the truth she'd always known. She'd even seen the marks he'd refused to acknowledge. Hearing him talk about it, though, shredded her heart, every revelation making her ache for what he'd suffered growing up. She also knew he wouldn't accept her sympathy now any more than he had then. So she gave him the only thing she could—total silence while he spoke.

"The person with the weapon is after one thing," he shared, referring to his father in such a vague sense as if that gave him distance, protection. "It isn't actually about the pain. It's about submission."

She couldn't hold back the flinch or a whimper of sympathy.

Elliot tipped her chin until she looked at him. "But you see, it's okay now. When I'm out there racing, it's my chance to win. No one, not one damn soul, will ever beat me again."

She held her breath, wrestling with what to do next, how they could go forward. This wasn't the time to pledge futures, but it also wasn't the time to walk away. Growing up, she'd always known how to be there for him. At this moment, she didn't have a clue.

The squawk of their son over the nursery monitor jolted them both. And she wasn't sure who was more relieved.

Her or Elliot.

Elliot barely tasted the gourmet brunch catered privately at a crowded café near the race day venue. With two hundred thousand people pouring into the small principality for the circuit's most famous event, there were fans and media everywhere. At least his friends and mentor seemed to be enjoying themselves. He wanted to chalk up his lack of enthusiasm to sleep deprivation.

Race day in Monaco had always been one of Elliot's favorites, from the way the sun glinted just right off the streets to the energy of the crowds. The circuit was considered one of the most challenging Formula One routes—narrow roads, tight turns and changing elevations made it all the more exciting, edgy, demanding.

And just that fast, Lucy Ann's words haunted him, how she'd accused him of searching out challenges. How she'd accused him of seeing her as a challenge. Damn it all, he just wanted them to build a future together.

What would she be thinking, sitting in the stands today with his school friends and their wives?

He glanced at her across the table, strain showing in the creases along her forehead and the dark smudges under her eyes. He wanted to take Eli from her arms so she could rest, but wasn't sure if she would object. He didn't want to cause a scene or upset her more.

With a mumbled excuse, he scraped back his chair and left the table. He needed air. Space.

He angled his way out of the room—damn, he had too many curious friends these days—and into the deserted patio garden in the back. All the patrons had flocked out front to the street side to watch the crowds already claiming their places to watch the race. But back here, olive trees and rosebushes packed the small space so densely he almost didn't see his old high school headmaster—now an Interpol handler—sitting on a bench sending text messages.

Colonel Salvatore sat beside his preteen son, who was every bit as fixated on his Game Boy as his father was on his phone. A couple of empty plates rested between them.

How had he missed them leaving the table? Damn, his mind wasn't where it was supposed to be.

Colonel Salvatore stood, mumbled something to his son, then walked toward Elliot without once looking up from his phone. The guy always had been the master of multitasking. Very little slipped by him. Ever.

The older man finally tucked away his cell phone and nodded. "We couldn't sit still," he said diplomatically, "so we're out here playing 'Angry Monkeys' or something like that."

"I'm sure you both enjoyed the food more here where it's quieter," he said diplomatically. "I could sure use parenting advice if you've got some to offer up."

Salvatore straightened his standard red tie. He wore the same color gray suit as always, like a retirement uniform. "Why don't you ask the guys inside?"

"They only have babies. They're new parents." Like him. Treading water as fast as he could and still choking. "You have an older boy."

"A son I rarely see due to my work schedule." He winced. "So again I say, I'm not the one to help."

"Then your first piece of advice would be for me to spend time with him."

"I guess it would." He glanced over at his son, whose thumbs were flying over the buttons. "Gifts don't make up for absence. Although don't underestimate the power of a well-chosen video game."

"Thank God we have the inside scoop with Troy's latest inventions." Maybe that's who he needed to be talking to. Maybe Troy could invent a baby app. Elliot shoved a hand over his hair, realizing how ridiculous the thought sounded. He must be sleep-deprived. "I'm a little short on role models in the father department—other than you."

Salvatore's eyebrows went up at the unexpected compliment. "Um, uh, thank you," he stuttered uncharacteristically.

"Advice then?"

"Don't screw up."

"That's it?" Elliot barked. "Don't screw up?"

"Fine, I'll spell it out for you." Salvatore smiled as if

he'd been toying with him all along. Then the grin faded. "You've had to steal everything you've ever wanted in life. From food to cars to friends—to your freedom."

"I'm past that."

"Are you?" The savvy Interpol handler leaned against the centuries-old brick wall, an ivy trellis beside him. "It's difficult for me to see beyond the boy you were when you arrived at my school as a teenager hell-bent on self-destructing."

"Self-destructing?" he said defensively. "I'm not sure I follow." He was all about winning.

"You stole that car on purpose to escape your father, and you feel guilty as hell for leaving Lucy Ann behind," Salvatore said so damn perceptively he might as well have been listening in on Elliot's recent conversations. "You expected to go to jail as punishment and since that didn't happen, you've been trying to prove to the world just how bad you are. You pushed Lucy Ann away by getting engaged to Gianna."

"When did you find time to get your psychology degree between being a headmaster and an Interpol handler?"

"There you go again, trying to prove what a smart-ass you are."

Damn it. Didn't it suck to realize how well he played to type? He took a steadying breath and focused.

"I'm trying to do the right thing by Lucy Ann now. I want to live up to my obligations."

"The right thing." The colonel scratched a hand over gray hair buzzed as short of Elliot's. "What is that?"

"Provide for our son... Marry her... Damn it, colonel, clearly you think I'm tanking here. Is it fun watching me flounder?"

"If I tell you what to do, you won't learn a thing. A

mentor guides, steers. Think of it as a race," he said with a nod—which Elliot knew from years in the man's office meant this conversation was over. Colonel Salvatore fished out his phone and headed back to sit silently beside his son.

Elliot pinched the bridge of his nose and pivoted toward the iron gate that led to the back street. He needed to get his head on straight before the race. Hell, he needed to get his head back on straight, period. Because right now, he could have sworn he must be hallucinating.

Beyond the iron gate, he saw a curly-haired brunette who looked startlingly like his former fiancée. He narrowed his eyes, looking closer, shock knocking him back a step as Gianna crossed the street on the arm of a Brazilian Formula One champion.

Lucy Ann usually found race day exciting, but she couldn't shake the feeling of impending doom. The sense that she and Elliot weren't going to figure out how to make things work between them before the end of their time together. Thank goodness Mrs. Clayworth had taken the baby back to the condo to nap, because Lucy Ann was beyond distracted.

Sitting in the private viewing box with Elliot's friends and the relatives of other drivers, she tried to stifle her fears, to reassure herself that she and Elliot could find a way to parent together—possibly even learn to form a relationship as a couple. That she could figure out how to heal the wounds from his past, which still haunted everything he did.

The buzz of conversation increased behind her, a frenzy of whispers and mumbles in multiple languages. She turned away from the viewing window and monitors broadcasting prerace hubbub, newscasters speaking in French, English, Spanish and a couple of languages she didn't recognize. She looked past the catering staff carrying glasses of champagne to the entrance. A gasp caught in her throat.

Gianna? Here?

The other woman worked her way down the steps, her dark curls bouncing. Shock, followed by a burst of anger, rippled through Lucy Ann as she watched Gianna stride confidently closer. Her white dress clung to her teeny-tiny body. Clearly those hips had never given birth. And Lucy Ann was long past her days of wearing anything white thanks to baby spit-up. Not that she would trade her son for a size-zero figure and a closet full of white clothes.

Above all, she did not want a scene in front of the media. Gianna's eyes were locked on her, her path determined. If the woman thought she could intimidate, she was sorely mistaken.

Lucy Ann shot to her feet and marched up the stairs, her low heels clicking. She threw her arms wide and said loud enough for all to hear, "Gianna, so glad you could make it."

Stunned, the woman almost tripped over her own stilettos. "Um, I—"

Lucy Ann hugged her hard and whispered in her ear, "We're going to have a quick little private chat and, above all, we will not cause a scene before the race."

She knew how fast gossip spread and she didn't intend to let any negative energy ripple through the crowd. And she definitely didn't intend for anyone to see her lose her calm. She hauled the other woman down the hall and into a ladies' room, locking the door behind them.

Once she was sure no one else was in the small sitting area or in the stalls, she confronted Elliot's former fiancée. "Why are you here?"

Gianna shook her curls. "I'm here with a retired Brazilian racer. I was simply coming by to say hello."

"I'm not buying that." Lucy Ann stared back at the other woman and found she wasn't jealous so much as angry that someone was trying mess with her happiness—hers, Elliot's and Eli's.

The fake smile finally faded from Gianna's face. "I came back because now it's a fair fight."

At least the woman wasn't denying it. "I'm not sure I follow your logic."

"Before, when I found out about you and the baby—"

Lucy gasped. "You knew?"

"I found out by accident. I got nosy about you, looked into your life…" She shrugged. "I was devastated, but I broke off the engagement."

"Whoa, hold on." Lucy Ann held up a hand. "I don't understand. Elliot said you broke up because of his Interpol work. That you couldn't handle the danger."

She rolled her dramatic Italian eyes. "Men are so very easy to deceive. I broke the engagement because I couldn't be the one to tell him about your pregnancy. I couldn't be 'that' woman. The one who broke up true love. The evil one in the triangle. But I also couldn't marry him knowing he might still want you or his child."

"So you left." Lucy Ann's legs gave way and she sagged back against the steel door.

"I loved him enough to leave and let him figure this out on his own."

If she'd really loved him, Gianna would have told him about his child, but then Lucy Ann figured who was she to throw stones on that issue? "Do you still love Elliot?"

"Yes, I do."

She searched the woman's eyes and saw…genuine heartache. "You're not at all what I expected."

Gianna's pouty smile faltered. "And you're everything I feared."

So where did they go from here? That question hammered through Lucy Ann's mind so loudly it took her a moment to realize the noise was real. Feet drummed overhead with the sound of people running. People screaming?

She looked quickly at Gianna, whose eyes were already widening in confusion, as well. Lucy Ann turned on her heels, unlocked the door and found mass confusion. Spectators and security running. Reporters rushing with their cameras at the ready, shouting questions and directions in different languages.

Lucy Ann grabbed the arm of a passing guard. "What's going on?"

"Ma'am, there's been an accident in the lineup. Please return to your seat and let us do our jobs," the guard said hurriedly and pulled away, melting into the crowd.

"An accident?" Her stomach lurched with fear.

There were other drivers. Many other drivers. And an accident while lining up would be slow? Right? Unless someone was doing a preliminary warm-up lap…. So many horrifying scenarios played through her mind, all of them involving Elliot. She shoved into the crush, searching for a path through to her viewing area or to the nearest telecast screen. Finally, she spotted a wide-screen TV mounted in a corner, broadcasting images of flames.

The words scrolling across the bottom blared what she already knew deep in her terrified heart.

Elliot had crashed.

Twelve

Her heart in her throat, Lucy Ann pushed past Gianna and shouldered through the bustling crush of panicked observers. She reached into her tailored jacket and pulled out her pass giving her unlimited access. She couldn't just sit in the private viewing area and wait for someone to call her. What if Elliot needed her? She refused to accept the possibility that he could be dead. Even the word made her throat close up tight.

Her low pumps clicked on the stairs as she raced through various checkpoints, flashing the access pass every step of the way.

Finally, thank God, finally, she ran out onto the street level where security guards created an impenetrable wall. The wind whipped her yellow sundress around her legs as she sprinted. Her pulse pounding in her ears, she searched the lanes of race cars, looking for flames. But she found no signs of a major explosion.

A siren's wail sliced through her. An ambulance navigated past a throng of race personnel spraying down the street with fire extinguishers. The vehicle moved toward two race cars, one on its side, the other sideways as if it had spun out into a skid. As much as she wanted to deny what her eyes saw, the car on its side belonged to Elliot.

Emergency workers crawled all over the vehicle, prying open the door. Blinking back burning tears, Lucy Ann strained against an arm holding her back, desperate to see. Her shouts were swallowed up in the roar of activity until she couldn't even hear her own incoherent pleas.

The door flew open, and her breath lodged somewhere in her throat. She couldn't breathe, gasp or shout. Just wait.

Rescue workers reached inside, then hauled Elliot out. Alive.

She sagged against the person behind her. She glanced back to find Elliot's Interpol handler, Colonel Salvatore, at her side. He braced her reassuringly, his eyes locked on the battered race car. Elliot was moving, slowly but steadily. The rescue workers tried to keep his arms over their shoulders so they could walk him to a waiting ambulance. But he shook his head, easing them aside and standing on his own two feet. He pulled off his helmet and waved to the crowd, signaling that all was okay.

The crowd roared, a round of applause thundering, the reverberations shuddering through her along with her relief. His gaze homed in on her. Lucy Ann felt the impact all the way to her toes. Elliot was alive. Again and again, the thought echoed through her mind in a continual loop of reassurance, because heaven help her, she loved him. Truly loved him. That knowledge rolled through her, settled into her, in a fit that told her what she'd known all along.

They'd always loved each other.

At this moment, she didn't doubt that he loved her back. No matter what problems, disagreements or betrayals they might have weathered, the bond was there. She wished she could rejoice in that, but the fear was still rooted deep inside her, the inescapable sense of foreboding.

Elliot pushed past the emergency personnel and… heaven only knew who else because she couldn't bring herself to look at anyone except Elliot walking toward her, the scent of smoke tingling in her nose as the sea breeze blew in. The sun shone down on the man she loved, bright Mediterranean rays glinting off the silver trim on his racing gear with each bold step closer.

She vaguely registered the colonel flashing some kind of badge that had the security cop stepping aside and letting her stumble past. She regained her footing and sprinted toward Elliot.

"Thank God you're okay." Slamming into his chest, she wrapped her arms around him.

He kissed her once, firmly, reassuringly, then walked her away from the sidelines, the crowd parting, or maybe someone made the path for them. She couldn't think of anything but the man beside her, the warmth of him, the sound of his heartbeat, the scent of his aftershave and perspiration.

Tears of relief streaming down her face, she didn't bother asking where they were going. She trusted him, the father of her child, and honestly didn't care where they went as long as she could keep her hands on him, her cheek pressed to his chest, the fire-retardant material of his uniform bristly against her skin. He pushed through a door into a private office. She didn't care whose or how he'd chosen the stark space filled with only a wooden desk, a black leather sofa and framed racing photos.

Briskly, he closed and locked the door. "Lucy Ann, deep breaths or you're going to pass out. I'm okay." His voice soothed over her in waves. "It was just a minor accident. The other guy's axle broke and he slammed into me. Everyone's fine."

She swiped her wrists over her damp eyes, undoubtedly smearing mascara all over her face. "When there's smoke—possibly fire—involved, I wouldn't call that minor."

Elliot cradled her face in his gloved hands. "My hair didn't even get singed."

"I'm not in a joking mood." She sketched jerky hands over him, needing to touch him.

"Then help me out." He stalled one of her hands and kissed her palm. "What can I say to reassure you?"

"Nothing," she decided. "There's nothing to say right now."

It was a time for action.

She tugged her hand free and looped her arms around his neck again and drew his face down to hers. She kissed him. More than a kiss. A declaration and affirmation that he was alive. She needed to connect with him, even if only on a physical level.

"Lucy Ann," he muttered against her mouth, "are you sure you know what you're doing?"

"Are you planning to go back to the race?" she asked, gripping his shoulders.

"My car's in no shape to race. You know that. But are you cert—"

She kissed him quiet. She was so tired of doubts and questions and reservations. Most of all, she couldn't bear for this to be about the past anymore. To feel more pain for him. For herself. For how damn awful their child-hoods had been—his even worse than hers.

Hell, she'd lived through those years with him, doing her best to protect him by taking the brunt of the blame when she could. But when the adults wouldn't step up and make things right, there was only so much a kid could do.

They weren't children any longer, but she still couldn't stand to think of him getting hurt in any way. She would do anything to keep danger away, to make them both forget everything.

At this moment, that "anything" involved mind-blowing sex against the door. Fast and intense. No fun games or pretty fairy tales. This was reality.

She tugged at his zipper, and he didn't protest this time. He simply drew back long enough to tug his racing gloves off with his teeth. With her spine pressed to the door, he bunched up her silky dress until a cool breeze blew across her legs. A second later, he twisted and snapped her panties free, the scrap of lace giving way to him as fully as she did.

But she took as much as she gave. She nudged the zipper wider, nudging his uniform aside until she released his erection, steely and hot in her hand. Then, he was inside her.

Her head thunked against the metal panel, her eyes sliding closed as she lost herself in sensation. She glided a foot along his calf, up farther until her leg hitched around him, drawing him deeper, deeper in a frenzied meeting of their bodies.

All too soon, the pleasure built to a crescendo, a wave swelling on the tide of emotions, fear and adrenaline. And yes, love. She buried her face in his shoulder, trying to hold back the shout rolling up her throat. His hoarse encouragement in her ear sent pleasure crashing over her. Feeling him tense in her arms, shudder with his own completion, sent a fresh tingle of aftershocks through her. Her body clamped around him in an instinctive need to keep him with her.

With each panting breath, she drew in the scent of them. His forehead fell to rest against the door, her fingers playing with the close-shorn hair at the base of his neck. Slowly, her senses allowed in the rest of the world, the dim echo outside reminding her they couldn't hide in here forever.

They couldn't hide from the truth any longer.

Even as she took him now, felt the familiar draw of this man she'd known for as long as she could remember, she also realized she didn't belong here in this world now. She couldn't keep him because she couldn't stay.

No matter how intrinsic the connection and attraction between them, this wasn't the life she'd dreamed of when they'd built those fairy-tale forts and castles. In her fantasies, they'd all just looked like a real home. A safe haven.

She loved him. She always had. But she'd spent most of her adult life following him. It was time to take charge of her life, for herself and for her son.

It was time to go home.

As Elliot angled back and started to smile at her, she captured his face in her hands and shook her head.

"Elliot, I can't do this anymore, trying to build a life on fairy tales. I need something more, a real life, and maybe that sounds boring to you, but I know who I am now. I know the life I want to live and it isn't here."

His eyes searched hers, confused and a little angry. "Lucy Ann—"

She pressed her fingers to his mouth. "I don't want

to argue with you. Not like last time. We can't do that to each other again—or to Eli."

He clasped her hand, a pulse throbbing double time in his neck. "Are you sure there's nothing I can do to change your mind?"

God, she wanted to believe he could, but right now with the scent of smoke clinging to his clothes and the adrenaline still crackling in the air, she couldn't see any other way. "No, Elliot. I'm afraid not."

Slowly, he released her hand. His face went somber, resigned. He understood her in that same perfect and tragic way she understood him. He already knew.

They'd just said goodbye.

The next day, Elliot didn't know how he was going to say goodbye. But the time had come. He sat on Aunt Carla's front porch swing while Lucy Ann fed Eli and put him down for a nap.

God, why couldn't he and Lucy Ann have had some massive argument that made it easier to walk away, like before?

Instead, there had been this quiet, painful realization that she was leaving him. No matter how many fairy-tale endings he tried to create for her, she'd seen through them all. After their crazy, out-of-control encounter against the door, they'd returned to the hotel. She'd packed. He'd arranged for his private jet to fly them home to South Carolina.

Lucy Ann had made a token offer to travel on her own, not to disrupt his schedule—not to distract him. The implication had been there. The accident had happened because his life was fracturing. He couldn't deny it.

But he'd damn well insisted on bringing them back here himself.

The front door creaked open, and he looked up sharply. Lucy Ann's aunt walked through. He sagged back in his swing, relieved to have the inevitable farewell delayed for a few more minutes. He knew Lucy Ann would let him be a part of his son's world, but this was not how he wanted their lives to play out.

Carla settled next to him on the swing, her T-shirt appliquéd with little spring chickens. "Glad to know you survived in one piece."

"It was a minor accident," he insisted again, the wind rustling the oak trees in time with the groan of the chains holding the swing. The scent of Carolina jasmine reminded him of Lucy Ann.

"I meant that kidnapping stunt your friends staged. Turning your whole life upside down."

Right now, it didn't feel like he'd walked away unscathed. The weight on his chest pressed heavier with every second, hadn't let up since he'd been pulled from his damaged car. "I'll provide for Lucy Ann and Eli."

"That was never in question." She patted his knee. "I'm glad you got out of here all those years ago."

"I thought you wanted Lucy Ann to stay? That's always been my impression over the years."

"I do believe she belongs here. But we're not talking about her." She folded her arms over the row of cheerful chickens. "I'm talking about what you needed as a teenager. You had to leave first before you could find any peace here. Although, perhaps it was important for Lucy Ann to leave for a while, as well."

There was something in her voice—a kindred spirit? An understanding? Her life hadn't been easy either, and he found himself saying, "You didn't go."

"I couldn't. Not when Lucy Ann needed me. She was my one shot at motherhood since I couldn't have kids of my own." She shrugged. "Once she left with you, I'd already settled in. I'm on my own now."

"I just assumed you didn't want kids." He was realizing how little time he'd spent talking to this woman who'd given him safe harbor, the woman who'd been there for Lucy Ann and Eli. He didn't have much in the way of positive experience with blood relatives, but it was undoubtedly time to figure that out.

"I would have adopted," Carla confided, "but my husband had a record. Some youthful indiscretions with breaking and entering. Years later it didn't seem like it should have mattered to the adoption agencies that he'd broken into the country club to dump a bunch of Tootsie Rolls in the pool."

Elliot grinned nostalgically. "Sounds like he would have made a great addition to the Alpha Brotherhood."

And might Elliot have found a mentor with Lucy Ann's uncle as well if he'd taken the time to try?

"I wish Lucy Ann could have had those kinds of friendships for herself. She was lost after you left," Carla said pointedly. "She didn't find her confidence until later."

What was she talking about? "Lucy Ann is the strongest, most confident person I've ever met. I wouldn't have made it without her."

He looked into those woods and thought about the dream world she'd given him as a kid, more effective an escape than even his favorite book.

"You protected her, but always saw her strengths. That's a wonderful thing." Carla pinned him with unrelenting brown eyes much like her stubborn niece's. "But you also never saw her vulnerabilities or insecurities. She's not perfect, Elliot. You need to stop expecting her to be your fairy-tale princess and just let her be human."

What the hell was she talking about? He didn't have time to ask because she pushed up from the swing and left him sitting there, alone. Nothing but the creak of the swing and the rustle of branches overhead kept him company. There was so much noise in this ends-of-the-earth place.

Carla's words floated around in his brain like dust searching for a place to land. Damn it all, he knew Lucy Ann better than anyone. He saw her strengths and yes, her flaws, too. Everyone had flaws. He didn't expect her to be perfect. He loved her just the way she—

He loved her.

The dust in his brain settled. The world clarified, taking shape around those three words. He loved her. It felt so simple to acknowledge, he wondered why he hadn't put the form to their relationship before. Why hadn't he just told her?

The trees swayed harder in the wind that predicted a storm. He couldn't remember when he'd ever told anyone he loved them. But he must have, a long time ago. Kids told their parents they loved them. Although now that he thought about it, right there likely laid the answer for why the word *love* had dried up inside him.

He'd told himself he wanted to be a better parent than his father—a better man than his father. Now he realized being a better man didn't have a thing to do with leaving this porch or this town. Running away didn't change him. This place had never been the problem.

He had been the problem. And the time had come to make some real changes in himself, changes that would make him the father Eli deserved. Changes that would make him the man Lucy Ann deserved.

Finally, he understood how to build their life together.

* * *

The time was rapidly approaching to say goodbye to Elliot.

Her mind full of regrets and second thoughts, Lucy Ann rocked in the old bentwood antique in her room at Carla's, Eli on her shoulder. She held him to comfort herself since he'd long since settled into a deep sleep. She planned to find a place of her own within the next two weeks, no leaning on her aunt this time.

The past day since they'd left Monte Carlo after the horrifying accident had zipped by in such a haze of pain and worry. Her heart still hadn't completely settled into a steady beat after Elliot's accident. Right up to the last second, she'd hoped he would come up with a Hail Mary plan for them to build a real life together for Eli. She loved Elliot with all her heart, but she couldn't deny her responsibilities to her son. He needed a stable life.

To be honest, so did she.

There was a time she'd dreamed of escaping simple roots like the cabin in the woods, and now she saw the value of the old brass bed that had given her a safe place to slip away. The Dutch doll quilt draped over the footboard had been made for her by her aunt for her eighth birthday. She soaked in the good memories and the love in this place now, appreciating them with new eyes—but still that didn't ease the unbearable pain in her breaking heart as she hoped against all hope for a last-minute solution.

Footsteps sounded in the hall—even, manly and familiar. She would recognize the sound of Elliot anywhere. She had only a second to blink back the sting of tears before the door opened.

Elliot filled the frame, his broad-shouldered body that of a mature man, although in faded jeans and a simple gray T-shirt, he looked more like *her* Elliot. As if this weren't already difficult enough.

She smoothed a hand along Eli's back, soaking in more comfort from his baby-powder-fresh scent. "Did you want to hold him before you go?"

"Actually, I thought you and I could go for a walk first and talk about our future," he said, his handsome face inscrutable.

What else could there be left to say? She wasn't sure her heart could take any more, although another part of her urged her to continue even through the ache, just to be with him for a few minutes longer.

"Sure," she answered, deciding he must want to discuss visitation with Eli. She wouldn't keep him from his son. She'd made a horrible mistake in delaying telling Elliot for even a day. She owed him her cooperation now. "Yes, we should talk about the future, but before we do that, I need to know where you stand with Gianna. She approached me at the stadium just before your wreck." The next part was tougher to share but had to be addressed. "She said she's still in love with you."

His forehead furrowed. "I'm sorry you had to go through that, but let's be very clear. I do *not* love Gianna and I never did, not really. I did her a grave injustice by rebounding into a relationship with her because I was hurting over our breakup." The carefully controlled expression faded and honest emotion stamped itself clearly in his eyes. "That's a mistake I will not repeat. She is completely in the past. My future is with you and Eli. Which is what I want to speak with you about. Now, can we walk?"

"Of course," she said, relief that one hurdle was past and that she wouldn't have to worry about Gianna popping up in their lives again.

Standing, Lucy Ann placed her snoozing son in his portable crib set up beside her bed. She felt Elliot behind her a second before he smoothed a hand over their son's head affectionately, then turned to leave.

Wordlessly, she followed Elliot past the Hummel collection and outside, striding beside him down the porch steps, toward a path leading into the woods. Funny how she knew without hesitation this was where they would walk, their same footpath and forest hideout from their childhood years. Oak trees created a tunnel arch over the dappled trail, jasmine vines climbing and blooming. Gray and orange shadows played hide-and-seek as the sunset pushed through the branches. Pine trees reached for the sky. She'd forgotten how peaceful this place was.

Of course she also knew she'd walked the same course over the past year searching for this peace. Elliot's presence brought the moment to shimmering life as he walked beside her, his hands in his pockets. She assumed he had a destination in mind since they still weren't talking. A dozen steps later they came around a bend and—

Four of her aunt's quilts were draped over the branches, creating a fort just like the ones they'd built in the past. Another blanket covered the floor of their forest castle.

Lucy Ann gasped, surprised. Enchanted. And so moved that fresh tears stung her eyes.

Elliot held out a hand and she took it. The warmth and familiarity of his touch wrapped around her, seeping into her veins. She wasn't sure where he was going with this planned conversation, but she knew she couldn't turn back. She needed to see it through and prayed that somehow he'd found a way for them all to be together.

He guided her to their fort, and she sat cross-legged, her body moving on instinct from hundreds of similar hideaways here. He took his place beside her, no fancy trappings but no less beautiful than the places they'd traveled.

"Elliot, I hope you know that I am so very sorry for not telling you about Eli sooner," she said softly, earnestly. "If I had it to do over again, I swear to you I would handle things differently. I know I can't prove that, but I mean it—"

He covered her hand with his, their fingers linking. "I believe you."

The honesty in his voice as he spoke those three words healed something inside her she hadn't realized was hurting until now. "Thank you, Elliot. Your forgiveness means more to me than I can say."

His chest rose and fell with a deep sigh. "I'm done with racing. There's no reason to continue putting my life at risk in the car—or with Interpol, for that matter."

The declaration made her selfishly want to grasp at what he offered. But she knew forcing him into the decision would backfire for both of them. "Thank you for offering again, but as I said before, I don't want you to make that sacrifice for me. I don't want you to do something that's going to make you unhappy, because in the end that's not going to work for either of us—"

"This isn't about you. It isn't even about Eli, although I would do anything for either of you." He squeezed her fingers until she looked into his eyes. "This decision is about me. Interpol has other freelancers to call upon. I mean it when I say I'm through with the racing circuit. I don't need the money, the notoriety. The risk or the chaos. I have everything I want with you and Eli."

"But please know I'm not asking that sacrifice from you." Although, oh, God, it meant so much to her that he'd offered.

He lifted her hand and kissed the inside of her wrist.

"Being with you isn't a sacrifice. Having you, I gain everything."

Seeing the forgiveness that flooded his eyes, so quickly, without hesitation, she realized for the first time how much more difficult her deception must have been for him, given his past. All his life he'd been let down by people who were supposed to love him and protect him. His father had beaten him and for years he'd taken it to shield his mother. His mother hadn't protected him. Beyond that, his mother had walked out, leaving him behind. On the most fundamental levels, he'd been betrayed. He'd spent most of his adult years choosing relationships with women that were destined to fail.

And when their friendship moved to a deeper level, he'd self-destructed again by staying away. He'd been just as scared as she was about believing in the connection they'd shared the night they'd made love.

She knew him so well, yet she'd turned off all her intuition about him and run.

"Life doesn't have to be about absolutes. Your world or my world, a castle or a fort. There are ways to compromise."

Hope flared in his green eyes. "What are you suggesting?"

"You can have me." She slid her arms around his neck. "Even if we're apart for some of the year, we can make that work. We don't have to follow you every day, but Eli and I can still travel."

"I know you didn't ask me to give it up," he interrupted. "But it's what I want—a solid base for our son and any other children we have. I'm done running away. It's time for us to build a home. We've been dreaming of this since we tossed blankets over branches in the forest as kids. Lucy Ann," he repeated, "it's time for me to come home and make that dream come true. I love you, Lucy Ann, and I want you to be my wife."

How could she do anything but embrace this beautiful future he'd just offered them both? Her heart's desire had come true. And now, she was ready, she'd found her strength and footing, to be partners with this man for life.

"I've loved you all my life, Elliot Starc. There is no other answer than yes. Yes, let's build our life together, a fairy tale on our own terms."

The sigh of relief that racked his body made her realize he'd been every bit as afraid of losing this chance. She pressed her lips to his and sealed their future together as best friends, lovers, soul mates.

He swept back her hair and said against her mouth, "Right here, on this spot, let's build that house."

"Here?" She appreciated the sacrifice he was making, returning here to a town with so many ghosts and working to find peace. "What if we take our blankets and explore the South Carolina coast together until we find the perfect spot—a place with a little bit of home, but a place that's also new to us where we can start fresh."

"I like the way you dream, Lucy Ann. Sounds perfect." He smiled with happiness and a newfound peace. "We'll build that home, a place for our son to play, and if we have other children, where they can all grow secure." He looked back at her, love as tangible in his eyes as those dreams for their future. "What do you think?"

"I believe you write the most amazing happily ever after ever."

Epilogue

Elliot Starc had faced danger his whole life. First at the hands of his heavy-fisted father. Later as a Formula One race car driver who used his world travels to feed information to Interpol.

But he'd never expected to be kidnapped. Especially not in the middle of his son's second birthday party.

Apparently, about thirty seconds ago, one of his friends had snuck up behind him and tied a bandanna over his eyes. He wasn't sure who since he could only hear a bunch of toddlers giggling.

Elliot lost his bearings as two of his buddies turned him around, his deck shoes digging into the sand, waves rolling along the shore of his beach house. "Are we playing blind man's bluff or pin the tail on the donkey?"

"Neither." The breeze carried Lucy Ann's voice along with her jasmine scent. "We're playing guess this object."

Something fuzzy and stuffed landed in his hands.

Some kind of toy maybe? He frowned, no clue what he held, which brought more laughter from his Alpha Brotherhood buddies who'd all gathered here with their families. Thank goodness he and Lucy Ann had plenty of room in their home and the guest house.

He'd bought beach property on a Low Country Carolina island, private enough to attract other celebrities who wanted normalcy in their lives. He and Lucy had built a house. Not as grand as he'd wanted to offer her, but he understood the place was a reflection of how they lived now. She'd scaled him back each step of the way on upgrades, reminding him of their new priorities. Their marriage and family topped the list—which meant no scrimping on space, even if he'd had to forgo a few extravagant extras.

As for upgrades, that money could be spent on other things. They'd started a scholarship foundation. Lucy Ann's organizational and promotional skills had the foundation running like clockwork, doubling in size. They'd kept to their plans to travel, working their schedule around his life, which had taken a surprising turn. Since he didn't have to worry about money, thanks to his investments, he'd started college, working toward a degree in English. He was studying the classics along with creative writing, and enjoying every minute of it. Lucy Ann had predicted he would one day be a college professor and novelist.

His wonderful wife was a smart woman and a big dreamer.

There was a lot to be said for focus. Although with each of the brothers focused on a different part of the world, they had a lot of ground covered. Colonel Salvatore had taught them well, giving them a firm foundation to build happy, productive lives even after their Interpol days were past.

Famous musician Malcolm Douglas and his wife were

currently sponsoring a charity tour with their children in tow, and if it went as well as they expected, it would be an annual affair. The Doctors Boothe had opened another clinic in Africa last month along with the Monte Carlo mega-rich Hughes family—their daughters along for the ribbon-cutting. Computer whiz Troy Donavan and his wife, Hillary, had a genius son who kept them both on their toes.

"Elliot." Lucy Ann's whisper caressed his ear. "You're not playing the game."

He peeled off his blindfold to find his beautiful wife standing in front of him. His eyes took in the sight of her in a yellow bikini with a crocheted cover-up. "I surrender."

She tucked her hand in his pocket and stole the toy from his hand, tucking it behind her back. "You're not getting off that easily."

Colonel Salvatore chuckled from a beach chair where he wore something other than his gray suit for once—gray swim trunks and T-shirt, but still. Not a suit. But they were all taking things easier these days. "You never did like to play by the rules."

Aunt Carla lifted a soda in toast from her towel under a beach umbrella. "I can attest to that."

Elliot reached toward Lucy Ann for the mysterious fuzzy toy. "Come on. Game over."

She backed up, laughing. "Catch me if you want it now."

She was light on her feet, and he still enjoyed the thrill of the chase when it came to his wife. Jogging a few yards before he caught her, Elliot swept her up into his arms and carried her behind a sand dune where he could kiss her properly as he'd been aching to do all day. Except his house was so full of friends and family.

With the waves crashing and sea grass rustling, Elliot kissed her as he'd done thousands of times and looked forward to doing thousands more until they drew their last breath. God, he loved this woman.

Slowly, he lowered her feet to the ground, and she molded her body to his. If there wasn't a party going on a few yards away, he would have taken this a lot further. Later, he promised himself, later he would bring her out to a cabana and make love to her with the sound of the ocean to serenade them—his studies in English and creative writing were making him downright poetic these days.

For now though, he had a mission. He caressed up her arm until he found her hand. With quick reflexes honed on the racetrack, he filched the mystery toy from her fingers. Although he had to admit, she didn't put up much of a fight.

He slid his hand back around, opened his fist and found…a baby toy. Specifically, a fuzzy yellow rabbit. "You're—"

"Pregnant," she finished the sentence with a shining smile. "Four weeks. I only just found out for sure."

They'd been trying for six months, and now their dream to give Eli a brother or a sister was coming true. He hugged her, lifting her feet off the ground and spinning her around.

Once her feet settled on the sand again, she said, "When we were kids, we dreamed of fairy tales. How funny that we didn't start believing them until we became adults."

His palm slid over her stomach. "Real life with you and our family beats any fairy tale, hands down."

* * * * *

A SPANISH
AWAKENING

KIM LAWRENCE

CHAPTER ONE

EMILIO swallowed his coffee, grimacing at the taste. It had gone cold. Knotting his silk tie with one hand, he finished up the coffee and headed out of the door. A quick glance at his watch confirmed that with luck and good traffic he could make it to the airport to meet Rosanna's flight and still be at his desk by ten—a very late start for him, but being the boss did have certain privileges.

There were people who considered his life was one long privilege.

Some went further, like the actress he had been meant to escort to a premiere the previous night. She had called him selfish—quite loudly.

Emilio had received the insult with a philosophical smile. Her good opinion meant nothing to him. They had not even slept together yet and he doubted now they would, even though she had rung back later, clearly regretting her outburst, to apologise.

Her efforts to ingratiate herself had left him as unmoved as her earlier tantrum. He actually thought she might have a point—maybe he was selfish. The possibility did not unduly bother him. Was selfishness not the upside of being single and not in a serious relationship?

Upside? Were there any downsides to being in a position where one did not have to consider the wishes of other people? Emilio could not think of any.

In the past he had done his duty and pleased others, namely his father. That unquestioning compliance had resulted in a failed marriage entered into when he was too young, stupid and arrogant to believe he could fail at anything.

On paper his father had been right. He and Rosanna had been the perfect couple, they had a lot in common, they came from the same world, and, most importantly from his father's point of view, his bride had been good breeding stock from a family who could trace their bloodline back *almost* as far as his own family.

Emilio slid into the driving seat of his car, his lips twisting into a bitter smile of recollection as he fastened his seat belt.

Luis Rios had been incoherent with outrage when the marriage he had promoted had failed. He had used every threat and bullying tactic in his considerable arsenal and had become frustrated when he saw none made any impression on his son.

His fury had turned to scornful contempt when Emilio had introduced the topic of love, suggesting mildly that the absence of it might be a possible reason for the short life span of the doomed marriage.

The irony in his voice had sailed—predictably—directly over his father's head.

'Love?' his parent had snorted contemptuously. 'Is that what this is about? Since when were *you* a romantic?'

The question had, Emilio conceded, been legitimate. It was true that his own attitude towards the hype around romantic love had always been at best condescending, at worst contemptuous.

He had continued to feel that way right up to the moment

he had found out the hard way that love was not an invention of overactive imaginations, that it was possible to look at a woman and know with every fibre of your being that she was *meant* to be yours.

The instant was indelibly seared into Emilio's memory, every individual detail of her breathless late arrival midway through the boring dinner carrying the scent of the warm summer night into the stuffy room with her.

His heart had literally stopped, which was crazy when you considered how many times he had seen her walk into a room previously, but in that moment it had been as if he were seeing her for the first time.

Wary of sliding into self-pitying mode, jaw clenched, Emilio pushed away the image of her face allowing the far less pleasing image of his father's face to fill the space it left. He no longer attempted to fill the empty space in his heart; he lived with it.

You didn't lose her, he reminded himself. She was never yours. Because the fact was it was all about timing and his had stunk.

He crunched the gears, wincing at the sound as he heard his father say, 'If you want *love*, take a mistress. Take several.' His father had sounded astonished that such an obvious solution had not occurred to his son.

Emilio could still remember looking at the man who had fathered him and feeling not even filial duty—there had never been affection—but coruscating revulsion that burnt through his veins like acid.

The idea of putting anyone through the humiliation his father had inflicted on his mother had filled Emilio with deep repugnance. Emilio might have entered into a marriage of convenience, but he had always intended to be faithful.

'Like you did, Papa?' It had been a tremendous struggle

to keep his voice level, but he had not struggled to disguise the anger and disgust he felt.

The older man had been the first to look away, but during that long moment their eyes had met a profound change had taken place in the relationship between father and son.

Luis Rios had never attempted to carry through with any of his threats to disown him, but Emilio would not have cared if he had. Part of him would have relished the challenge of building a life away from the financial empire his great-grandfather had begun and each successive generation had built upon.

It had been shortly after this event that his father had stopped taking any active part in the business, retiring to the stud where he bred racehorses, leaving Emilio free to put in place wide-ranging changes with no opposition. Changes that meant the global financial downturn had left the Rios brand virtually untouched and the envy of many rivals. People had begun to speak enviously of the Rios luck.

That luck appeared to be working in his favour as he drove into what appeared to be the only vacant parking space a full ten minutes before his ex-wife's flight was due in.

Emilio walked towards the terminal building feeling glad as he passed by a group of vociferous placard-carrying air-traffic controllers that he was not here to catch a flight. The building was filled with anxious and, to varying degrees, angry people who clearly were.

He spared a sympathetic thought for them before his thoughts turned to the reason for his presence. He sighed, wishing he shared Philip's apparent belief that one word from him would somehow magically remove any obstacle in his friend's path to romantic fulfillment. Still, some of the things his friend had said had made it seem that there were things that had been left unsaid.

Emilio had not seen Philip Armstrong for almost a year, so it had been a surprise to see his old friend walk into his office yesterday.

Emilio gave a sardonic smile—it had not been the last!

He chose a vantage point where he would see Rosanna and allowed his thoughts to drift back over yesterday's extraordinary conversation.

'There is a problem.'

It was not a question. A person did not have to be an expert at reading body language to see that there was something wrong in Philip's world.

'I've never been happier.'

The gloomy reply made Emilio's lips twitch. 'It does not show.'

'I've fallen in love, Emilio.' If anything, the Englishman's gloom seemed even more pronounced as he explained the source of his great joy.

'Congratulations.'

Missing the sardonic inflection, Philip produced a dour 'Thanks.' Adding, 'Oh, I don't expect *you* to believe it. I've often wondered, you know…?'

'What have you wondered?' Emilio asked, mystified but not inclined to take umbrage from the underlying antagonism that had crept into the other man's manner.

'Why did you ever get married?' he said bitterly. 'It's not as if you were—'

'In love?' Emilio suggested without heat. 'No, I was not. I am presuming you did not come here to discuss my marriage.'

'Actually, I did, sort of,' Philip Armstrong conceded. 'The thing is, Emilio…'

Emilio repressed his impatience.

'The thing is, I want to get married,' the Englishman revealed in a rush.

'That is surely good news?'

'I want to marry your wife.'

Emilio was famed for his powers of analytical deduction, but he had not seen this one coming!

'You're shocked. I knew you would be,' his old school friend announced with darkly pessimistic gloom.

'I am surprised,' Emilio corrected honestly. 'But if I was shocked, would it matter? Rosanna has not been my wife for quite some time. You do not require my blessing or my permission.'

'I know, but the thing is I think she feels guilty about finding happiness.'

'I think you are imagining things,' Emilio said, wondering if he ought not at some level to feel a little jealous.

He didn't. He was still fond of Rosanna, but then that had been the problem: he had been *fond* of Rosanna just as she had been *fond* of him. It was one of the many things they had in common, and they had both agreed that mutual respect and common interests were a much stronger foundation for a successful marriage than anything as transitory as romantic love.

Madre di Dios, he really had been that stupid!

The marriage had, of course, been doomed, but Emilio had been spared the painful task of telling Rosanna that there was 'someone else'. He hadn't needed to agonise over it, she had taken one look at him and known.

Women's intuition, or had he been that obvious?

What he had not been spared was the overriding sense of guilt—irrational, some might have said, considering his wife had been already unfaithful to him—that and the nasty taste that came with failure in any form.

It had been drummed into Emilio in his cradle that an integral part of being a Rios was not contemplating failure. It was a lesson he had learnt well. Divorce was not just failure, it was public failure, and that had been tougher to take than his wife's confession she had slept with someone else months after they had exchanged vows.

Emilio had been a lot more tolerant of her weakness than he had his own, and in his eyes the fact he had not been physically unfaithful did not make him any less culpable.

Before issuing the public statement on the divorce they had told their respective families, to prepare them. His father's reaction had been predictable and Emilio had been able to view his final ranting condemnation with an air of detached distaste that had clearly incensed his parent further.

What had been far less predictable was the viciously hostile response of Rosanna's family—that had been a genuine shock to him, but not, quite clearly, to her.

It had come out during the heated exchange that unbeknown to him his father had agreed to pay the blue-blooded but broke Carreras family a large sum of money on the marriage and another equally large sum when the first offspring of that union was born.

Under the impression that her attitude had been similar to his own when they had married, he could now see that his bride's motivation had been less to do with pragmatism and more to do with coercion and parental pressure.

It certainly explained Rosanna's initial refusal of a divorce when he had floated it. At the time he had been mystified, but now he realised that she was more afraid of being disowned by her money-grabbing family than living a lie.

It was the reason that, though supporting the official line of mutual decision, amicable divorce, blah…blah, Emilio had not made any effort to deny the rumours that had hinted heavily that his infidelity had caused the rift.

It was not totally a lie and it made things easier on Rosanna, as did the sum he paid the Carreras family out of his own funds.

The media, having created the story, had waited, headlines at the ready, confidently anticipating a lover or lovers to surface once they realised their sordid stories were lucrative. Of course none had because the person he had left his wife for remained oblivious to her role in these events.

Any woman seen with him immediately after the divorce would run the risk of being labelled the other woman, but patience in the circumstances was, he had reasoned, if not a virtue, certainly a necessity if he wanted to protect the reputation of the woman he had fallen for.

So he had waited a decent interval, or almost—there were limits to his patience—before he made any move: six months for the divorce to be finalised and six months for the dust to settle. The only minor problem he'd anticipated that day had been his inexperience at courtship; Emilio knew about seduction but he had never wooed a woman.

The dark irony of it almost drew a laugh from him— almost. It was hard to smile at anything related to the day he had had his heart broken and his pride crushed simultaneously.

In hindsight he was now able to appreciate that the injury to his pride had caused the most damage. He was embarrassed that for a short time he had done the predictable bitter and railing-at-fate thing, but he had reined in those emotions, walled them securely up—a man had to put a time limit on such self-indulgences—and got on with his life.

There had been a certain dark irony in Philip's comment of, 'If you could fall in love with someone, I'm sure Rosanna could move on.'

'With anyone in particular?'

'God, no, anyone would do.' Emilio's laughter brought his attention back to his friend's face. 'Sorry,' he said with a self-conscious grimace. 'I've had a sense of humour bypass. It's just I know we could be happy, but Rosanna— I think she won't be able to move on until you're with someone...'

'I have hardly spent the last two years living the existence of a monk.'

'I know that and I'm sure most men would envy you,' Philip admitted. 'I did. The thing is, Rosanna thinks that underneath you're not really that shallow, not that I think you're shallow.'

'I'm relieved,' Emilio responded gravely. 'So you are asking me to fall in love to make your love life easier. I'm sorry, Philip. I would do a lot for you but—'

'I know. I don't know what I expected. The thing is I'm pretty desperate.' The driven expression shining in his blue eyes was a reflection of that desperation. 'I'd do anything for Rosanna—cut my hair, for starters.'

The comment drew a laugh from Emilio. 'I am impressed.'

'I'm serious. It's time to settle down. No more wandering the world for me. I'm going to get respectable. If Rosanna wants me to, I'd even go and work for Dad, become a suit, swallow the silver spoon and be the son he always wanted me to be.'

'Would the opportunity arise?'

'Are you kidding? Dad would love it if I came crawling back with my tail between my legs. He's built up his empire to hand it over to his heir.' He grinned and directed a finger at his own chest. 'Me.'

'You are hardly an only child.'

Philip conceded this point with a shrug. 'I suppose if Janie had been interested in the business the fatted calf might not await me, but she never was and it's not likely she will be, having become the face of that perfume. It's real spooky to see your little sister staring at you from magazine covers and advertising boards.'

Emilio dismissed the elder of the Armstrong sisters with a shake of his head. 'I was thinking of Megan.'

The sight of a familiar figure snapped him back to the present, catching his gaze as he scanned the busy concourse searching for his ex-wife.

He had thought of Megan and now she was here!

Despite the fact she appeared to have dropped a couple of dress sizes—a circumstance he did not totally approve of—and acquired a fashionable gloss to match the new poise in her manner, he knew Megan Armstrong immediately.

Of course he knew her. Emilio, not a man given to exaggeration, believed totally he could have located her blindfolded in a room of a thousand beautiful Englishwomen!

It was enough, he reflected, to make a man believe in fate. Of course, Emilio did not believe in signs or cosmic forces, but he did believe in following his instincts.

If he followed his at that moment it might get them both arrested. A smile that did not soften the predatory glow in his eyes flickered across his face as he thought, It might be worth it.

CHAPTER TWO

'But I need you here tonight!'

Megan was not surprised to hear the aggrieved note tinged with truculence in her boss's voice.

Charlie Armstrong had not made his millions by allowing little things like air-traffic controllers' strikes to stand in his way and he expected his staff to display an equally robust response to such obstacles to his wishes, even when that member of staff was his daughter.

Actually, *especially* when that employee was his daughter!

'Sorry, Dad.'

'What use is sorry to me? I need—'

'But it looks like I'm stuck here,' Megan inserted, her calm, unruffled tone affording a stark contrast to her father's haranguing bellow. 'I'll book into a hotel here and catch the first flight out tomorrow,' she promised.

'And when will that be?'

Megan glanced at the slightly scratched face of the watch that encircled her slim wrist. Not an expensive item but as far as Megan was concerned utterly invaluable, it had belonged to her mother, who had died when she was twelve.

'It's a twenty-four-hour strike so 9:00 a.m. tomorrow is the earliest flight.'

'Nine! No, that is simply not acceptable!'

'Acceptable or not, Dad, short of sprouting wings I'm grounded, and before you suggest it, the trains and cross-channel ferries are booked up.'

'By people with foresight.'

Megan resisted the impulse to retort by people who were returning home after the international football tournament, knowing that an excuse, legitimate or not, would not soothe her father when he was in this mood.

She let him vent his displeasure loudly for another few minutes, responding with the occasional monosyllabic murmur of agreement when appropriate while she allowed herself to be carried along by the seething mass of bodies, fellow stranded travellers who were all heading in the same direction, towards the exit.

Getting a taxi was going to be a nightmare. Megan mentally prepared herself for a long wait. Maybe she should simply camp out in the airport overnight?

'And don't expect me to fork out for fancy hotels. Being my daughter doesn't mean you can take advantage of the situation. I expect the same level of commitment from you that I would expect from any of my—'

As she tuned out the lecture she had heard many times before Megan's attention strayed around the crowded space heaving with a cross-section of humanity.

The air left her lungs in a fractured gasp as recognition jolted through her body with the fizz of an electric shock. *'Oh, my God!'* she breathed, pressing a hand to her heaving chest.

'What? What is it?'

Megan squeezed her eyes shut, but still saw the face that had caused her to haemorrhage the composure that had become her trademark.

It was not a face that was easy to banish!

She took a deep breath, looking up in guilty acknowl-edgement towards the young man who had nearly tripped over her when she had come to a dead halt without warning. 'I'm so sorry.'

'No problems,' said the backpacker, losing his air of ir-ritation and producing an engaging smile as he took in her slim figure, gleaming, glossy brown hair and English-rose heart-shaped face. 'Do you want a hand with that bag?'

Megan, who was already drifting away, didn't register the offer as she glanced back towards the door through which she had seen the tall figure framed, her emotions a mixture of heart-thudding excitement and trepidation.

It was empty.

Had she imagined it? Her glance swung to left and right, moving over the swathe of heads. Emilio Rios was not the sort of man who blended into a crowd.

'What is it, Megan? What's wrong?'

'Nothing, Dad, I'm fine,' she lied, well aware that her reaction to someone who bore a fleeting similarity to some-one who probably had forgotten she existed had been, to put it mildly, way over the top.

'Well, you don't sound fine!'

It was mortifying. In a matter of seconds she had re-gressed to the cringingly naïve and self-conscious twenty-one-year-old she had been the last time she had seen him. If her feet had not been nailed to the floor she would have turned and run, exactly the way she had eventually done on that occasion.

Now how crazy was that?

She had not seen the man for almost two years and he had probably forgotten both her and the rather embarrass-ing circumstances of their last meeting.

All the same, she was glad she had only imagined him.

Megan took evasive action to avoid a baggage trolley

being wheeled straight at her before replying to her father's comment. 'It was nothing. I just thought I saw someone, that's all. Look, I'll have to go now. I'll ring you later when I've booked in somewhere.'

'Saw who?'

Megan took a deep breath and swallowed, the name emerging huskily from her dry throat. 'Emilio Rios.'

'Emilio!'

'Or someone who looked like him.' This was Madrid. There were a lot of dark, dramatically handsome men; some were even several inches over six feet. Why assume that man she had seen for a split second had been him? It could have been anyone.

The realisation made some of the tension leave her shoulders.

'No, it could be him, you know,' her father mused. 'He has an office in Madrid.'

It would have been harder to mention a capital where there was not a building bearing the Rios name. Emilio was accounted by some in the financial world to be a genius, by others to be incredibly lucky.

In Megan's opinion, to be as successful as he was he had to be both, with the added essential ingredient of utter ruthlessness thrown in!

The tension back with bells on, Megan heard her father add, 'The Rios family estate is nearby, magnificent old place.' The awe in the voice of a man who lived in a stately pile with more rooms than Megan had ever counted suggested the Rios Estate really was something out of the ordinary.

'Well, if he was here he's gone now,' she said as much for her own benefit as her dad's.

'I stayed there once when Luis and I were negotiating

a deal. My God, that man was slippery. Did you ever meet Emilio's father?'

'I thought he was a bit of a snob, actually.'

'No, not a snob,' her father disagreed, sounding irritated by her outspoken appraisal. 'Just very old-school and immensely proud of his family heritage, and who can blame him? They can trace their history back centuries. You know, this Madrid stopover of yours might not be such a bad thing after all.'

Deeply distrustful of the thoughtful note in her father's voice, Megan frowned and said warily, 'You think so?'

'I'll ring Emilio.'

A loud announcement on the speaker system drowned out Megan's wailed protest of, 'Oh, God, no, don't do that!'

'I've lost touch since Luis retired. This could be the perfect opportunity to reconnect, and I'm sure Emilio could arrange accommodation for you.'

'I wouldn't want to trade on our relationship.'

Ignoring the sarcasm of her retort, Charles mused thoughtfully, 'The Rios family have strong South American connections, connections that could be very useful if the Ortega deal proves viable. Actually, even if it doesn't there are—'

Shaking her head, Megan cut her father off mid-flow. *'No.'*

'What do you mean?'

'I mean, no, I will not butter up Emilio Rios for you.'

'Did I ask you to?' her father said, sounding suitably bewildered and hurt by the accusation.

'Emilio Rios was Philip's friend, not mine. *I* don't even like the man.' Two years ago he had been well on the way to becoming a carbon copy of his aristocratic, aloof father. By now he had probably become equally stuffy and pretentious.

There was nothing like being lauded as a genius to confirm a person's belief in his own infallibility, and having beautiful women throw themselves at your feet was not exactly going to encourage humility, she reflected sourly.

'You used to follow him around like a puppy.'

The reminder brought a flush to her cheeks. 'I'm not twelve, Dad.' Actually, she had been thirteen when her brother had brought home his college friend, who had been the most beautiful young man she had ever imagined, let alone laid eyes on.

He had been kind.

Later he had been cruel.

'And anyway, he *definitely* doesn't like me.' This was not a stab in the dark; it was actually an understatement. Two years on the memory of his blighting scorn no longer had the power to make her feel physically sick. Though she was a little way off laughing at it.

'Don't be stupid, Megan. Why would he not like you? I doubt if you even registered on his radar back then.'

Is that meant to make me feel better? Megan wondered.

'I did have hopes he might have fallen for Janie.'

Why not? Megan thought. Everyone else had, or so it had seemed to her when she had watched, with wistful envy, her beautiful half-sister make male jaws drop wherever she went.

'But I think that marriage of his was a done deal when they were both in their cradles. But that's over and it's different now. You've turned into quite an attractive young woman. No Janie, obviously.'

Obviously, Megan thought, and her twisted smile was more philosophical than cynical as she said, 'You mean I lost twenty pounds.' There was less of her but suddenly she was a lot more visible, at least to male eyes. 'Look, Dad, I have to— Hold on, Dad,' she added, turning in response to the pressure of a hand on her shoulder.

The expression of polite enquiry on her face melted into one of wild-eyed panic as she tilted her face up at the man standing at her shoulder.

He was the reason why she was suddenly not being jostled. People did not jostle Emilio Rios. It wasn't just his physical presence, which was considerable, it was his aura.

'*You!*' Oh, God, how long had he been standing there? The thought that he had been listening made her feel queasy.

Emilio Rios smiled and Megan's lips parted. She had no control over the tiny sigh of female appreciation that emerged from her throat. Fortunately the level of noise in the place drowned it out.

The smile did not reach his dark eyes, just deepened the fine lines fanning out from the corners, leaving the gleaming depths intent as without a word he framed her face with his big hands.

A myriad emotions swirling in jumbled psychedelic chaos through her head, Megan stood immobile as she felt the warm brush of his breath against the fluttering pulse at the base of her neck, then the downy softness of her cheek as his dark features blurred out of focus as she struggled to escape the magnetic tug of his unblinking stare.

Logic told her this was not happening, but it was. This wasn't a dream; it was real. Dreams were not hot; he was. Across the inches barely separating them the heat of his body seeped through the fine creased linen of her jacket.

Say something! Do something?

She did neither, but he did.

Emilio bent his head and covered her mouth with his.

Scream, kick him, bite him, said the voice in her head.

Instead she melted into him, her soft body moulding sinuously against the lean, hard length of him. Her lips parted with a silent sigh, not just allowing but inviting the bold, erotic penetration of his tongue.

Need and enervating lust rolled over her, sweeping her along in its wake as she clung to him, her arms sliding around his middle.

The crowds faded, her sense of self faded, all that remained was the taste of him filling her mouth, the texture of his warm lips. The hunger inside her responding with mindless enthusiasm to the erotic probing advances of his tongue.

Then just as abruptly as it had begun it stopped and she was standing there deprived of the heat of his body, shaking and feeling pretty much as if she had just been run over by a truck.

Megan's hands balled into fists at her sides.

'Mr Rios,' she croaked. 'I was just talking about you.' She raised the phone that she still held in a white-knuckled grip.

He just kissed you!

Two years had not changed him. He looked perhaps a little leaner, a little harder, the angles and planes of his incredible face perhaps more sharply defined, but essentially he was still the same.

But you're not that Megan, you've moved on, she reminded herself.

He just kissed you.

Emilio stood waiting for his breathing to return to something approximating normal and watched her, fascinated to see denial this close up. Megan was addressing her remarks to some point over his left shoulder and her attractive contralto voice had an audible edge of hysteria. The open neck of her blouse didn't quite hide the pulse that beat at the base of her throat.

Struggling to control the hunger rampaging through his body, he avoided looking at her mouth, deciding it would not help the painful issue of his arousal, which remained painfully obvious—also painful!

Kissing in public places had some definite disadvantages.

You've met a lot of good-looking men, Megan, she told herself. You can look at him and not turn into a gibbering idiot. You do not worship this man from afar. He cannot injure you with an unfair accusation and harsh word. He has no power at all over you any more because he's just a good-looking man you used to slightly know because he went to school with your brother.

Just a man who made it a struggle to breathe when she looked at him and all that scalp-tingling stuff. Her glance swept downwards as she rubbed her forearms to dispel the goose bumps that in the heat of the terminal building had broken out over her body like a rash.

Face it, Megan, a man like Emilio is never going to be just a man, not with a mouth like that. But that didn't mean she had to humiliate herself by drooling.

'I know, I heard you.'

Somewhere above the hum of noise and the pounding of her heart as it struggled to batter its way through her ribcage, Megan was conscious of a voice, a vaguely familiar voice, calling Emilio's name.

If he heard it he gave no sign, he just continued to stare silently down at her with an expression on his face that she struggled to interpret.

'You just kissed me.'

He angled a dark brow. 'I was beginning to think you hadn't noticed.'

'I'm ignoring it.' Or not dealing with it? 'Like I ignore troublesome, irritating bugs.'

'So you do not like me?'

The possibility did not appear to have dented his armour-plated confidence, she thought, struggling to recover her shredded composure, or at least close her mouth—it was so *not* a good look.

Relax, she told herself.

It was not *like* or anything similarly tepid that Emilio felt as his eyes moved across the soft contours of her upturned features. Soft was the right word, he decided, allowing his eyes to briefly drop as far as her visibly heaving bosom before returning to her face, soft and feminine.

The colour of her eyes had always fascinated him, a deep shade of topaz, though at this moment only a rim of that remarkable colour remained around her dilated pupils. Her skin was incredible. Under the spreading dark stain on her smooth cheeks it was milk-pale and totally flawless. Did that milky pallor extend all over?

He watched the muscles in her pale throat contract as she blinked and gave her glossy head a tiny shake and lifted her chin to a defiant angle before opening her eyes. Emilio, identifying the 'don't mess with me' look on her face, felt a buzz in his blood that had been absent for a long time as he silently accepted the challenge.

He would dearly love to mess with her.

Megan was familiar with powerful men and their generally fragile egos. Experience had taught her that great men's egos responded well to a well-chosen word. She had averted many a potential meltdown with a placatory word, a compliment.

This was a situation she was more than capable of coping with, which begged the question—why wasn't she? Why was she standing there like an idiot?

Powerful, successful men liked to be told they were wonderful as well as the next person—possibly more, because they took it as their due.

She took a deep breath that eased the tightness in her aching chest, opened her mouth and heard herself say, 'No. No, I don't like you at all.' Not the sop to his ego she had intended.

'You do not know me, although you think you do.'

Megan's edginess materialised as hostility as she tilted her chin. 'Very profound, but actually I don't want to know you,' she blurted childishly. 'And if you kiss me again I will—'

Emilio arched a questioning brow and smiled down into her upturned face. 'You will what?' he enquired with interest.

Megan inhaled and thought, Good question. 'Just don't!'

Not a threat likely to make him gibber in fear, but it was preferable to the more candid response of, *Kiss you back!*

She watched his eyes glitter in response to the warning, not with anger, not with amusement, but with something else she could not put a name to. Megan struggled to keep her eyes on his face as the nameless something made her stomach dissolve into a liquid, molten mush.

'That came from the heart.'

Aware that the organ in question was trying to batter its way through her ribs, she glared at him.

Megan heard his name again and began to turn her head towards the sound, but a long brown finger laid against the curve of her jaw prevented her.

The unexpected contact sent a shudder through her body and dragged a shocked breath from her lungs.

She wanted to slap his hand away.

She wanted to tell him she had no desire to know him.

She wanted to tell him to stop looking at her like that.

'Stop looking—'

As his mouth covered her own for a second time the strength left Megan's body in one whoosh. If one hand had not curled like a supportive steel band around her ribcage, dragging her body up against his iron-hard thighs, she would have slid to the ground.

When he released her she was breathing hard as she blinked up at him. 'I told you not to do that.'

'What can I say? It's the challenge and also your mouth. It was made for kissing.'

Taking the phone from her grasp, Emilio lifted it to his ear and, still holding her eyes, spoke into the mouthpiece.

'Rios here.'

Megan slanted an angry glare at his face and held out her hand.

'Ah, Charles. Yes, she is here with me now,' Emilio said, ignoring her silent demand, and continued to speak, responding to what her father was saying, his voice oozing almost as much insincerity as his mocking gaze.

'No, don't worry, I will take care of her. No need, it is not a problem, Charles.' A taunting grin in place on his lean face, Emilio turned to evade the hand that tried to snatch the phone from him. He waved an admonishing finger at her face and directed a wolfish smile at her indignant face as he raised his voice and said, 'It is a total pleasure and no trouble at all. Yes, and Megan sends her love.'

Love was not the emotion stamped on Megan's face

when she attracted the attention of several people within earshot as she yelled, 'No, I don't!'

Finally able to grab the phone, Megan snatched it from his hand and lifted it to her own ear, struggling to regain some semblance of control. 'Dad?' she said. 'I don't need to bother Mr Rios, I'm—I'm... He's gone,' she said, directing an accusing look up at Emilio's dark face.

'Your father is a busy man.'

'My father is—' Megan bit back the unflattering reading of her father's character and glared up at Emilio.

'He can relax now he knows you have someone to look after you.'

'I don't need anyone to look after me, and my father knows it. He just wants me to be nice to you because you have contacts that he...' Realising belatedly the extreme indiscretion of her goaded retort, she closed her lips firmly over further tactless disclosures.

Emilio's lips thinned as his nostrils flared in distaste. Who needed an enemy when you had a father like Charles Armstrong? A man who had never really grasped the fact that a father's duty to his children was to protect and shield.

Armstrong used anyone, including members of his own family, if it gave him an advantage.

'Just how nice does he expect you to be to me?'

Megan responded to the comment as if it had been a slap, catching her breath and drawing back. The subsequent blast of fury that sizzled along her nerve endings blinded Megan to the sympathy in Emilio's dark eyes.

She lifted her chin and glared up at him. 'My father does not ask me to have sex with men who can be useful to him.'

'Though he'd not be likely to kick up a fuss if you decided to.'

'I have sex with men because I want to.'

So far she had not wanted to, but Megan saw no reason to share this information with Emilio Rios; even if she had, she doubted he would have believed her.

Ironic, really—the world thought she was a bit of an iceberg, a reputation she found it comfortable to hide behind, but Emilio Rios thought she was some sort of sex-mad tart.

Two years ago her initial gratitude at being rescued from a situation that had escalated dangerously out of control had changed to wretched misery when he had looked at her with contempt and treated her to a blighting lecture on the dangers of leading men on.

Acting as though she were some sort of sexual predator!

Sexual predator!

At that point Megan hadn't even had a real boyfriend. The man Emilio had rescued her from had not been her date. He was a lecturer, quite old to her mind, and she had treated his kind offer of a lift home from the graduation party, when the boy who had promised her an early lift home had become drunk and incapable, as just that—kind.

How was she meant to have known that he had been drinking too? She hadn't had a clue until he had put his foot down through the village, then, after making her extremely uncomfortable with comments loaded with sexual innuendo, instead of taking her to the house where her father was hosting a party for his business partner—all the family were under orders to attend—he'd pulled up on the long tree-lined drive leading up to the house and tried to kiss her.

During the rather undignified tussle that had followed Megan had tried to remain calm, but she had been close to panic when the door had been dragged open to reveal Emilio.

Her relief had been short-lived.

'So how about me?'

She looked at him blankly as she pushed away the memory of that night. 'How about you what?'

Emilio arched a sardonic brow. 'Do you want to have sex with me?'

Heat flashed through Megan. She was insulted, she told herself, not excited. She hung on to her temper with difficulty and pretended to consider his insolent question. 'You got a spare million?' Word was he had several.

His brows lifted. 'You value yourself highly.'

Megan flicked the ponytail that lay against her neck and responded with a cool assurance she was about a million miles from feeling. 'I'm worth it.'

'Then maybe we could work something out. I'm not averse to paying for quality,' he drawled.

The sexual tension soared as they stared at one another, neither willing to back down. But before this absurd negotiation went any further a voice cut across the seething silence.

'Emilio?'

CHAPTER THREE

MEGAN turned her head. The woman standing there was tiny, barely an inch above five feet. The last time she had seen the petite brunette the older woman had been wearing a ring; today her hand was bare, but nothing else, it seemed, had changed.

Rosanna Rios was still the most beautiful woman she had ever met. Never a hair out of place, she looked like a porcelain ornament with big brown eyes, a rosebud mouth and delicate nose. She had the sort of delicate fragility that aroused the protective instincts in men.

'I did call, but you were…' she raised a darkened brow and lifted her enquiring gaze to Emilio as she teased '…occupied.'

Megan felt her stomach muscles tighten as she watched Emilio brush the smooth cheek offered him with his lips.

'I had no idea at all.' Rosanna turned to smile at Megan, adding with a smile tinged with relief as she turned back to Emilio, 'I'm glad things are finally working out for you.'

Megan, puzzling over the soft-voiced aside, waited for Emilio to set the record straight. Instead she heard him ask his ex-wife if she was being met.

'I was.' Rosanna scanned the crowds, a delicate frown

furrowing her smooth brow. 'But he appears to have been held up.'

'Can we offer you a lift?'

Megan, frowning at the *we* and the misleading message it sent, watched as Rosanna shook her head. 'I'll wait.'

Emilio shrugged and placed a hand lightly between Megan's shoulder blades, acting as if he hadn't noticed when she flinched. 'If you're sure?'

Megan flashed him a 'what the hell are you up to?' look, which he responded to by dropping his head to whisper softly in her ear, 'I'll meet your price.'

The mortified colour flew to Megan's cheeks as she blurted loudly, 'I wasn't serious and you know it.'

'You really shouldn't make offers you don't intend to follow through with,' he chided, adding, 'Sorry, Rosanna, we're being rude.'

'*You're* being rude,' Megan gritted.

Rude, and extremely manipulative.

'No apologies necessary. Are you two arriving? Or were you planning a romantic trip?'

'We are not together,' Megan protested in a belated attempt to set the record straight. The breathlessness of her delivery, due in part to the fingers that had begun to massage the tight area at the back of her neck, did not add weight to her claim.

The casual intimacy of his action sent a quiver of raw sexual awareness through her body.

Emilio hooked a thumb under her chin. 'You're tense, *querida*.' He disapproved with a frown that left his dark eyes warm with concern.

'I can't imagine why,' she retorted.

The ironic retort drew a laugh from Emilio, who allowed the hand that lay against her waist to slide lower to the firm curve of her bottom. 'Megan was planning to fly home, but it looks like I have her here for a little longer.'

Rosanna gave a sympathetic grimace. 'Bad luck.'

'Good luck for me.'

'I was lucky. I arrived on an early flight.'

'How long have you two been…?'

Megan, aware of Emilio's eyes on her face, struggled to manufacture an amused smile for the other woman. 'No, we're not, that is… He's joking.'

Emilio came to her rescue. 'We are just good friends,' he said with an 'if you believe that you'll believe anything' smile.

Rosanna smiled. 'Of course.'

'No, really we're…'

Emilio placed a finger to her lips.

The contact made her pupils dilate.

'Relax, Megan.' His deep voice, huskily suggestive of unspoken intimacies, shivered across her oversensitive nerve endings. 'Rosanna understands, and she is not going to report back to anyone,' he soothed, lifting a stray hank of hair from her cheek.

A hazy, distracted expression drifted across his face as he rubbed the silky strands between his fingers before tucking them behind her ear.

Megan swallowed and struggled to maintain a façade of calm while her thudding heart tried to climb its way out of her chest cavity.

Mesmerised, she stared at him. She did not register the time lapse before he pushed her hair from her face. She was too busy registering unpleasant things like the almost painful clutching of her stomach muscles and the rush of heat that raised her core temperature by several uncomfortable degrees.

His hand did not fall away. Instead he touched her ear

lobe, seeming to notice the amber studs in the gold setting for the first time. His dark, thickly lashed eyes drifted downwards to the hollow of her throat where a pulse fluttered visibly against the tender blue-veined white skin.

Any residual guilt he might have felt for exploiting the situation had long vanished. It had been a long time coming, but Megan Armstrong was going to be his and he was going to make her forget every man she had ever been with—and, *Madre di Dios*, he was going to enjoy every second of it!

His fingertips barely brushed her, but even the suggestion of contact sent a shiver of sensation across the surface of her skin. She was frozen to the spot by a wave of enervating lust that was terrifying in its strength.

Hating the feeling of being utterly helpless and not in control, Megan hid behind the sweeping half-moon fan of her dark lashes and, like a drowning man clinging to a straw, repeated, *You'll laugh about this later*, over and over in her head.

'I like those,' he said, making her shiver as he touched, not just the earring, but the thin layer of skin behind her ear, and Megan realised it really was an erogenous zone.

God, I've got erogenous zones!

She met his dark intent gaze and thought, God, I've got a problem!

Her hand came up to push his away—that had been the intention at least. Instead she somehow ended up with her fingers curled over his and stayed there for an awkward heart-thudding moment.

'They were my mum's.'

Her eyes dropped from his uncomfortably perceptive gaze a moment before they filled with emotional tears. The earrings were one of a handful of physical reminders she had of her mother, along with her watch and the creased and grainy snapshot of herself as a baby held in her mother's arms she carried in her wallet.

'They match your eyes. Did your mother have golden eyes too?' His voice flowed over her like honey.

She was startled by the question; the eyes in question flew to his. He wasn't really interested, she told herself. This little byplay was presumably for Rosanna's benefit—like the kisses.

'Yes, she did. I…I look like her.'

'Then she must have been a very beautiful woman.'

Megan felt her heart give a traitorous thud and forced herself to look away. He looked genuine but he was about as sincere as a politician running for re-election; she would be a fool if she lost sight of that fact.

Twisting her earring, she turned to the older woman. 'Look, it was nice to see you again but I'm running late.'

'Of course, and it was very nice to see you too, Megan,' she said warmly. 'Philip often speaks of you.'

'You speak to Philip?'

A look of consternation crossed the older woman's face. 'I, well—'

Emilio cut across her. 'I hate to interrupt, ladies, but—' he tapped the face of the watch on his wrist and angled a significant look at Megan '—this is why we are running late. You talk too much.' Grabbing her arm, he dropped a kiss on Rosanna's cheek and headed for the exit, virtually dragging Megan along with him.

She angled an angry look up at his lean face. 'What do you think you're doing?'

'I am rescuing you from an awkward situation.'

Megan loosed an incredulous hoot as they emerged in the fresh air. She pulled away from him and stood, hands on hips, glaring at him.

'An awkward situation of your making.'

He flashed a grin and held out an arm towards her. 'The car is this way.'

Megan didn't move. 'Goodbye.'

He studied her face for a moment before sighing. 'Look, we can—'

'Do this the hard way or the easy way,' she slotted in.

'Tempting, but no, I was going to say we can stand here debating this, but in the end you will accept a lift because the alternative is a very long wait.' He nodded towards the long queues beside the empty taxi ranks. 'And you are, I am led to believe, a practical woman not given to cutting off her very pretty nose to spite her beautiful face.

'Besides, I promised your father I would take care of you.'

'And you are a man of your word?'

'It hurts me you doubt it.' The silence stretched as he watched her struggle. 'Of course, if for some reason you are afraid to get in a car with me…?'

Her chin went up. 'Of course I'm not afraid,' she scoffed.

CHAPTER FOUR

ANGRY that she had allowed herself to be manipulated into accepting this lift—a two-year-old could have seen through his tactics—Megan maintained her tight-lipped, frigid silence until Emilio had negotiated the congested traffic around the airport.

'I think you owe me an apology.'

'You do? For what exactly?' he said, sounding interested.

'You kissed me.' Annoyingly, she could not say it without blushing. She just hoped he was too busy avoiding some suicidal cyclists to notice.

Emilio arched a brow and flashed a quick wolfish grin in her direction. 'I have not forgotten. You expect me to apologise for kissing you?'

Megan shook her head. 'I've already forgotten the actual kiss,' she lied, hoping but not expecting to bruise his ego. 'I expect you to apologise for using me that way to make your ex jealous.'

Emilio looked startled by the interpretation. 'Jealous?'

'And all that effort and it didn't even work. Face it, Emilio, she didn't care.' Possibly, Megan mused bitterly, because Rosanna knew all she had to do was click her pretty fingers and Emilio would come running. 'I have to admit I'm disappointed.'

'With my kissing?'

Megan, who had no intention of going there, ignored the interruption. 'I thought you were supposed to be the great authority on women, a regular Casanova...'

'You seem to take a great interest in my sex life.'

The taunt brought a flush of colour to her cheeks, but Megan didn't drop her gaze as she countered, 'It's hard to avoid it.'

He looked momentarily confused before his mouth twisted into a grimace. 'That damned article. How long is that damned thing going to haunt me?'

The look of disgust that flashed across his face made her laugh.

'Haunt?' she said, pretending confusion. 'I thought it was very flattering. Some of the things she said you did I didn't know were physically possible. May I give you some advice?'

'If that advice is don't sleep with women who confide intimate details to tabloids and trashy magazines, don't waste your breath.'

Emilio took very little interest in what was written about him, good or bad, but he was actually a long way from feeling the amused indifference his manner suggested, for this particular article had been, not only incredibly tasteless and salacious, but totally untrue.

He would have won any prosecution he brought against the magazine that published it, but such a course would have inevitably prolonged the public interest. Instead he had bitten the bullet and chosen to remain silent on the subject, waiting for it to go away.

'It wasn't,' Megan admitted. 'But it seems sound advice.'

'Only if you actually did sleep with the woman in question.'

Something in Emilio's voice brought her frowning scrutiny to his face. 'And you didn't,' she realised. 'But she said…?'

'And you believe everything you read in trashy magazines?' he asked sardonically.

'No…' she conceded doubtfully.

'Just everything you read about me?'

Megan aimed a killer look at his profile. The man, she brooded darkly, always had to have the last word.

'That advice—what was it? I would like to hear it, if only to prove to you that I actually have an open mind. So what pearl of wisdom would you like to share with me?'

'You want to know? Fine! I'm no expert—'

Emilio gave a lazy smile. 'I can feel a *but* coming on.'

'Do you want to hear what I have to say or not?'

He produced an unrealistically meek expression and mimed a zipping motion across his lips.

'*But*—it seems to me that kissing someone else is not the best way to win back a wife.'

There was a long silence before he filled it.

'You really think that is why I kissed you?' The next time he intended to make his intentions clearer—always easier when you didn't have several hundred people watching you.

She arched a brow and adopted an expression of amusement. Inside the laughter was noticeably absent as she said, 'And you're trying to tell me you were just overcome with uncontrollable lust when you saw me?'

Not for the first time she wondered what it would be like to be one of those women who did just that to men. Did that make her very shallow?

'I suppose you know that it was totally pathetic. I should

have called Security!' Instead I kissed you back, which was a really great idea.

'People kiss in airports.'

'Not like that!'

'You did not exactly beat me off with a stick.' Emilio struggled to concentrate on the road ahead as the memory of her soft curves moulding themselves to his body rose up to torment him.

'Quite the opposite. Now, why was that, I wonder?'

'I felt sorry for you.' Pleased with the way the explanation had tripped off her tongue, she added, 'You know, you really should get a life for real. Rosanna clearly has.'

Actually it wasn't at all clear. Megan could see that Emilio would be a hard act for any man to follow, even the most self-confident of men.

'Yes, she has. I believe we will be getting an invite to her wedding any day now.'

'She's getting married!' This information went a long way to explain Emilio's performance, especially if he was still in love with his ex-wife.

Megan squashed the flash of sympathy she felt for him. It might explain why, but it did not begin to excuse the way he had used her.

'It is in the cards, though not certain as yet. You sound surprised?'

'I am.'

Not as surprised as she had been when she had learnt that the couple who had seemed a perfect match on every level were breaking up. Up until the moment that the divorce had been announced Megan had anticipated a dramatic reconciliation, but the Rios divorce, like the break-up, had been low-key and bizarrely amicable based on what they called a mutual decision.

But had that mutual, civilized, still-good-friends routine

been a way to save face? The Rios family name came not only with a clearly superb gene pool, she thought, sweeping a covert glance through her lashes at Emilio's clear-cut patrician profile, but also some far less attractive things.

Things like family tradition and pride. How would divorce have gone down? In many ways the Rios family had not moved on very far from the Dark Ages, and they didn't do divorce. When it came to pride the Rios family had a lot more than their fair share.

For the first time she found herself wondering just how mutual the divorce had really been. Had it in reality been forced on him?

She flashed a speculative look at Emilio's profile, wondering if he too had been anticipating a passionate reconciliation?

'I thought marriage to you would have put her off the institution for life! It's almost as much of a mystery as why she married you in the first place.'

'Is it?' he said, looking at her mouth.

The insolent scrutiny made Megan shift uneasily in her seat. 'She seems quite sane.'

He continued to stare at her mouth until, unable to bear it a second longer, Megan yelled, 'Will you keep your eyes on the road?' They were stopped at a set of lights. 'And nobody gets married to someone because they are a good kisser, if that's what you're implying.'

'I am relieved you noticed. Actually, my talents extend beyond kissing.'

Megan dragged a hand jerkily down the front of her blouse, growing more agitated by the second. 'I really don't want to know!' she choked, dropping the pretence of an amused façade.

Her directive stemmed the flow of details, but not the

flow of visual examples of his *talent* slipping through her head.

'I should have waited for a taxi,' she muttered under her breath. 'God alone knows why I got in a car with you.'

'Possibly because you were hoping I'd kiss you again?'

Her slender shoulder lifted in a shrug and she sneered, 'No audience here, so I feel safe.'

He lifted one shoulder, but admitted modestly, 'I am not the exhibitionist you appear to think. I actually do some of my best work in private.'

His deep, throaty drawl sent Megan's imagination into free fall. She gasped as shameful heat flooded the sensitive juncture between her legs. 'Not with me!' she retorted as she pressed a button to open the window, pressing it again with a certain amount of desperation when it did not immediately respond.

'We do have air conditioning, you know.'

Megan stuck her head out of the window and breathed deeply. 'It's not working.' She found it extremely doubtful that a cold shower would have worked for her at that moment.

She was bewildered and alarmed by the ease with which he could arouse her physically. It was bizarre, but the excitement in her veins seemed to grow in direct proportion to the antagonism she felt towards him.

Emilio shifted gears and the powerful monster he drove shot forward, straining at the leash as the traffic began to move once more. He felt some sympathy for the machine's frustration; his libido was straining at the leash.

'You know what they say, *querida*—never say never.' His sideways glance touched her heaving bosom. 'You gave every appearance of enjoying yourself when you kissed me.' Her response had delighted him.

'That was not a kiss.'

'It was not?'

Megan chewed fretfully at her full lower lip and stared stubbornly out of the window. 'It was…a reflex,' she retorted in a driven voice.

'Indeed. I can only say that you have the best…*reflexes* of any woman I have ever come across.'

The window beckoned again.

When she pulled her head back in she pushed the mesh of hair from her eyes and observed with a spite that was totally uncharacteristic for her, 'I should have told Rosanna that, far from being an *item*—like anyone is going to believe that,' she inserted with a scornful sniff. 'I can't stand the sight of you!'

'Is it such a good idea to allow this to become personal?'

Megan stared at his patrician profile in disbelief. Was the man for real? 'It already is personal. It got personal the moment you k…k…you kissed me!'

'I too have excellent reflexes.'

Lips compressed, she directed her gaze on her hands clenched primly in her lap, thinking, Do not go there, Megan. 'I just bet you do,' she snarled, watching her knuckles blench white.

She flashed him a look of exasperation. 'Is it so impossible for you to believe that I can't stand the sight of you?'

'I believe that your reaction to me is not mild, and neither, for the record, is mine to you.' Before she could analyse the message within his cryptic utterance he continued, 'But I was referring to your comment…something along the lines of—"like anyone would believe that." Why would anyone *not* believe that we are lovers?'

Megan slung him an irritated look. 'I have a brain and

I like to be exclusive. Also I look nothing like a Barbie doll.'

'Ouch! So much for sisterly solidarity! You really should not judge by appearances, Megan.'

'You're right, *I'm* the superficial one.'

His grin flashed and her own smile faded. It would be an exaggeration to call the spiky atmosphere warm, but she was conscious that a worrying element of intimacy had developed.

Megan could have done without knowing he could laugh at himself; it made despising him all the more of a struggle. She needed out of this car and fast! God only knew what had possessed her to get in to begin with.

Like you don't know?

Ignoring the unhelpful contribution of the knowing voice in her head, she cut short the inner dialogue and said, 'Look, you can drop me at the first hotel we pass, if that's not a problem?' If it was a problem she could always jump out of the moving vehicle. It could not be a more painful experience than this conversation.

'Without feeding you first?' He shook his dark head in reproach.

'That really isn't necessary. I ate breakfast,' she lied brightly. 'And it isn't lunchtime.' She glanced at her watch and realised it was barely nine-thirty. It felt as though she had been in the car for hours.

His dark brows twitched into a straight line above his hawkish nose. 'You are very hung up with time,' he drawled.

'And you must be a very unique billionaire businessman if you have time to snack and watch the grass grow,' she retorted tartly.

'I work, but I am not a slave to routine.'

'Congratulations on being a free spirit, but I'm still not hungry.'

'You think your time would be put to better use counting the minutes until the planes start flying again? You're stuck here—I suggest you make the most of it. Madrid is a beautiful city, though being a native I must admit to some prejudice on the subject,' he conceded with a fluid shrug. 'Do you like architecture, history...?'

'Why—are you offering to be my guide?' She leaned back in her seat and thought, Gotcha, as she wondered how long it would take him to discover a very full diary.

It might amuse Emilio Rios to buy her breakfast, he might even feel he was obliged to do so because of her manipulative parent's request to look after her, but spending an entire day with her would definitely not be his idea of an efficient use of his time.

'Why not?'

The cynical smile playing about her lips vanished. 'I wasn't being serious!' She watched his brows lift in response to the horrified vehemence of her tone and added, 'And even if I did want to sightsee, by the time I check my emails my dad will have found me one or two things to do,' she promised, flashing a wry smile.

'Then don't check your emails.'

The simple logic made Megan blink as she stared at him as though he were from another planet. 'You might be your own boss, but I'm not. My dad does not have a great opinion of slackers.'

'And are you a slacker?' he wondered, making his interest sound academic.

Megan's response was not academic, it was indignant. 'I am not!'

One corner of his mouth lifted and the amusement extended to his dark eyes. 'You are the boss's daughter—that must give you a certain amount of latitude.'

'Being the boss's daughter means I have to prove I can do more than paint my nails—' She turned her head, a suspicious frown forming on her smooth brow. 'Are you trying to wind me up?'

His grin flashed. 'Yes, the ruffled-feather look suits you.' His eyes dropped to her emotionally heaving bosom. 'Realistically, Armstrong isn't going sack you to prove his egalitarian credentials, is he?'

'If I didn't pull my weight he might. But…' she gave a shrug and conceded '…probably not.'

'Because you're his daughter.' He raised a brow in response to her laugh and came to a halt as the second set of lights ahead changed. '*Not* because you're his daughter?'

Her eyes connected with the dark-eyed glance that flickered her way. 'While I'm working for him, to some extent he still controls my life.'

A small silence followed this unemotional explanation as Megan considered a situation she had been thinking about a lot of late.

'So if he sacked you he'd lose that power?'

Megan nodded, turning her head his way as she agreed with this analysis. 'Exactly.' It wasn't until her glance flickered his way and she saw his expression that she realised what she was discussing and more importantly with whom!

Her eyes shot saucer-wide as she gave a dismayed croak. Had she gone mad? She kept her own counsel on certain subjects; she had not even confided her recent half-formed plans to her best friend.

'So now you know all about my dysfunctional family—not a very fascinating subject, so do you mind if we change it?'

Emilio, who knew a lot more about her family than she

suspected, watched the rosy glow wash over her fair skin and his expression hardened as his thoughts drifted back to a specific section of his conversation with Philip that he had brooded angrily over long after his friend had made his farewells the previous day.

CHAPTER FIVE

'WHY is the idea of Megan being groomed to take over the company a joke?'

Philip grinned, then stopped. 'You're serious,' he realised.

It was a struggle to contain his impatience in the face of the Englishman's open-mouthed amazement. 'Why would I not be? It is my understanding that your sister is being groomed to take control one day.'

'How would you know that? Unless you have been secretly following her progress.' Philip grinned at his own joke.

'We have a proactive policy with recruitment. We are always on the lookout for the brightest and the best,' Emilio explained.

'You thought of offering Megan a job?' The possibility appeared to render her brother tongue-tied with amazement.

'She is exactly the sort of candidate we target.' Not directly obviously—such preliminary approaches were made through the aegis of an agency.

'Megan! *Our* Megan?'

'She did graduate top of her class.' Had any of her family actually noticed?

If they had it would be the first time. A quiet member

in a family of large and noisy personalities, Megan had perfected the art of fading into the background to such a degree that she seemed startled when someone actually noticed her.

Emilio had felt his anger rise as he recalled how pathetically grateful she'd been when she had been included by her family.

'Megan always was a bit of a swot,' Philip recalled with an affectionate grin.

'The same has been said of me, but I would call it focus. It is a quality I find essential in those working for me.'

'So you wanted Megan to... Did she refuse you?'

'I was given to understand through an intermediary that she was not available.'

'Megan being headhunted—that's a tough one to get my head around. She's bright, of course she is...I just never thought...'

'Well, your father must have if he's grooming her—'

'He's not,' Philip cut in.

'How can you be so sure?'

'I know my dad. Oh, he's probably told her that he will—that would be his style,' Philip admitted. 'But let her take over...?' He shook his head. 'No way, never in a million years.'

'Why not?'

'Well, for starters, in case you've forgotten, she's a girl.'

'I had noticed she is a *woman*.'

'Dad can talk the talk when it comes to women in the workplace, but at heart he's a chauvinist.'

'You implied that he would not have been unhappy if Janie had shown an interest.'

'Sure, Janie's always been his favourite, and she's—'

Emilio was taken unawares by the level of anger he

was forced to suppress as he prompted coldly, 'You were saying.'

Maybe he hadn't suppressed it all because Philip looked wary as he responded. 'Dad took Megan in when her mum died, but at the end of the day she was...'

'The maid's daughter.'

'I don't think that way,' Philip protested, flushing. 'But Dad does. And her mum was the *housekeeper* before she got herself pregnant.'

Emilio schooled his expression into neutrality. He had no idea why the sordid story made him so furious. It wasn't as if such things had not occurred in his own family. The only difference being that no member of his family would have ever acknowledged the child of such an unequal union, even if she had been left alone after the death of her mother.

To give Armstrong his due he had recognised his responsibilities even if it had taken twelve years for him to do.

He could only imagine what it had been like for a child brought up in what, according to Philip, had been a pretty tough housing estate in an industrial town to be removed into a totally foreign environment among people she did not know.

People who did not value the gift they had been given.

Megan's glance moved from his long fingers drumming an impatient tattoo on the steering wheel to his profile. The taut lines of his face suggested Emilio wasn't very happy, the tension was rolling off him in waves.

'I hate driving in heavy traffic too. You can't wonder that road rage happens.'

Her soft contralto voice dragged Emilio free of his dark reflections. He turned his head and felt something squeeze tight in his chest as he read the sympathy in her face and all his submerged protective instincts rose to the surface.

'I do not feel rage towards the road.' Just every person who has ever hurt you. 'But you still carry on working for him?'

The abrupt and seemingly unconnected angry addition made her start slightly and blink in confusion.

'Dad?'

He nodded abruptly.

'Why wouldn't I?' No longer an impression—the anger he was projecting was very real.

'So you don't mind that by your own admission he tries to manipulate you.'

'Manipulate is a strong word,' she retorted with manufactured optimism in face of his bewildering level of disapproval.

Not strong enough in Emilio's view for a father who had no interest in his daughter's potential being fulfilled, just her usefulness to him. Did she realise that he had no intention of ever letting go of the golden carrot he dangled?

'If he will not sack you, why worry?' More to the point, why carry on working for the guy?

'There are worse things than being sacked,' she retorted.

'Such as?' he asked, reminding himself that what went on between Armstrong and his daughter was none of his business.

'What is this—twenty questions?' she asked crankily. 'If you must know he'll make an example of me.' She could hear him now: *Just because you're my daughter, Megan.* 'Something suitably humiliating, a public dressing-down, a demotion, at least on paper.'

Her job description and salary might change, but Megan,

who knew despite her father's complaints that she was good at what she did, doubted her workload would alter.

'But as I'm going to be a good girl and refuse your very *tempting* offer of breakfast,' she said, masking the disturbing truth with sarcasm, 'it's kind of academic. And don't pretend to be disappointed. Admit it—you can think of better ways to spend your days than showing me around the tourist sights.'

'I can think of better ways to spend my day,' he admitted, looking at her lips and thinking about several of them; all involved a bed and none featured clothes.

She had never imagined any different, so the anticlimax she felt at his admission was totally irrational.

The lights changed and, while Megan was considering the subtle but important difference between brutal honesty and plain bad manners, Emilio drew away.

At least he had finally dropped the subject. Megan was gazing out through the passenger window, beginning to loosen up slightly when he said something that tipped her over into heart-racing panic…as she found it preferable to designate the erratic thud of her heart as it climbed its way into her throat.

'And are you always a good girl, Megan?'

It could have been an innocent question, but not when it was delivered in a throaty drawl that came direct from an erotic fantasy. Not hers—she didn't do fantasies, erotic or otherwise. She was a girl very founded in reality—a girl who right now was shaking.

Did he like his girls bad?

It was bad she had thought the question; at least she had not said it.

She stared at him feeling as though she had slipped into some sort of trance. This conversation, the entire morning, it was all so surreal. She inhaled deeply, getting an unsettling dose of the male fragrance he used along with the sustaining oxygen. God, Megan, get a grip, girl, or failing that get out of this car!

'Always,' she confirmed in a cold little voice—shame about the tremor.

A disturbing smile tugged the corners of his mobile mouth as his glance dropped to the hands clenched in her lap. 'Good girls don't bite their fingernails.'

Unable to stop herself, she slid her hands under her thighs to hide the shameful condition of her fingernails. 'I don't…' She bit off the futile denial and lifted her chin, turning her defiant golden stare on the hands curved lightly around the steering wheel.

Strong hands, hands that were good to look at, much like the rest of him, she suspected. Her amber eyes were glazing as she stared fixedly at his long, tapering brown fingers and nails that were, of course, not bitten, but neatly trimmed. In her head she saw those long brown fingers, dark as they slid over pale flesh.

She clenched her jaw and pushed the image away.

'I bite my nails—so what? I suppose *you* think that it's an external manifestation of some sort of unresolved conflict. Well, think again—it's just a habit.' And one that Megan now intended to cure herself of for good. She had intended to before, but this time she *really* would.

'I just thought you might be hungry,' he returned mildly.

'I'm always hungry,' she admitted without thinking.

The wistful note in her voice drew a smile from Emilio. 'Then that settles it.'

His response drew Megan's attention to his face. 'Settles what?'

'I don't recall you being this belligerent. Low sugar levels?'

The confident assertion drew a snort from Megan. 'There's nothing wrong with my sugar levels.' It was a great pity the same could not be said of her hormone levels, which had been running riotously out of control since Emilio had appeared.

Since he'd kissed her.

The memory she had tried so hard to suppress rushed over her. It was like walking headlong into a solid wall of heat. It stole her breath, her skin prickled hotly, low in her pelvis things tightened. Megan shuddered, her eyes darkening as she remembered the moment his tongue had stabbed deep into her mouth, the abrasive contact making her melt.

Eyes glazed and misty, she half lifted a hand to her lips, then, catching his dark stare, let it fall away.

She took some comfort from the realisation that she was not likely to be the only female whom he had this effect on.

Don't start thinking you're anything special, Megan. You're creased, cranky and the last person in the world he wants to be lumbered with.

So why didn't he dump you in an airport hotel?

She was too warm in her linen jacket, air conditioning or not. Her covetous gaze moved resentfully up from his gleaming shoes. She had not got very far before her resentment fell away, and the emotion that replaced it tightened like a fist in her chest—she might not be special, but Emilio was!

There was a ribbon of colour across his cheekbones accenting the sharp, sybaritic curve as their stares briefly connected.

The challenge in his made her heart beat faster as she let her lashes fall in a protective mesh over her eyes.

'All right, you can buy me breakfast, but nowhere too

posh. I look scruffy.' What could be the harm eating in a public place? And it might be nice to see a part of Madrid that was not her hotel room.

'I had thought we'd go Dutch, but...'

Despite herself, Megan found herself laughing.

CHAPTER SIX

MEGAN lagged a little behind as she followed Emilio into the building. They had crossed the foyer and entered a lift before her preoccupied brain made a fairly obvious leap.

'This is not a restaurant.'

As she spoke the glass doors closed with a silent swish and the elevator rose silently. Megan, who was not fond of heights, did not take the opportunity to look down into the greenery-filled atrium below.

'Smart and beautiful.'

Very beautiful, but not obvious, he mused, studying her face. She had classic English-rose beauty, her face a perfect heart shape, her pale complexion flawless. It was the sort of face that might not leap out of a crowd, but great, actually *fantastic*, bones and once you started looking you found you couldn't stop.

Or is that just me?

She was about as far removed from the plastic production-line beauty that most of the females he encountered boasted, but then she had what cosmetic enhancement and beauticians could not give. Megan had class; quiet, understated class.

Unaware of his scrutiny, Megan slung him a dark look, smoothed her hair and tried to slow her rapid, shallow, audible inhalations as the elevator came to a smooth halt.

She was uneasily aware that vertigo only explained part of her breathing difficulties.

'Annoying and sarcastic,' she countered, directing what she hoped was a cool, calm look up at him. 'What is this place, Emilio?' And why wasn't the damned door opening? she wondered, sliding a stressed look at the button on the wall behind him.

She wasn't claustrophobic and the space was far from cramped, but if the door didn't open soon she wasn't sure how long she could resist the strong impulse that was telling her to push him out of the way and punch in the instruction necessary herself or, failing that, bang on the door for help.

Emilio continued to stare as he gave a shrug of disinterest. The building, situated in one of Madrid's most exclusive residential areas, had been an investment, one that he had actually forgotten he had made until his ever-efficient PA had pointed out that the penthouse apartment being empty could be an obvious solution to his temporary housing situation.

'I live here.'

Megan's stomach went into a lurching dive as she digested this information in silence. *'Live?'* She was able to keep the panic from her voice, but not her tawny eyes, as she stared at a point midway up his broad chest. 'Live as in…?'

He looked amused by the question. 'Live, as in I go home to at the end of the day.'

Her eyes dropped as the sarcasm in his voice brought a flush to her cheeks. Agreeing to eat with him in a public place with people around was one thing, but this was not what she'd signed up for!

For God's sake, Megan, she counselled herself crossly,

act your age. How long could it take to swallow a cup of coffee and gulp down a pastry?

What was the alternative, run away like a frightened kid?

Emilio Rios, she reminded herself, could literally have any woman he wanted. He's not lured you to his apartment to make a pass at you!

The recognition *should* have made her feel happier.

It didn't. It wasn't that she wanted to be someone else, she was happy being herself, but it would have been nice to know what it felt like to exude that indefinable something that made men notice you *that way*.

Men?

Or was it one specific man she wanted to notice her?

Megan closed down the line of thought, drawing a firm line under the ludicrous flow of speculation. She was a practical person, not given to wishing for things she could not have, and no amount of wishful thinking or Chanel suits were going to give her what women like Rosanna were born with.

As for wanting to be *noticed* by Emilio Rios... She pressed a hand to her stomach where a fluttering had joined the hollow feeling; even the *thought* of such a thing made her feel queasy.

Or something!

'We could go to a restaurant if you prefer?'

Megan found herself responding to the challenge, imagined or otherwise, in his voice.

'No, this is fine.' She glanced down at her watch, silently trying to calculate how soon she could make an escape without looking rude.

Five minutes tops to gulp down coffee and a pastry, Megan reckoned, though actually what was so bad about appearing rude? It wasn't as if he would recognise polite conversation if it bit him on his bottom.

'You're not on the clock. Relax.'

'I am relaxed,' she gritted, plastering on a determined smile.

Emilio, who had seen nervous bridegrooms who looked more relaxed, did not comment. 'You seemed surprised that I have an apartment. What did you think—I sleep at my desk?' he asked, sounding amused.

Her golden eyes swept upwards. 'Wherever you sleep, I'm sure it's not alone.'

'And that bothers you?' He framed the question slowly, his perceptive gaze trained on her face.

Megan found his expression unreadable, but she couldn't shake the crazy conviction he could read her mind.

'Bother?' Her slender shoulders lifted in an uninterested shrug. 'It's none of my business what you do or with whom.'

'But I'm guessing that doesn't stop you having strong views on the subject,' he drawled ironically.

'I have none whatsoever,' she retorted without a blush.

She was just glad that there was no Josh to challenge her lie.

She hadn't even realised that she zeroed in on every reference to Emilio she came across until her flatmate Josh had pointed it out after she had had delivered a few juicy quotes from an offending article, and then, despite his clear lack of interest in the subject matter, had thrust it under his nose.

'How does her dress stay up? That's what I'd like to know.'

It was clear from the red-carpet shot of the couple that Emilio knew how it came off. The woman was plastered up against him like glue.

'Mioaw!' Josh laid the paper aside without looking at it and carried on drinking his coffee. 'Why the interest in this guy, Megan?'

'I'm not interested.'

He arched a brow. 'And judgemental, which isn't like you.'

'I'm not—' Innately honest, Megan was unable to complete the sentence. 'Well, Emilio can be pretty judgemental himself.' And with an awful lot less cause! She recalled his lecture on the last occasion they had met, despite the fact that she had been the victim of an unwanted pass and he had treated her like some sort of tart.

'Really? That sounds interesting.'

'Well, it wasn't,' she said discouragingly. She had no intention of dredging up the humiliating subject for Josh or, for that matter, anyone else.

She had put it very firmly behind her.

'He is just a friend of Philip's.'

'For someone who's not interested you seem awfully concerned about who he's sleeping with.' Josh, his blue eyes gleaming, angled a speculative look at her flushed face. 'Were you two ever…?'

'No, we were not!'

Chuckling, Josh held up his hands. 'I just thought maybe he was the man.'

'What man?'

'The one responsible for your nun-like existence.'

'I have a healthy social life—'

Josh cut across her protest. 'And zero sex life, and don't try and deny it, sweetheart, the walls are extremely thin. You could no more have a secret affair than I could.'

Knowing a defensive comment would prolong the teasing, she had maintained a dignified silence, but it had started her thinking.

Perhaps she did think a little too much about Emilio Rios?

He was not even part of her life any longer. He had been a friend of Philip's, not hers, so there was no reason for him to contact her. They lived in very different worlds.

Pushing away the memory of that embarrassing conversation, she looked Emilio in the eyes and added, 'But I'd sooner not read about it while I'm eating my breakfast.' She pursed her lips primly. Tales of a person's sexual stamina were not, in her opinion, suitable reading for any time of day.

Emilio arched a brow as he wedged his broad shoulders up against the glass wall of the elevator as he studied the top of her glossy head.

The urge to run his fingers across the smooth conker-brown surface and allow the glossy strands to slide through his fingers was almost impossible to resist.

Megan had renewed her study of the carpeting.

She mightn't have strong views on whom he slept with, but he was certainly bothered by whom she spent her nights with, he conceded wryly. If Philip was right about the boyfriend moving out—and Emilio did not think that was an unreasonable conclusion to draw from his comment that *Megan was thinking of moving as her present place was too expensive now Josh had moved out*—it seemed hopeful that this Josh was no longer one of that number.

Having managed to remain blasé while convincing him she cared not at all about whom he slept with or where, Megan felt the colour rush to her face the moment their eyes connected.

'Do you live alone?' You just carry on digging that hole, Megan! And why not jump in for good measure?

'I do. How about you?' he asked casually.

'Yes, I do.' Megan cleared her throat and added, 'I was wondering, is there a problem with the lift?'

It was actually pretty hard to sound casual when you were trying not to inhale his scent—not scent in a perfume sense. Although soap and shampoo were definitely involved, mingled in there with the more disturbing fragrance was a scent of warm male and Emilio.

She forced a breath into her oxygen-deprived lungs and shuddered with the effort.

'Are you all right?'

The mocking light had faded from Emilio's eyes as, concern etched in the furrows on his broad brow, he took a step towards her. Her skin was as pale as paper, the only trace of colour remaining in her face the rich tawny gold of her wide-spaced eyes.

Megan shadowed the action, her own hasty step backwards bringing her shoulder blades up against the wall of the elevator.

Her reaction sent Emilio's dark brows in the direction of his ebony hairline as he raised both hands to his chest, palm flat out to her. 'Relax. What on earth did you think I was going to do?' he asked, his lean face taut with impatience.

Relax—wasn't bad advice to take if she didn't want to give the impression she was a raving lunatic.

Embarrassed, she peeled herself away from the wall. 'You startled me,' she retorted, a defensive note of complaint in her voice.

'Clearly. I have seen rabbits less jumpy than you.' His eyes narrowed to speculative slits as he slowly scanned her face. 'Anyone would think you are scared of me.'

The velvety rasp in his deep voice had a tactile quality like raw silk. She had no control over the shudder that slid the length of her spine like the stroke of a finger. In her mind the phantom finger was long and tanned and— Stop it, Megan!

Ashamed and exasperated by her escalating physical reaction to every aspect of him, Megan studiously avoided making eye contact as she gritted her teeth.

'*Scared?*' She lifted her chin and laughed at the suggestion. 'I'm sure you make grown men cry, but not me,' she conceded. 'But—' She stopped. He had made her cry, but only the once.

Refusing to allow her thoughts to slip back to an occasion that rated pretty high in her 'the worst moment in my life' league, she sketched a tight smile and added, 'Not today anyway.'

And never again. She would never again allow him to make her feel sordid and grubby.

Emilio looked at her mouth and felt the desire in his veins burn hotter as he thought to himself today would not be soon enough for him.

He had always prided himself on his ability to keep his libido on a leash. There had only ever been one woman who had breached his defences and she was standing here now, standing here wanting him as much as he did her, so he was damned if he was going to deprive himself of the unspoken invitation that glowed in her incredible golden eyes when she looked at him.

A nerve clenched in his cheek as his mask of composure threatened to slip. The scorching sexual tension between them was stronger than anything Emilio had ever experienced in his life—she *had* to be feeling it!

Or was he projecting his fantasies onto her?

The question surfaced and was immediately quashed. He exhaled. He knew when a woman wanted him; she *was* feeling it.

Megan wanted him.

The question he ought to be asking, he told himself, was

why, given the overwhelming, almost primal attraction between them, was she putting on this ludicrous act?

Did she think she could pretend that it wasn't happening and it would go away? Why would she want it to?

He dug his fingers into his close-cropped hair and tried to think past the sexual frustration pounding in his skull and other parts of his anatomy.

The Megan he knew had an engaging candour and here she was acting like some shy virgin, which he knew she wasn't.

A girl who looked like Megan did not go through college without drawing a lot of male attention. In retrospect he could see that it should not have been a surprise to him when her flat door was opened by a half-naked man with a quiz-show-host smile—he turned out to be a doctor—and eyes that were too close together.

And yet it had been a surprise. It had been a total bombshell! Emilio had felt as though someone had just gut-punched him, but of course *someone* hadn't, the humiliation had been totally self-inflicted.

A child could have predicted this, but he hadn't. He had spent a year anticipating this moment, covering, or so he'd thought, every angle, but not once during that time had he thought she would be with someone else.

The guy, clearly very much at home, had invited him in, explaining Megan was in the shower.

Emilio had declined the offer.

Could this be simply out-of-control hormones? Megan lifted a hand to her buzzing head. Maybe he was right— maybe her sugar levels were low. It was better than the alternative—better than admitting that she had zero defences against the sizzling sexual charge he exuded.

'It...it h-hasn't opened,' she stuttered, staring at the closed door.

She heard him curse, the low savage imprecation loud in the confined space as he banged the heel of his hand on the control panel. 'Why on earth didn't you say that you suffer from claustrophobia?' he demanded, scanning her pale classic profile.

'I don't,' she protested, too slow-witted to accept this perfect excuse to explain her odd behaviour.

'So what's wrong with you?' he asked, scepticism mingled with irritation.

Again Megan's tongue bypassed her brain. 'You—' She stopped, then was inspired. 'I was just surprised you live somewhere like this. I always pictured you living in some sort of ancient mausoleum filled with antiques, a town version of your little place in the country.'

He tipped his dark head in a concessionary nod to the suggestion, and straightened up to his full impressive height as the glass doors of the private elevator silently opened into a very white space. Not that she was actually noticing; she was too busy asking herself why she was here.

Like you don't know?

Ignoring the sarcastic contribution of the snide voice in her head and the hard knot of illicit excitement low in her belly, Megan fought her way through the mind-fogging confusion in her head.

Sexual attraction, Megan told herself, was a kind of insanity, and should be treated as such. Knowing her weakness, she reasoned, gave her a degree of control.

Her tawny eyes were drawn in the direction of the tall, silent figure watching her. The silence stretched.

The invitation had been for breakfast, she reminded herself, and that was why she was here. She wouldn't let anything happen again; she would eat and leave. Sure, he had kissed her in the airport and had appeared not to want to stop, but that had been an act. For Emilio kissing her had not been a big deal.

Only it was to her. It was a very big deal to be kissed by Emilio Rios, but she would have died before she'd confess as much to him.

'You did not look surprised, you looked…' He paused, considering the question and, much to her dismay, her mouth.

Unhappy, not just about the way he was staring, but also the idea of him relentlessly pursuing the question to its conclusion, she rushed to fill the developing silence.

'Oh, all right!' She sighed, lifting her hair off her neck with her hand as she pursed her lips and evinced a show of reluctance before admitting, 'You might have been right. I do need feeding.'

For a split second she thought he was going to push, then to her relief Emilio grinned. His smugness, she decided, struggling to drag her stare from the curve of his sensually full lower lip, was infinitely preferable to him guessing the lustful direction of her thoughts.

'I am always right, and I do possess the sort of home you speak of,' he admitted, stepping through the door into the white apartment.

CHAPTER SEVEN

MEGAN moved to follow Emilio and hesitated, unable to shake the irrational conviction that by stepping over the threshold she would be committing herself to more than breakfast, which she wasn't, but what if he thought…?

What if he had more planned than breakfast? She had no doubt that he took sex as casually as he did kisses.

How was he to know she didn't?

She knew she was here for breakfast, but who was to say he did? He might assume that she knew breakfast was some sort of code for sex.

'We could do the restaurant option if you prefer. You did say you looked too much of a mess to be seen anywhere…*posh*,' Emilio reminded her. 'I thought you would appreciate the lack of strangers being traumatised by your appearance.' Strangers did not fit in with his plans for the rest of the day, as he pictured her tangled skein of glossy hair spread out on a pillow.

'Traumatised…' she choked. Her flashing golden eyes narrowed in his face. Indignation had carried Megan across the threshold without realising it until the door did the spooky swishy thing behind her, making her jump, and she momentarily transferred her anger to the inanimate object.

'You afraid that being seen in public with a female who

hasn't got her surgically enhanced boobs on show will be bad for your reputation?' she charged scornfully as she glanced downwards, adding, 'What's wrong with the way I look?'

It was a question that Megan almost immediately bitterly regretted issuing.

As his gaze drifted downwards Emilio reined in his lust with difficulty.

She stood there rigidly, her heart pounding against her ribcage, her stomach churning as his dark eyes made a slow, insolent journey from the top of her head to her toes, then at an equally leisurely pace made the return trip.

Emilio swallowed, his head jerking backwards fractionally as he snapped himself clear of the sensual fog.

'You were the one who was unhappy with the way you look.' At his sides he forcibly unclenched his long fingers.

Time, it seemed, had not lessened the strength of the primal emotions that she had shaken loose in him two years ago. He had wanted her then and he still did...

'You didn't have to agree.'

He frowned. 'Don't put words into my mouth,' he said, staring at her lips still swollen from his kiss.

The husky caution brought Megan's gaze helplessly zeroing in on the area under discussion. She felt her anger slip away as a silent sigh lifted her chest as she shook with the memory of his kiss.

The texture of his warm lips as they moved over her mouth, the lust, slammed through her body making her literally rock back on her heels.

She blinked hard to banish the memory, her control worn paper-thin as she nibbled nervously at her full lower lip, unwittingly riveting his attention to the lush curve.

'You want me to tell you you're beautiful?'

Megan flushed. 'Of course not.'

'I would hardly be the first man to tell you this.'

Emilio had never considered himself a possessive man. He had never been guilty of double standards when it came to the subject of any healthy young woman exploring their sexuality.

It turned out that this enlightened attitude only worked when the woman in question was not Megan.

'Sure, I stop traffic on a regular basis. So, why are you living here if you have a palace or something, or is this where you bring your...?' She stopped, the hot colour rushing to her cheeks.

He arched a brow. 'My...?'

'Nothing.'

Her mortified mumble drew a grin that lightened some of the tension in his lean face. 'Relax, this is not a love nest. I am temporarily homeless, while the experts sort out a bad case of dry rot. A man needs somewhere to lay his head and this location is not inconvenient,' he explained, watching her expression as she completed a slow three-hundred-and-sixty-degree turn.

'I see, you're slumming it.' Some slum! The place was a bachelor's paradise, loft-style living with modern art on white walls, acres of gleaming chrome, leather and high ceilings.

It said nothing to her about the man who lived there.

'You like it?'

'I'm sure it's every boy's dream to live somewhere like this.' If this place did not boast every techno gadget on the market she would eat her designer handbag—actually, her very good rip-off handbag.

Emilio responded to the smiling put-down with a lazy grin. The place was no fulfilment of a dream, it was a convenience and nothing more.

'I have not been called a boy for some time.'

Megan's superior smile wilted as their glances locked; the breath snagged in her throat.

She was not surprised. There was nothing even vaguely *boyish* about the man standing there. He radiated male arrogance like a force field. He was all man, all hard sinew and muscle. He couldn't have been harder if he'd been hewn out of granite, but he wasn't stone, he was flesh. Warm flesh.

The tight knot of desire low in her belly tightened so viciously that she gasped, looking away to hide the desire she felt must be written all over her face.

Emilio was a walking advertisement for masculinity and raw sex. Why was she thinking about sex, raw or otherwise?

Panic suddenly gripped her. 'I don't know what I'm doing here.' Her head came up in response to the hand on her shoulder.

'Yes, you do, Megan.'

Trapped by his dark compelling stare, she swallowed, her cheeks hot as she said in a small voice, 'You offered me breakfast.' The pause that followed her statement stretched her nerves to the breaking point.

'So I did.'

Relieved that he hadn't suggested her reasons for being here were far less clear-cut or innocent, she tried to resist the pressure of the hand on her shoulder that urged her down into one of the leather upholstered chairs.

'Relax.'

He needed to stop telling her that—how on earth could she relax?

He loosened his silk tie and slid off his jacket, flexing his shoulders as if to alleviate some unseen tension in the muscles of his neck as he flung it on a sofa. Megan watched through the inadequate protective screen of her lashes as the action strained the seams of the white shirt he wore.

Her stomach muscles flipped and tightened another disturbing notch in response to the suggestion of restrained power and the faint shadow of body hair visible through the thin fabric.

Was his skin that same deep burnished gold all over?

An image flashed into her head of her fingers moving across the surface. The illusion was strong, so tactile that she had to remind herself it wasn't real, but the tingle in her fingertips and the surge of liquid heat between her thighs were.

Megan, appalled and ashamed by her sexual awareness of him, sucked in a deep breath as she tried to focus on what he was saying.

'So what's the verdict?'

Flustered and embarrassed that he had caught her mentally undressing him and worse, Megan shook her head and echoed warily, *'Verdict?'*

'On the apartment.'

Megan, barely able to conceal her relief, embraced the far safer subject of the interior design with enthusiasm. 'Oh! Very tasteful,' she said, turning her head and seeing, not the room, but the image in her head of Emilio minus his shirt. 'But I'm not really into the minimalist look,' she admitted. 'Or technology.'

'What are you impressed by?' He arched a brow. 'A man who can cook?'

'You can cook?'

The shock in her voice drew a laugh from Emilio. 'I will let you be the judge of that,' he said, rolling up his sleeves to reveal hair-roughened sinewy forearms.

It was clear that Emilio knew his way around a kitchen. As she watched him Megan found herself wondering how well he knew his way around other places. Was he equally skilful in the bedroom? she wondered, watching as he whipped the eggs he had cracked into a bowl.

Shocked and ashamed at the direction of her thoughts, she lowered her gaze and wondered what was happening to her.

'You don't have to do this, you know. A coffee and a pastry or something would be fine.'

'I know I don't have to do this. I want to do this, and coffee and a pastry?' He snorted scornfully. 'I hope that is not your idea of a meal.'

'I don't have a lot of time for food.'

'You should make time for the important things in life.'

'I used to eat out quite a lot at a little place near where I live, but not so much since Josh—' She gave a sigh. Life was a lot duller and quieter since her flatmate and best friend had decided to do a stint with an aid agency.

Her expression softened as she recalled his embarrassed response when she had said how much she admired his decision to quit his job to work in a Third World country.

Paying his debt to society and easing his conscience, he'd said, before he sat back and drew his fat consultant's pay cheque.

She jumped, startled by the loud clatter that came from the kitchen area.

'Sorry, I dropped it,' Emilio said, putting the stainless-steel implement he had just picked up off the floor into the dishwasher.

A hard light of steely determination shone in his eyes as he began to whip the egg whites. It was his intention that, not only would Megan not smile dreamily when she thought about her ex, she would forget he ever existed!

Megan watched as he beat the hell out of the eggs. The

annoyance on his face seemed pretty out of proportion with the incident to Megan, but then who knew? Maybe he was a bit of a diva in the kitchen.

It was half an hour later when Megan sat back in her seat and gave a sigh as she licked the butter from her fingertips. 'You can cook. That was delicious.'

'It was only eggs.' He dismissed the feather-light creation with a self-deprecating shrug and filled her coffee cup. 'Wait until you try my pasta al fungi porcini, and my clams have received rave reviews.'

The smile faded from Megan's face. 'I'm sure they have.'

His comment was a timely wake-up call.

She'd been in danger of feeling special, but she was sure he made all women feel special. Maybe cooking was a tried and tested part of his seduction technique? Not that Emilio needed to feed a woman to get her into bed, she admitted bleakly.

Emilio studied her expression with a frown. 'What's wrong?'

She shook her head and avoided his eyes. 'Nothing.'

'Do not lie to me, Megan, or yourself.'

'What do you mean by that?' she flared. 'I'm not lying,' she contended stubbornly. 'Thank you for the breakfast, Emilio, but I—'

A whistled sound of irritation escaped his clenched teeth. 'From where I'm sitting you have a problem. I think you're in danger of developing a seriously bad relationship with food. Are you feeling guilty because you have eaten?'

She looked at him and thought, I'm feeling guilty because I can't look at you without thinking of you naked.

'Of course not. I promise you I do not have an eating disorder.'

'Not now maybe,' he conceded. 'But these things can be insidious.'

'Food is just not that important to me.'

'Food is not important to all people,' he conceded, leaning forward as he planted his forearms on the table. 'But you are not one of them. Eating is a sensual pleasure. You take pleasure in food because you are a sensual person. Why deprive yourself of this pleasure to fit some stereotypical image? Why fight nature?

'When it comes to food, the question,' he contended, 'is not what time is it, it is are you hungry?'

Megan glared at him in total exasperation. 'Of course I'm hungry. I'm always hungry!' she yelled.

Didn't the stupid man realise that she was fighting nature that had decided in its infinite wisdom that she should be ten pounds heavier? 'As for eating, when I'm hungry if I ate what I *liked* I'd be...'

Emilio, aware that he had hit a raw nerve or possibly several, turned his chair around, dragged it nearer to hers and straddled it. 'Less cranky?'

'Very funny,' she snapped, unappreciative of his smart retort, a comment that could only be made by a person who had never worried about their weight.

Her eyes skimmed scornfully down his body. Either he had iron discipline or an enviably efficient metabolism.

Even fully clothed it was obvious he didn't carry an ounce of excess flesh on his lean frame. He was all hard muscle and sinew.

The butterfly kicks that fluttered in the pit of her stomach made her hastily avert her gaze.

'Do you think I'm a size ten by accident?'

'I wondered if you had been ill,' he admitted.

Megan's jaw dropped as her head turned back towards him. Her amber eyes sparkled with incredulous wrath as she got to her feet.

'I look ill?' It was always ego-enhancing to be told you looked wrecked by a man who, in her head, had been the standard of physical perfection she measured his entire sex by since she was a teenager.

Emilio grinned. He was not oblivious to the danger in her voice, but he was not a man who thought it a virtue to play it safe.

In his opinion a rush of adrenaline made life more interesting and reminded a man he was alive. His eyes followed the swish of her free hair as it settled in a glossy frame to her heart-shaped face. Actually, now that he thought about it, there had been precious few adrenaline rushes in his life of late.

When was the last time he'd clashed with anyone? When was the last time anyone had openly disagreed with him?

And it wasn't just professionally. Even the women in his life censored out any of the contents he might not like before they spoke, never even considering that he might appreciate the challenge of an opinion other than his own.

'You look a little...*faded.*' His eyes slid to her pink lips and he swallowed. 'Like a crushed rose.'

The odd note in his deep voice brought Megan's frowning regard to his face. 'Rose?' she echoed, fighting off the crazy rush of pleasure.

He nodded. 'One who needed a long cool drink or, in this case, breakfast.'

'You're obsessed by food!' she complained, thinking it was better than what she was obsessed by!

It wasn't even as if she were not a very sexual person;

the contrary was true. It was as if that airport kiss had pressed some off switch to the on position!

'No, that is you,' he countered, watching the play of expressions as they moved across her expressive face. It wasn't just her hair that had slipped, it was her composed mask too.

'I'm not obsessed with food.'

Just your mouth and, for that matter, the rest of you!

Switching off the inner commentary, but not before the guilty colour had rushed to her cheeks, Megan dropped her gaze to her hands clasped in her lap.

What was going on? She didn't have thoughts like this.

'A person,' he came back confidently, 'is only obsessed by what they are deprived of.'

Megan's head came up. 'What do you mean by that? I'm not deprived of anything!' she yelled, her defensive voice bouncing off the high ceiling.

He held up his hands in mock surrender, the sardonic gleam in his dark eyes making her shift uncomfortably in her seat. 'I'm delighted to hear it, though some people might think the lady protests too much?'

Lips pursed, Megan shrugged and did not respond to the gentle taunt. 'I simply show a bit of self-control where food is concerned.'

Self-control... Emilio's sloe-dark eyes drifted towards her mouth. Her lips were bare; he remembered the hint of strawberry in the gloss that he had kissed away. Without adornment they were naturally rose-tinted, and amazingly lush, their softness so inviting he struggled to think past the loud buzz in his head and the stab of desire that sliced through him like a knife.

He lifted his gaze, meeting her eyes through the mesh

of his eyelashes. 'Self-control has its place.' Like in an airport.

The ripple of sensation Emilio's sinfully seductive throaty purr set in motion passed through her entire body from her scalp to her curling toes.

Megan, her eyes melded to his smouldering stare, endured the moment breathing through the nerve-shredding sensation. It passed, but the aching lump lodged like a chunk of broken glass in her throat remained.

'I...' Megan was unable to tear her eyes free of his mesmeric stare, and her voice faded. Her lips continued to move, but nothing emerged but a whispery sigh.

When the sexual tension had been in the background she had been able to pretend it wasn't there. That was no longer possible. In the space of a heartbeat it had become an almost visible presence, humming like a high-voltage charge in the air between them, swallowing up the oxygen so that she struggled to breathe.

'Though sometimes it is good to let go.'

Megan, hand pressed to her throat, struggled to catch her breath. She compressed her lips, angry with him for playing games and herself for being such a sucker for his not very subtle tactics, and there was no way in the world it was accidental. Was this some sort of game for him?

'I really wouldn't know. I don't...'

'What? You never let that lovely hair down and throw caution to the wind? Some men could view a statement like that as a challenge.'

'Certainly I let my hair down, but only with people I trust.'

'You think I would take advantage?' Emilio sighed inwardly. She was right.

The predatory gleam in his dark eyes sent a secret shiver down her spine. 'I'm really not interested in finding out.'

Her declaration of indifference drew a low chuckle from him. The scarily attractive sound made Megan bite the inside of her cheek.

'You are probably...' he mused, studying her with an intent expression that made Megan want to cover her face with her hands.

'Probably what?' she snapped when the dramatic pause stretched beyond bearable limits.

'The worst liar of any woman I have ever met.'

Her eyes flew wide. 'I am a *very* good liar!' she cried, bouncing to her feet.

Megan gave him the evil eye when her unthinking indignant rebuttal drew another throaty chuckle, of the incredibly sexy variety, from him.

'What's that on your mouth?' Emilio asked, no longer looking amused as he got to his feet and reached out towards her face.

Megan reacted to his hand like a striking snake, her heart beating a furious tattoo as she ducked away from his touch.

He raised an eloquent brow in response to her instinctive action as, feeling foolish, Megan slid her eyes from his.

'What's what?' she said, lifting a hand to the corner of her mouth. Her finger came away smeared red. 'Oh, it's nothing,' she said dismissively as she fished a tissue from her pocket.

His dark brows twitched into a disapproving straight line above his hawkish nose. 'It looks more like blood to me.'

Megan rolled her eyes. Talk about overreaction. 'Why are the Spanish so dramatic?' she asked, clicking her tongue in irritation as she added, 'It's a microscopic speck of blood. If you must know, I bit myself,' she admitted, wishing something would distract his attention from her mouth.

To have his dark-eyed scrutiny trained with unblinking intensity on her lips was sending her nervous system into frantic overdrive.

'That was not a clever thing to do,' he mused, leaning in close—too close—and taking the tissue from her hand.

Their fingers brushed before she could take evasive action and then she didn't want to. A shiver wafted across the sensitised surface of her skin making all the downy hairs stand on end.

Her nostrils flared in response to the scent of his body: warm, musky male smell overlaid with the clean scent of the spicy soap he used.

Struggling against the tide of enervating heat that washed through her, Megan, who was sure her struggle was written across her face in neon, did not make the mistake of meeting his eyes.

Instead she trained her eyes on his strong jaw, close enough to see the dark rash of stubble and the faint white scar that angled upwards in the direction of his cheekbone.

'I'm not clever.' The words came out a husky whisper as she thought, No, I'm insane, as in certifiable.

The flash of insight did nothing to halt the growing fluttering sensation of excitement low in her stomach. She caught her lower lip between her teeth, swallowing hard as her covert glance flickered across the strong angles and planes of his incredible face.

'But you are a very good cook.'

'Would you like some more?'

She shook her head. 'If I ate what I wanted when I wanted I'd be ten pounds heavier,' she said honestly. 'And a lot of those pounds would be on my boobs and hips.'

'And that is a problem?'

The anger sizzled up out of nowhere. Her hands

clenched into tight fists, squeezing the blood from her whitened knuckles. She was suddenly so angry she couldn't breathe.

'Yes, as men appear to measure a woman's availability and her morals by the size of her breasts!' she yelled, pressing her hands flat on her heaving C-cup bosom, still able to see Emilio's expression when she had turned to him with tearful gratitude, thanking him for saving her.

CHAPTER EIGHT

Two years had passed, but Megan could recall the entire scene in painful, mortifying, word-perfect detail that time had not dulled—if anything time had intensified the humiliation.

Ironic, really—if Emilio hadn't arrived when he had, if instead she had been able to extricate herself from the situation with a few of the dirty tricks that her brother had said no girl should be without, the incident might now have faded to a memory. Maybe she'd even have been able to smile at it.

But the memory hadn't faded. Instead it had grown in her mind out of all proportion. It had lost none of its ability to tie her stomach into nauseous knots because Emilio *had* walked in, or, rather, past the parked car. He had flung open the car door with a force that had almost wrenched it from its hinges.

Megan's initial relief had rapidly morphed into shock mingled with dismayed confusion as she'd registered the expression on Emilio's lean face. In Megan's mind her brother's handsome Spanish friend with his excitingly different background and charming accent had always epitomised urbane, sophisticated charm.

The golden skin drawn tight across the strong bones of his face, raw, brutal fury etched into every plane and angle of the hard lines of his patrician visage, the man with the blazing dark eyes had seemed like a stranger.

He had responded to her escort's drunken slurred protests with a storm of staccato Spanish before he had literally dragged the man from the car and vanished into the trees with him.

Megan never knew what happened during the five minutes Emilio was gone. But next time their paths had crossed at the university her lecturer had forgotten the ultra-cool image he liked to cultivate and run, gown flapping, in the opposite direction like a scared rabbit.

When Emilio had returned she had already got out of the car and had been relieved to see the explosive fury had vanished. He seemed calm, cold even.

She had gathered her courage in both hands and levelled a wary look at his face, still able to remember his anger, still seeing a stranger when she looked at him. But her dignified thank-you had been genuine, even though she had wished it had been anyone else but Emilio who had rescued her from the mortifying situation.

'Did you *want* saving?'

The response bewildered her until she saw his expression.

The scorn and aristocratic disdain etched on his patrician features made her cringe. She felt crushed by his scorn. It was bad enough that the man she had had a secret crush on since she was a kid had witnessed the grubby sordid scene, but that he could think she had *wanted*... If she could have crawled out of her skin at that moment Megan would have. She stuttered in her eagerness to correct him.

'No...no, that is, yes, you can't think that I wanted... Of course I—'

'You were a fool.'

Unable to deny the scathing denouncement, she shook her head and blinked back tears. Did he think she didn't know that? Did he think she needed it rubbed in?

As she stood there she silently prayed for the ground to open up and swallow her—maybe even out loud; that part remained a little vague. But it didn't so she simply had to stand and endure the contemptuous study, nailed to the spot with scorching humiliation, mortified beyond belief as the sweep of his disparaging stare moved from the top of her glossy head to her feet shod in a pair of high-heeled ankle boots.

'You say you didn't want anything, but appearances suggest otherwise. You look like you've been poured into that top, and as for the jeans…'

Megan dragged down at the rounded high neckline of the shirt she wore today under her business suit, closing her eyes as she still recalled the condemnatory glow in his eyes as his sweeping gesture had encompassed the V-necked black T-shirt—black because she'd thought the colour was slimming—before sliding to the dark denim jeans, the brand and style that all her friends had been wearing without being accused of flaunting anything.

'What reaction did you expect?' Megan heard him ask as she focused her attention, not on the condemnation in his eyes, but the nerve in his lean cheek that was clenching and unclenching.

He stabbed his long fingers into the dark waves of his thick hair and released a string of expletives in Spanish, sounding and looking nothing like the quietly authoritative man who had always been kind to her and, even more amazingly, appeared interested in what she was doing, possibly because he had lovely manners.

'As for getting into a car with a boy who had been drinking…'

His sneering disdain made her see red. 'He's not a boy, he's a lecturer.'

'Do the university authorities look kindly on their lecturing staff dating their students?'

'It wasn't a date, he was just—'

'I saw what he was just doing, and if you choose to have casual sex it might be a good idea to remember that drunks have a very slender grasp of safe sex!'

The accusation horrified Megan. 'He wasn't—'

'Are you saying he had not been drinking?'

'No, I'm…' She shook her head, struggling to equate this cold, cruel critic with the person who had always had a kind word of encouragement for her in the past.

Her miserable silence seemed to incense him further.

'Have you been drinking also?' he asked, his hooded gaze suspicious as he studied her face.

At that point a small burst of defiance, long overdue it seemed in retrospect, came to Megan's aid.

Planting her hands on the curve of her hips, she thrust out her chin, tossed back her hair. 'If I wanted to have a drink, so what?' she challenged, her voice husky as she forced the words past the aching emotional lump in her throat.

'It's not illegal, you know. I'm over eighteen.'

'This is not about *legality*, it is about self-respect.'

Megan, unable to stand there and take the sheer breathtaking unfairness of the cutting condemnation, choked back a sob and yelled, 'I wasn't attending an orgy! It was just a few friends, a university thing… Actually, it's none of your business. You're not my father.'

Inexplicably, or so it seemed to Megan, he took her response as a tacit admission of guilt.

'So you have!' His eyes closed, he let his head fall back, exposing the long line of his brown muscled throat as he inhaled deeply, then slid apparently unwittingly into his native tongue, ending the tirade with a biting, *'Well?'*

Well, what? she thought. 'I had one glass of wine,' she admitted after a fulminating silence. 'I said I'd get a taxi, but he offered—'

'How did you expect the man to react when you look like that? It's an open invitation to…to…' The rest of the insult was delivered once more in his native tongue, but this time a crushed Megan definitely got the gist!

'I said no.'

'Clearly not loudly enough. He said…'

'What did he say?'

'He said you were gagging for it.'

Megan, white-faced, pushed away the images crowded into her head and refocused on the present.

'I prefer to steer clear of the D-cup she's-gagging-for-it look.' As she spoke she saw the flash of shocked recognition in his eyes and wished the words unsaid.

Her intention had always been, should he ever refer to the subject—admittedly unlikely—to shrug it away as though she barely recalled it. The last thing she wanted was Emilio to guess what sort of indelible impression the incident had had on her.

'You are speaking of that night when that little loser made a pass.'

His retrospective take on the evening drew a laugh from Megan. 'You mean that innocent victim I led on?' She bit her lip and thought, Could you sound any more bitter, Megan?

A nerve clenched in his lean cheek.

If it had been anyone else she would have interpreted the look that flashed across his face as discomfiture, but this was Emilio Rios, who did not know the meaning of awkward.

He dragged a hand down his jaw and expelled an irritated-sounding sigh. 'I was angry that night.' He had been angry that entire weekend, from the moment she had walked into the room the previous evening smelling like summer and looking like warm, inviting sin, looking as if she were made for him.

The forced admission made her laugh. 'I'd never have guessed.'

Even now the memory of his loss of control shook Emilio. He had never before or since come closer to totally losing it. The red haze had consumed him totally.

'The situation was…'

She angled an interrogative brow as his voice trailed away to a growl.

'I did not handle the situation well.'

As apologies went it was pretty feeble. 'Being my brother's mate did not make you the guardian of my morals and you had no right to judge me!'

'I did not judge you. I was trying to protect you, Megan.'

'You made me feel grubby.' She saw the flash of shock in his eyes and dropped her gaze.

'That was not my intention.'

Not his intention, but the result nonetheless. 'It doesn't matter. It was a long time ago.'

'Not so long ago and it clearly does matter,' he said, feeling intense guilt as he studied her face.

'Look, let the subject drop. Like I said, it was a long time ago.'

'My actions were…not acceptable.'

He had been more out of control than he had ever been at any other time in his life.

When the guy had bleated out the clichéd defence and even tried to suggest Megan had not meant no, Emilio had come closer than he even liked to admit to himself to choking the life out of the sleaze.

It had not occurred to him until now that he had vented his frustration on Megan. Frustration that had been building the entire weekend. When he had come back and seen her standing there, the tears on her cheeks, her hair tangled and her mouth bruised from another man's kisses, all that frustrated sexual hunger and guilt he had been keeping under tight control for the entire weekend had exploded.

'And then some.' His remorse seemed genuine, but Megan was not prepared to let him off the hook just yet. 'I think, Megan, that you—'

She held up her hand. 'Don't bother, I know what you think about me. You made yourself quite clear at the time, practically telling me I was a little tart who was a danger to the moral well-being of the entire male population for a hundred-mile radius.'

'Don't be ridiculous. I didn't say anything like that.' Their eyes connected and he shrugged, admitting, 'All right, I might have given that impression, but that was only because…'

'Because you were disgusted by my *slutty* clothes. Well, as a matter of fact, they weren't. They were perfectly ordinary things for—'

'Jeans, very tight, and the clingy black top. It kept slipping off your shoulder—your bra strap was pink,' he recited. His dark eyes drifted towards her mouth as he continued to catalogue. 'Your lipstick was pink too. It was smeared.' He swallowed convulsively before adding in the same flat, colourless tone, 'And your lip was bleeding.'

Until he'd seen the blood he had been holding it together quite well. All right, not *well* as such, but he had been keeping his more primitive instincts in check. But those tiny beads of red on her skin had made something snap inside him.

Megan's jaw dropped. 'You still remember.' And in detail. Even she didn't remember what colour her lipstick had been that night. Her ensemble appeared to have been so truly awful that it had imprinted itself on the memory of a man who had perfect taste.

Actually he had perfect everything, she thought, concentrating on her resentment that rose in direct proportion to the perfection, rather than the liquid rush of excitement low in her belly.

Her legs were jelly, inside her bra her breasts chafed painfully against the lace. Stop acting like you don't have a choice, she told herself. There's always a choice.

Her moment of rebellion lasted as long as it took for her gaze to wander back to his mouth.

She struggled against a wave of lust. It was insane, she thought, running the tip of her tongue across the curve of her dry lips, but when it came to being a total pushover that theoretical choice was just that—theoretical.

The way Emilio made her feel was one thing in her life that she had no choice about!

She was stuck with loving the way he looked. Loving the way he sounded, the way he smelt, the way he moved… Actually love was perhaps the wrong word to accurately convey the visceral intensity and power of the effect he had on her.

On the other hand, maybe *love* was exactly the right word.

Megan's pupils dilated with shocked rejection as she pushed away the dangerous thought and narrowed her wandering focus to one little triangle of olive-toned tanned skin at the base of his throat. Even that tiny section of skin set in motion a stream of erotic conjecture.

This was so unfair. What chance did she have? Linen didn't dare crease on him. In a fair world it ought to be illegal for any man to be this good-looking.

Conscious that the silence had lengthened, she dragged her thoughts away from the steamy place they were in danger of returning to and angled a hostile stare up at his face.

'Have you got a photographic memory or something?' Was the embarrassing moment never going to be allowed to die?

'No, I do not, but I have excellent recall for some things.' The weekend he had realised that he had been a blind fool had lingered in his mind.

'I didn't look *that* bad. Did I?' She bit her lip, hating the fact she sounded as if she was asking for his approval.

And you're not?

The question made him blink. *'Bad...?'* Emilio ejaculated hoarsely.

He shook his head. The rest of the world looked at Megan and saw an incredibly beautiful woman, but what, he wondered grimly, did she see when she looked in the mirror?

Had that boyfriend of hers been too busy admiring himself in the mirror to make her see she was stunning? His opinion of the man, never high, now zoomed to below zero. As for that family of hers, he brooded darkly, they had a hell of a lot to answer for!

On his visits to the Armstrong household over the span of several years, Emilio had been forced on numerous occasions to remind himself it was not his business as he watched the attempts of Philip's little sister, not to win approval or praise from her family, but simply to be noticed.

Doomed attempts, obviously it went without saying.

The Armstrongs were a loud, egocentric bunch too busy with their own lives to show any interest in anything else, especially the new and painfully unsure member of the family.

'There's no need to yell,' Megan bellowed, then looked shocked. She was not in the habit of raising her voice, as much as the last hour belied that fact.

From the expression on his dark face she had the strong feeling that Emilio was equally unaccustomed to being yelled at.

On another occasion his astounded expression might have amused her, but at that moment she felt as though she might never laugh again.

Emilio swore under his breath, the muscles along his strong jaw tightening as his scorching dark gaze swept across the features turned up to him. Being furious with her was not reducing the level of his painful arousal. If anything it was feeding the desire that licked through his veins like a forest fire, out of control—did he want to control it?

Emilio shifted his weight in a futile effort to ease the pain in his groin. This was not a moment for deep analysis. He could barely string a sequence of intelligible words together, let alone indulge in self-analysis of the complex mixture of emotions that he was struggling with.

Megan, her head tilted to one side, watched through the veil of her lashes as he dragged a shapely brown hand through the ebony strands of his gleaming dark head. Her level of fascination with his fingers, the size, elegance, strength and shape of his hands, was beginning to escape her control.

What control? asked the ironic inner voice in her head.

'*Por Dios*, there is every need to shout,' he contended,

studying her flushed face with an air of scowling disbelief as he fought to subdue the protective feelings that surfaced when he saw the reflection of whatever inner battle she was fighting shining in her eyes.

It was easier to focus on his anger.

He *knew* she was feeling the erotic charge that hung heavily in the air between them. How could she not? It almost had a physical presence.

Why was she fighting it? Why couldn't she just relax and let it happen? His jaw clenched in frustration. It was as if she couldn't get past the fact he'd been the one to rescue her from an unpleasant and potentially dangerous situation.

Was it because he'd seen her vulnerable? Did that not mesh with the cool, controlled image she obviously wanted to project?

He dragged a hand down his jaw and decided it was useless to try and figure out her reasoning because, quite clearly, there was none.

CHAPTER NINE

'WAS I drunk?'

The simmering hostility in Emilio's manner as much as the abrupt question made Megan blink. 'What?'

His dark eyes flashed. 'Was I forcing myself on you? *Por Dios*, no, I was not!'

'I never—'

'So at what point did I become the bad guy?' he demanded, cutting across her.

'I never—'

'The fact is you were lucky I was there, but you're too stubborn to admit it! You are just as stupid now as you were then!'

Megan's chin went up at the insult. Eyes narrowed, she threw back her head, glaring up at him with simmering hostility. 'And you are just as arrogant and judgemental.'

A hissing sound of irritation escaped his clenched teeth. 'Also, do you know,' he drawled, 'how incredibly boring this ugly-duckling routine of yours is?'

Megan's amber eyes lit up like beacons with anger. 'Oh, I'm *so* sorry to bore you.' If she'd been some long-legged lissom beauty with plastic boobs attached to a skeletal clothes-hanger frame he would no doubt make allowances for an IQ in single figures.

Emilio's teeth audibly ground in response to her sarcastic insincerity.

'Of course, if I had known I was expected to *entertain* you, I'd have made more of an effort—worn a funny nose, perhaps?' she suggested, pressing the tip of her finger to her small, classically perfect nose.

He gave a hard laugh and watched as her hand fell, revealing the delicate purity of her features only spoiled from being textbook classical by the generosity of her lips. Emilio, his eyes glued to the full, lush curve, did not think it spoiled anything.

It took every ounce of his strength not to grab her and crush her mouth under his. He inhaled sharply through flared nostrils and snarled.

'Do not be absurd!'

His dismissive, plain nasty attitude fed her anger and sense of growing resentment. 'So I'm assuming for "absurd" read anyone who says anything you don't like?'

Which couldn't, she reasoned darkly, be something that happened very often. The problem with Emilio Rios was that people were willing to cross oceans, let alone roads, to avoid antagonising him, and from where she was standing it was easy to see why.

He had not gained the reputation of being a bad man to get on the wrong side of by accident! And he did look pretty magnificent if you liked your dark and moody with an edge of danger.

And she, it turned out, did!

As Megan watched a shaft of sunlight from an angled skylight hit his face. He had no reason to fear the unforgiving light; there were no flaws or shortcomings to be revealed.

He was perfect.

A furrow of concentration appeared between Megan's

feathery brows as her rapt gaze lingered on the hard angles and hollows of his patrician face, the strong, sculpted contours emphasised by the dusting of dark hair sprinkled already over his clean-shaven jaw. She wondered how it would feel against her skin and shivered, unable to tear her rapt gaze from his face.

He was nothing short of breathtaking to look at!

'You make a great deal of effort to be rude to me, *querida*. I wonder why?' he mused.

'It's no effort, believe me, and don't call me that,' she snapped, her discomfort increased by the casual endearment.

Privately she conceded he did have a point. Where was the diplomacy she was famed for? Winding Emilio up was a bit like getting into a tiger's cage and throwing sticks at it.

A person had to expect the tiger to leap so the question remained why? A mental image of Emilio falling across her body flashed into Megan's head, the erotic fantasy so powerful that she could actually feel the weight of his body, the heat of him bearing down on her.

The effort of expelling the erotic intrusion wrenched a soft grunt from her aching throat that drew a quizzical look from Emilio.

Megan decided to avoid tiger analogies for the foreseeable future and took refuge in hostility—*again*.

'What can I say? My job entails being pleasant to men who have to be told at regular intervals how marvellous they are. I'm on my own time.' Her dad might disagree on that detail, but then nothing she had done so far today was going to make him break out in song. 'I don't have to play nice.'

A white line of anger appeared around the sensual outline of his sculpted lips as Emilio drew himself up to his full intimidating height.

'I am not your father,' he snarled, totally incensed by the implied comparison she made with a man he despised.

Megan, aware she had been appallingly indiscreet, not to mention unprofessional, began to back-pedal furiously. 'I didn't mean Dad, just men in a position of power generally,' she finished lamely.

Emilio ignored her protestations. 'And I do not,' he imparted grimly, 'need my ego stroked.'

How about other parts?

Shocked, not just by the shameless question that popped into her head, but the accompanying images that followed the thought, Megan dropped her gaze from his as she felt the shamed colour fly to her cheeks. She was not the sort of girl who went around mentally undressing men.

'It's the effect you have on me,' she mumbled, struggling to find a plus side to this situation. He couldn't read her mind, though sometimes when he looked at her she did get the uncomfortable feeling that she had no secrets from him.

'It was not my intention to...' His voice faded as she began to nibble nervously at her full lower lip.

The silence stretched way beyond dramatic pause and into nerve-shredding territory until finally Megan could bear it no longer.

'Not your intention to what?'

Her voice dragged Emilio from the hot place his thoughts had gone. He blinked and met her eyes, still imagining her lips parting to allow his tongue deep inside.

'Not my intention to—' He paused again and exhaled slowly.

He could have said lose the thread...lose the plot... Both, to his intense shock, were true. He could sit in a high-powered meeting that went on into the small hours and when others faded, not miss a beat, stay on top of every detail discussed, some buried in a mass of techno babble, yet he looked at Megan's mouth and his brain was mush.

Emilio chose to fast-forward the conversation. 'I find your self-deprecating attitude annoying. You are a beautiful woman and, believe it or not, I was trying to help that night, not judging.'

Megan gave a derisive hoot. 'Sure you weren't.' *Beautiful?* Her stomach muscles did a shimmy as she directed a wary look at his face, waiting for the punchline and telling herself not to start seeing or hearing things that weren't there.

'It was not your clothes that night,' he said abruptly, 'though they were enough to—' He inhaled, turning his hand away sharply, providing Megan with a view of the nerve pulsing in his hollow cheek and the cords of tension standing out in his brown throat.

'Of course, I can see the sense of power you had discovered must have been intoxicating,' he conceded, struggling to be fair-minded and failing big time as he thought of Megan enjoying her feminine power in the arms of men like that creep he had dragged from the car.

As he remembered the fear in the said creep's eyes he smiled thinly, not regretting having put it there—at least he knew there would be one less guy supplying willing arms.

She gave a baffled shake of her head, confused as much by his strained manner as his peculiar choice of words. *'Intoxicating?'*

'You'd pretty much been invisible at home all through your adolescence and, I assume, school.' Recalling the slights and snubs he had witnessed and imagining the ones he had not, Emilio struggled to keep his voice impassive.

'Thanks.' Megan finally saw where he was going with this. It was always good to be told you were a needy and pathetic outsider. 'So you're suggesting at some point I morphed into an equally pathetic attention seeker with self-esteem issues.' She wasn't sure which was worst.

His lips twisted in a spasm of impatience. 'Don't spin my words. I'm *saying* that the tables were turned. You weren't the one doing the vying. It was not surprising that, after years of being overlooked, being the focus of male attention should go to your head. You wouldn't be the first person deprived of parental approval to confuse sex with love. Sex is only ever a short-term fix.'

The expression in his eyes when he drew this bleak conclusion made Megan wonder if this was personal.

Was Emilio thinking of the women he had slept with since his marriage collapsed when he spoke of short-term fixes? Was Rosanna the only woman he had ever loved? It was obvious after the airport debacle that, whatever he said, he was not over her.

'It is hard to recover your self-respect, Megan, once you have lost it.'

'Is that a polite way of saying you think I'm a tart?'

'Do not put words in my mouth,' he responded irritably.

Megan gave a bemused shrug and stared up at him. For a man with the reputation of infallibility, she reflected grimly, when Emilio got it wrong he got it wrong big time!

'And you got all that from the colour of my lipstick! Amazing, you're even smarter than they say.'

The muscles around his jaw tightened at her mock admiration. 'Oh, so I'm meant to believe you didn't have the *faintest* idea what you could do to me…a man, looking that way.'

'Do to a man?' Her eyes widened. The expression

smouldering in his deep-set eyes made her heart kick up several more uncomfortable notches. 'Me? Sure,' she drawled, coating her words with protective cynicism as she batted her eyelashes like crazy and struck a provocative pose, hand on hip. 'It's such a burden being irresistible. Ouch,' she yelled, pulling back as his fingers closed like an iron band around her wrist.

The touch was light and the effect on her nervous system totally disproportionate. 'This habit you have of putting yourself down before someone else does is one you should try to break.'

'I don't—' Emilio watched the flash of recognition in her eyes before they fell from his.

'That hurts,' she lied, wincing not in pain but at the breathy sound of her own voice.

Emilio was breathing hard as he brought her hands together and pressed them, palms sealed, between his.

It was a moment before his gaze lifted from their entwined fingers. The blaze of hunger in his eyes as they connected with her own made Megan's insides dissolve.

'So does wanting a woman so much you can't think of anything else, so much that you can't function!' he growled, jerking her roughly towards him until they stood thigh to thigh.

They were so close now that Megan could hear his heartbeat, or was that her own? His hands had moved to the small of her back, leaving her own trapped between their bodies. She might have struggled to work out where he ended and she started, except he was harder...*much* harder. The muscular thighs she was pressed against had as much give as oak-tree trunks.

Shaking her head to clear the dreamy, light-headed sensation, she forced herself to recognise the abrupt rise in her core temperature for what it was: a hormone rush—God, a hormone avalanche!

She struggled hard to inject a note of humour into her response. 'Your concern for your fellow man does you credit, but I promise to behave and never wear pink lipstick again.'

'I have no concern for them.' Emilio dismissed the mental well-being of one half of the population with an expressive sneer. 'And,' he added, gritting out the words with force, 'I don't want you to behave.'

'You don't?' she whispered.

His glittering eyes held hers. 'Not at all,' he confirmed in a deep smoky voice that sent shivers of anticipation down her spine.

Emilio wanted her to misbehave—with him.

She said it twice in her head and it still didn't seem real. Did she even know how to misbehave in the way he clearly expected? Her eyes drifted to his gorgeous, incredibly sexy mouth and suddenly her lack of experience felt less important as need swelled inside her, tightening into a hard fist of hot desire in her belly.

Emilio was the one man whom she had always been prepared to sacrifice her principles for. She had frequently told herself she was lucky he had never asked her to. That way, she had reasoned, she had no regrets—what she also did not have, but had not previously acknowledged, were no memories.

Now he was standing there, not asking directly but sending some pretty explicit messages, unless she had disastrously misinterpreted his thinly veiled comments and the gleam of sexual intent in his eyes was a figment of her overheated imagination.

She checked. That gleam looked real. It felt real, she

thought as a fresh shiver rippled through her body. At that moment it hit her that it *was* real; she wasn't dreaming.

What am I doing?

Belatedly Megan's self-protective instincts kicked in and her head dropped forward, causing her hair to fall in a silky screen around her face.

Space, she told herself. I need space and I need *not* to say, Take me!

Do not say it, Megan!

She bit down on the shameless words. She remained dumb but couldn't put the space plan into action as her feet remained nailed to the floor.

She felt the sweat trickle down her back and realised with horror that if anything she was leaning into him, not pulling away. Her body just wasn't listening to what her head was telling it.

Her body had its own agenda!

And to make the situation even more unbearable her brain might have closed down but her senses were painfully alert. Being this close to him, being able to smell him, feel the heat coming off his body, was physically painful.

She started shaking like someone with a fever. The intensity of the need pounding through her terrified her. It was utterly and totally outside her experience.

Had he noticed? Of course he had. The knowledge that she was trembling with sheer lust would presumably confirm his conviction she was a bed-hopping tart.

CHAPTER TEN

'WOULD you like to not behave with me?'

This time the invitation left no room for misinterpretation.

Megan felt vulnerable, exposed and excited all at the same time. 'It really isn't that simple.' A person standing on the brink of a precipice stepped back; they did not jump—so why was every atom in her body screaming, Jump?

'It is.' There was no trace of uncertainty in Emilio's voice.

But then why would there be uncertainty in his voice? This was simple for him: he felt an attraction and he acted on it. He had no moral dilemma, no trust issues, no deep fear of having his heart broken.

'Has someone hurt you, Megan?'

His question triggered her self-protective instincts.

'No. There are no great dramas in my life.'

He looked unconvinced by her response, but was quickly distracted. 'Your skin is so soft,' he said, looking at her mouth. 'And I have dreamed of your mouth.'

She lifted her head and groaned. 'It's not even dark!'

Emilio threw back his head and laughed. The deep, attractive sound lowered the sexual temperature but the respite was brief. A moment later he was looking at her, his teeth bared in a white, wolfish grin, and the expression of predatory intent written into every line of his lean face as he looked down at her sent the sexual temperature zooming off the chart!

'Are you a lights-out girl?'

She was a good-book-and-a-mug-of-cocoa girl, but even had she felt inclined to confess this Megan doubted he would have believed her.

'While I agree darkness has an allure,' he continued in the same deep, seductive, throaty purr that made the downy hair on her neck and arms rise and the skin they covered tingle. 'It breaks down restraints and frees up the imagination.'

Megan, whose imagination had broken free of all her own restraints, her eyes sealed to his, began to pant softly. She couldn't seem to draw enough air into her tight, aching chest.

'I find visual stimulus very—'

With a cry she pulled her hands out from between their bodies and clamped them over her ears, closing her eyes and yelling, 'We weren't talking about your sexual predilections!'

A static silence followed her outburst. Megan stood there with her eyes tight shut, knowing she had pretty much blown her I've-been-here-done-this-got-the-T-shirt card!

'No, we were talking about yours.'

At the quiet but firm correction her eyes flickered open. She angled a wary look at his face and immediately felt her defences crumble as she read tenderness mingled in with the driven hunger in his lean face.

'I would like to know what pleases you.'

The answer did not require much thought and Megan felt her knees give as the truth emerged uncensored from her lips. 'You!'

Heat flared hot in Emilio's eyes in response to her whispered admission.

Megan could not understand a word of the flood of liquid, passionate Spanish that flowed from his lips, but she listened raptly, observing with a mixture of anticipation and apprehension the smile of gloating male satisfaction that curved his sensually sculpted lips.

'I don't know what you just said, but—'

He cut her off, which was possibly just as well because Megan hadn't the faintest idea what she wanted to say. What sort of *but* was appropriate after you'd just told a man that he virtually embodied your sexual fantasies? There was actually no virtual about it—he did!

'I said I intend to please you,' he promised thickly.

Megan's heart lurched wildly further south; the liquid heat between her thighs throbbed. She never doubted for a moment that he could fulfil his promise and she couldn't wait—it was what she wanted.

It was what she'd always wanted.

You can't have what you want. You can just have a tiny piece of it. Will that be enough?

Megan lifted her chin and silenced the whisper of doubt in her head. You had to take a risk. Life was short and when it threw the possibility of something precious your way it would be churlish, not to mention stupid, not to grab it with both hands!

The alternative was always wondering what if? Megan didn't want what ifs. She wanted Emilio. She wanted Emilio heavy on top of her; she wanted him inside her.

For the first time she allowed herself to look at him without trying to disguise what she was feeling. The sensation was simultaneously liberating and scary, but since when was anything that involved Emilio uncomplicated?

'I want you so badly, Emilio, I can't stand up.'

Megan heard the sharp intake of his breath and sighed as his long fingers slid into her silky hair. Her head fell back, the expression in her golden eyes hazed by a sheen of lust as he slid a supporting second hand into her hair and angled her face up to him.

'You are so beautiful—that face, that body.'

Megan saw the raw hunger in his eyes and tasted for the first time some of the female power he had spoken of—it felt pretty good. She wanted to tell him it was the first time she'd felt this way, that he was the first man who—

Her eyes widened. God, she had to warn him that she hadn't done this before it went any further, even at the risk of her confession ruining the mood. The possibility of that happening made her hold back, but only for a moment. If he had a problem with her inexperience it was better to know now, not later down the line.

Rejection later on really would be crushing.

'Do you remember that night in the car?'

Emilio swore softly under his breath at the reintroduction of the subject.

Obviously he remembers, stupid, she told herself. He thinks it's the event that triggered your moral downfall.

'Well, I know that it looked—'

'I remember that that night I came this close...' he interrupted, bringing his face within a whisper of hers.

Megan's eyelids drooped. She could feel the waft of his warm breath on her skin, on her mouth. The thought of confession slipped from her head as lust and longing shuddered through her body. She stared transfixed at the fine lines around his eyes, the gold tips at the end of his otherwise ebony eyelashes. Her heart ached. He was the most breathtaking, perfect thing on the planet and he wanted her.

'This close?' she parroted, fighting her way through the sensual fog in her head.

'To throttling the bastard,' he explained matter-of-factly.

Not following this instinct had taken a large chunk of will power, but the effort had faded into insignificance beside the will power he had needed to tap into to stop himself taking Megan in his arms to comfort her.

The sight of her standing there, white-faced and shaking, looking so vulnerable and fragile, had awoken every protective instinct he had and some new ones. While she had struggled not to cry he had struggled to keep his distance.

Emilio hadn't allowed himself to even touch her.

He couldn't. If he had he knew it wouldn't have stopped at comforting.

He had been tempted. *Dios*, but he had been so tempted standing there, fighting against his baser instincts, especially given the status of his relationship with his then wife playing in a loop through his head.

Little snippets of the beginning of the end of his marriage slid into his head now.

'I understand,' Rosanna said when she discovered he had removed his things from the room they shared.

'And are relieved?' he asked, genuinely curious, and taking no satisfaction from her obvious distress.

Emilio felt a lot of responsibility for what had happened. His mindset when he had entered into the marriage had not differed from how he would enter into any other contract.

With the benefit of hindsight he could see that this had been a mistake—this wasn't any contract.

Mistake number two had been not factoring in the

emotional factor, not allowing for the possibility that, despite what she had said, Rosanna needed more than he had been prepared or able to offer.

What had happened had been inevitable.

The suggestion made his errant wife look uncomfortable. 'I wasn't dissatisfied with what we had. That isn't why I slept with—'

Emilio took pity on her. 'It's all right, I don't want a score out of ten, Rosanna, and I don't want to know his name.'

'I know you don't. If you'd loved me you would have.'

'I never—'

'I know you didn't,' she cut in quickly. '*He* didn't love me either, but he said that he did, and I needed to hear that even if it was a lie,' she admitted sadly. 'Don't look like that, Emilio. Don't be sorry for me. I'm not asking you to sleep with me. I don't expect it, and I do realise that you will need—when you do I won't make a fuss.'

'So you are giving me permission to have sex with other women?'

'It's a sensible solution.'

Cold-blooded and clinical were the words that slid unexpectedly into Emilio's mind; they were two things that he had been accused of in the past. And mostly those accusations had been justified, so why now did settling for a dispassionate solution make him feel discontent?

Why did he think it was settling? *Settling* implied there was a better option. He knew there wasn't—marriage was by definition flawed, at best a compromise.

'More sensible than a divorce?'

She looked at him, white with anxiety under the perfect make-up he had never seen her without. 'But you agreed we could make this work.'

'I agreed that a divorce would be messy. I agreed that we

make better friends than lovers. I agreed that domesticity is not something I am suited to.'

'You haven't met anyone?' she began tentatively. 'Someone special?'

The idea amused him. 'I have met no one I wish to have sex with and, even if I had, I have no desire to leap into another marriage,' he promised, believing it.

They left it like that.

When six months passed and he had not taken up the offer of guilt-free cheating, he did pause to consider the situation. Six months was a long time and he was a man with a healthy sex drive. He recognised channelling his energies, no matter how successfully, into work was not a long-term solution to the problem.

Did his reluctance to even acknowledge a problem existed stem from the fact he still thought of sex outside marriage as *cheating*?

It was not a distaste of cheating that held him in check when he looked at Megan that night and burnt with a primal need to make her his.

It was the knowledge that following through with his instincts, taking advantage of her at a moment like this would make him no better than the man he had just sent packing.

The idea filled him with repugnance; for the first time in his life he wanted more than sex. He did not want some sordid hole-in-the-corner affair; he did not want their relationship to be tarnished with his past mistakes. He knew he had to be patient.

Despite his reputation for infallibility, Emilio had made bad decisions in the past. While he did not advertise that, neither did he agonise over it; he shrugged and moved on.

But the decision he made that night to be patient had not

been one he had been able to shrug away. It had tortured Emilio for two years.

He never made the same mistake twice.

Emilio was going to make Megan Armstrong his. He was going to make her forget every man she had ever known. Determination hardened to steel inside him. The need to claim her had not lessened with time, but deepened—she was going to be his.

He ran a finger down her smooth cheek, smiling as he felt her shudder. He breathed in the fragrance of her hair and allowed the scent of apples to flood his senses.

'I did not warm to the man,' he explained.

Megan, deep in the sensual thrall, responded to the wry admission with a vague, 'Who?' The warmth of his breath on her ear lobe was sending shivers of sensation all the way down to her curling toes.

He brought his face close to hers until their noses were almost touching. 'The clown you were fighting off in the car.'

'I *was* fighting him off,' she said, thinking, Kiss me, please kiss me. Every second he didn't was sheer torture.

'I know.' He lifted his head fractionally and hooked a thumb under her chin, tilting her head from side to side as he studied the soft curves of her face with an expression of ferocious fascination. 'I should have throttled him,' he mused thickly. 'I *really* wanted to, but not as much as I wanted to do this.'

Without warning he grabbed her bottom, his big hands curling over the feminine curves as he hauled her upwards and hard against his body, sealing them from waist to thigh.

Megan's eyes flew wide, the breath leaving her body in

a gusty sigh as she registered the bold imprint of his rock-hard erection as it ground into the softness of her belly.

'Oh, God!' she groaned as a rush of liquid heat exploded inside her. 'You wanted… That night… But you were married.'

His mouth twisted into a smile that left his dark eyes cold. 'Do you think that a piece of paper stops a man wanting another woman? You of all people should know that isn't so, Megan.'

She flinched at the reference. 'So you're saying if it did I wouldn't exist,' she said quietly, trying not to be shocked by his admission. Maybe some men shouldn't get married. Especially highly sexed ones like Emilio.

He kissed her then, hard and possessively, the bruising pressure of his lips driving the breath from her lungs, his tongue probing deep into her mouth. Megan's arms slid around his middle as she clung, kissing him back wildly, without finesse, just with a hunger that equalled his.

When he finally lifted his mouth from hers it took several seconds for her head to clear, for a tiny sliver of sanity to filter back.

'You're going to do that again, aren't you?' Not that much sanity.

He smiled, his liquid, dark, incredible eyes fastened on to her face absorbing every detail as he ran his fingers down her throat. 'That's up to you.'

His reply frustrated her. 'Do I have to beg?'

No wonder he looked so smugly confident; he had to have had women begging him all his life.

God knew Megan didn't want to be another notch on his bedpost, but if she had to beg she would. Where Emilio was concerned it seemed she had no pride.

'You have to tell me you want me as much as I want you.'

She began to turn her head, her lips trembling. 'Because you don't know.'

The bitterness in her voice brought a frown to his face. 'Because I need to hear you say it.'

She couldn't bear it. Every cell in her body craved his touch. 'I want you, Emilio.'

His nostrils flared as he moved in to bite her lower lip, breathing in her warm womanly smell as he nipped his way towards the corner of her mouth. 'But if you prefer to go sightseeing…' he teased, running his tongue along the sensitive skin of her inner lip. Her moan of pained protest drew a fierce grin from Emilio. 'Though I should point out that my bedroom is much closer…'

If they got that far it would be a miracle. He was clinging to what control he had with his fingernails. To have her shaking with lust for him was incredible and her wild response had blown him away. All he could think about was burying himself in her.

Megan's head fell back to look into his lean face. Her eyes were half closed, her cheeks flushed. 'Bed, please.'

A low growl vibrated in Emilio's throat as his hold tightened, his arms like steel bands around her ribcage as he bit and nuzzled his way up the exposed curve of her white neck.

Megan went limp in his arms, her eyelashes fluttering like butterfly wings against her flushed cheeks, her toes brushing the ground as Emilio walked blindly across the room to the bedroom door, his lips moving up the curve of her throat.

He reached the door and her lips at the same moment. Keeping his dark eyes trained on her face, his mouth a tantalising whisper from her own, Emilio hefted her higher into his arms as though she weighed nothing, an arm scooping her bottom as he swung her upwards. She shivered, some buried primal instinct in her responding to the raw power revealed in his casual action.

CHAPTER ELEVEN

'Kiss me, Megan!' Emilio rasped, and kicked open the door, the instruction and action blending seamlessly into one.

The door hit the wall behind with a loud crash, the vibration of the impact rippling around the apartment as Megan, her eyes glowing, grabbed his face between her hands and pressed her warm lips to his.

Her enthusiasm drew a growl of approval from his throat, then as she slid her tongue experimentally into his mouth, tentatively and then with more confidence, she felt a shudder run through his lean body.

She stopped kissing him long enough to moan, 'God, you taste so good.'

Emilio's eyes darkened dramatically. *'Madre de Dios!'*

'Is something wrong?' she asked anxiously. He looked like someone in pain.

'Wrong?' he echoed. He looked at her, his brilliant eyes fierce but tender, the muscles in his brown throat visibly working as he swallowed, struggling to control the primal hunger pounding through his body. 'No, things are very right. You wish to taste me, you shall,' he told her thickly. 'But not until I have sampled every inch of your delicious body.'

The throaty promise planted a mental image in Megan's head that made her skin prickle.

His long-legged stride brought them to the bed in seconds. Megan's eyes were closed and her arms still fastened around his neck as he lowered her onto the bed.

As she sank into the mattress Megan opened her eyes.

Emilio curved over her, motionless; his breath came harder as he looked down at her. 'You're beautiful,' Emilio slurred, his voice thick with desire. 'I've never in my life needed anything as much as I need you.'

The husky confession sent a thrill through Megan's tense, aching body. She waited, her heart beating frantically in anticipation as she stared into his glowing midnight-dark eyes.

She wanted his touch, she ached for his kisses, she wanted him with a fierce urgency that scared her. For a second she wanted to retreat from it, push him away, but she made herself accept it, embrace it.

In that moment her last doubts vanished in a blaze of certainty.

This was what she wanted. The *rightness* of it made no sense, but that didn't matter. Unable to communicate the ache of inarticulate yearning that brought the threat of tears to her eyes, Megan raised her arms, stretching her finger towards him in a silent plea.

The gesture cut through Emilio's last shred of control. A growl locked in his throat, his face set in a strained mask of primal need. He caught her hands, raised them to his lips and pressed his lips to each palm in turn before he sat down on the edge of the bed.

Retaining her hands in his, he placed them against his chest.

Megan could feel the heat of his body through his shirt. With a soft cry she pulled herself into a sitting position and began to fumble with the buttons on his shirt with frenzied urgency. Her hands were shaking so much that the simple task was beyond her.

'Let me.'

A hand in the middle of her chest sent Megan back against the pillows.

Megan watched through half-closed eyes, her throat dry and aching as he slipped the buttons of his shirt, his actions tantalisingly slow.

The fabric parted to reveal his taut muscled torso, his broad, well-developed chest and flat, muscle-ridged belly. His skin gleamed like beaten copper.

Megan gasped. 'Oh, God!' and ran her tongue across the surface of her dry lips.

There was predatory confidence in his smile as he fought his way out of his shirt and flung it across the room.

Megan couldn't take her eyes off him. His skin glowed and he didn't carry an ounce of surplus flesh on his sleek, muscular body.

He almost casually pinioned her hands either side of her head before settling his long, lean length down beside her. There was nothing casual about the searing heat of his stare as ran his tongue up the exposed curve of her neck.

'You taste good.'

He lowered his head towards her, but at the last second stopped just short of her mouth and looked deep into her eyes, part of him wanting to prolong the moment he had waited for.

'Please kiss me, Emilio.'

The husky plea snapped the last thread of his shredded control. A deep groan emerged from his lips as he sealed his mouth to hers, pressing her limp body deep into the mattress with the force of his kiss.

Megan gave a soft moan of yearning as her lips parted

under the hungry, demanding pressure. The sound was lost in his mouth as his tongue stabbed deep, the erotic incursions drawing a series of mewling sounds of pleasure from her throat.

'This is crazy.'

He trailed a series of moist, open-mouthed kisses down her throat. 'You want me and I want you. Is that crazy?'

'Yes, it is, but I think I like crazy.'

He levered himself up a little to allow himself easier access to the buttons on her blouse. He started at the bottom and worked his way upwards, holding her eyes, watching her gasp as each one gave way.

Megan squeezed her eyes closed and held her breath as he peeled the fabric aside. At the sound of his rasping intake of breath, her eyes shot open.

He was staring transfixed at her body; desire burned in his eyes like twin flames. '*Por Dios*, but you are lovely,' he breathed, his expression almost reverent as his glance licked down her pale body.

She glowed. Her skin was as pale as alabaster, not cold, but warm. Megan was warm. Emilio wanted to bury himself in her warmth, feel it close tight around him.

Megan shivered, the earthy appreciation in his deep voice sending an erotic thrill through her body. She shivered again and bit her lip, oblivious to the pain as he traced a line with his finger down the middle of her stomach before laying his big hand across the curve of her stomach.

Then, holding her eyes, he unclipped the front catch on her bra.

His eyes left her then, and she heard the breath leave his lungs in a long, sibilant hiss. His eyes glittered with passion as he curved his shaking hand around one soft, pink-tipped mound, drawing an earthy moan from her throat as he rubbed his thumb across the engorged peak before taking it into his mouth. All the time his fingers were stroking her delicate skin with erotic skill that made her burn up inside with the nameless need that gripped her.

She writhed in a sweet torment, her response to his skilful caresses uncoordinated, the words that slipped from her lips unintelligible in the hot haze of passion.

One hand stayed curved possessively around her breast as he lifted his head and looked deep into her passion-glazed tawny eyes before he bent his head, his tongue dipping inside the parted pink sweetness between her lips, drawing a series of weak cries of pleasure from Megan.

He slid a hand around her back, drawing her up off the bed while he freed the blouse and bra from her shaking body. One arm wrapped around her narrow ribcage, the other pressed behind her head, he lay down, drawing her down beside him.

The first skin-to-skin contact was shocking, then, after the shock faded, addictive. Megan's mind emptied, she stopped thinking, acting on the dormant instincts that surfaced as she pressed her breasts against the hard barrier of his hair-roughened chest.

Emilio continued to kiss her, one deep drowning kiss blending into the next.

When he eventually drew back the naked desire shining in his dark eyes sent a fresh pulse of desire slamming through her body.

'Hold that thought,' he said thickly as he rolled on his back. Megan's instinctive protest stilled as she watched him unfasten his belt, lifting his narrow hips off the bed to slide them down his thighs, then kick them away.

His boxers received the same treatment.

Megan felt the hot colour score her cheeks; he was aroused and he was magnificent! Heat pulsed, spreading from her core through her body, and the dragging, heavy sensation low in her pelvis became a physical pain. She couldn't take her eyes off him.

Emilio saw her staring and didn't seem to mind. In fact on physical evidence her unconcealed awe appeared to arouse him further—something she would have imagined was impossible!

He swung his legs around the side of the bed, his movements as graceful and sinuous as a big cat, each action emphasising the controlled strength and power of his body. She wondered at his complete lack of self-consciousness, her covetous gaze following his progress around to her side of the bed.

By the time he stood over her she was so aroused by the erotic image he presented that breathing was a struggle. Each laboured inhalation she drew made her full breasts quiver.

Without a word he bent down, one knee braced on the bed, and slipped a hand under the waistband of her skirt. The contact of his fingers on her burning skin sent a shiver along her sensitised nerve endings.

She closed her eyes as he slid her skirt down her thighs, then closed them tighter still as he removed her tiny briefs.

'Look at me, Megan.'

Megan prised her heavy lids open and gazed up at him, mute with helpless longing.

Raw need burning in his eyes, Emilio took her fingers and curled them around his erection. 'This is how much I want you,' he slurred.

It was, Megan thought, quite a lot!

She stroked him, her fingers tightened around his throbbing length. Emilio closed his eyes and groaned before gritting his teeth and removing her clever fingers forcibly before he ran his own fingers along the silky curve of her inner thigh, smiling with primitive satisfaction to hear her gasp, then moan as he parted her legs, opening her to him.

He kneeled over her. She was the most beautiful thing he had ever seen, ravishing. The need inside him was pounding in his head, wiping every thought but the need to possess her from his mind.

His entire being was focused on one thing—making her his, binding her to him.

As he kneeled between her legs he was unable to resist the lure of her quivering swollen lips. He kissed her lips hard, then the curve of her belly, before his smoky dark eyes meshed with her slumberous golden gaze.

He reached between her legs, her body arched in response to the intimate touch, the slick heat he discovered there, the knowledge that she was ready for him, and then finally her husky plea of, 'Please, Emilio,' broke his control.

His face contorted in a fierce mask of driving need, he settled between her legs, his body curved over her.

Megan felt the push against her silken barrier and tensed at the exact moment he slid into her. The cry of shock and pain was wrenched from her throat.

Above her he froze. He had felt the resistance at the last moment and understood what it meant, but it had been too late to pull back.

'Relax,' he soothed, kissing her neck.

'I'm… You're…' A long sigh left her throat as her tense muscle unclenched and began to expand to accommodate him. The sensation was incredible and as he began to move very slowly the fibres inside her responded to the friction, sending hot fingers of sensation rippling through her entire body.

'Oh, yes!' she sighed, grabbing his shoulder for support as she relaxed into the rhythm as he sank deeper into her.

Sweat slicked Emilio's body as he fought with every fibre of his being to control his thrusts, though in that final moment when he felt the deep contractions of her climax build he let go and slammed into her, feeling his explosive release and a moment later the guilt.

CHAPTER TWELVE

FINALLY Emilio rolled off her. Megan missed the weight of him pressing her into the mattress. Without the heat of his body the air-conditioned air felt cool on her hot, sweat-slick skin.

Megan, her breathing still all over the place, turned her head on the pillow. Emilio lay beside her on his back, one arm curved above his head. His eyes were closed and he was breathing deeply; his chest rose and fell in sync with each shallow breath. Megan rested her cheek in the crook of her arm, her expression rapt as she followed the play of muscles sliding below the golden glistening surface.

Everything about him fascinated her.

She reached out a hand to touch his skin and drew back. So far he hadn't said a word. Was that normal? Should she be bothered by his silence?

How crazy was this? Minutes earlier they had been intimate in a way that should have shocked her but hadn't; now she was scared of touching him in case it was the wrong thing.

Megan chewed her lower lip fretfully as the doubts crowded in. Had he fallen asleep?

Perhaps he would expect to find her dressed or even gone when he woke up? The instincts that had kicked in earlier had definitely switched off.

It was ironic—when she might have expected to feel some uncertainty there had been none, except for that brief moment when she was sure that they were simply not compatible in a purely dimensional sense—she had been very pleased to be proved wrong.

Beautifully wrong!

She might no longer be a virtuous virgin, but she still had no clue how a person was meant to behave post-lovemaking.

She glanced around the unfamiliar bedroom with the vast bed and modern art on the walls almost guiltily, as though she were a voyeur intruding on a scene in someone else's life.

But this wasn't happening to someone else, it was happening to her. Had happened.

No wonder it seemed surreal. *I spent the morning in bed with Emilio Rios*—now how weird did that sound? Actually, not so weird at all. A person, it seemed, could adapt awfully quickly to some things.

But she couldn't allow herself to lose sight of the fact that for Emilio this was just sex. While in one sense his pragmatic approach to his physical needs and appetites shocked Megan, in another way she did kind of admire his painful honesty.

It would never be possible for her to match his honesty, she thought, refusing to acknowledge the lonely ache in her heart—time enough for that later. To him she was a one-night or any rate one-morning stand, so wanting more was a stupid waste of time.

She had always wanted more from him. God, it really did stink when your first crush turned out to be your last!

She had always been his for the taking; he just hadn't felt the urge to reach before today. Megan blinked away the hot tears burning behind her eyes and gave a fierce frown as she told herself that for once in her life she would not think about tomorrow.

Her eyes made a covetous sweep of his body. A natural athlete's body, long and lean, it was a sculpted, breathing miracle of taut muscles, hard bone and glistening, satiny bronzed skin. A tiny sigh of appreciation left her lips; he really was beautiful!

And he had done beautiful things to her.

And tomorrow he would be doing them to someone else.

The pucker between her arched brows smoothed out as she firmly pushed away the thought. She swallowed, refusing to acknowledge the ache in her throat—why spoil a perfect moment?

She rolled onto her side, watching the rise and fall of his chest as Emilio sucked air deep into his lungs through flared nostrils. There was not the slightest suggestion of softness in any part of his lean, hard body. She exhaled a shaky sigh and thought, This *is* perfect.

He was perfect.

As she watched him, need unfurled from the tight knot of nameless emotions locked in her chest. She had imagined she was in love with him, but the man she had fallen for had never really existed. She had been infatuated with a fantasy.

She had seen the real Emilio Rios the night he had ripped her character to shreds, not a kind man, but dangerous and capable, as she knew to her cost, of being cruel.

She tried to work out the attraction. She knew it wasn't just his amazing face or athlete's body. Emilio projected a raw power, an intensity that drew her like a moth to a flame.

Scratch the surface of polished sophistication he was famed for and there was something primitive, a danger that should logically have made her run. Instead Megan found his earthy magnetism impossible to resist.

Throat thick with emotion that shone in her amber eyes, she responded to the compelling need to touch him. She reached out, tangling her fingers in the light fuzz of hair on his chest before trailing her fingers slowly in the direction of his flat, muscle-ridged belly. She had never imagined feeling this greedy fascination with a man's body, but she was utterly enthralled by everything, from the texture of his skin to the faint quiver of muscles just under the satiny surface she stroked.

The dark fan of his ebony lashes lifted slowly from the sharp angle of his cheekbones.

Megan held her breath.

Emilio turned his head.

Their eyes connected, liquid brown on topaz.

She could not read the expression in his dark eyes but she could feel the waves of strong emotion rolling off him, not something she had anticipated.

Neither had she anticipated the wave of paralysing shyness, not after the intimacies they had just shared and the total lack of inhibition she had displayed. She lay there aware of every imperfection, feeling horribly exposed and vulnerable, wishing with every ounce of her being that she could recapture the liberating pleasure in her own body she had experienced while they had been making love.

Emilio's stare had not wavered from her face. The intensity of his unblinking regard was starting to be unsettling, but suddenly overwhelmingly conscious of her nakedness Megan reached down for a sheet to cover herself.

The next seconds were a blur. One moment she was clumsily attempting to grab the sheet, the next her hands were pinioned above her head.

'What are you doing?'

'I should get dressed.' It was pretty hard to hit a casual note, but Megan thought she did quite well given the circumstances. 'I'm sure you have things to do, a busy schedule, and I should touch base with D—'

'You should stop babbling.'

'I'm not babbling,' she protested.

His broad shoulders lifted fractionally. 'All right, talking nonsense.' His dark eyes dropped from her face, sliding slowly down her body.

The insolent, sexually overt scrutiny made her stomach muscles twist in excitement.

'I do have things to do.' His eyes glittered as he bared his white teeth in a fierce smile. 'All of them include you, and clothes are not involved. Your body pleases me. I find it utterly and totally exquisite. You will not hide it from me. You should be proud of it and enjoy it as much as I intend to.'

The explosive quality in his fierce stare made her shiver, then cry out when without warning he pressed his face against her breasts, the stubble on his chin abrading the smooth, sensitive skin, but not in a bad way.

He thinks I'm beautiful.

Her breath came in a series of shallow gasps as, eyes half closed, she watched through heavy eyelids his dark head against her body, her back arching as his tongue began to whip slowly across the peaks of her breasts, still painfully sensitised from their recent lovemaking.

When he loosed her hands to cup one quivering peak she tangled her fingers in his dark hair, pushing through the ebony strands still damp from their recent exertions to cradle his skull and hold him against her.

They stayed in his hair when he lifted his head and grinned down at her.

'Also there is no point trying to hide from me in a bed this small.'

The bed was vast but she let it pass. 'I wasn't trying to hide,' she protested.

He arched an ironic brow, making her eyes slide guiltily from his.

'I was cold.'

'Cold?' Emilio laid his hand possessively on the soft feminine curve of her stomach. Megan started and trembled at his touch, shifting restlessly under his hand, but not wanting it to go away.

'You do not feel cold to me.' He leaned across her, sealing his mouth to hers as he kissed her, and he ran his hands down the silky skin of her thighs, wresting a whimper from her throat.

'Not cold at all.'

Eyes closed, her head fell to one side as he began to nuzzle her neck.

Emilio's head lifted, but his eyes remained riveted on her raspberry-pink thrusting nipples, wet and gleaming from his recent ministrations, dark against the milk-pale skin of her perfect breasts. With the utmost reluctance he clenched his jaw and tore his gaze free of temptation.

'We have things to talk about,' Megan heard him say with some unease.

She opened her eyes. 'I thought you were a man of action, not words.' Would the challenge successfully divert him?

It didn't. Emilio saw through her tactics. 'Nice try,' he admired sardonically. 'And I am tempted,' he admitted with a smile that made her heart flip. The smile was absent as he added in a voice stripped of the sexy smokiness, 'But we will talk. Your economy with words and my actions could have hurt you.'

He stopped and moved a hand across his face. She was shocked when his hand fell away to see his face contorted in a grimace of self-loathing.

'*Did* hurt you,' he added sombrely.

Megan was shaken by the dark anguish she saw reflected in the shadows of his incredible eyes. 'No…' she protested. 'No, you didn't.' The memory of the moment of pain had already faded, supplanted by the incredible pleasure that had followed.

The muscles in Emilio's brown throat stood out corded with tension as he dragged a hand jerkily across the surface of his dark hair, making it stand up spikily in front.

It was, she decided, a good look on him, but then any look was good on Emilio. God, but I am so besotted.

'Do not lie to me, Megan,' he rasped throatily as he caught her jaw between his long fingers and angled her face to him.

Megan struggled to judge his mood; his enigmatic expression gave nothing away. 'I'm not—'

'You have never been with a man before.' The shock still fresh in his mind, Emilio struggled to frame the words. 'It was your first time.'

If he pursued the theme too far Megan knew there was a real danger of her revealing more than was sensible.

The last thing she wanted was Emilio knowing that she had only been a virgin, not because she was virtuous or even that she had major hang-ups about sex, but because… God, how could she admit, without sounding incredibly old-fashioned, that she'd made a choice early on not to have sex outside marriage?

Megan had simply never been able to imagine being intimate with a man she didn't have a strong emotional connection with.

The man she slept with would be the man she fell in love

with, and as the only man she'd ever fallen for had been married she had accepted it might never happen and she was fine with that, or so she had told herself. There was more to life than sex and there were few things worse in life, it seemed to her, than sex with the wrong man.

There had been a lot of wrong men for her mother, a parade of 'uncles' whom Megan could recall appearing and disappearing at intervals. The eternal optimist, Clare Smith had always embarked on a new relationship believing it was *the* one, only to end up crushed and heartbroken when things fell apart.

As she got older and recognised the destructive pattern Megan, not sharing her mother's optimism, had begun to dread seeing a new man appear. Some of the youthful anger she felt had been aimed at her mother; she wished very much now she had been more understanding.

'Why do you need a man?' she had yelled. 'Why can't I be enough?'

The stricken look on her mother's face had stayed with her and she had never had an opportunity to retract it. Her mother had slipped off a crowded pavement at rush hour and under the wheels of a passing bus.

A hissing expletive left Emilio's lips as, face dark with wrath, he stared at her, the muscle in his lean cheek spasmodically clenching and unclenching.

He looked ready to implode.

Megan struggled to respond to the blunt statement of her virginal status without blushing and failed. 'Guilty as charged,' she joked in an attempt to play the subject down.

Megan bit her lip. So much for lightening the mood!

'You think this a joke?' he grated. 'Your first time should be *special*.'

Megan stared and thought, And he thinks it wasn't?

'I may not have used the word,' she told him in a voice that shook with the emotions she was struggling to suppress, 'but if you're talking *special* as in unique and outstandingly brilliant, I do seem to recall saying something along those lines, quite loudly actually.'

'You're blushing, all over.' The discovery appeared to distract and amuse him, though a moment later he was looking darkly sombre once more as he picked up a theme that Megan found acutely uncomfortable.

'Your first time only happens the once, and…and I…' His face contorted with a grimace of self-disgust, he broke off and dragged a hand down his jaw. Hearing the sound in his head, he felt as if he'd never be able to forget her sharp cry. His voice dropped as he accused, 'You wept.'

Silently, and he had held her shaking body and felt like a total animal.

Megan laid a tentative hand on his shoulder; his muscles felt rock-hard and rigid. 'It wasn't because you hurt me,' she protested, stunned by his reading of the situation.

'If I had known—' His jaw clenched; the knowledge that he had hurt her felt like a blade sliding between his ribs. 'But how could you be… *Why?*'

Megan groaned and scanned his face. 'You're not going to let this go, are you?'

He looked at her as though she had just announced she was actually a Martian. *'Let it go!'* He'd waited two years for that moment and when it had happened he had blown it! When he thought of the way he had… *'Por Dios!* I think you owe me an explanation,' he announced grimly.

Her eyes slid guiltily from his. *I'm yours and I love you. I actually pretty much always have*, was a fairly accurate summing-up of the situation, but she doubted it would go down too well.

'Why the hell didn't you tell me that you—?'

Her voice tight with humiliation, Megan cut across his incensed demand. 'You didn't seem all that interested in conversation at the time.'

The line of colour across the angle of Emilio's cheek-bones deepened as their glances clashed. Even now the air between them hummed with a sexual tension that was almost tangible. Despite the intensity of their lovemaking it had not even taken the edge off his hunger for her.

He did not need reminding that his actions had been ruled by his own selfish carnal desire, a carnal desire that after two years of denial had been stripped to its primitive and most basic form.

It had been a point of pride with Emilio that he had never been a victim of his hormones. He had certainly never lost control in bed before, and now the one time he should have shown restraint with a woman, when he should have been gentle, he had snapped. His relentless, ravenous need for her had made him utterly blind to her inexperience until that last moment.

There must have been clues? How had he missed them? Missed the opportunity to make her initiation special.

'And you were not acting like a virgin,' corrosive shame made him retort defensively.

'Know a lot about virgins, do you?'

His eyes narrowed as his eyes drifted to her tender lips still swollen from his kisses. 'Nothing, as it happens,' he said, thinking it seemed he also knew even less about women, or this one at least.

'You're making a big thing of nothing. Being a virgin isn't like having a contagious disease. It's not obligatory to go into isolation.' Her mouth settled into a mutinous line of defiance as she tried to hide her hurt. 'I'm sorry you feel cheated and short-changed but I'm not about to say sorry.'

His brows lifted. 'What are you talking about now? *Cheated...*?' he asked irritably. 'You are not making sense.'

Face scrunched in an effort to hold back the tears that threatened to spill over, she lifted her chin and blinked hard.

'Well, so sorry,' she drawled, 'if I've lost my edge of clinical objectivity, but I've never been in this situation before.'

'And you think I have?'

'Yes, I get it, you don't need to spell it out.' She had been slow but the penny had finally dropped. She knew why he was acting this way. 'You thought you were getting someone who knew what she was doing in the bedroom and instead—' she broke off to give a loud sniff and passed a hand across her suspiciously bright eyes as she gulped '—instead you got me.'

She heard the unattractive, self-pitying whine in her voice and shook her head, mumbling, 'Even you could not have got it perfect your first time.'

He probably had. Megan closed her eyes, hating the woman he had got it right with.

Torn between frustration and tenderness, Emilio levered himself into a sitting position with the fluid grace that typified all his actions.

'Have I got this right?' he asked, placing one hand beside her head as he looked down at her. 'You think I feel *short-changed*? *Short-changed?*' he repeated, shaking his head as he added something, not appearing to realise he had slipped into his native tongue, and laughed. 'The way your mind works, *querida*, is a constant source of amazement to me. Listen, you may not value what you gave me highly, but I do.'

CHAPTER THIRTEEN

MEGAN'S eyes slid slowly up from the expanse of golden
chest she was staring at. 'You value?'

She parroted the words like someone speaking a foreign
language.

Emilio nodded and framed her face between his long
brown fingers, smoothing the strands of hair spread around
her face from her brow. 'I am your first.' The sheer impos-
sibility of it still shook him. 'Do you know how that makes
me feel?'

Her eyes darted from side to side, refusing to meet his.
'Annoyed?'

'Privileged.'

She froze at the throaty rebuttal, her eyes heavy, lids
half closing as he touched her cheek. The tremor she felt in
his fingers as they brushed slowly across the downy curve
shocked her.

Her lips, soft and warm and so incredibly sweet, trembled under his as he kissed her softly.

'And in shock,' he admitted, pulling back. 'I still don't
understand how it is possible.'

Arm curved above her head, she watched as he propped
his broad shoulders against the carved headboard. Taking a
deep breath, she pushed the tangled strands off her hot face

with one hand and, anchoring the sheet over her breasts with the other, pulled herself up into a kneeling position.

'Because you thought I slept my way through college?'

The suggestion drew a dark frown from Emilio. 'No, because you've been living with a man for two years.' And though he had buried it deep, the knowledge had driven him out of his mind. He took a deep breath, let the anger pass through him and released it; despite a lot of practice he had never quite perfected the technique.

'A man!' Megan sank deeper into confusion.

'All right, live-in lover, boyfriend, whatever he was to you.'

Megan sat back on her heels, lifting a hand to balance herself as the mattress shifted. She was totally at sea. Live-in lover? She had barely had a date!

'What are you talking about? I haven't been living with a man!' She stopped, her eyes widening in comprehension, before sliding back down in the bed with a laugh and a billowing of silken sheets. 'You're talking about Josh?' She chuckled.

He arched a brow, his focus drifting as his eyes were drawn to the outline of her body against the silk. She gave a sinuous wriggle. All he had to do was reach out and lift the sheet... He swallowed as he struggled to banish the image of her smooth, naked body from his head.

The effort made sweat break out along his upper lip.

'There were others?' He immediately recognised the irrationality, given the topic under discussion, of his jealous question. More? There hadn't been any!

'What is this about?'

Emilio looked down at her lying there, looking like a wild-haired wanton angel, and felt a pulse of desire throb through his body. 'That's what I'm trying to find out. This *Josh*, he—'

Megan's brows twitched into a perplexed line. Her fingers restlessly tugged at the sheet. 'What is this thing you have about Josh? You sound as if you don't like him.'

'I have no thing about *Josh*. I'm sure he was perfect, but...'

'Pretty much,' she admitted. It was a view shared by all her female friends. They had all bemoaned the fact that the perfect men were always gay.

The smiling insertion drew a dark frown from Emilio. 'You lived with the man!'

His accusing manner and bewildering interest in the subject of her ex-flatmate was beginning to make Megan feel angry. 'It's hardly a crime to share a flat with someone and I'm not on trial,' she added, growing more bewildered by the second—his condemnatory attitude. 'What has living with Josh got to do with anything?'

'You have been living with the man for two years. What am I to think you spend your time doing? Playing Scrabble? *Por Dios!*' His upper lip curled in a derisive sneer as he shook his dark head slowly from side to side. It was inexplicable to him that any man could live under the same roof as Megan for two hours and not make love to her—this man had spent two years!

She stopped, her startled stare flying to his face as the penny finally dropped. 'Josh—my boyfriend!'

'What was he waiting for—your wedding night?' Emilio growled.

The question touched a nerve with Megan. 'And would that be so weird?' she asked him sharply.

Emilio stared at her. 'In one word—yes.'

'Well, call me weird but actually that was my plan up until an hour or so ago.'

It turned out it was easy to have lofty principles when there was no temptation. Not that she regretted her change of heart for a millisecond.

He swore under his breath.

'Well, I don't expect you to understand,' she conceded with a sleepy yawn. Her time clock had to be seriously skewed. 'Look, the fact is it's true that I didn't ever plan having sex before marriage, but that's not the reason I hadn't slept with Josh. I didn't sleep with Josh because I am really not his type.'

Emilio frowned skeptically. To his mind Megan was every man's type.

'I mean *really* not his type.'

Emilio stiffened. 'You're saying…?'

Megan nodded, amused by the look of amazement on his face. Propping her chin on her hands, she shook her head and teased, 'For a smart man you can be awfully slow sometimes.'

Emilio exhaled a long, slow breath. It whistled through his clenched teeth before he framed a grim smile. 'It certainly looks that way.'

'I really miss Josh.'

A few minutes ago this wistful statement would have roused Emilio to blind fury. Now he was able to offer a sympathetic smile and murmur, 'Gay?' Just to double-check the facts.

'Yes, my perfect flatmate was gay. He has gone to do aid work overseas. Josh is lovely. You'd really like him.'

She chattered on, blissfully unaware of the thoughts going through the head of the man beside her.

Gay! The guy he had spent a year being jealous of, twelve months torturing himself imagining the other man with Megan, and the guy was gay.

Did irony get any darker than that?

'Emilio?'

The questioning lilt in her voice roused him from his bitter reflections.

He rolled towards her.

'How did you know I shared a flat with Josh?'

'Philip must have mentioned it and I assumed.'

Rachel nodded. 'That must be it,' she agreed as she leaned across him, the tips of her breasts brushing his chest as she stroked his cheek. 'Wait until I tell Josh in my next letter.'

'Nobody writes letters,' he said, tangling his fingers in her hair.

'I do. There's something about putting a fountain pen to paper that's more personal,' she mused.

'Nobody saves themselves for their wedding night either.'

'Don't worry about it. I don't expect you to propose, Emilio. Marriage is not meant for men like you.'

She blinked in bewilderment as she found herself exiled from his arms. She turned her sleepy stare on Emilio, who was sitting upright in bed with his arms folded across his chest. He looked magnificent and inexplicably furious.

With a resigned sigh she pushed her hair back from her face and propped her chin on the heel of her hand. 'What's wrong?'

'What do you know about *men like me*? And what exactly would I be incapable of understanding?'

'Sorry, I didn't mean to generalise,' she soothed.

'But now you have—'

'I'm not judging,' she promised earnestly. 'And I'm sure you did love Rosanna, but you said yourself that being married didn't stop you from feeling sexually attracted to other women, and I'm sure most men are, but they don't act on it. You did.' The worst torture in the world, it seemed to Megan, would be to watch the man you loved cheat on you. 'You obviously tried not to be unfaithful.'

Emilio stared at her in amazement as she gave his shoulder a comforting pat.

'It's a fact of life that some men are simply not suited to monogamy or marriage.' She pushed away the sadness and added with a wicked laugh, 'But you do make the most perfect lovers.'

'We try,' Emilio husked, pulling her into his arms. 'We try. This time,' he promised, 'it will be better.'

'I don't see how,' Megan said honestly, though the idea of trying to achieve the impossible did hold its attractions.

He fitted his mouth to hers, one hand cupping her breast, the other stroking the smooth curve of her thigh.

'I'm going to touch you everywhere,' he whispered thickly. 'I'm going to taste all of you,' he told her as he slid his tongue between her parted lips. 'Everywhere,' he said, kissing her closed eyelids. 'All of you.'

Megan prised her eyelids open. She was breathing hard. 'You'll own me,' she whispered, thinking, You already do.

His dark eyes glowed with approval as he slid down her body. 'Believe it.'

Her entire body was bathed in a rosy glow of arousal as he parted her legs. Her heart thudded heavily as his hand slid between them, pushing them further apart, opening her up to him.

She gasped, her hips lifting from the bed at the first intimate touch.

'Relax. We're going to take our time, *querida*,' he soothed, stroking his tongue wetly along the silky skin of her inner thigh.

Megan closed her eyes and said, 'Oh, God, you're incredible.'

It was a theme she returned to on several occasions during the next couple of hours, because, true to his word, Emilio did take his time. He took her to the brink of paradise several times before he finally slid on top of her and led her screaming over the top into the waiting golden glow of fulfilment.

As they lay side by side, their bodies trembling and slick with sweat, he turned his head and grinned at her. 'I'd ask how it was for you but I think I already know. Who'd have guessed you were a screamer?'

'I'm just an excellent actress, that's all,' she teased, curling happily up to his side. 'Next time, Emilio, I wouldn't mind being the one driving you a little crazy.'

'Works for me. I have no problem at all with a woman in charge.'

It was a couple of hours later that Megan was woken by the sound of the door hitting the wall. She blinked to see Emilio approaching, bearing a tray.

He laid it on the bed.

'What's this?' she said, looking at the array of cold meats, cheese and crusty bread laid out.

Emilio pulled the cork on the bottle of red and filled two glasses. 'It's a picnic in bed.'

'I really don't have an eating disorder, you know.'

'You have expended a lot of energy.' Her blush made him grin. 'Any athlete will tell you that taking on fuel at regular intervals is essential to maintain performance.'

Glancing at the food, Megan realised without the prompting of her rumbling tummy that she was hungry. 'Shouldn't we get up? It's…' She glanced at the face of her watch and gasped. 'My God, we've been in bed all day.'

Emilio appeared unperturbed. 'Yes, deliciously decadent, isn't it? I could get used to it.'

I can't let myself, she thought.

Pushing away the sad thought and telling herself to just enjoy the moment, she sat up, pushing her hair from her face with both hands.

'I am quite hungry,' she admitted.

'I love watching you eat,' he said when she was allowing herself to be tempted by another piece of cheese. 'You do it with such…relish.'

'You mean I'm greedy.'

'So am I every time I look at you.'

'I feel so guilty.' She saw the flash of annoyance cross his face and added quickly, 'Not about the food or the sex, but it's a weekday and I haven't done a scrap of work. It's all right for you—you're your own boss.'

'Has it occurred to you that you could be too?'

She flashed him a surprised look. 'As a matter of fact, yes, it has.'

'You should. You're obviously not stretched now. You are capable of much more.' He hesitated. 'I know that your father might say that—'

'He'll hand the reins over to me?' she interrupted with a laugh. 'Oh, I know that's never going to happen. I'm a woman and I'm only accepted as an Armstrong up to a point, but I've learnt a lot working for him and made some very useful contacts.'

And he had been worried Armstrong was taking advantage of her. It turned out that Megan was no doormat. Emilio chuckled low in his throat.

'I'd ask you to come work for me, Megan, but it's a rule of mine not to mix business and pleasure.' With a low growl he lunged for her, rolling her underneath him. 'And you are definitely pleasure.'

CHAPTER FOURTEEN

MEGAN put down the gloss she was applying to her lips. She very much hoped to challenge, with a little bit of help from a tall Spaniard, the manufacturer's claim that it lasted for twenty-four hours, and fished her mobile from her open bag on the floor where it was ringing stridently.

She checked the caller identity and her brows lifted in surprise. She sat down on a linen hamper, telling herself not to assume the worst—it might not be bad news.

Though experience tended to suggest it would be. The last time her brother had rung he had lost his passport and all his money; the time before he'd rung from the casualty department, where he'd ended up after coming off his motorbike.

Unless in a scrape of some sort it was rare for her brother to return a call, let alone take the initiative. Typically, she thought, her smile becoming wry, he had chosen the worst time possible to make contact.

'Hi, Megan, and before you ask I'm fine.'

'I'm glad to hear it. Look, I'd like to chat, Phil, but this isn't actually a very good time,' she admitted, smiling to herself as she glanced towards the door, her stomach giving a little shimmy in anticipation as she thought of it opening any second to admit Emilio.

Her eyes half closed and her breath came a little faster

as an image of him standing in the doorway slid into her head. She was utterly powerless to control the response of her body to the mental image.

She had not seen him for three minutes tops and she already missed him. She smiled, recalling his response when she'd looked into the mirror and exclaimed, 'I look awful!' Privately she thought she looked pretty good for someone who had spent the best part of the day in bed.

'Is this where I'm supposed to say, no, you look fine?'

She pursed her lips and glared at his reflection in the mirror with feigned antagonism. 'Would it have hurt to tell a white lie?'

His glorious eyes smiled back at her. 'It wouldn't have been a white lie, *querida*, it would have been a massive lie.'

Megan struggled to adopt an indifferent expression. While she appreciated honesty as much as the next person, there was a time and a place and a limit to her new-found confidence.

'Because you don't look fine, you have never looked fine in your life. You are utterly breathtaking.' The carnal glow in his stunning eyes deepened as he elaborated on this theme in a voice that trickled over her like warm honey. 'Luscious, and incredibly sexy. The only flaw I can see is that you have too many clothes on,' he decided, flicking the collar of a blue chambray shirt she had appropriated from his wardrobe because, while she had become a shameless version of the Megan that awoke that morning, she was not as comfortable with the entire walking-around-naked thing as Emilio was.

It was possible nobody was as comfortable as him, she decided, unable even to glance at his tall, lean, perfectly sculpted body without feeling a heat prickle across the surface of her skin in response to the raw power and sheer animal grace he exuded. It helped slightly that he had pulled on a pair of silk boxer shorts.

He seemed massively amused when, in response to his accusation that she wasn't listening to him, she was driven to yell, 'What do you expect? I can't think while you're walking around like *that*!'

She discovered it was empowering to be told you looked sexy by a man who was the definition of the word.

But before she was able to enjoy the sensation and possibly tempt him to elaborate on the theme further he took charge and pulled her up from the dressing table stool where she sat. Grabbing her overnight bag from the floor, he dropped a hand on her slender shoulder and, ignoring her half-hearted protests—God, but she was putty in his hands—he steered her towards the room she sat in now.

A bathroom, but like none Megan had ever encountered, it was a marble-floored, decadently appointed space complete with a vast shower that had more gadgets than a space shuttle, and in centre stage, raised on a pedestal, was an enormous antique copper bath.

She was unable to repress an exclamation of admiration.

'You like, then?'

The way she saw it there was nothing not to like. 'My favourite room in the place.'

'I thought that was the bedroom.'

Megan tipped her head, intending to respond to his sly teasing remark, but was momentarily knocked off balance to discover, not the taunting amusement she had anticipated on his lean face, but a curiously intent expression.

'It's not the décor that made an impression in the bedroom.'

His heavy-lidded eyes darkened at the shy admission.

'While I don't think your looks can be improved on—'

the compliment made her flush with pleasure '—I could probably do with freshening up, though I admit I rather like the smell of you on my skin.'

She stared at him, her eyes enormous, quite shockingly aroused by his comment. 'I must smell of you too.'

'Then perhaps we should share the bath.'

Megan, her mind filled with the image of floating in that fabulous bath with him, hastily assured him that she had no strong objections to this idea. The fact was she had no objections to anything Emilio chose to do to her so long as it involved physical contact; she was already a total junkie for his touch.

Emilio excused himself, promising that the phone calls he needed to make to clear the rest of his day would only take a few minutes and suggesting she fill the tub in his absence.

The tub was filled and scented with some of the oils she had discovered, and she had been wondering whether to get into the water now or wait for Emilio to return when the phone rang, by which point she was leaning towards getting into the water, if only to see Emilio's reaction when he walked in. Though that would mean wasting the cute matching undies set she had already slipped on in the hope of having him take them off—it was a tough choice.

Tough choice? Strip or be undressed?

God, where was Megan Armstrong, the Megan Armstrong who barely knew how to flirt?

And who was the wanton hussy who had taken her place?

'Is Dad working you too hard?'

Megan, struggling to focus on what her brother was saying, gave a non-committal grunt.

'Silly question, of course he is,' her brother added, answering his own question, which suited Megan fine. If she could get away without telling an outright lie she would prefer to.

'Fine, I'll make it quick, you little workaholic.' He continued talking even faster than normal—which was very fast. 'I just had to ring, to say thank you. You really are a good sport.'

'I am?' Megan said, searching her memory for something she might have done recently that would deserve her brother's gratitude.

Nothing immediately sprang to mind. It was true she did intercede to smooth things over sometimes when hostilities flared up between Philip and their father. But things had been pretty peaceful lately. His son wearing a tie the last time he visited had put Charles Armstrong in a good mood for a month.

'I suppose it was Emilio's idea, and as usual,' he observed with an admiring chuckle, 'he was spot on the money.'

A bemused Megan shook her head, tensing at the name. 'You think so?' Her thoughts raced. How on earth did he know she was with Emilio?

'Oh, God, yes. It was a brilliant idea. I mean, if Rosanna knows he's with someone else whose name he actually knows she can move on with her life, hopefully in my direction.'

Megan's jaw dropped as she struggled to cope with the shocks that were coming thick and fast—Philip and Rosanna. Things were getting seriously *Twilight Zone*.

'Though you and Emilio!' He seemed unable to control his amusement any longer, and her brother's voice became suspended by laughter.

As she listened to Philip's incredulous laughter echoing down the line Megan sat there, the sick feeling in the pit of her stomach growing.

'I suppose it was a case of it's so crazy it must be true. I mean, it's not the sort of thing you'd make up unless you were a brilliant strategist like Emilio.'

'Oh, yeah, he's brilliant.'

Oblivious to the irony in her voice, Philip continued to congratulate her. 'Well, he had your help and however you pulled it off, little sister, I am very grateful. I suppose, when you think about it, you and Emilio wouldn't be any more crazy than me and Rosanna, but I love her, Megan, I really do.'

Megan closed her eyes and thought, God, I hope not! She really didn't want to see Philip get his heart broken. And if Emilio had decided he wanted his wife back that was inevitable. Emilio would let nothing stand in his way. Her brother had a great many excellent qualities; he was nice, but what woman, given the choice between nice and Emilio, was going to choose nice?

'I had no idea,' she said honestly. 'What I don't really understand is why you went to Emilio in the first place.'

'Other than habit, you mean.'

'You're not teenagers any more, Philip,' she said, a shade of irritation sliding into her voice.

'I suppose it does seem a bit weird, and I wasn't sure if I actually thought he could help, I just figured maybe if they talked… Closure and all that. But you know Emilio, he never lets you down, does he? Rosanna is totally convinced that you two are together and that's what matters. You must have put on quite an act. I wish I'd been there to see it.'

'You were about the only person that wasn't.'

'Well, don't tell Rosanna you noticed. According to her you two didn't have eyes for anyone but each other. In your own private world, she said,' he quoted. 'She also kept saying she didn't know why she was surprised, because when you thought about it it was obvious. Any idea what she meant?

'Not that it matters,' her brother continued. 'The thing is she can finally let go because she thinks you two are love's young dream. I think, Megan, that she's finally able to put her marriage behind her, now that she thinks Emilio is happy. Anyway, cheers, I'll let you know how things go. I'm just going to give Emilio a ring to say thanks.'

'I can save you the bother, Phil,' she said brightly. 'He's right here. Hold on a sec, I'll get him for you.'

Emilio had just finished filling the second champagne flute and was preparing to carry them into the bathroom with him when he heard the door open. He turned, glasses in hand, as Megan walked into the room, phone pressed to her ear.

His smile was not returned. A man did not have to be particularly intuitive to see that Megan was not happy. He wondered what had occurred in the few minutes they had been apart to account for her change of mood, but only in passing—his attention was focused on admiring how sinfully sexy she looked in a pink bra and a minuscule pair of matching silk shorts trimmed with lace.

His throat dry, his body hardening in lustful appreciation, he watched her advance, each angry step making her breasts jiggle gently under the silk.

Presumably she had not hated him when she had put on that outfit, unless she had intended to give him heart failure. Now she looked as though she would have preferred a more hands-on method of murder.

When she'd walked into the room the look she'd fixed him with was icily aloof, but by the time she had stalked across the room it had moved on to full-blown fury.

She paused about a foot short of him, still appearing to listen to the person speaking on the phone.

Emilio's lashes rested against the sharp angle of his jutting cheekbones as his heavy-lidded glance dropped down her smooth curves.

'You really do know how to make an entrance, *querida*,' he slurred admiringly.

Megan gritted her teeth. Even reminding herself that she hated him did not prevent her body responding of its own accord to his voice.

'Though if that's the outfit you were thinking of wearing for dinner, I think perhaps we should order in.'

Belatedly Megan realised that she had been so eager to confront him that she had forgotten what she was wearing, or, rather, what she wasn't!

She covered the mouthpiece with her hand. 'I'm not hungry,' she snapped, adding, just in case there were any doubts, 'For food, or you! And the only thing I need ordered is a taxi. Ask him yourself.'

Snarling the last disconnected remark in what he assumed was in response to what the person on the other end of the line was saying, she produced a saccharine-sweet smile and with no warning lobbed the phone at him—not gently.

Emilio managed to catch it in his free hand, only slopping a little champagne in the process.

'Well caught,' Megan admired, taking a glass. Holding his eyes, she took a deep swallow, then, wiping the moisture from her lips with the back of her hand, she made a sharp turn and walked stiff-backed towards the bathroom, resisting the temptation to run.

Just before she vanished inside she yelled over her shoulder, 'And stop staring at my bottom!'

Emilio chuckled throatily. 'Admit it, you'd be insulted

if I could.' His smile faded as she closed the door with a loud click.

There was zero chance of her being offended and zero chance of him letting Megan walk away. Eyes narrowed, he weighed the possibility of scaring her off by revealing his intentions. On balance he decided it was worth the risk. After two years of wasted time Emilio wasn't about to waste another minute.

He lifted the phone to his ear. 'Yes, Philip, I am here. Yes, she did say bottom.'

Five minutes later Emilio let himself into the bathroom.

Megan was standing at the mirror above the washbasin using some unladylike language as the slide she was trying to secure her hair with at the nape of her neck slithered along the silky strands onto the floor.

She picked it up and continued with her task, deciding to ignore his smouldering presence. A good idea in theory, but not actually easy to follow through with when the presence you were ignoring consisted of six feet five inches of solid bone, muscle and potent masculinity.

The sexual charge of his presence scorched its way across the room towards her. It would have been easier to ignore walking into a brick wall.

She was almost relieved when he broke the charged silence and spoke.

'At least you didn't lock the door.'

But she had unfortunately got dressed. He wondered if the pink things were still on underneath; he had every intention of finding out.

Megan slung him a dark look over her shoulder and was annoyed to see that he looked insultingly at ease with his broad shoulders propped casually against the wall. He didn't even have the decency to look defensive.

'Only because there isn't a lock.' Tongue caught between her teeth, her expression one of fierce determination, she finally managed to get the wretched slide to stay put.

With a little grunt of triumph she spun around chin high to face him, her expression a study of haughty disdain as she said, 'You could have knocked.'

The suggestion made him laugh. 'I think not.'

'Because the normal rules that govern society don't apply to Emilio Rios.'

Instead of responding to her sneering provocation, Emilio, a distracted expression in his dark eyes, produced a seemingly unconnected comment. 'The nape of your neck is very sexy—did you know that?'

Megan, hating herself for responding to the throaty comment, gave an indifferent sniff and lifted a protective hand to the area under discussion.

'We're not talking about my neck.' But he was still staring at it.

'I was.' He blinked and gave his head a shake as if to clear it. 'Look, I'm sorry to keep you waiting.'

'Don't flatter yourself,' she rebutted, her amber eyes flashing with antagonism. 'I wasn't waiting.'

Emilio acknowledged her cranky response with the sardonic elevation of one winged brow and continued as though she hadn't spoken. 'But explaining your presence to your brother required some—'

'Tact?'

'Patience.'

Of which Emilio had rapidly run out.

Rather than placating Philip, he had found himself delivering a few home truths. He had pointed out that the show of concern for his sister's welfare, as touching as it was, had kicked in pretty late in the day, and for the record he did not need to be told that Megan was not like the girls he normally dated. As for what she was doing in his apartment, he had left Philip in no doubt that it was none of his damned business.

'You should have mentioned I wasn't meant to tell him we had sex.'

His brows lifted. 'Did you?' he asked, sounding more interested than alarmed.

Megan picked up the hairbrush she'd just been using from the glass vanity unit above the basin and dropped it into her open holdall. 'It's not something I'm likely to boast about.'

The muscles around his angular jaw tightened, but she ignored the warning signs.

'I don't like to broadcast my mistakes. God knows why—'

'You slept with me? You gave me your innocence? We both know why, Megan.'

Megan's eyes fell from his. This was somewhere she could not go—not now, not if she wanted to cling to what shreds of dignity she retained.

'I doubt,' she muttered, 'Philip expected you to go as far as have sex with me to help him with his love life. God!' she exclaimed, her voice aching with disgust. 'Did this have *anything* to do with me?' she asked, banging her chest palm flat against her heaving chest.

'Oh, no, I was thinking about your brother the entire time we were making love,' he drawled. Shaking his head, he dragged a hand across his dark hair and ejaculated, *'Madre di Dios!'* He regarded her with an expression of utter incredulity. 'What are you talking about, woman?'

'I'm talking about spiking any chance Philip has with Rosanna and making Rosanna jealous.' She could see from his point of view it was a win-win situation.

'Leaving aside the why would I want either of these

things to happen, how exactly would sleeping with you achieve them?' Emilio levered his broad shoulders from the wall and took a step towards her, shrugging off his relaxed façade.

'It's glaringly obvious,' she contended.

Emilio was, Megan realised as their eyes connected in the mirror, pretty mad.

'Are you denying he asked you to intercede on his behalf with Rosanna?' Megan took a blind step backwards, reluctant to admit, even to herself, that she was daunted by the anger glinting in Emilio's eyes.

'Why would I deny anything? Are *you* denying you begged me to have sex with you?'

Megan compressed her lips and glared at him. 'It's always nice to be considered a charity case.'

'I've always considered you more of a challenge. By the way, Philip also extended an invitation to dinner. I refused on both our behalves.'

'I don't need you to do anything on my behalf!'

He adopted an expression of innocent enquiry as he countered, 'You wish to go to dinner with Rosanna and Philip?'

'He didn't really invite us, did he?'

'No.'

Megan gave a frustrated snort and spun away from him, causing her hair to break free again. With a sharp cry of frustration she dropped to her knees, but Emilio was faster than her; his long fingers closed around the errant item a second before she reached it.

Megan was unable to control her instinctive reaction as she pulled her hand back from his with the caution normally reserved for contact with white-hot metal.

Fully expecting him to make some sarcastic comment,

she was relieved but cautious when, squatting back on his heels, Emilio held his open palm out to her.

'Pretty,' he said, running the pad of his thumb over the antique tortoiseshell hair ornament.

Her relief evaporated when his dark lashes lifted from the razor-sharp angle of his high cheekbones. The expression in his deep-set dark eyes as he subjected her hair to an equally intense study sent a convulsive shudder up her spine.

Megan arranged her features in a prim expression, inhaling deeply to clear the fuzzy feeling in her head, and said, 'I like it.' Thinking, But not as much as I like your mouth.

The corners of his mouth curved upwards into a smile, but as his glance continued to move across the soft brown waves that surrounded her face it faded. 'But not as pretty as this.'

He stretched his hand towards her and every instinct of self-preservation she possessed screamed, Do not let him touch you!

But other, stronger instincts won out. They always would. Like it or not, the fact was he owned her body.

His long fingers barely brushed the skin of her forehead as he pushed a shiny strand from her eyes but the electric charge that zigzagged through her body felt like a lightning bolt.

'I prefer your hair loose,' he admitted, thinking of how it had looked spread out on the pillow around her flushed face. Thinking of burying his face in it, recalling the sensation of the silky strands brushing against his skin as she bent over his body.

Feeling his control slipping, Emilio banished the line of thought but could not resist touching her hair one more time.

Megan flinched away. 'Well, that's it, then,' she cried,

reaching out and snatching the hair slide from his open palm.

She rose jerkily to her feet and stared at it for a moment before slinging it wildly over her shoulder. She was close to tears and not sure who she blamed for this situation most—Emilio or herself.

So she hadn't known about Rosanna and Philip. She had known he'd kissed her at the airport for Rosanna's benefit, and she'd come with him anyway, knowing no matter how hard she had tried to pretend otherwise exactly where it was going.

But having it spelled out to her by Philip was a different matter. 'I will never tie my hair back again,' she declared, striving for ironic mockery and delivering instead something a lot closer to frenzied panic, possibly because the husky addition of, 'because I live to please you,' was uncomfortably close to the truth.

'Are you going to tell me what I've done to upset you?'

The quiet words sent a fresh flash of anger through Megan.

'Let me think…' she said, adopting a mystified expression as she pressed a finger to the suggestion of a cleft in her firm, rounded chin. 'Could it be something to do with the fact I don't much like being used? How do you think I felt having my brother thank me for playing along with your *brilliant* idea? He called me a good sport!'

His lips sketched a quick smile. 'Yes, that sounds like Philip.'

She searched his face. 'Don't you feel even slightly guilty?'

'What exactly should I feel guilty about, Megan?' His feral smile flashed, sexual and dangerous.

'You are utterly unbelievable!' she breathed, his indolent

pose incensing her further. The man was totally and completely shameless, she decided, shaking her head in disbelief. 'The fact that you can even ask that,' she said in a voice that quavered with anger.

'Philip thinks you're a great guy.' She shook her head, gave a bitter laugh and regarded Emilio in disgust.

Emilio folded his arms across his chest and studied her flushed, vivid little face, his expression softening as he watched her blink back tears from her glowing eyes.

Not for the first time he cursed the inconvenient timing of Philip's call. 'And you do not?'

'Me?' she said, sweeping the make-up she had used earlier to make herself look good for him into her open bag with her forearm.

'You do not think I'm a...*great guy*?'

She glared at him, felt the helpless longing roll through her and snarled, 'I think you're a selfish, manipulative rat!'

'Don't hold back now, say what you think,' he drawled with deceptive affability.

'Like you care what I think. You,' she accused, 'don't care what anyone thinks about you.'

It had been true.

It still was to a degree. The good opinion of others had never mattered to Emilio. He did not need people to love him.

He still didn't need people's approval or love—just one person's.

'But for the record I think you're cold, calculating and callous.'

His dark eyes glinted dangerously. 'Great alliteration,' he admired. 'But don't stop there when it's just getting interesting. How exactly am I...' he paused and selected an insult at random '...calculating?'

'You went to the airport to meet Rosanna.' Pretending to be Philip's friend and all the time intending to stab him in the back. 'And you kissed me!'

'True, but as I didn't know you would be there you can't really call my actions calculating. Now opportunistic…?' He shrugged his impressive shoulders, causing the powerful muscles in his chest to bunch beneath his satiny skin.

'You know exactly what I mean!' she snarled.

He directed a narrow-eyed considering look at her angry face.

The prolonged scrutiny began to make Megan feel uncomfortable and her scowl deepened in direct proportion to those feelings of discomfort. If I'm not careful, she reflected grimly, I'll be the one apologising!

Not that she expected for one minute that Emilio would apologise, but he could at least have the guts to acknowledge he'd done something wrong.

'I doubt very much if *you* know what you mean, but I have to say a pout actually looks pretty good on you.'

Her chest swelled wrathfully. 'I do not pout!'

His grin was deliberately provocative as he corrected his previous observation. 'Maybe not *pretty* good—make that very good.'

Megan sniffed and did not rise to the obvious bait as she regarded him coldly. 'It's bad enough you used me to make Rosanna jealous, but Philip doesn't have a clue you want her back, or at least don't want him to have her if you can't.'

'Have you ever thought of writing novels—I'm thinking fantasy here.'

Megan pointedly ignored his attempt to divert the conversation.

'He thinks you want him and Rosanna to be happy. He doesn't have the faintest idea about your hidden agenda.'

'And you think you do?'

Megan's last faint but persistent hope that she might have it wrong was extinguished when he didn't even attempt to deny her accusation.

'Yet despite that you are here with me.'

'That situation can change very quickly.' The retort, she knew, would have carried more weight if she had swept from the room.

So why aren't you?

'Philip is right. I would like to see Rosanna happy.' Whether the man to do this was Philip he was unsure. Emilio hoped so, but at that moment it was his own future happiness that dominated his thoughts and actions.

'And you think getting back with you would make her happy.'

'Being with me never made Rosanna happy.' And Emilio blamed himself for not realising it earlier. 'And that went doubly once she realised that I was in l—'

'Realised you were sleeping your way through the female population of Europe!' she interrupted shrilly.

A nerve clenched in his lean cheek before he flashed a quick sardonic smile as he drawled, '*Not* what I was about to say.'

Too angry to register the ironic inflection in his voice, Megan sneered. 'I suppose you're going to promise to be faithful to her.'

Emilio inhaled, his dark eyes flashing. 'You have finished?'

As she met his level stare Megan felt an irrational flicker of guilt. He was the one who should be feeling guilty, she reminded herself, and nothing she had said was not the truth.

CHAPTER FIFTEEN

'I was never unfaithful.'

'Sure you weren't…' Megan's voice died away as her eyes reconnected with Emilio's level stare. A flicker of confusion crossed her face that changed to astonishment as she gasped. 'You're serious!'

He dipped his head in curt acknowledgement.

'So if there weren't other women, why did you split up?'

Emilio studied her face for a long, thoughtful moment before he responded. Was it unreasonable, he wondered, to expect her to not think the worst of him, to allow for the possibility he might be the good guy, or at least attempting to be, just once?

'While I find it fascinating to be viewed as some sort of evil genius hatching diabolical plans and bending people to my will—' he drawled.

'Oh, no, you're one of life's innocents!' And he hadn't answered her question.

'No, Megan, that is you. Do you really imagine for one moment I kissed you at the airport because I wanted to make my ex-wife jealous, or help out your brother? I didn't plan on seeing you there any more than you planned to kiss me back. We did what we did because, *Dios*, do I have to spell it out? We have just spent the day in bed having the most incredible sex of my life!'

Clearly it was only a figure of speech, but even as she counselled herself not to take him too literally Megan had to snatch in a breath and grab the shelf beside her as her knees began to wobble, the excitement surging like a tide through her, and all the time painfully conscious of the excitement unfurling, hot and liquid, low in her pelvis.

'It may have been the *only* sex of your life,' he conceded, his lips twisting into a self-condemnatory smile—not only did he not regret this amazing discovery, he felt a knee-jerk rush of primal, possessive satisfaction as he thought about being Megan's first, her *only* lover.

Did that make him a total bastard?

'But you can't tell me that it—*I*—didn't move your world a little too.'

Megan stared back at him and shook her head mutely. She knew that today had changed her and her life for ever; she knew now what it was like to love a man, and even though Emilio wasn't talking about love he was right about one thing: her world had moved. Actually it had tilted on its axis.

His chin tilted to an arrogant, challenging angle. 'You can't look at me without wanting to rip off my clothes.' His liquid eyes darkened as they meshed with hers. 'You tremble when I touch you.'

It was clear from Emilio's expression that he was inviting her to respond, but Megan felt the words of denial locked in her emotionally congested throat. If she started speaking she was afraid she wouldn't be able to stop.

When it became clear she wasn't going to rise to the challenge he had thrown, Emilio sighed and dragged a hand down his strong shadowed jaw. 'You could meet me halfway. But fine…yes, I went to the airport with the intention of speaking to Rosanna, but I did not agree to act as a go-between for Philip. However,' he conceded, 'when we spoke yesterday I was concerned. I realised that he had a point. There were issues in our marriage that were perhaps not fully resolved.'

Megan, thinking, Like you being in love with her, did not bother to hide her scepticism. 'You didn't do much talking that I saw.'

'That is because I became distracted.' His eyes sought and found hers and the anger shining in the dark depths morphed into a potent blend of hunger and sensual appreciation.

Megan, who had no control over the tide of warm colour that washed over her skin, felt her stomach muscles flutter. Her helpless physical response to the sexual message in his eyes did not stop there. She was just glad that he could not see those other, more embarrassing physical responses.

'What distracted you?'

One corner of his mouth lifted, that crooked smile…it never failed to make her heart ache.

'You know the answer to that, Megan. And for the record you still are. You'll still be distracting me when I'm old enough to know better.'

The realisation did not appear to make him happy as, visibly leaking patience, he stalked with pantherlike grace to the other side of the room and slammed his hand against the wall before pressing his forehead to the cool tiles and breathing a heartfelt, 'Give me strength!'

After a moment he lifted his head, exhaling as his attention immediately switched back to Megan. As he read the expression on her face the furrow between his dark brows deepened.

The mixture of heady exhilaration and grim determination that had carried him through the day faded as he registered the wariness in her eyes. The idea that Megan could ever be afraid of him pierced him like a blade.

'I'm sorry...you...'

Megan didn't know what was more shocking: hearing Emilio say sorry or seeing him at a loss for words.

The natural hauteur in his manner was pronounced as he revealed abruptly, 'I am not accustomed to explaining myself.'

Her brows lifted. 'Imagine my amazement and, let me guess, you don't intend to start now.'

But it seemed he did intend to start.

'I do not want to resurrect my marriage, and Rosanna did not divorce me because I had been unfaithful. She divorced me because she knew I had fallen in love.'

The colour slowly seeped from Megan's face until even her lips were blenched white. The words, the last ones in the world she had imagined to hear coming from Emilio's lips, hung in the air between them.

She looked at Emilio, who had not moved an inch since he had made his shocking declaration. His lean face was shadowed, his expression unreadable; Emilio's dark lustrous stare remained trained on her pale face.

'You fell in love?' Why had this possibility never occurred to her?

His response echoed the sentiment. 'Is that so difficult to believe? You think I am not capable of feeling such things?'

Megan gave an awkward shrug. 'Of course not, no, I... just...' Her voice dried.

'It was not something I planned to happen. It was not actually something I believed possible. I felt in fact vastly superior to people who based their marriage on a temporary chemical imbalance, which in my mind equated to temporary insanity.' His lips twisted into a self-derisive smile as he admitted his previous arrogance with a disbelieving slight shake of his dark glossy head. 'I did not believe in something I could not see and taste and feel—then I did feel. I felt—' He stopped and swallowed, his bleak gaze sliding from hers.

Watching this man who had always appeared to be in charge of, not just himself, but everything else, display his vulnerability evoked a swell of empathy in Megan that was physically painful. She felt his struggle to rein in his emotions as deeply as she would have felt a blade sliding into her own heart.

The shocking realisation that he had had his heart broken was deeply disturbing on many levels, not least because she felt envious of the woman with whom Emilio had had the affair that had ultimately resulted in his marriage break-up.

Which left the question—why weren't they still together? Had the affair burnt itself out or was there another reason?

A reason that accounted for the haunted look in his dark eyes?

The nerve in his hollow cheek continued to clench and unclench. 'My feelings were not relevant—'

Not relevant, she thought, but evidently strong. 'Of course they were.'

'I was not free to act on them, because by that time I had already entered into a marriage of convenience.'

Megan braced her shoulders against the cool tiles of the wall; the alternative was falling down in a heap.

'Convenience? This is the twenty-first century. People don't— And anyway you and Rosanna were—' She stopped and lifted a shaky hand to her spinning head. 'God, I need a drink.'

Without a word he held his hand out.

For a moment Megan stared at it. Emilio waited, his expression hardening as she shook her head in a negative motion from side to side. Fighting to retain his upbeat mood in the face of her rejection, he was about to let it fall when she reached out and snatched at it, her small finger curling tightly around his.

Emilio had switched on a couple of lamps. The big room was illuminated by their soft glow that cast shadows across his face, emphasising the sheer perfection of his strong sculpted features.

The champagne in the glass she nursed had not lost its fizz. Megan dragged her eyes from his face and directed her gaze instead at the golden bubbles as she drew her knees up to her chin and took a deep gulp.

'Obviously it's none of my business.' She took a careful sip and looked at him over the rim of her glass. His response was a faint smile that told her nothing.

'And obviously you don't have to talk about it if you don't want to.'

He lifted a satirical brow and approached, bottle in hand.

'But you did bring up the subject,' she reminded him defensively.

'I did, didn't I?' Not at all in the manner he had intended, but he'd been reacting to events rather than anticipating them all day, and reacting in a way that was totally uncharacteristic.

Megan held a hand over her glass as he tilted the bottle.

She realised his glass was untouched, but then she could recall Philip once commenting during their college days that he'd never seen Emilio tipsy, let alone drunk!

'No, thank you.' The moment the well-mannered refusal left her lips the farcical quality of the scene hit her.

She bit down on her trembling lip to hold in the bubbles of laughter that welled in her throat.

'Care to share it?'

'I'm being served champagne by a man wearing silk boxer shorts who looks like—' Her glance swept from his toes to his glossy head, taking in all the perfect bits in between, and she felt her imagination go into overdrive and provide her with a slide show of seriously distracting images.

'Like?' he prompted.

Megan shifted her position, arranging her skirt modestly across her knees as she struggled to ignore the shameful liquid heat that flamed between her legs.

'Well, like you!' she burst out, frustration making her voice unattractively shrill.

In other words, perfect!

'Surreal does not even come close to describing all this. I feel like I've slipped into someone's fantasy.' She stared at his bronzed chest, watching the muscles glide beneath his satiny skin, and thought, Mine!

A glint appeared in his expressive eyes as he surveyed her flushed face. 'I could take offence at being treated like a sex object.'

'Which would be hypocritical considering the fact you enjoy flaunting your...your...'

'Almost as much as you enjoy looking, *querida*,' he taunted.

Megan, her cheeks burning, expelled a long shaky sigh as he vanished into the bedroom. A moment later he reappeared, zipping up a pair of faded jeans. His white shirt, which hung open, he made no attempt to fasten.

He held his hands wide. 'Better?' he asked, his gesture

inviting her opinion as he approached, his intention clearly to take the seat beside her on the vast sofa.

Megan breathed through a wave of paralysing lustful longing and experienced a moment's panic. 'We'll talk if you stay over there.'

'What,' he asked, looking torn between amusement and annoyance by her edict, 'are you talking about?'

'I'm talking about no touching.'

'No touching?' he echoed.

She shook her head. 'Touch me and I'm out of here.' *Touch me and I'm toast.* 'I know you think that all you have to do to close down any discussion is to kiss me, but—'

'Presumably, considering your rather elaborate precautions, I'd be right.'

Megan's amber eyes flew wide with indignation. 'That wasn't what I said—'

He arched a brow. 'No?'

Realising that was *exactly* what she'd been saying, she closed her mouth, wishing she could think of a smart line that would wipe that unbearably smug expression off his face.

'Naturally a man is always pleased to realise that he is actually irresistible.'

'Just stay over there, Emilio, please,' she begged, too weary to fight herself and him at the same time.

Their eyes held, for a moment she thought he was going to refuse, then he shrugged and turned, lowering his lean, rangy frame into a chair a few feet away.

He stretched his long legs out in front of him and, resting his chin on steepled fingers, arched an enquiring brow. 'Better?'

She nodded, thinking it wasn't better at all.

'You know, Megan, you can build as many walls as you like, I will—'

'Huff and puff and blow them down?'

He gave an appropriately wolfish grin. 'And leave myself open to the insult I am all hot air? No, I would remove your walls brick by brick, Megan.'

He didn't need to. With a cry she leapt up and flew across the room to him. She couldn't recall why she had put him at a distance, why they needed to talk—so she could hear more about some other woman? Was she out of her mind? She pressed her body to his, wrapping her arms around his neck.

'I don't want you not to touch me. I can't bear it,' she confided in an agonised whisper. 'Can I stay here tonight, with you?'

His slow smile was fierce and possessive, an emotion echoed in his kiss. 'What made you think that you were ever going anywhere?' he asked, sweeping her up into his arms.

CHAPTER SIXTEEN

MEGAN sat hunched forward, wrapped in a blanket of silent misery all the way to the airport. It seemed to take hours because, despite the hour, the early morning traffic was heavy and they got snarled up several times.

The taxi driver apologised in heavily accented broken English for the delays and reiterated his promise that he would get her to the airport on time to catch her flight.

Clearly misinterpreting the reason for his passenger's tension, he reeled off a list of statistics he had clearly memorised for such occasions that demonstrated flying was the safest form of transport.

Normally Megan would have tried to respond to his friendly overtures using her basic Spanish. It only seemed good manners to her to attempt to use the language when you were in a country. This time she didn't. She was afraid that if she opened her mouth she would start crying.

A hysterically weeping woman might not come under the heading of security threat, but she was not willing to take the gamble and risk being barred from the flight.

So she smiled and nodded instead and wondered again what Emilio would do when he woke up and found her gone.

Had he listened to his father's message?

She closed her eyes, hearing again the diatribe recorded on the answer machine.

The first half had been in Spanish, but as she had returned from the kitchen, her glass of water in hand, the speaker had slid unconsciously into English, a language he was equally fluent in, at least when it came to curses, which had liberally peppered his comments.

She had tried hard not to hear, even going so far as to hum softly to herself as she hurried through the room to drown out the sound of the voice she had identified as belonging to Luis Rios.

Emilio's father was clearly furious.

Then she had heard her father's name and stopped.

'Charles Armstrong was on to me half an hour ago. It turns out he gets the early edition of the damned British tabloids. Of course *he* was more than happy with the connection and shamelessly hinting at marriage plans—the man is deluded, but that is no reason to offend him. He can be useful to you and he does have influence in certain circles.

'What were you thinking of? You kiss the girl in an airport terminal packed with people with mobile phones, of course you end up on the front page. I've no doubt at all it will be all over the Internet. I can only hope there is nothing more incriminating out there.

'My son and a girl who is the daughter of some cleaner. *Por Dios*, what were you thinking of? If you're going to get involved with one of the Armstrong girls, did you have to make it the bastard? The other at least has some sort of pedigree. What have I told you? Bad blood will out! Well, I insist that it ends now. If not I will have no compunction in disinheriting you.'

The diatribe had continued, but by that point Megan had heard enough. She had dragged on her clothes, pausing only to take one last look at Emilio's sleeping face before she had left the building and hailed a cab.

Would he be angry or secretly relieved when he found she was gone and read her note?

She had her answer to the depressing question a lot sooner than she anticipated.

Having paid off the driver, she was walking towards the terminal building when a shadow fell across her. She automatically turned her head, just in time to see a tall figure clad in a black biker leather jacket remove his helmet.

'We cannot carry on meeting like this, *querida.*'

The sound of his soft accented drawl hit Megan with the impact of a thunderclap. Shock held her immobile. Totally paralysed, she gazed up blankly at the tall, rampantly male figure exuding masculinity from every pore and thought, He can't be here.

Logically he could not be here; she had left him sleeping. Was she hallucinating, or had she lost her mind?

Dragging a hand across his tousled dark hair, Emilio bared his teeth in a smile that left his dark eyes angry and cold as he stepped directly into her path, removing his designer shades as he did so, to pin her with a stare with the same penetrating quality as surgical steel.

People were staring, not because he was doing anything, just because he was Emilio—he was really here.

'You...here... I don't... How?' Megan stammered, barely able to hear her own voice above the pounding of her overstressed heart. 'Note... My note, it...' Frustrated by her inability to form a sentence, she stopped trying and lapsed into miserable silence.

Emilio arched a brow and took her arm, sliding the bag she carried from her shoulder. 'I always said if I ever found a woman who travels light I would not let her go.'

Her gaze made a slow journey up the long, lean length

of him. She released a fractured sighing gasp. He looked like a walking advert for mean, lean and dangerous—a leather-clad fallen angel.

'You have a motorbike?'

'It allows me more flexibility than a car does.'

Megan lifted a hand to her spinning head. 'I feel—not good.'

As he subjected her face to a searching, unsympathetic scrutiny Emilio felt his anger fall away and protective instincts rush in to fill the vacuum. She looked so incredibly fragile, the ribbons of soft colour along her cheekbones only accentuating her ghostly pallor, it physically hurt him to see her distress.

'You're not going to faint.'

Her outrage stirred in response to this typically heartless statement. 'Serve you right if I dropped dead at your feet.'

'That's more like it,' he approved, taking her elbow.

Megan, still in shock, responded to the pressure without thinking.

There was a time lag before she realised they were walking in the wrong direction. She directed a worried gaze up at his stern profile.

'My flight, it's…?'

Emilio carried on walking.

'Emilio.' She stopped dead. Short of dragging her, which she did not put past him, he would have to listen to her now.

He flashed an impatient look down at her before continuing to scan the rows of parked cars in the distance.

Watching him, Megan was conscious of details she had previously missed, like the pallor of his normally vibrant-toned olive skin and the lines of tension bracketing his mouth.

She pushed her disquiet aside, telling herself that all those things could be simply a result of sleep deprivation rather than anything more sinister, and goodness knew he had had very little last night. Cheeks flushed, she lowered her eyes and gritted her teeth as she forcibly expelled the erotic images from her head.

Better to worry about herself. If anyone was capable of looking after himself, it was Emilio.

'The car should be here,' he announced after consulting the metal-banded watch on his wrist.

She avoided the obvious question. 'Look, Emilio, I don't know how or why you're here but I left a note. I should be at check-in and—'

'I know you left a note.' A muscle clenched along his jaw. 'You have delightful manners, and excellent hand-writing, but neither are the reason I spent the last twenty-four hours in bed with you.'

The earthy disclosure sent a slam of desire through Megan's body. Lowering her eyes in the vain hope of dis-guising her reaction, she heard him say, 'I fully intended to spend the next twenty-four in much the same manner.'

This time there was absolutely no question of hiding her reaction.

She moaned a weak, 'Oh, God, Emilio!' And lifted her passion-glazed golden gaze to his. 'You can't say things like that to me.'

'Why?' He angled a satiric brow and smiled down into her face. 'It's true. Are you trying to tell me you don't want to go to bed with me?'

Megan flushed to the roots of her hair and cast an ago-nised look over her shoulder. Emilio had made no attempt to lower his voice and they were now attracting a great deal of attention.

'Will you lower your voice?' she hissed. 'People can

hear you.' And some enterprising person might snap a photo again.

Anger flashed across his face. 'Pity you cannot.' He might not have *said* the words, but he had told her in every other way possible that he loved her.

He had stripped his soul bare, broken the ingrained habit of a lifetime and lowered his defences to let her in, making himself vulnerable in the process.

She had frustrated his plans to make a formal declaration—a formality as far as he was concerned—by falling asleep in his arms after their last exhausting session of wild lovemaking.

To wake up and find her gone had been the low point of the last twenty-four emotionally turbulent hours. He had thrown on his clothes in a blind fury, fully intending when he picked up the ringing phone on his way to the door to slam it down.

Then he had heard his father's querulous voice saying, 'You haven't responded to my message.'

He had slammed the phone down then and listened to the message. What he heard confirmed his suspicions and explained pretty much why she had left, but where?

If in doubt it was Emilio's habit to follow his first instincts—he headed for the airport. He was confident that his motorbike and his knowledge of the city would considerably cut down on the journey time. The only problem being he had no idea how much of a head start Megan had on him.

He had actually been there less than five minutes before he saw her. His initial relief was followed by an equally intense rush of blind anger. How could she think that his father's threats meant anything to him? That he gave a damn who her mother was?

* * *

'Do I have to spell everything out for you?' he growled. 'Come,' he added, taking her elbow again, this time in a firm grip.

'My flight.'

He ignored her.

Megan struggled to inject a little common sense into the proceedings. 'Emilio, you can't kidnap me in broad daylight.'

'Kidnap implies coercion. You want to come with me,' he asserted confidently.

She bit her trembling lip and swallowed the lump of self-pity lodged in her throat. Was she destined to become one of those bitter people railing at the deal fate had dealt them?

She lifted her chin. 'A person cannot always have what they want.' Compared to others she had a lot: her health, friends, a good job.

But not Emilio!

Under the circumstances it was hard to feel suitably grateful.

Without warning Emilio halted, oblivious to the other people on the congested pavement. He cupped her chin in his hand and tilted her face up to him.

'But you want to stay with me?'

Emilio, a stranger to insecurity, despised himself for voicing the question, but he couldn't help himself.

The lie stayed locked in her throat. Instead Megan found herself nodding, her misted gaze missing the triumph that blazed bright in his eyes at her admission.

'It's been lovely.'

'*Lovely?*' Not the first word or even the last that sprang to his mind when he thought of the last twenty-four hours.

'I've really enjoyed myself, but duty calls. I have to

get back. Perhaps I could visit some time?' Oh, God, I'm babbling.

'On a friends-with-benefits basis?' He vented a hard laugh. 'Shall we check our diaries?' The mockery in his voice was savage as he shook his head and added, 'I think not, *querida*.'

'I didn't mean that. I meant...' She passed a hand across her eyes and admitted, 'I have no idea what I meant. Why did you have to come?' she wailed, past caring by this point if she attracted attention. 'Why couldn't you just let me go without a fuss?'

'I made that mistake once.'

Before she could question this cryptic statement or wonder about the odd, driven expression on his face, Emilio spotted what he had been looking for in the distance and changed direction.

'Come!'

Literally swept along, she had no time to think about resisting his imperious command; she was too busy trying to keep up with his long-legged pace.

She was panting by the time they reached the long, low, gleaming limousine.

'This is yours?'

He nodded.

'But what about your motorcycle?'

'It is hard to have a conversation while wearing a helmet.' He threw his own into the back seat and spoke to the uniformed driver who had emerged from the driver's seat when they appeared.

After exchanging words with Emilio in Spanish, he nodded courteously to Megan as he opened the rear passenger door and stood to one side.

Megan did not respond to the unspoken invitation. She

turned instead to Emilio, who stood there visibly oozing impatience at the delay.

'I don't want to talk to you.'

'I talk, you listen, whatever.'

Unprepared for his hands-on approach to the situation, Megan let out a soft shriek of protest as he scooped her up and placed her bodily inside the vehicle.

Ignoring both her shriek and the lucky punch she landed on his shoulder, Emilio slid in beside her and calmly indicated to the driver that they were ready to leave.

'I'm not ready!'

Her shrill protest went ignored by both men.

Megan smoothed down her skirt and turned in her seat to level a furious look at his impassive face.

'This is ludicrous. What do you hope to achieve by kidnapping me?'

'We have already established it is not kidnap, and as for what I hope to achieve—I suppose a degree of sanity.' His dark eyes skimmed her face as he sighed and admitted, 'It might be a long time before I let you out of my sight.' He would be afraid of closing his eyes for fear of her vanishing while he slept.

'Very funny.'

'I was not attempting to amuse you.'

'Has it occurred to you that someone might have snapped that little scene back there?' she asked him, nodding over her shoulder.

Emilio settled back in his seat and, taking advantage of the space offered by their luxurious transport, he stretched his long legs out in front of him and unzipped his leather jacket.

'Like yesterday morning, you mean.'

Megan stiffened, guilty colour flooding her pale face.

He knew she'd listened in and was probably furious about the invasion of his privacy.

'It wasn't deliberate. I didn't mean to listen to the message,' she told him earnestly. 'I was just going to get a drink of water when the answer machine kicked in. I was coming back to bed and then I heard Dad's name. I thought there might be a problem at home.'

Instead she had discovered that she was the problem.

'What an amazing relief. I thought for one awful moment that I was lumbered with the sort of woman who checks her man's emails and text messages.'

'I wouldn't— I—' Her wide indignant gaze flew to his face and she stopped. 'You're not serious.' Of course he wasn't serious—he'd called himself *her man*.

He gave a crooked smile. 'You think…?'

Her eyes fell from his. 'Have you spoken to your father? Is he still angry?'

'Probably.' He gave an uninterested shrug. 'My father is generally unhappy about something or other.'

Realising that he was downplaying the situation out of consideration for her feelings, Megan covered his hand with hers. 'It's all right, Emilio,' she soothed, producing a bright brittle smile to prove the point. 'It's nothing I haven't heard before.'

She stopped, a fractured sigh escaping her parted lips as he covered her hand, sandwiching it heavily between the two of his.

'It is something that you will not hear again!' he growled.

Ribbons of feverish colour appeared along her cheekbones as she gave a little laugh and stopped trying to tug her hand free. 'He's right, I am…a…b—'

Emilio cut across her in a voice that vibrated with outrage. 'Do not say it!'

Megan winced at the volume. 'All right,' she said, taken aback by the intensity of his response. 'But you have to remember your father is of a different generation. Things like that matter to him—'

'It is not a matter of age, it is a matter of ignorance. You will not make excuses for him.'

'All right,' she soothed. 'I won't. Can I have my hand back?'

'No.'

His brooding expression as he stared at her intensified the dark fallen-angel look and made her hopelessly receptive heart skip several beats.

'You will ignore anything you heard my father say,' he instructed grimly. There was menace in his expression as he scanned her face, exuding offended masculine aggression. 'How dare he?'

It was becoming clear to Megan that this was more about Emilio's relationship with his father than her. She wondered how the older man could not realise that issuing edicts to a man like Emilio was the equivalent of waving a red rag to a bull!

Emilio was the sort of person who would not give an inch if pushed, even if it was against his best interests. He was just too stubborn for his own good.

'I thought you might react this way. That's why I left.'

He arched an interrogative brow. 'What way would that be?'

He had no idea what was going on in her head, but he seriously doubted that she was about to say, You were blind to everything except the compelling need to find me and bind me to you.

She didn't.

'Admit it, Emilio, if you hadn't been determined to prove to your father that he has no control over you, you wouldn't have hared off after me this way. But, point proved—do you think you could take me back to the airport?'

Emilio vented a harsh laugh and dragged a hand through his hair. 'The way your mind works is a continual source of fascination to me.' Not to mention frustration. 'So if we follow your logic, if my father had told me to marry you I would have shown you the door to prove a point?'

'I'm not saying you'd go that far, but—' She stopped, her throat drying as he leaned in towards her.

His eyes were trained on her mouth as he said softly, 'I think you will find that there is no limit to how far I would go to protect what is mine.'

'You don't think your father would really disinherit you, would he?'

A sound of frustrated incredulity whistled through his clenched white teeth as he drew back. 'I am not talking about money! My father's threats mean nothing to me. He said he would disinherit me when I got divorced and my response was then what it would be now—I said, "Fine, go ahead."'

'You called his bluff.' A risky policy, but then Emilio was a born risk taker.

'Blackmail only works if you care about the thing that is being threatened.' His broad shoulders lifted in a shrug. 'I enjoy what I do, and I'm good at it, but if it vanished tomorrow and I had to start again I would not lose any sleep. My father, however, who is enjoying his retirement, has some very expensive hobbies—I am very good at making money and he enjoys spending it.'

'So he wouldn't disinherit you.' Megan gave a sigh. 'Well, thank God for that, but if necessary I'll speak to him myself and explain there's no chance of us…you know, of me polluting the Rios gene pool or anything.'

Aware that her laugh had a hollow, unconvincing sound,

she struggled to inject more conviction into her voice as she added, 'That it was just, you know…'

'No, I do not *you know*. Perhaps you would like to tell me *you know*.'

'Just sex, casual sex.' She saw anger flame hot in his eyes and, lifting her chin to a defiant angle, cried, 'What… what have I said now?'

A pulsing silence followed her question.

Emilio struggled to speak past the knot of anger lodged in his chest. 'I know about just sex. I have had just sex, you have not.'

'Great sex, then,' she admitted in a small voice.

A muscle clenched along his jaw. 'We made love, Megan.'

She felt his hand tighten over hers until it hurt, but she barely registered the pain. She couldn't take her eyes off his face and the impossible, incredible things she was seeing in his eyes.

'I've dreamt about making love to you for two years.'

Megan's stomach took a lurching dive. She stared at him, her head spinning. She was feverishly shaking—literally shaking from head to toe in reaction to this amazing statement.

He lifted the hand under his and, still holding her eyes, raised it to his lips. 'But the reality, *mi esposa*, was much, much better than dreams.'

The throaty confession sent a shudder through her body.

'Emilio…I don't understand…' I'm the one dreaming, she thought, not allowing herself to believe the possessive, tender glow in his eyes meant what she wanted it to mean.

'Do you think I don't know that?' He groaned. 'You are without exception the most clueless woman it has ever been my misfortune to fall in love with.' He stared into her face, drinking in the beauty of her delicate features like a starving man. 'Actually, the only woman I have ever fallen in love with.'

She started to shake her head. That was wrong; she knew that was wrong. 'But you loved… You still love… the woman who—'

'You still don't get it, do you?' He framed her face in his big hands. 'I fell in love with you, Megan. You are that woman.' The relief of having finally told her after two years' delay sent a rush of adrenaline through his body.

The low hum of confusion in her head had become a loud buzz. Megan, hardly daring to move, slowly lifted her wary gaze to his face. He was totally still, not an eyelash flickered, not a muscle moved as, deathly pale, he looked back at her with eyes that glittered with a febrile intensity.

'Me?' Was this a joke? If so it was in the worst possible taste. 'But you left your wife, you—' She stopped, the moment of comprehension causing the blood to slowly seep from her face until she was parchment pale. 'That was me?'

'Is you,' he corrected huskily. 'Why is that so hard for you to believe?'

He dabbed his thumb to the tear running unchecked down her cheek, his smile so tender that more tears welled in her eyes. Her heart felt full enough to explode.

'But you didn't like me.'

Her protest was lost in his long, lingering, tender kiss.

Finally Emilio lifted his head, but only fractionally. He stayed close, close enough for their breaths to mingle as they stared in silence at one another.

If I'm dreaming, Megan thought, I definitely don't want to wake up.

She slid her hands under his leather jacket, pulling herself closer as she pressed her hands flat against his chest, feeling the warmth of his skin through the cotton of the T-shirt he wore underneath, feeling the heavy, strong, hypnotic thud of his heart through her fingertips.

'You feel real.' He felt marvellous.

Emilio smiled and nipped gently at the full curve of her lower lip with his teeth.

'And you feel delicious,' he said, sliding a hand under her skirt and along the smooth, silky skin of her outer thigh. Megan caught her breath sharply. 'You have the most incredible skin.'

Megan felt regret when he removed his hand. If he had decided to make love to her in the back of this limo with only a tinted-glass panel separating them from the driver it would not have crossed her mind to stop him. She would have gone out of her way to assist him!

The realisation came with not a scrap of shame.

'But, Emilio,' she said, frowning as she struggled to sort out the puzzles and unanswered questions in her head, 'I don't... How... That weekend.'

'That weekend,' he said heavily.

'You snubbed me. You barely spoke to me and then you told me I was a tart!'

'That weekend I *couldn't* look at you.' Dark colour stained his cheekbones as he forced himself to meet her gaze now. *'Por Dios,'* he groaned, pulling back from her, his face dark with the remembered pain as he dragged not quite steady hands over his sleek dark hair.

'I couldn't even trust myself to be in the same room as you for fear of giving myself away! To make it worse I *knew* that you were attracted to me.'

'I knew it!' she cried, leaning back in her seat and clapping a hand to her forehead, feeling utterly mortified in retrospect. 'I knew you knew. It was awful—you made me feel so...so... When I sat next to you at dinner that first night I couldn't breathe... I really thought I was having a panic attack or something. There were freesias on the window sill—I can't smell a freesia now without hyperventilating!'

'I do not remember flowers, but I do remember you arriving late during dinner looking so...' Sucking in air through flared nostrils, he sighed and shook his head. 'It was as if I was seeing you for the first time. You took my breath away.

'But I fought it. I was not willing to admit even then that such a thing was possible. Love was a fantasy, my life was planned, my work, a wife who made no emotional demands on me. Emotional detachment makes life easy, but I didn't realise until that night how lonely it can make you too.'

Moved beyond tears by the husky confession, she reached up and touched his cheek lovingly. For this strong, self-contained man to acknowledge, let alone confess, any weakness must, she knew, have taken great courage.

'And when I caught that loser in the car with you I knew, *I knew*, and I wanted you so much that not touching you was like some sort of— It was sheer torture. It—'

He stopped, his startled expression morphing into one of desire as Megan grabbed his face between her hands and pulled him towards her.

Nose resting against his, she closed her eyes and breathed in his warm male smell, then fitted her mouth to his. For a split second he did not respond to the pressure of her lips, then with a groan he kissed her back with a fierce hunger and bruising urgency that awoke an equal hunger in her.

'Wow!' She breathed in shakily when they drew apart.

'Indeed...wow!' Emilio echoed, looking almost as shaken as she felt.

Megan turned her head and kissed the hand pressed to her cheek before she held it there. 'Why didn't you touch me, Emilio?'

'I was married.'

'Of course.' She blushed that she needed reminding—reminding that Emilio was a man of honour and finding himself in such a situation must have been incredibly difficult. 'But afterwards, when you were divorced, why on earth didn't you...?'

He arched a brow.

'Come and get me,' she said simply.

'I did,' he admitted. 'After a decent interval passed—the last thing I wanted was anyone calling you the other woman—I came to your flat intending to sweep you off your feet and into my bed.' One corner of his mouth curled upwards into a self-derisive smile. 'It never even crossed my mind that you would not be there waiting for me.

'So I was not prepared for your door to be answered by a half-naked man of more than average good looks who informed me you were in the shower.'

'Josh!' she exclaimed.

He nodded. 'Your gay flatmate, yes, I know this now, but at the time I jumped to the obvious conclusion,' he admitted. 'It is never pleasant to feel a fool or have your heart and hopes crushed.

'I felt—' His apologetic glance swept across her face. 'It was totally irrational, I know, but in my mind you had betrayed me. My pride would not allow me to follow my instincts and take you from this man. I told myself you would do the running the next time. Deep down I think I never lost hope there would be a next time.

'Then when Philip let slip that your lover, or so I thought, had moved out, I felt... Let's just say I was not unhappy for your loss. The next day I went to the airport to assure Rosanna that there was no need to feel bad that things hadn't worked out for me with the woman she knew I had not pursued because we were still married. I spent the journey to the airport thinking of you and suddenly there you were. I was not thinking about Rosanna or anything when I kissed you.

'I just followed my instincts. If only I had followed my baser instincts when your friend opened the door that day the last year might have been very different.'

The pain and self-recrimination on his face made her tender heart ache. 'I was jealous of all the skinny, beautiful women I saw you photographed with,' she confessed. 'And no matter how hard I dieted I never looked like them.'

'Por Dios!' he ejaculated, looking horrified. 'I would never want you to look like those women. I love your curves. It is as a woman should be—warm and soft. And you will never diet again,' he announced firmly.

His vehemence made her smile. Her smile faded as she looked into the face she adored and declared with husky sincerity, 'I really do love you, Emilio.' Her golden eyes glowed as she ran a loving finger over the roughened curve of his cheek.

'And I love you.'

The kissing lasted until they drew up outside the building that housed Emilio's temporary accommodation. Neither occupant of the back seat noticed the car had stopped and the discreet driver made no attempt to announce the fact.

Megan laid her head on his chest and sighed with pleasure. 'And the good thing is when I leave the firm and set up on my own I'll be able to come to Madrid a lot more often, and maybe you will be able to come over to London occasionally too?'

She angled a look of tentative enquiry at his face.

'But surely you will set up your business here? In the short term I can help you with any language problems, though obviously enrolling on an intensive language course would be the obvious course of action.'

'You want me to move here… Are you asking me to move in with you, Emilio?'

He shook his head. 'I am asking you to marry me, *mi esposa*. I thought that was a given.'

Megan gasped. 'Not to me.'

'You wish time to think about it?' He glanced at his watch. 'Will three seconds suffice?'

Megan's expression of solemn shock melted into laughter as he delivered his outrageous offer.

'It will have to suffice, *querida*, because I have been waiting for your answer for two years and every extra second is taking a year off my life.'

He was right; the knowledge made her relax. Why stress over a choice she had already made?

'Well, I wouldn't want that because I want my husband to be around for a very, very long time.'

Emilio released the breath he had been holding—holding, it seemed to him, for two years. 'You will not regret this. I promise you, Megan, that you will not regret this,' he cried, pulling her to him and raining kisses on her upturned features. Finally he found her mouth and the last long, languid, achingly tender kiss lasted a very long time.

It was Megan who pulled out of his arms with a laugh. 'I have just realized—not when you were kissing me, obviously.' There was no room for anything but Emilio in her head when he kissed her. 'How long have we been here— not in the car, in Madrid?'

Emilio consulted his watch. 'Almost twenty-four hours exactly.'

'Do you realise I have been in one of the most vibrant, colourful cities in the world for twenty-four hours and all I've seen of it is the airport and your apartment? God, we've arrived back and I hadn't even realised.'

'That is indeed truly shocking!' Emilio agreed, tongue firmly in cheek. 'I feel I should share more shocking news. I do not have sightseeing trips planned for the immediate future.'

Her lips twitched as she adopted an innocent expression. 'What do you have planned?'

A wicked smile that made her pulse race split his dark features. 'Come with me, *mi querida*, and I will show you.'

Megan grinned back and took the hand he offered. This was one offer she had no intention of refusing. 'Why not? Madrid will still be here tomorrow.'

'Also next week.' The teasing smile faded from his handsome face as he took her hands in his. 'And so will I. I will always be here for you, Megan.'

The simple statement meant more to Megan than the vows they would soon exchange with equal solemnity. She nodded and said in a clear voice that shook with the depth of the emotions she wanted to convey, 'And I will always be there for you Emilio.'

Tears of emotion glowed in her eyes as Megan allowed him to lead her out into the morning sun and her new life.

LET'S TALK
Romance

For exclusive extracts, competitions
and special offers, find us online:

- **f** facebook.com/millsandboon
- **𝕐** @MillsandBoon
- **◎** @MillsandBoonUK

Get in touch on 01413 063232

For all the latest titles coming soon, visit
millsandboon.co.uk/nextmonth

MILLS & BOON

THE HEART OF ROMANCE

A ROMANCE FOR EVERY KIND OF READER

MODERN

Prepare to be swept off your feet by sophisticated, sexy and seductive heroes, in some of the world's most glamourous and romantic locations, where power and passion collide.
8 stories per month.

HISTORICAL

Escape with historical heroes from time gone by. Whether your passion is for wicked Regency Rakes, muscled Vikings or rugged Highlanders, awaken the romance of the past.
6 stories per month.

MEDICAL

Set your pulse racing with dedicated, delectable doctors in the high-pressure world of medicine, where emotions run high and passion, comfort and love are the best medicine.
6 stories per month.

True Love

Celebrate true love with tender stories of heartfelt romance, from the rush of falling in love to the joy a new baby can bring, and a focus on the emotional heart of a relationship.
8 stories per month.

Desire

Indulge in secrets and scandal, intense drama and plenty of sizzling hot action with powerful and passionate heroes who have it all: wealth, status, good looks…everything but the right woman.
6 stories per month.

HEROES

Experience all the excitement of a gripping thriller, with an intense romance at its heart. Resourceful, true-to-life women and strong, fearless men face danger and desire - a killer combination!
8 stories per month.

DARE

Sensual love stories featuring smart, sassy heroines you'd want as a best friend, and compelling intense heroes who are worthy of them.
4 stories per month.

To see which titles are coming soon, please visit

millsandboon.co.uk/nextmonth

JOIN US ON SOCIAL MEDIA!

Stay up to date with our latest releases, author news and gossip, special offers and discounts, and all the behind-the-scenes action from Mills & Boon...

 millsandboon

 millsandboonuk

 millsandboon

It might just be true love...